THE STORM BOYS SERIES

COLLECTION

N.R. WALKER

COPYRIGHT

Cover Art: N.R. Walker
Editor: Boho Edits
Publisher: BlueHeart Press
Storm Boys Series © 2023 N.R. Walker

ALL RIGHTS RESERVED:

WARNING

Intended for an 18+ audience only. This book contains material that maybe offensive to some and is intended for a mature, adult audience. It contains graphic language, and adult situations.

TRADEMARKS:

All trademarks are the property of their respective owners.

AUTHOR NOTE

This series is strictly fiction. Actual bureaus of meteorology do not work like this in real life. The author is very aware.

There has been creative licence taken in regards to weather tracking, prediction systems, and any/all meteorological practices mentioned herein.

It's just a fun and crazy ride intended for entertainment purposes only. Please enjoy it for what it is.

Also please note with Australian English the plural for antenna is antennas, not antennae. We also use vice instead of vise, and further instead of farther.

For reference, Storm Boy and Mr Percival, as mentioned in this book, is from a much-loved Australian classic novel (by Colin Thiele, 1964) and movie (1976 and 2019).

Thank you for reading!

SECOND CHANCE AT FIRST LOVE
OUTRUN THE RAIN
INTO THE TEMPEST
TOUCH THE LIGHTNING

THE STORM BOYS SERIES

COLLECTION

SECOND CHANCE AT FIRST LOVE

PREQUEL

BLURB

Paul Morgan has been running his luxury camping tour business in Kakadu National Park for the last five years. Taking small groups glamping, hiking, climbing, and swimming. It's been a busy five years, a hard five years, as he tried to forget the man he left behind.

Derek Grimes pushes people away—a self-preservation reflex. Because they can't break his heart if he breaks theirs first, right? Five years on, lost and lonely, he tracks down the one and only love of his life. Maybe seeing how Paul had moved on will help Derek move on too . . .

Paul can't believe it when a familiar name pops up on his client list, and Derek can't believe how good Paul looks, or just how happy living his dream job has made him. The spark between them never waned, but five years on, they've learned a few things about themselves and what they want.

They could have everything they ever dreamed of—if they're prepared to trust each other. Because a second chance at first love comes but once in a lifetime.

THE STORM BOYS SERIES PREQUEL

SECOND CHANCE AT FIRST LOVE

CHAPTER ONE

PAUL

I TIGHTENED THE RATCHET GRIP ON THE BACK OF MY CRUISER and went back for the canisters of water. I'd done many five-day tours, taking groups of tourists from all walks of life out in the wilds of Kakadu National Park. It was my job, my business, and I loved it.

But I was nervous today.

I'd read the manifest, double checking all insurances and permits were in order. I was taking four individuals. Two women from Norway—both in their twenties, backpacking around Australia. One Australian woman in her fifties—an avid bushwalker, ticking Kakadu off her long list of conquests.

And Derek Grimes.

Thirty-three-year-old from Darwin, amateur astronomer.

My ex-boyfriend.

There could only be one Derek Grimes, thirty-three years old from Darwin who liked astronomy, right?

It had to be him.

It had to be.

Did he know I was running this tour specifically? That

he'd be stuck with me for five days in the remote scrub of the tropical Top End?

Well, he was about to find out.

Instructions were to be at the meeting point in Darwin by seven am. From there, we'd drive out to the national park and do some sightseeing on the way. It was also so I could stock up and get essential supplies in Darwin before we left. And it was also the last stop of civilisation before venturing out into the vast, vast parklands. If they wanted a Coke or any kind of fast food, it was now or never.

We'd spend all of day one travelling, stopping to see the Mitsuaki Tanabe rock carving site, then on to the Mary River stop to see the crocodiles and have lunch. From there, I'd be taking them to my camp. It was a good hour off the main road, on a dirt track that was mostly inaccessible when the weather turned to shit. It was a solid first day of mostly touristy things, with a lot of hiking, and everyone was always glad to get to camp in time for dinner and an awesome sunset that only Kakadu could put on.

August was the dry season, which was peak tourist season. That didn't mean it never rained; it just meant it wasn't tropical monsoonal storms every afternoon.

And the next five days were supposed to be good weather. A bit of rain, not stinking hot and humid, but still hot for some. It was the Top End, after all. Most tourists underestimated just how hot and humid it got here, and what those kinds of temperatures did to the human body.

Some days were so bad, being locked in a sauna would be a reprieve.

But I loved it.

I loved the heat and humidity and the enormity of the most beautiful wilderness on Earth. I didn't even mind the mosquitoes, the wild water buffalo, the crocs, and other critters. But mostly, I loved the lack of people.

Even the limited crowds of Jabiru Visitor Centre in peak

tourist season were enough for me. You can have your cities and rat races. Give me open space any day.

Give me anywhere where there is no chance of running into ex boyfriends who reminded me of how much I fucked up . . .

The first two of my client group turned up. Marit and Kari, backpackers from Norway. They both had long blond-ish hair plaited down their back, sun-kissed skin, wide blue eyes, and excited smiles. They'd been in Australia for five weeks and were loving every minute of it. They wore shorts and singlet tops, and I liked that they wore sensible walking shoes. Given they'd been backpacking for five weeks, they were well-accustomed to the Outback and Top End, and I was happy about that.

Next to arrive was Norah. With an H, as she was quick to remind me. She was fifty-six years old, from Sydney, and had done hiking trails all over the world. She came prepared, or so she said. Her backpack was expensive, but it looked well-used. She wore sensible hiking clothes and boots, which made me happy—I'd seen some ill-prepared and stupid people wear even stupider clothes out here—but she was already wiping sweat from her brow, and it wasn't even seven o'clock in the morning. And it was August, one of the milder months.

I'd have to keep an eye on her and make sure she stayed hydrated, for sure.

"Norah, this is Marit and Kari," I said, making introductions. They'd be spending the next five days together in the middle of nowhere, and I was glad they all seemed pleasant enough. I tapped my clipboard. "We're just waiting on one more."

The one I was both dreading and so very excited to see.

The one that had my stomach in knots . . .

"Oh, here comes someone," Marit said, nodding over my shoulder.

I turned around to see him walking toward us. He was

carrying a duffle bag in one hand and a telescope case in the other. It was him, all right. God, he looked good. Still as handsome as ever. His dark hair was longer than it used to be, shaggy on top and was still damp. Just showered, maybe? The sleeveless shirt showed off his broad shoulders and defined biceps and a new tattoo. His chiselled jaw and his dark eyes . . .

Zeroed in on me.

Just short of reaching us, he stopped dead in his tracks. His duffle bag landed at his feet, fingers tightened on the handle of his telescope case. His jaw ticked. For a second, I thought he might have swallowed his tongue. "You?" he breathed.

"Nice to see you again too, Derek."

He sighed, looking back at the visitor centre, probably wondering if it was too late to cancel.

"Oh. You know each other?" Marit asked, her eyes wide.

I gave her a bright smile. "You could say that. It's been years though, right Derek?"

Derek mumbled something I didn't quite catch. It was probably just as well.

"Drop your bag at the tailgate," I said to him. "If you're still coming with us, that is."

He glared at me for a long second, and I wondered if he was about to bail. The tic in his jaw always gave him away. But he huffed as he brushed past me, and I had to bite back a smile. I made very quick introductions, and while they made small talk, I went to the back of the Cruiser to stack their bags. Resting my hands on the tailgate, I paused to catch my breath.

Derek.

The only man I'd ever loved.

Still as gorgeous as he had ever been.

This was going to be a very interesting five days.

Get it together, Paul. Be professional. What happened between you was a long time ago.

I could do this.

Easy as.

Right?

God, why did he have to look so good? Why did he have to smell all fresh-showered and have damp hair that hung into his eyes?

And why did he still have to look at me like he wanted to kill me?

Five days, Paul.

How bad could it be?

CHAPTER TWO

DEREK

I THOUGHT I WAS PREPARED.

I thought I was prepared to see him. I knew he was out here running these tours. I'd asked around. I'd stalked his social media. He'd made his dream come true, doing what he'd always wanted to do. I always knew he would. He was determined and driven.

And gorgeous.

And selfish.

The outdoor life seemed to serve him well. More rugged now, tanned, and with muscles that came from working hard. His light brown hair was short, his chest broad in his khaki uniform shirt, his thighs and calves thick down to his work boots.

I wasn't prepared for how good he'd look.

I wasn't prepared for the pang and stab of longing and regret.

And the anger.

I wasn't at all prepared for that.

But there he was, hot as hell with a smile I'd missed more than I'd realised.

He used to smile at me like that.

I was still in a bit of a daze as we all piled into his Cruiser. The crew-mover kind, fitted out like an army truck, or as if he was fully prepped for the zombie apocalypse.

"So how do you know each other?" Marit asked.

Her question struck me out of my thoughts and my gaze darted to Paul. I was sitting in the back opposite him, with a clear view of the side of his face. He had a small scar on his cheekbone that he hadn't had before . . .

I wonder how he got that.

When I hadn't answered, he did. "Ah, we used to work together in Darwin. A long time ago."

His eyes cut to mine in the rear-view mirror.

What he said wasn't a lie. We *had* worked together in Darwin years ago. That was how we'd met.

What he'd left out was that we'd also lived together. For two years. We'd met as co-workers at a bar and I'd needed to find a new place when my lease was up. He was looking for a roommate. We fell into stride with each other and then fell into bed.

But like he'd said, that was years ago.

I gave a nod. "Yeah, that sounds about right."

Sounded about wrong too, but whatever . . .

I checked my phone, noticing the bars of reception deplete the further we drove. Paul spoke most of the way, giving a sightseeing tour as we made our way deep into the park, first on tarred roads, then on dirt trails. Vegetation went from savannah woodlands to wetlands and then onto the lowlands. Towering rock walls, gigantic termite mounds, every tree and palm you could name. And Paul could name most of them.

First stop was the rock carvings, which were interesting and all, just not really what I was here for, but I was still glad to see it. It was good to see the three women enjoy themselves and, of course, getting to see Paul in his element.

I gave him some space, kinda hung back a bit.

He waited for me, a confused and uncertain look on his face and obviously decided to leave me alone.

Not that I could blame him.

The way we'd left things five years ago wasn't great.

Correction.

The way *I'd* left things five years ago wasn't great.

I didn't want to rush him. We had five days, after all, and I didn't want to ruin the whole thing on day one.

Next stop was the river cruise with the jumping crocodiles. I took a seat away from the edge of the boat, and after Paul got the two Norwegian girls and Norah—with an H, as she'd told everyone several times so far—settled in, he spoke to the staff on the boat for a few minutes. He clearly dealt with them regularly because they were all smiles.

He really had a whole new life now.

New business, new job, new friends.

New life.

New boyfriend, probably.

That twisted in my belly enough to make me feel nauseous. What did I expect? What we'd had together was five years ago. Of course he would have moved on.

It's just you that can't move on, Derek.

I wasn't sure what coming out to see him was going to achieve. A stupid fairy tale reunion was a pitiful dream, I could see that now. So maybe at best, I could see with my own two eyes that he'd moved on and that I should do the same.

"You feeling okay? Lookin' a little pale. If you don't like boats, you should have said."

His voice was so familiar. I hadn't heard it in years, yet after just a few hours, it felt as if I'd never missed a day.

I'd missed him every day.

I let out a breath and glanced at him before nodding toward the front of the boat. "Nah, I'm okay." It wasn't like I could tell him the uneasy feeling was because I was imagining him having a new lover. "You do know that teaching crocodiles to jump out of the water for food isn't a good idea."

He grinned. "They tell people not to dangle over the sides and of course they never listen. Until they see the crocs jump up like that."

I shook my head. Stupid tourists. Actually, stupid tourism operators who thought of it. I pointed my chin to a group of people who were keeping clear of the edge. "Wanna bet they're locals?"

Paul chuckled, and with a sigh, his smile faded. "I saw your name on the group manifest. Wondered if it was you."

"The one and the same." I also wasn't about to tell him that I'd found out which tour operation he ran and chose it specifically so I could see him. So I lied instead. "Got a bit of a surprise seeing you."

He nudged me with his elbow. "I could tell by your face."

The shock on my face when I'd seen him had nothing to do with surprise. It was that he, after all these years, was standing right in front of me. Even more handsome than he ever had been.

Five years later, like an eternity and no time at all had passed.

"How've you been?" he asked.

"Okay," I replied. "Pretty good. How about you? Got your dream job, I see."

He flinched like my words had found their mark. I hadn't meant to sound so bitter. "Yeah. Been doing this for over four years now. I love it." He looked at me then. "What about you?"

I shrugged. "Much the same."

"Still at the bar?"

I snorted. "No. Office job. It's as bad as it sounds."

"But no nights and weekends or bar fights, right?"

I almost smiled. "Right."

He kinda smiled, and we watched the tourists marvel at the crocodiles for a while. "Still into the stars, I see," he said, giving me a smile. "Is that a new telescope?"

I nodded. He'd never really understood my fascination with the night sky. Hell, I didn't either, really. But he'd never thought it was weird or foolish like other people did, and I was still grateful for that. "Yeah. I've had it for about two years now. Someone said I needed to see the view from Kakadu." I shrugged again. "So here I am."

No one had told me to come to Kakadu. It was all my doing. Tracking him down, using it as an excuse to see him again. And, like he could see right through my bullshit, he stared at me for a long beat, his gaze searching mine. I don't know what he was looking for. The truth, probably.

"It's pretty spectacular," he said.

My pulse quickened—his effect on me still had a stronghold. Especially this close to me, where I could feel his body heat, smell his deodorant. Before I could form any words to speak, the crowd of idiots watching the crocodiles jump all squealed, and both Paul and I turned at the sound.

"Has anyone ever fallen in?" I asked.

"Not that I know of." He shot me a half-smile. "I did hear of a guy that needed to be choppered out of a canyon this year. Tried to take a selfie with a brown snake."

I snorted. "Play stupid games, win stupid prizes. You know, Darwinism is a thing."

He chuckled. "I try and instil a common-sense approach with my clients."

I nodded to the crowd. "Well, you better go have a chat with Norah with an H. She's about to get a fast-tracked membership to the left-handed society."

He looked over and, sure enough, there was Norah, first in line with the crocs. Paul sighed. "Ah, jeez." Then his eyes met mine again. "It's good to see you again, Derek."

Then he got up and went over to the crowd and I tried to catch my breath.

It hadn't gone terribly. In fact, it was a miracle he'd even spoken to me at all, so I was taking it as a win.

I still didn't know if he was seeing someone. Or hell, he could even be married for all I knew.

There was that sick feeling again.

Needing to distract myself, I got up and stood at the handrail. I figured if someone was going to lose a limb, then I'd want the best view possible.

CHAPTER THREE
PAUL

Derek hadn't changed much at all. He still had that dark gallows humour. He was still the brooding type, still a pessimist by nature, still pouty and still cute as hell.

I had so many questions to ask him.

He said he had an office job now, which didn't seem like him at all. But there was something else in his eyes. A resignation, a sadness. He'd always been a wallower. His glass was always half empty. That's just how he was.

He still had no tolerance for stupidity, and he never was a fan of people in general. But he'd always been insightful and thoughtful, and the few he let into his world, he treated like kings.

He didn't trust easily, and I'd thrown that back in his face.

Well, inadvertently. I hadn't meant to hurt him so much. But he'd trusted me, and I'd left him.

I could only imagine the wreckage I'd left behind.

He'd have put up more walls, maybe hated people a little more. And for that I was sorry.

He really was a wonderful guy—once you got past the prickles and barbs. I'd always said he was like a Bougainvillea: beautiful and sweet, thrived in the right conditions, but covered in thorns that would tear you to shreds with one wrong move.

He seemed even thornier now, and maybe that was my fault.

But still, it was so good to see him.

The crocodile cruise ended without any fatalities—thank god. We had some lunch where we got to know each other a little more. I got the feeling Marit spoke better English than Kari because she did most of the talking, and Norah became the mum of the group. She was nice enough, just had a very strong personality. Derek didn't say much and kept himself a safe distance from conversations. He wasn't rude, just happy to stick to his introverted self.

And we were soon back on the road, leaving the Arnhem Highway before we got to Jabiru and headed off-road. I gave the clients a bit of a guided tour, pointing out sights of interest and answering any questions.

My camp was a permanent campsite, with what one might call luxury or 'glamping' tents. They were technically eco-domes with solar power. Each had an elevated wooden floor, a camp bed or two, power outlets, and mesh walls that could open up to let in the breeze. They were spacious enough, had a small private bathroom each, and were decked out with fairy lights for ambience, with a small deck out the front to take in the spectacular view.

There was a common covered area where we'd do all our cooking and eating and a fire pit for the cooler nights. The campsite was on top of a ridge looking out over the wetlands, which weren't too wet at this time of year. There were rocky escarpments to the right, quite a hike up to the top but worth it for the view. And there was a nice billabong and swimming hole further along the track to the left.

It was the perfect spot.

Not a soul for miles, which some people found a little worrying. I freaking loved it.

I had everyone grab their bags from the Cruiser with instructions. "Tent number one is a double so, Kari and Marit, that's you. Norah, you're in tent two. Derek, you're in tent three. I'm in tent four if you need me. There is always fresh fruit, crackers, and water in the communal kitchen. Help yourself at any time."

I gave them rules and instructions about safety and reminded them to never leave the camp without a backpack with water and emergency supplies. Even if they only intended to walk for five minutes. There was no room for mistakes out here.

None.

They all nodded and went off to their allocated tents. Giving them some time to get settled and freshen up usually gave me enough time to unpack the Cruiser. I plugged in the satellite phone to charge as I always did, and put the supplies away.

I found Derek standing at the edge of the campsite, looking out at the view. It was green wetlands to the horizon. Simply amazing. "Is this actually the Never Never?"

I almost laughed. Everyone knew that name from Crocodile Dundee. "No. That part of the park is about a hundred kilometres southeast of here."

He nodded. "It's impressive. I can see why you like it here."

"You should see it in the wet season," I said. "Electrical storms all afternoon. The whole sky is a light show. The wetlands come to life. There's nothing like it."

His gaze cut to mine before he turned back to the view. "Can you get here in the wet season? I thought it'd be cut off."

"I live here," I admitted. "All year round. I spend very few nights away. The roads aren't great, and when the rains hit, there's very few visitors or tourists. Not up here where we are, anyway. The wetland tours still run. I do have a guy that comes this way in the wet season. He chases storms and studies them. Likes the lightning, apparently. Sometimes he'll stay here if the roads are impassable."

"He likes lightning? Is he insane?"

"No. He's a nice guy, actually. A bit of a wildcard, but you'd have to be to be setting metal equipment up in a lightning storm, right?"

His eyes flinched, hardening at the horizon. "Is he . . . are you . . . ?"

Am I . . . what?

He didn't finish the sentence, and before I could ask, Norah appeared by our sides. "Now, that's not exactly a terrible view," she said. "Any direct walking trails from here?"

Distracted by her question, I explained where the trails were, showing her which was best, longest, shortest etc, which of course just fuelled more questions. When I looked back, Derek was gone.

Is he . . . are you . . . ?

Was he trying to ask if the storm guy and I were a thing?

Tully Larson was a nice guy. Late twenties and yeah, maybe he was cute. But I had no idea if he could be interested because I had no intention of acting on it.

I hadn't acted on any impulses in a long time. I'd been busy, for one thing. Sure, I'd tried to have some one-nighters not long after Derek and I broke up. But they didn't feel right, just left me feeling hollow and empty, like I was trying to fill a void that could never be filled.

A Derek kind of void.

So I gave up trying after that. I hadn't looked at or touched anyone since.

"Tonight we'll be hiking up to the top of the escarpment," I told Norah. "It's not exactly arduous and I'm sure it'll be easy for you, but I promise you the view is worth it."

"I'm sure it'll be a walk in the park," she said, waiting for me to catch the pun. "Get it?"

I faked a laugh. "Oh yes, a nice and easy walk in the national park."

She preened a little, and she told me how she'd hiked the Overland in Tasmania last year. She'd also done Machu Picchu and had hiked some of the Appalachian Trail in North America as well as some walking trails in England along Hadrian's Wall, just to name a few.

It was remarkable, yes. And she certainly had some fascinating stories, which I was going to hear all about over the next five days, I was sure. But she was nice, if not a little preachy, and Marit and Kari were super friendly, and along with Derek, I was happy with the small group of clients. Everyone was amenable, pleasant enough.

But I really just wanted some alone time with Derek.

I wanted to talk to him, ask him about everything that he'd done these last five years, how everyone in his life was going, and what was the reason for the pools of sadness in his eyes.

"Who's up for a small hike to the top of the ridge?" I asked the group, pointing to the rocky outcrop that framed the righthand side of the campsite. "A picnic and a Kakadu sunset for our first night here. How does that sound?"

Everyone was in agreement, excited even. Except for Derek. He nodded and shrugged, but to use the word excited would be a stretch. "Sure," he said.

"Let's leave in thirty minutes," I said, making a point of checking my watch so they would too.

I packed some fruit salad, and cheese and crackers, and the plastic wine flutes that we could drink our juice or water from. And as we began our hike, I led the way with Norah behind me, then Marit and Kari, and Derek was last.

I hadn't planned it that way, but it actually worked well.

The escarpment had natural rocky steps, but the climb

was vertical, and everyone had a backpack with their standard emergency water and supplies. Not heavy like an army kit but not light by any means. When I got to the top of the ridge, I helped pull each of them up the last step. The women were sweaty and puffing a little, and admittedly so was I. Derek seemed to be doing it easy, his biceps bulging as he pulled himself up. I held my hand out for the final step. He looked at my hand, then to my face, before he took my hand, somewhat begrudgingly.

His grip was strong and familiar, yet new all over again.

He dropped my hand first and brushed past me to join the others near the far edge, taking in the magnificent view. It was green national park for as far as the eye could see—to the horizon in all directions.

"Oh wow," Derek said.

Marit and Kari were grinning, taking photos, and Norah was already taking in landmarks for hiking and marking out where she wanted to go.

I set the blanket out and unpacked the picnic from my backpack. We sat around, eating the fruit and cheese, sipping juice, and watching the sky morph into vibrant pinks and oranges, then purples that had to be seen to be believed. It was almost other-worldly, and quite often the tourists who came here were first amazed but would often fall silent as the palette of soft colours washed over them.

I'd seen every single sunset and sunrise for four years, and they never got old.

They never would.

"I'd like to bring my telescope up here," Derek said. "Maybe tomorrow night." We were packing up and heading back down before it got too dark.

"We can come back later tonight," I suggested. If he'd wanted to come alone, well, that was out of the question. No one hiked alone out here. No exceptions. "But it's been a busy day. If you'd like to wait until tomorrow, that's fine."

"Oh." He baulked. "Uh, I just thought I could come back—"

"No one hikes solo," I said, offering my hand to Kari, who was going down the escarpment first. She smiled as she took the first step down, then Marit, and then Norah. They each took my offered hand and when it was Derek's turn, I held out my hand with a smirk.

He rolled his eyes and ignored me, taking the first step unassisted.

I would have been offended if I hadn't caught the hint of a smile.

"Tomorrow might be better," I said. It had been a long day, after all. "You can set up your telescope at camp tonight. Might be a good introduction," I said as we got to the bottom of the climb. "Then tomorrow night we can come back up here."

Derek gave a nod, not too pleased, but he didn't push, thankfully.

I went to the front of the line. I never let any guest dictate our schedule, so there'd be no arguing. And if I was being honest, as nice as some alone time with him on top of the ridge under the stars sounded, I wasn't sure I was ready for that. "I'll cook us some dinner first."

The plan was dinner and clean up, then we'd sit in the camping site in front of our tents, under the stars, looking out across the darkened valley below. I always lit a small camp-fire, not for the warmth but more for the experience. I boiled a billy of tea, like the Australian bushrangers used to do, and the clients loved it.

It was the perfect way to relax after a long day.

Kari and Marit were first to call it a night. They thanked me for a wonderful first day and disappeared into their tent. Their lights went out shortly after.

Yet Norah stayed.

She was nice, I couldn't deny it. The strong personality

type with opinions, but she was also smart and well-travelled, and normally I'd have enjoyed her stories. But my gaze kept drifting to Derek, who was basically ignoring us and looking up at the night sky.

I really just wanted some alone time with him, and the longer Norah talked, the longer the night dragged on, and the more I could feel my time running out. Like a clock was ticking down in my head, knowing my time with Derek was so limited . . .

"Oh, Derek," I said, as if I'd just remembered. "You might want to set up your telescope away from the campsite, away from the lights. Not too far though." I got up, effectively ending my conversation with Norah. "I'll grab the lantern."

Derek checked his watch. "It's a bit early," he said. "But I can already see so much out here."

"Wait until you get away from light pollution," I said, bringing the lantern out to him. "You wouldn't think a campsite would make much difference, but it does."

He smiled at me and my pulse quickened. The kind of carefree smile he used to have all those years ago. The one I saw in my memories, in my dreams . . .

"I'll just grab my backpack," Norah said.

Oh, great.

She was coming with us.

"Good idea," I said, aiming for a smile, even though it felt like a grimace.

"You're still a terrible liar." Derek was smirking at me. "Were you hoping for some alone time with me?" he murmured, but there was a glint of honesty in his eyes.

I hadn't realised just how much I was hoping for some alone time until it occurred to me that I wasn't getting it.

"Don't flatter yourself," I hissed at him.

He laughed, and my god, I'd missed that sound. But Norah was back before I could reply. She had her backpack on and her LED lantern in her hand. She was like a girl scout sponsored by a camping outlet. It was kinda fun. I showed her my lantern, which was like hers just ten times more powerful. "Are we ready?"

She nodded eagerly, and Derek rolled his eyes.

I led them to a cleared spot in the scrub I thought might be good. Just far enough away so the lights weren't a bother but close enough to hear if Marit or Kari needed me.

I set the lantern down while Derek set up his telescope. He'd always loved the stars and the vastness of space. Quite often I'd wake up to an empty bed and find him sitting in the backyard of the place we'd rented with his old telescope, his view looking ever upward.

I never thought to ask him what exactly he was looking for.

Or if he ever found it.

He used to say he'd just look at everything and nothing. I never questioned why he searched the skies. I just accepted that he did.

"Your new telescope looks pretty flash," I said as he set it up.

"Uh, thanks," he said. "I've still got the old one. But I can see more with this."

"Uh, Paul?" Norah said. "What wildlife is nocturnal out here?"

She was looking into the scrub, which was more of a wetland/lowland forest. There were trees, ferns, tall grasses, and a whole cacophony of wildlife that we couldn't see—but they could undoubtedly see us.

"There's a lot," I said. "Lots of mammals, frogs, lizards." I wasn't mentioning wild pigs and bats.

"Are there any crocodiles here?"

"I wouldn't have brought you here if there was," I said. "And I wouldn't be standing here."

She seemed to relax for a bit . . . until she thought of something else. She spun to me, her eyes wide, her face pale by the stark LED lantern. "Cassowaries?"

"You mean velociraptor turkeys with helmets?" Derek replied, not looking up from his telescope eyepiece.

I snorted but quickly reassured Norah. "No. There aren't any cassowaries here. And they're not nocturnal."

"But there are snakes and goannas," she added.

"This is Australia," Derek answered flatly. "So, yes. There is." He stood back from his telescope and gestured to Norah. "Take a look."

She wasn't as tall as him, so she had to pull it down a bit, but as soon as she put her eye to the eyepiece, she gasped. "Oh my god."

Derek grinned at me, and the warmth of it curled around my belly.

Norah looked up at Derek. "Is this for real?"

"Sure is."

She looked again for a few seconds, then stood back, wide eyed and excited, and let me have a look.

And holy shit.

I could see . . . everything. I could see it all.

So many stars. Countless. Bright and close, magnificent and unbelievable.

Like a disco ball or a snow globe or . . . There were no adequate metaphors.

"It's like nothing I've ever seen," I whispered. I turned back to Derek. "This telescope is way better than your last one."

"I know, right?" he said, taking the telescope again, putting his eye to the piece. "It's like a front-row seat on the Hubble."

I'd hate to think what his new telescope cost. "Did you get it from NASA?"

He chuckled. "Not quite." He was quiet then for a few moments. "It's even more breathtaking from here." He moved the telescope so he could pan across the Milky Way; he was looking for something, clearly. He grinned when he found it. "Oh wow."

He held it still and fixed the scope so it didn't move. "Here. Take a look at this."

Norah had another look and she gasped again. She was, quite surprisingly, speechless. She looked up at Derek, amazed. "Another first to add to my list," she said. "Of all the things I thought I'd see in Kakadu, Saturn wasn't one of them." She looked back through the scope. "I've never seen anything so beautiful."

My eyes drifted to Derek's. His longish hair fell to his eyes, the muted lantern light catching all his features like a monochrome photo against the blackness around him.

I'd never seen anything so beautiful either.

"Here," Norah said. "Take a look."

Derek and I pretended we hadn't just been staring at each other. I put my eye to the eyepiece and looked.

And stopped breathing. What I was looking at literally stole my breath.

I glanced over at Derek, awe clear on my face. He smirked in return, like he'd known this secret all along.

"Jesus," I mumbled, looking back through the telescope.

It was Saturn and its rings in all its celestial glory. Like every high-definition photograph I'd ever seen, only better.

And with my own eyes.

"You look at these every night?"

When he didn't answer, I turned back to face him. He nodded. "Yeah."

"Derek," I whispered. "I'm . . ." I didn't know what I was. "Wow."

His smile was timid, personal somehow. And I wished we were alone. I wished Norah wanted to go back and it could be just me and him . . .

But instead, she began to tell me of the Northern Lights

she'd seen in Iceland. She talked while Derek kept his eye to the telescope, and I kept my eyes on him. The way his jaw cut the dark night behind him, the column of his neck, how his long fingers handled the telescope with such care.

My mind took me back to our lives together. Him laughing in the shower, him moaning in my ear . . .

"Paul?" Norah asked, her voice cutting into some very private memories.

"Sorry? I was a million miles away."

"I just asked if you've ever seen the Southern Lights?"

"No. Not yet. Maybe one day."

Norah began telling me about the time she was in New Zealand, and I caught Derek's smile as he went back to looking through his telescope.

It wasn't long after that he began packing up.

"Did you want to stay?" I asked. "I can walk Norah back to camp and come back."

His eyes cut to mine. "Nah, it's okay. Been a long day."

So we walked back to camp. Barely fifty metres really, but it was through the scrub. When our tents came into view, my stomach began to tighten. Knots and butterflies, nerves and anticipation.

"Well, goodnight," Norah said, heading for her tent. "See you all bright and early."

Derek and I stopped. He glanced at his tent, then at me. For the longest moment, we stared at each other.

"Derek, I . . ."

"See you tomorrow," he said, turning and disappearing into his tent, the zippered door a finality in the silence.

I stood there for a second, trying to catch my breath. And it was only day one . . .

Yeah, we were definitely gonna have to talk.

CHAPTER FOUR

DEREK

Christ, this was a bad idea.

When it was just me and him, the air between us crackled with tension. He had to be able to feel it. I wasn't imagining it. The way he looked at me, hot and familiar, but guarded now. Like he'd moved on and it was too late. Like he was sorry, but it was too late.

He'd mentioned the storm-chasing guy. The one who would come and stay with him.

I should have known he'd find someone new. I mean, Paul was a great guy. Handsome, funny, hard-working. He was running his own successful business. He was living his dream, and he'd never looked happier.

Who wouldn't want him?

I was pissed that Norah had joined us, but as I lay there staring at the tent ceiling, I was probably glad she had.

Because the second we were alone, Paul was about to tell me that it was good to see me, but . . . It was good to catch up, but . . . He was glad I was doing okay, but . . .

I didn't want to hear it.

My heart wasn't up for that.

Not on day one.

Day two wasn't shaping up to be much better.

We had a breakfast of bacon-and-egg sandwiches, coffee, and juice. Paul packed up our lunches, stacked everything into his Cruiser, and off we went again.

Our first stop was driving into the wetlands to a bird-watching spot, and it was pretty good. I wished I'd brought my smaller telescope from home, though there were binoculars for tourists to use. There was a flourish of different birds to see, and it wasn't even the wet season.

It wasn't what I'd come here to do, but it was interesting and good to see at least once. I liked listening to Paul talk about things he was passionate about.

It was a good reminder that he'd spent years learning his trade and that he was different to the Paul I used to know.

A good reminder, yes. Painful, but good.

After that, we drove along some bumpy path until the track basically ended with a turning circle and what was probably supposed to be a parking bay. "We walk from here," Paul said.

And walk we did.

It was a warm day and a touch humid, though Marit and Kari were sweating and flushed; Norah was red in the face. Paul kept an eye on her, and she kept saying she was fine; she just wasn't used to hiking in tropical climates. And that was probably true. Every place she'd talked about hiking before was colder.

"Don't worry about me," she said, drinking her water. "If the elevation and steepness of Machu Picchu didn't kill me, Kakadu won't either."

Paul had laughed along with her, but I could tell he was keeping a close watch on her.

Paul and I were used to this climate, both being Darwin locals. In fact, it was pleasant weather for us. I was glad Norah hadn't chosen to visit in January.

The billabongs were beautiful, and I could see why they

were popular. We hiked around to the far edge, and I wondered why Paul had suggested that when another group of tourists arrived soon after us. He'd definitely picked the best spot.

Marit and Kari went in the water first, laughing as they dived under. Norah gave me a nervous nod. "Are you going in?"

"Yeah. Guess I will," I said, dumping my backpack.

"There aren't crocodiles, are there?"

"Nah." Not the saltwater kind, anyway. I didn't say that out loud, even though it was right on the tip of my tongue.

Paul bit back a smile as if he could read my mind. "No, there are no crocs here," he said.

So, with a nod and seeing the tourists on the other side were also going in, Norah waded out into the water.

"Does she really think you'd bring them to a croc-infested waterhole?" I asked. "Anyway, she's more likely to meet an inland taipan here than a croc."

Paul snorted. "Don't say that."

I pulled off my socks and shoes and pulled my shirt over my head. Paul's gaze went straight to my chest, and I could tell he tried not to look, but the ink caught his eye.

"That's new."

It was a spray of pink, purple, and orange across my heart, with fine geometric lines in the shape of a trapezium.

I nodded. "So is the one on my back." I walked out into the water, giving him a full view of the new tattoo there. No one who ever saw it knew what it was, not without asking. It just looked like a large intersecting mass of triangles: fine lines, a geometric design.

A map of the stars, covering half my back.

Paul knew though.

He wouldn't know the significance, but he knew what they were at least. Probably the only person in my life who *would* know.

I dove into the water. Cool and refreshing, and exactly what I needed to clear my head. I swam out to where Kari and Marit were. Norah was floating on her back, drifting, looking up every so often to check where she was.

"Norah said your telescope is very good," Marit said. "She said we should look tonight. If that's okay?"

"Yeah, absolutely." The more people the better. It meant less chance of Paul and me being alone.

Coming here to see him had been a mistake. And even though it hurt and even though it was not the outcome I'd wanted, maybe I could use it as closure.

He'd moved on, and it was time for me to do the same.

Lunch was chicken and salad on bread rolls, with some cut fruit and juice. "Do you carry all this?" Kari asked, nodding. "Heavy to carry, yes?"

Her English wasn't perfect, but Paul was good at encouraging her to speak more often. He was so good at this job.

"Yeah, it's heavy," he agreed. "But it's good exercise. No need for a gym membership." He flexed his biceps with a grin. "And it's always lighter going back, which is the most important part."

My mind was still replaying his biceps flexing to realise that yes, he did have to carry all the food and drinks. Maybe that was why he insisted we each carry our own water, at least.

I kinda felt bad though.

The women decided on a short walk around the edge of the water to the rocky outcrop on the far side, but I was happy to sit in the shade. "I'll watch our camp," I said. "You guys go."

Paul studied me for a second. "Are you sure?"

I nodded, avoiding his eyes. He'd always been able to see right through me, and I didn't want him to see my truth right now. "Yeah. You go."

The three women were waiting for him, but with an unsure glance my way, he turned and met them on the path.

I watched as they disappeared into the scrub, and I sighed.

Dammit.

It was confusing, that was for sure. The way he'd look at me, or the way I'd catch him looking at me, was laced with a familiar heat. But then it was gone as quick as it had appeared.

The chemistry we'd always had was still there. The heat, the spark. The desire that saw us fall into bed far too easily. That connection had been missing from my life for five years, and it was back, itching under the surface the second I laid eyes on him.

But what good was it now?

If he did have another guy in his life, then all this anguish was for naught. But I needed to talk to him. I needed to clear the air, once and for all.

Only then would I be able to move on.

We got back to camp on dusk. Everyone had an hour or so before dinner, so I set my telescope up on the small porch in front of my tent. I could hear the low murmur of Marit and Kari talking. It wasn't in English so I could tune them out easily. And Norah was soon punching out some Zs in her tent.

Paul's tent was more of a luxury canvas cabin. It was still technically a non-permanent fixture, as I was certain permit restrictions insisted on in the national park, but it would take some more effort to remove his than the glamping tents. I could hear him moving around in his cabin, which I supposed was his home now. He lived out here, in the remote wilderness.

I didn't know if I thought he was crazy or if I envied him.

I was leaning toward the latter.

I envied the hell out of him.

Not wanting to travel down that lonely road, I looked

through the eyepiece of my telescope and set my sights on things far, far away.

My memories betrayed me with something Paul had said to me years ago.

You're always focused on things so far out of reach, but you can't see what's right in front of you.

It was one of the last things he ever said to me. Before he left me. Before I pushed him away.

Those words haunted me still.

And maybe that was why I was here. To see what had been right in front of me.

To see what I'd lost.

Maybe part of me liked the pain . . .

"Whatcha looking at?" Paul's soft voice was right beside me. I hadn't heard him come over.

"Oh." I sat back. "Uh, just the moon."

"Just the moon," he repeated. "Nothing out of this world."

I almost smiled. "Was that a joke?"

He smirked, his eyes soft. "Can I see?"

I fixed the scope and gave him room so he could look. He was quiet for a second. "Jeez. You weren't kidding. That's like the actual fucking moon."

I snorted at that. "It is."

He was quiet for a second, his focus on the view in the telescope. "Why are you focused on that crater?"

"It's the *Mare Tranquillitatis*," I replied. "Or the Sea of Tranquillity."

Paul looked at me then. "That's a pretty name."

"It is. That's me, though. Still focused on things so far out of reach that I can't see what's right in front of me."

Paul's gaze flashed with recognition. With hurt.

"Yeah, look, Derek. I'm sorry."

"You don't need to apologise. You were right."

He turned to the view across the valley and sighed. "The

same could be said about me. I was so focused on what was on the horizon, I didn't look at what was passing me by."

"But you're happy now," I asked, though it really wasn't a question.

"I mean, sure."

"With your storm guy?"

Paul's head turned so fast I thought I heard his neck crack. "What?"

"Oh, Paul," Marit said. "There you are. Can I ask you something? Do you mind? With the shower." She imitated turning the tap on. "The . . . handle. Is no water."

"Ah, yes," Paul said. "The tap. I know what you're going to ask." He stepped off my deck and headed toward her tent. "There's a valve . . . you have to be careful or there'll be a water fountain out of your sink."

They disappeared into her tent and I went back to looking at outer space. Past the moon, slowly zooming in on the unreachable stars. Things were so much easier up there. The emptiness, the vastness.

The silence.

Where things weren't complicated.

Where the loneliness didn't hurt.

Dinner was quiet. Well, they all talked but I stuck to myself, like I usually did, and afterwards, Norah asked me if I was going stargazing again, up to the ridgeline like I'd mentioned the day before.

"Sure," I said. Then glanced to Paul. "If that's okay?"

I kept forgetting this was his business and I was a guest here. I needed to ask if it was okay first.

"Yeah," he said with a shrug. "Can't see why not."

"You two should come," Norah said to Marit and Kari. "The view through the telescope is amazing."

Oh goodie. Another group activity.

I repressed a sigh. I didn't mind them coming, I really didn't. I appreciated their enthusiasm for astronomy. It was nice that they were excited about it instead of rolling their eyes or mocking me, like some people did back home.

It was just something I normally did by myself.

It was always just me and the stars, the way I liked it.

It was personal and private.

Unless it was just me and Paul. I wouldn't have minded that.

But we were all going, apparently. And that was okay. I actually liked this group. There was no loudmouth, no raging extroverts that needed noise, or anyone who complained about every little thing.

I was grateful for that.

Sure, Norah liked to talk and tell her stories, but she wasn't overbearing. And when she started on her 'when I was trekking in Peru' stories, I could easily tune her out.

Like now.

We'd climbed up the escarpment, Paul had brought some picnic blankets and snacks, so while they sat around chatting, I set my telescope up.

I pretended it took a little longer than it really did, selfishly taking in the night sky by myself while I had the chance. I zeroed in on Saturn again, given it was the perfect time of the year to see it from here. It was clear and bright and very beautiful.

"Kari? And Marit?" I gestured to the telescope. "Want to see something amazing?"

They came over, Marit looking first. She gasped and turned her wide eyes to me, then she looked back in the eyepiece. Then she let Kari have a turn, saying something to her in Norwegian, and Kari's excitement matched her friend's.

Then Norah had a turn, and Paul stood back, smiling. "Want to see?" I asked him.

His warm smile and soft eyes made my insides curl. "Maybe later."

Oh.

Was that . . . was that an invitation?

I wasn't sure.

"What is your favourite?" Marit asked. She waved her hand across the sky. "Of all the things."

"The Orion Nebula," I answered immediately.

I could feel Paul's gaze on me, but I avoided his eye contact at all costs.

"Can you show us?" she asked, her eyes as wide as her smile.

"Sure. It might take me a little while to get the focus right." I'd never looked at it from this exact spot before, after all. "Give me a few minutes?"

They went back to the picnic blankets, lit only by a few muted camping lanterns. The wind was picking up, a cool and welcome reprieve. And I put my eye back to the telescope and set my sights on the north-western sky.

"The Orion Nebula, huh?" Paul asked quietly. I hadn't heard him come up beside me. He offered me a canister of water. I took it and had a sip. "The tattoo on your chest."

My eyes met his in the dark.

He recognised that?

"How did you know what it was?"

"I didn't. Not when I first saw it. But when you said it was your favourite." He shrugged, looking out into the vast darkness below. "I knew it was something star related. The purples and pinks, with the geometrical lines."

I held the eyepiece of my telescope. "Take a look," I murmured.

He stepped in close so he could look through the eyepiece.

I didn't step back. I let him into my personal space, feeling the heat of his skin close to mine.

He looked at the nebula, then he looked at me. He glanced down to my chest, above my heart, to where the tattoo was under my shirt. "Your tattoo. It looks just like it," he whispered.

"It was born from a cataclysmic disaster. It has a black hole in its centre, holding it all together with a disproportionate gravitational pull. It pulls everything into its heart and decimates it." My voice hitched, so I swallowed so I could speak. "Like me."

He didn't say anything, but even I could see the sadness on his face in the dark.

I let out a slow breath, trying to steady my voice. "It's light-years away. Pretty to look at. Complex, misunderstood, and completely unreachable. And it's destroying itself." My nose burned with unshed tears. "Like me."

Paul shook his head. "Derek." He breathed my name, so soft and gentle it almost carried away on the breeze.

"I don't know why I came here," I admitted. "I missed you—"

"I'm not seeing anyone," he blurted out. "The storm guy isn't . . . I haven't . . . not since you."

I couldn't believe what I was hearing. I wasn't sure I'd heard him properly or even what he meant.

I shook my head. I didn't know whether to laugh or cry.

"Me either," I managed to say, my chin wobbling. I sucked back a breath and faced away from him. I wasn't any good at talking about feelings and shit. Never had been, which was the reason for this whole mess. "Fucking hell."

Paul's hand touched my arm. Firm, warm. Familiar. "We will talk," he murmured.

I nodded because that was all I was capable of doing. I noticed the girls were silent then and staring at us. "Found the nebula," I said, my voice stronger than I expected. I stepped back away from the telescope, away from Paul.

I needed some space and time to process what had just happened.

He wasn't seeing anyone. Hadn't seen anyone since me.

What did that mean? That he'd been too busy? Or that I'd left as big a hole in his life as he'd left in mine?

As the three women took it in turns to gasp and marvel, I practiced some measured breaths and even took a few sips of water.

Paul folded up the picnic blankets and stashed the food containers into his backpack. I walked over and handed him his water canister.

"Hey, just real quick," he said quietly. "When you said you shouldn't have come here, what did you mean? Cause it kinda sounded like you knew I'd be here."

Well, shit.

"Uh . . ."

He stood up straight and cinched the backpack drawstring. "Yeah." He pointed between us. "You and me? We're gonna talk."

CHAPTER FIVE

PAUL

I COULDN'T LET HIM DO THIS. HE WAS STILL THE SAME OLD Derek. Still gorgeous, still the brooding, sulking type, still closed off and still unable to talk about anything important.

Like emotions and feelings.

And the truth.

I couldn't let him derail every-fucking-thing again. Not like last time.

Did I blame him for our relationship imploding?

Not entirely. Because I was the one who'd walked away.

But his inability to talk about how he felt, what was troubling him, what hurt him, was a huge blinking neon fucking warning sign.

I knew he had his reasons not to trust people. I knew the stories about his fucked-up childhood and his fucked-up father, but what I didn't know was how to help him.

How was I supposed to help him when he refused to admit he needed saving?

Now here he was, five years later . . .

Here we both were. Five years had passed, yet we were both stuck grasping at dry sand. The harder you held on, the harder it was to hold.

I couldn't let him do this again.

It needed to be different. And it needed to be different from the get-go.

I didn't even know what we were or what our futures held. My life was here now. My business, my future. Where he fit into that, I had no clue.

We really needed to talk.

Which wasn't easy given the other clients were here, and I needed to be with them almost every waking minute of the day.

Which left night-time.

We never had any trouble *communicating* at night, if you know what I mean. When the lights went out and we found ourselves alone, our bodies communicated just fine.

That had never been an issue for us.

And maybe that was the problem. Maybe the sex was so good that we just forgot we had to talk like adults.

So that had to change as well.

No sex until we cleared the air.

If sex was even on Derek's agenda . . .

And from the way he was looking at me when we got back to camp, I was pretty sure it was. He was trying to catch my eye, trying to have a silent conversation in front of the others, trying to get a minute alone.

I took the food containers into the communal kitchen to wash up and he pretended to refold the picnic blankets. Norah was hanging out by the fire pit, so Derek kept his voice down. "Can I see you?" he murmured. "When everyone's gone to bed. I can come to your tent . . ."

I turned to face him. "To talk. And talk only."

He winced but gave me a nod. "Yeah, of course."

"Can I help with anything?" Norah asked.

I gave her a warm smile. "Nope, all done. But thanks for the offer. I'll be heading to bed shortly, so it'll be lights out soon." I checked my watch. "Say ten? We've got another early start tomorrow."

Those instructions were more for Derek, and with a glance at him as I walked away, he gave me another nod.

I cleaned up my cabin, not that anything was too messy, but living in such small quarters, everything had to be in its place. I scrubbed my face and brushed my teeth, then changed into my pyjama bottoms and shirt. They were kind of hokey, given they were old-man PJs with my company logo monogrammed on the breast.

I waited for Norah's light to go out, then Derek's, knowing he wouldn't be far away.

My belly was full of butterflies and slippery knots. A small part of me wanted him to not show up, but a larger part of me was just about beside myself so when there was a gentle rap on the door, I almost jumped out of my own skin.

I opened the door, and Derek's pale silhouette in the moonlight made him look hauntingly beautiful.

I stood aside and he came in, not sure whether to sit or stand. He wiped his hands on his thighs and licked his lips.

"Take a seat," I said, gesturing to the sofa. I pulled the seat at my table out for me, figuring the distance—as small as it was—would do us good.

He sat and let out a long, steady breath. I was expecting him to not speak or to offer very little, like he used to do. But he just started to talk and, like a dam where the weight of the water was too much to bear, the wall cracked and the words spilled out.

"I knew you were here," he said. He spoke to the floor, to his fidgeting hands. "I kept track of your social media. I followed the leads and found your business here. Sounds creepy. I'm sorry. But I had to know you were okay, and I knew you didn't want to talk to me. It wasn't like I could have called . . ."

"You could have," I whispered.

He flinched and he took an unsteady breath. "I haven't been doing too good since you left." His chin wobbled a bit, but I knew he needed to say this. He needed to get this out. "I mean, I wasn't doing too good before you left either, and I know I fucked up. I pushed you away. I push everyone away. It's what I do, and I'm trying to not do that anymore." He grimaced. "I got a job in an office. I hate it, but it pays the bills. It's stifling and soul-crushing, and every day I dream of leaving. I envy you for doing what you always dreamed of doing. I know I told you that you were foolish." He shook his head. "I was scared of losing you, and I lost you anyway. You couldn't be the one to leave *me* if I pushed you away. I should have encouraged you to do this. I should have told you how proud I was of you." His breath trembled and his eyes met mine. Glassy, wet, vulnerable. "I'm so sorry for everything I said. For everything I did to hurt you. I don't know why I came here. I needed to see you. I thought maybe if I did see you, you'd either tell me to fuck off or I'd see how you'd moved on without me, and maybe then I could finally move on too."

He shook his head and a tear fell down his cheek.

"But I . . ." Derek swallowed hard and put his hand up, like he needed a minute. He recomposed himself. "This isn't easy for me. Nothing like this is easy for me. I can't talk about this shit. But I'm trying, Paul. I'm trying."

"I can see that," I said, unable to speak above a whisper. I wanted to touch him, to hold his hand. But he needed to say this, and frankly, I needed to hear it. "Take your time."

He nodded. "I thought if I came here and saw that you were happy, that maybe you had a new boyfriend, that it'd be the closure I needed. Because I've been stuck. I can't move on. Not from you or from what we had. From what I threw away. I've been so lost. I didn't know what else to do." He put his hand to his heart. "But then I came here, and I saw you. And you looked at me and you smiled."

Another tear fell down his face. He wiped it away.

"Maybe it'd be easier if you hated me," he said, crying now. "I could understand that. I could deal with that." Then he shrugged. "I would deserve that."

"No you wouldn't," I murmured. "Derek, what happened between us was not your fault. We both threw it away."

"I shouldn't have said what I did."

"And I shouldn't have either," I countered. "We were young and hurting. Our lives were changing, and we didn't know how to deal with that. I don't hate you. I could never hate you."

His gaze cut to mine. "You don't?"

I shook my head. "Never." I took a deep breath, now it was my turn to talk. "I wanted to start my own company. I saved money, I studied business. I had plans. You knew that. We talked about it all the time."

He nodded.

"It didn't have to mean the end of us. It just meant things would change, and that scared the shit outta you."

He nodded, another tear falling.

"I'm trying to be better. I want to be better."

"It's not a terrible flaw," I said quietly. "I knew you. I knew you were freaking out and all those horrible things you said were just barbs you put up to protect yourself."

His face crumpled and he began to cry. "I'm so sorry."

"I'm sorry too, Derek. But it's not all your fault. I could have tried harder too. I could have told you to pull your head out of your arse. I could have dragged you out here. You would have bitched and complained, but you would have done it. And it would have been hard. And we would have struggled in the early days. It wasn't easy. Hell, it's still not. But we would have done it."

He looked at me, confused. Which was probably fair, because I didn't even know what I was saying.

"We both could have tried harder," I said. "And I'm sorry we didn't."

He nodded then. "Me too."

We were quiet for a moment, letting the dust of our pasts settle around us.

He spoke first. "I haven't dated anyone else. I haven't even looked. I just couldn't. I never got over you. In my mind, you were this perfect time of my life that nothing will ever compare to." He managed a sad smile. "Kinda like looking at a galaxy that died a million years ago, but we can still see it because the light hasn't reached us yet. In hindsight, it's spectacular and brilliant. But in reality, in real-time"—his chin wobbled again—"it's no longer there."

God, his words . . . he'd always had a poetic way with words.

I ached to touch him, and against my better judgement, I went and sat beside him and took his hand. It was warm and strong, familiar yet new. "We can't change what happened. The words we said, the heartache. What's done is done. But I'm glad you're here. I'm glad we can talk about what happened. For both our sakes. For us to both move on."

"I don't want to move on," he whispered, his hold on my hand tightening. "I want to go back."

"But we can't. We're not those two guys anymore."

He shook his head, eyes welling with more tears. "What are you saying?"

"Derek, we're not those two young kids anymore. We worked nights behind a bar and dreamed during the day. We were so in love. We were reckless with it. We had something so wonderful, but we didn't understand just what we had. And that's exactly what young love is. What a first love is."

"My only love," he mumbled.

His words hurt me. The look of sadness on his face hurt me.

"Mine too. I've never loved anyone else. Not before, not

since." I held his hands in both of mine. "I wish I knew the answers. I wish I knew how to fix this. But I don't know what you want, and I don't know what I can offer. But Derek, we can't go back. We can't go back to how we used to be, because it would just all end the same."

He was staring at that in between space. At the floor, at his memories, I wasn't sure. He pulled his hand away and swallowed hard. "I get it. I do. I understand. Thank you," he mumbled. "For talking tonight. It was good to clear the air. And maybe now I can move on."

Wait a minute . . .

"Derek, stop," I said, maybe a little more harshly than I'd intended.

His gaze darted to mine, but he recoiled a little.

This right here. This right here, where he assumes the worst, shuts up like a clam and withdraws into himself . . . ugh. Frustrating as hell.

But he was trying.

And he did say what was on his mind earlier, and he'd said it well. Even though it was hard for him.

I could see he was trying.

"Derek, what do you want?" I asked. "Tell me right now. What did you come here for? Give me your best-case scenario."

He shook his head. "I don't know. I just don't know. I wanted . . ." He licked his lips and tried again. "I wanted you to not hate me. I wanted you to forgive me. To tell me it was okay. To tell me you . . ."

"To tell you what?"

He winced again, but man, my emotions were running high, my patience was worn thin. "You wanted me to tell you what, Derek? Enough of the not-saying-shit out loud. We're not kids anymore. So no more childish games. We're adults." Goddammit. I was mad now, and I tried to keep my voice down. "We need to be able to say shit out loud. So tell me. What did you want me to tell you?"

"I wanted you to tell me you still loved me!"

His outburst was made louder by the silence that followed. He sucked back a breath that was a half sob. "I wanted you to tell me you never moved on. Like I hadn't. I wanted you to tell me there was a hole in your life like there was in mine. I wanted you to tell me you still loved me because I'm still in love with you. I tried not to be, and I thought I'd just made up this illusion of who you were, like you were some perfect guy, and I hoped I'd get here and realise it wasn't true. You couldn't possibly be as perfect as I remembered, but then I get here and . . ." He waved his hand at me, up and down. "You're more perfect than I remember."

Oh wow.

Okay. I wasn't expecting the L word . . . considering he couldn't even tell me that when we were together.

"And it's made everything so much worse," he added quietly. "Because now I know. Now I know that you are everything I need, but it's too late." He let his head fall back, blinking and trying to breathe through his tears. "I'm sorry. I'm not used to saying this shit out loud. God, it hurts."

I tried to steady my breaths. My heart was hammering, aching.

I hadn't expected this. I hadn't expected him to turn up at all. Least of all pouring his heart out to me in ways he'd never been able to before. I hadn't expected him to still love me.

I hadn't expected to welcome hearing it. It made me happy. Cautiously, maybe even sceptically. But happy, none-theless.

"Do you think you could get used to saying it?" I asked, threading his fingers with mine.

He looked at me, confusion mixed with hope in his dark eyes. "What?"

"I don't know what the answers are, Derek. But seeing

you here . . ." I shook my head slowly. "You're as beautiful as you ever were. As poetically tortured as you ever were."

He made a face, half-smile, half twisted pain.

"You were my first love," I admitted quietly. "I never got over you. I thought of you often. Wondered what you were doing, if you'd moved on."

He shook his head again. "I couldn't."

"Me either."

His gaze fixed on mine. "Paul?"

"I'm not saying yes. I'm not saying I know what any of this means, because I don't. But I'm so fucking glad you're here. It's stirred up a lot of memories and emotions and I'm not sure what to make of it." And that was the honest truth. "But it's not a no. I don't know what it is. But I'm interested in finding out."

He looked at me, eyes wide, disbelieving, and full of tears. "Do you mean that?"

I nodded. "There's gonna be some terms and conditions. Like a whole fucking list. And we're going to start with talking. Actual conversations about what we want and what we expect."

He nodded, but another tear escaped down his cheek. "I just want to be with you. In whatever capacity, whatever it takes." He wiped his cheek with the back of his hand. "I've never known peace except when I'm with you."

Oh man.

My heart ached for him. I put my hand to his cheek. "Derek, your peace needs to come from here," I said, sliding my hand down to press against his chest.

He frowned, his whole face a mask of sadness. "I know. But it's easier when I'm with you. Just being near you makes it easier."

I wanted to kiss him. I so badly wanted to press my lips to his, to take even the smallest of his burdens. But we weren't there yet.

His eyes searched mine, as if he was looking for permission.

I took his hand, and holding it in both of mine, I moved an inch or two away, our legs no longer touching. "I don't want to fall into bad habits. It'd be so easy to just fall back into bed, but then we'd never talk about anything. And there's a lot we need to sort out."

He nodded, and he even smiled a little. "I want to tell you everything, but there isn't much to say. I've been treading water since you left. Barely keeping my head above the surface."

"Was coming to see me like a sink or swim type of thing?"

Derek's gaze met mine, intense and honest. He nodded. "Exactly like that. I had to try and move on, except I didn't know how. I thought if I could just see you . . . If you weren't as perfect as my memories made you out to be, or if you were with someone new." He shrugged. "But there you were, still the same, but different. Hotter than you were. Not sure how that was possible cause you were always pretty fucking hot."

I snorted out a laugh. "Thanks."

"But you were happy," he continued, smiling at me. "You were that ray of sunshine that had been missing. I've had nothing but gloomy skies and . . . grey. Everything's been so grey. And you . . ." He searched my face. "You stood there by your Cruiser in your sexy Steve Irwin outfit like a ray of fucking sunshine."

I chuckled. "Steve Irwin?"

"The khakis," he replied. "I like them, don't get me wrong. Not sure on the PJs though."

I looked down at my clothes. "Hey, these are my professional pyjamas. When I first started, a storm came through in the middle of the night and took a branch down near tent one. There was an almighty crack and someone screamed. I ran out wearing some boxer briefs. And not a stitch more. Needless to say, the next day, I ordered some professional pyjamas online. That way, if I have to run out in the middle of the night, I'm wearing something a little more professional."

"I'd prefer the boxer briefs," he murmured.

I knew that look he was giving me.

I cleared my throat and squeezed his hand. "And this is why we need to talk. As much as I want to kiss you right now —" I shook my head. "—I don't want to make the same old mistakes."

He looked at the floor again and chewed on his bottom lip for a while. "What do you want to know? I'll tell you everything. I've pretty much recapped the last five years. I did nothing. I saw no one. My dad's back in jail again, so that's something new, I guess. Well, not new. But you know what I mean. I rent a one bedder in the city. It's okay, nothing flash."

I didn't really mean that kind of stuff, but I was glad he told me. "Sorry about your dad."

"I'm not."

I wasn't either.

"I've got some money saved," he said with a shrug. "I don't go out and I don't drink, so whatever I earn just sits in my account. I bought the new telescope. And that's it. There's nothing else to tell. I wasn't lying when I said I was stuck, Paul. I'm just . . . stuck. Treading water, getting nowhere."

I took a deep breath and exhaled slowly. "And what do you want to do now?"

His gaze cut to mine. "I want to be with you."

"But how?"

"I don't know."

"Where will you live? What about your job? Your unit in Darwin?"

Derek shook his head. "I don't know," he whispered.

"Are you even talking about dating again? Or just friends?"

"I don't know," he said, more desperate this time. "What I want is you. What we had. Boyfriends, lovers, living together.

I would kill for that. But I'll take whatever I can get. And that sounds pitiful, I know, but you know what? That's where I'm at. I needed to tell you that I'm sorry, and to beg and grovel if I had to."

Letting go of his hand, I brushed a strand of hair off his forehead. "You don't need to beg. I'm glad you're here. I meant it when I said that. I'm sorry for how things ended with us too. We were just young and pigheaded, and too proud to admit what we needed. But we're older now. I'd like to think we know better."

He nodded quickly, but there was a hint of fear and uncertainty in his eyes. "I don't know how to make it work, like you said. Logistically, I have no clue. I didn't come here with a plan. To be honest, I was expecting you to laugh at me and tell me to fuck off."

I nudged my shoulder to his and chuckled. "I was just glad it was you and not some other Derek Grimes on my guest manifest. I wanted it to be you."

His eyes searched mine, a smile pulling at the corner of his lips.

"And you're willing to figure it out? For real?"

"I am."

His smile was breathtaking.

"But," I cautioned, "things will be different this time. They have to be."

He nodded. "I know."

Then he looked at my mouth, and he licked his lips.

I laughed and stood up. "Uh, yeah." I walked to the door and let out a loud breath. "I think I mentioned taking things slow a few times, and you looking at me like that doesn't help."

With his hands on his knees he stood up slowly, a smirk on his lips. "Looking at you how?"

"You know damn well." I opened the door for him. "Goodnight, Derek."

He pouted, but it was playful and shy. He walked to the door, standing closer to me than he had to. "Goodnight," he murmured, his voice low and rough.

I grabbed his arm, stopping him from leaving. I pulled him closer, our bodies pressing together. I looked at his lips, at his beautiful, smirking lips, then at his eyes. They were dark and swirling with familiar heat and pleading.

And all the permission I needed.

I slid my hand around the back of his neck and pulled him in for a kiss. It was hard stubble and soft lips, open and teasing, but no tongue, no tasting.

He grunted, and when I pulled back and put some distance between us, he whined.

"See you in the morning," I said, my voice betraying me.

He put his hand to my chest. Surely he could feel my heart thumping against my sternum, and from his smile, maybe he did. "Thank you, Paul."

The next morning, I was running a little later than I'd have liked. I'd barely slept. My mind kept replaying the kiss, his eyes, his smile.

It was a physical and emotional effort to have him leave my cabin last night. But it had been the right thing to do.

As much as my body disagreed, my heart and my brain were in charge this time.

Breakfast was a bit rushed, not that Marit or Kari noticed, and Norah didn't seem to, either. But Derek slipped into the communal kitchen and came to the sink, shoving his hands into the water and bumping me out of the way. "I'll finish washing up," he said. "You seem a bit frazzled this morning."

I would have growled at him if he wasn't right. In fact, I appreciated his help. "I was a bit slow out of bed this morning," I admitted. "Didn't sleep too well."

His gaze shot to mine. "Oh? In a good or bad way? Not like a having-second-thoughts lack of sleep."

"No." I ignored the heat in my cheeks. "More of a couldn't-get-someone-off-my-mind kind."

He raised an eyebrow, smiling, just as Marit came in. "Can I help with anything?"

"No, it's okay," I said quickly. "I was just about to load up the Cruiser."

"Oh, I can help with that." She decided she was helping whether I liked it or not. So I had her help me, and soon enough we were on the road for our day's adventure.

It was a lot of hiking, and though it was mostly flat, it was still humid. Getting close, you could hear the waterfalls and the river, and it ramped up the excitement. As soon as everyone walked through to the clearing and saw the amazing scenery, they soon forgot about how long and hot the hike was. The waterfalls made it worth it though.

It was one of my favourite spots.

Derek seemed to smile a bit more today, and he hung around me more. He even helped me carry stuff.

He also waded out into the water with Norah for one final dip before heading back. The walk back to the Cruiser was never as much fun as the walk to the waterfalls. Everyone was tired, the late afternoon sun was hot, the air getting humid.

A storm was rolling in across Kakadu. Not like the summer electrical storms, but the clouds were dark, the air thick.

When we got back to camp, everyone opted to freshen up with a cool shower, so I pulled out the camping chairs and sat them at the edge of the drop off. I served up some cheeses and crackers with grapes and juice, and I deliberately put Derek's telescope next to my chair so he'd sit next to me. When he walked out, he saw it and smiled at me in a way that made my heart knock against my ribs.

His damp dark hair hung in his eyes, his tanned skin the colour of honey in the stormy sunset.

I wanted to drag my teeth across the back of his neck. I wanted to taste his skin, see if it was as delicious as he smelled . . .

"Yeah, of course," Derek said. I realised then that my mind had been in the gutter and I'd missed the conversation. He took out his telescope and set the sights across the horizon, then they all took it in turns looking at the trees and wetlands that carpeted the scene before us.

The storm rolled in over the horizon, dark clouds of purple and orange with sparkling pockets of lightning and we could smell the downpours of rain in the distance.

It was an incredible sight.

It was a magical moment.

I cooked our BBQ dinner, and the five of us stayed there in our camping chairs watching over the world until long after the sun had set.

Derek shared his telescope around and his knowledge of the stars above us until Norah went to bed first, followed soon after by Marit and Kari.

"So, it's just us," he whispered.

"It appears so."

He sighed. "It's easy to see why you live here. This," he murmured, nodding to the darkness that now lay out before us. Then he gestured to the camp. "And this?"

"It's pretty amazing, isn't it?"

"Yeah."

He was quiet again for a while. Some crickets chirped and a hawk cried somewhere not too far away. He turned his gaze to me, a peaceful smile on his face. "You asked me what I wanted. Just this; you and me, and nothing else. That's what I want."

It was a nice dream.

But reality and finances would probably disagree.

He seemed to read my mind. "I don't know how to make it happen. But this is what I want."

I reached out and squeezed his hand. "If you want it bad enough, you'll find a way."

"Yeah, okay," he said, getting up. "I'm turning in. I'll see you in the morning."

It was so abrupt and curt, I was taken by surprise. "Yeah, okay," I said to his back. He was halfway to his tent already.

He jumped up onto his deck, opened the door, and stopped. "Ah, Paul?" he yelled.

I was up and out of my chair and right behind him in a second. My first thought was a snake . . .

He had water pouring out of his bathroom and onto his bed.

I dashed in and shut the water off. The shower valve had been shut off, and the basin spout had very deliberately been turned at the perfect angle to spray his bed.

I shot him a dirty stare. "Derek?"

"Oh no," he said flatly. "My bed's all wet. Looks like I'll need to sleep in someone else's bed . . ." He shrugged. "Say, in yours, perhaps?"

CHAPTER SIX

DEREK

Did I sabotage my bed? Yes.

Was I sorry?

Not one bit.

Paul was kinda mad, and I should have felt bad about that, but I threw my bag down on the floor of his bedroom and grinned at him. "Oh no. There's only one bed."

He was trying not to smile. "You did that deliberately."

"I don't know what you're talking about."

He raised one eyebrow. "Derek."

"You said I needed to action a plan. So I did. You said I needed to be more honest about what I want and how I feel. So I was."

"With words."

"We're talking, aren't we?"

He sighed and ran his hand through his hair. "I should make you sleep on the couch."

I looked at the couch. "I mean, I will if you want me to . . ." Then I looked at him. "But you don't want me to. The way you kissed me last night . . . I had to do something."

His gaze narrowed, trying to be mad at me, but when I laughed, he rolled his eyes and sighed. "We still need to talk."

"So let's talk. In bed."

He rolled his eyes again. "Derek, we—"

"I mean it. Talk only. I don't want you to be mad at me for doing what I did, but we have limited alone time together, and I don't want to leave here in a few days with things left undone."

He stared at me. "You really just want to talk?"

"Yes. If that's what we need to do, then yes."

He was sceptical, or probably flat out didn't believe me, and I couldn't blame him. Our sex life before had always been hot and electric, and I was usually the one to instigate it. Sex was easier than dealing with responsibilities and emotions and shit.

This time would be different.

It had to be.

"If I'm getting a second chance," I said quietly, "then I'll do anything in my power to not fuck it up. I meant what I said before, Paul. I'm serious about trying to do this right."

"And you call coercing yourself into my bed the right thing to do?"

I pulled my shirt over my head. "I said I was trying to do the right thing. But I'm still me."

He ogled my chest for a bit, then snapped out of it. He snatched up his pyjamas, went into his bathroom, and closed the door. When he came out, I was in his bed. "I take it from the book on your bedside you still sleep on the right side of the bed."

He tried to glare at me, but with another long sigh, he walked to his side and pulled back the cover. "I'm still mad at you."

I snuggled down and, facing him, folded my arm under my head and smiled. "You're still sexy when you're mad."

He ignored that, turned the lights off, got into bed, and pulled the covers up to his waist. He stared at the ceiling for a few moments, then turned onto his side to face me. "Your hair's longer."

"Not deliberate," I said with a shrug. "Just kinda stopped caring about a lot of things."

He reached over, and with the gentlest of touches, he brushed a strand of hair from my eyes. "I like it," he murmured. "And the tattoos."

I studied his eyes and, even in the dark, I could see honesty staring back at me. Sure, it was hard to say this stuff out loud, but I could trust him. I'd always been able to trust him. And I was safe with him. "I've been trying to fill the void, ya know? Trying to find something to fill the hole in my life. Tattoos seemed like a good idea. I love the ones I have, but . . ." I sighed. "The fix was only temporary."

He slid his hand over mine. "I'm sorry you had it tough."

"Did you?" It was a stupid question to ask, but I had to know. "Did you struggle at all?"

"Of course I did. I was heartbroken. I was busy, which helped. And I loved that I could channel my energy into getting this all set up. It took a while . . ." He frowned. "The nights were the worst. Lonely, and the quiet and remoteness made me wonder if you were right. If I was crazy for throwing everything away and chasing a dream."

I flinched. "I'm sorry I said that. And you know it wasn't true." I threaded our fingers. "I was just scared, to put it bluntly. You wanted to move on and leave me behind. I just needed to hurt you like I was hurting. It was childish, and I regret every word I said."

"I never wanted to leave you behind. I asked you to come with me. My plan was for you and me to do this." His lip pulled down. "But you didn't want it."

I let go of his hand and rolled onto my back. Telling this to the ceiling instead of looking into his eyes was so much easier. "I was scared. I was scared of change. I was scared of the unknown. Of failure. And you know why. Growing up with my dad . . . my entire life was an unknown." I swallowed down the lump in my throat. "And then I met you, and I had the first permanent things in my life. A job, food, a house."

"Hey," Paul said, reaching over for my hand again. "Look at me."

He waited for my eyes to meet his.

"I know. It's why I never blamed you." He shook his head, sadness etched on his face. Even the darkness couldn't hide it. "I blamed me. I fucked it up because I didn't try hard enough. I should have fought harder to show you, to prove to you."

I rolled back onto my side to face him properly, our knees bumping. "It wasn't your fault."

He sighed. "No. It wasn't yours either. We were just young, like I said. That's all. We didn't know how to handle it. We didn't talk enough. I should have told you every day that I loved you, that you were worth it."

Tears burned in my eyes. "I should have . . . I didn't . . ." I let out a shuddered breath. "I should have told you too."

He smiled, the silver moonlight outlining his face. "It's not too late for us. Seeing you again, having you here with me, it's like no time has passed at all, Derek. And I'd be lying if I said that didn't scare the shit outta me."

"I want it to be like it was. I want that with you," I whispered. "But you're right. Things need to be different this time. I need to be better this time. At saying shit out loud."

He chuckled warmly. Sleepily. "And I need to be better too." He put his hand to my cheek. His rough, warm hand felt divine. He stroked my cheek with his thumb, then pulled me in for a soft kiss. "Goodnight, Derek."

"Night, Paul. I'm not sorry about my bed."

He didn't open his eyes, but he did smile.

And I watched him sleep. Almost scared to close my eyes in case this was all some stupid dream.

Could it have been this easy?

It wasn't easy, Derek. You warred with yourself for a year about doing this. You struggled every minute of every day.

But he said he wants me back. Just like that.

Yeah, funny what happens when you decide to be a grownup and tell him how you feel.

I sighed, knowing there was no point in arguing with myself anymore. Overthinking and closing in on myself to shut everything else out had got me through most of my childhood. And it had served me well. But that was before Paul. That was before finding true love, finding someone who thinks I'm worth their time.

I didn't need to protect myself anymore.

I had to open myself up, as scary as that might be, and let him in.

Properly this time.

Forever this time.

Watching him, studying the lines of his face in the dark, I knew he was sound asleep. So I snuggled in a bit closer, and closer still, until his arm slid around me and pulled me close. With my head on his chest, his arms around me, it was the safest I'd felt in years.

I smiled into his neck and closed my eyes and breathed him in.

I slept like a baby.

***

I woke up to a smack on the arse. "You gotta get up," Paul said.

I opened one eye. He was showered and dressed, and I was spread out in his bed, hugging his pillow instead of him. I whined. "Mmm."

"The others will be awake soon. I'm starting breakfast early. We've got a busy day today."

I groaned again, rolled over, and kicked back the sheet.

His gaze went straight to my morning wood. He grunted, and I chuckled, still half asleep. "Don't blame me. I was having a very good dream and hugging your pillow that smells a lot like you."

He seemed stuck for a second, like his brain was glitching out. He wanted to stay but he knew he had to walk away. "I'll be . . . cooking breakfast."

"I'll be jerking off in your shower."

He tripped over his own feet, stumbled through the doorway but kept walking, grumbling as he went.

I chuckled and rolled out of bed.

In all seriousness, he did have a job to do. And also, in all seriousness, I did jerk off in his shower, imagining my hand and the warm, soapy water were his mouth. It only took a few strokes and a very vivid imagination, a replay of some of my favourite memories, and remembering his arms around me last night.

It was a pretty quick shower.

I got dressed, hoping to slip out of his tent unnoticed. I took one step out of the door and Marit and Kari both stopped dead on their way to the communal kitchen. Kari nudged Marit, and Marit smiled as if her suspicions proved correct.

"Morning," I said brightly. Then I yelled out to Paul. "I, uh, I couldn't find the . . . thing."

Paul looked up from the hotplate. "What?" Then, seeing the two girls, he shot me a wild look, his face a shade of red. "Oh. Okay. Uh, thanks."

We were terrible actors.

I made a beeline for my tent to avoid any awkward conversations, and to also assess the damage.

It wasn't so bad. Just a bit of water. We'd thrown towels on the floor last night, so I threw those towels into the bathroom for now. But the bed . . . well, it was wet through.

I stripped the bedding and lifted the mattress, carrying it out to the front deck.

Marit and Kari were clearly surprised, and Norah stood up. "Oh, what happened?"

"My bed got wet," I explained. "No big deal."

Marit cocked her head. "You wet the bed?" The language barrier wasn't embarrassing at all.

"No, no," I said, ignoring the grin on Paul's face. "Not wet like that. The tap and the valve in the bathroom . . ." I did the lever-hand action Marit did the other day so she'd understand. "It's no big deal."

"Oh, where will you sleep tonight?" Norah asked.

"Paul's got a spare bed. It's fine," I said dismissively, hoping they'd drop it.

By Marit and Kari's smirks, I think it might have been too late anyway.

"Breakfast is ready," Paul said a little too loudly. He gave me a 'please shut up' look before he turned his smile to his guests.

Breakfast was great. Back home, I'd have been lucky to choke down a coffee for breakfast on my way to work, but out here, getting up with the sun and having a full breakfast, then doing activities all day, outdoors in the fresh air . . . well, it was invigorating.

I felt like a different person.

Being with Paul and clearing away our pasts certainly had something to do with that. But being out here, surrounded by sunshine and wilderness . . . it was something I could get used to, that was for sure.

Paul said I needed a plan.

If we were going to move forward, I needed to figure out a sustainable way to do that.

To earn money, to pay my way, to help him.

If I wanted it bad enough, I'd find a way.

And I did want it. It was all I wanted.

"You okay?" Paul asked me quietly. We'd set off on our day of adventure, this time taking in Indigenous cave and rock art, and we were getting ready to hike in to the site. "You've been kinda quiet. At breakfast, on the drive out here."

I slid the backpack out of the back of the Cruiser. "Just thinking."

"About?"

"Making this happen," I said, lifting the full weight of his backpack. "Christ, this is heavy. Are you training for the Special Forces?"

He laughed. "Not quite."

"Here, turn around." I helped him put on the backpack. "Did you want me to take something out of here for you? I could halve your carry weight."

He shifted the bag on his back until he was comfortable. "Nah, I got it. I'm used to it now."

I mean, it certainly explained his physique. Hauling a twenty-five kilogram kit bag through the scrub, climbing over rocks and up and down rough terrain was no small feat.

I turned him around, not really giving him an option. I unclasped his backpack and took out the first aid kit and the top two insulated containers of food. It wasn't much, maybe five or six kilos at most. But surely it had to help.

"If I had a bigger backpack," I said, shoving them into my bag.

Paul tried to be annoyed but he relented a smile. "Thanks."

We began the hike in, Paul at the front, then Marit, Kari, and Norah, then me. It was getting warm, and this hike was all scrub. There were no overhead trees, no canopy for shade. We stopped a few times for water, and once Paul stopped, his hand up like a marine, and he pointed to his right.

There were two wallabies about twenty metres away. Marit and Kari were most excited, and they managed to snap some photos before the wallabies hopped away. Further along there was a huge goanna, maybe two metres long from its nose to the tip of its tail. Marit, Kari, and Norah were *not* excited to see that.

Paul put his arm out in a keep-back fashion, and we all sighed with relief when it sauntered off into the scrub.

It was so freaking awesome.

Better than my soul-sucking office job. Every day there was like purgatory, and I could kick myself for ever thinking Paul was crazy to want to do this.

I wondered if I could do it with him.

I wondered if he'd think that was a good idea.

Even if that was my Plan A, I'd still need a Plan B, C, and D.

I'd need contingencies to prove to him I was serious, that I'd thought it through. That I'd exhausted every possible option before I had to leave in two days.

Two days.

God. I wasn't ready to say goodbye again. Even if it wasn't permanent, even knowing I'd be seeing him again soon, it wasn't enough.

I didn't want to leave in two days.

The destination for the day was the site of some Indigenous rock art. There was a sheer rock face and trees that afforded some much-appreciated shade, an impressive overhang, a lookout, and a cave that was more of a slit in the ancient sandstone, all spotted with rock art. There were wooden paths to protect the ground, and the rock art itself was fenced off to stop people from trying to touch it.

It was sacred and beautiful and utterly amazing to think it was over tens of thousands of years old.

We took a moment to sit in the shade and take it all in. "It's peaceful here," I mused. Norah nodded, and Paul gave me a small, approving smile.

"It is. The First Nations people here, the Gundjeihmispeaking people, call this place Burrunggui," Paul said. "And according to traditional owners, this was shaped by Ancestral beings in the creation period of the Dreaming. They would meet here, prepare food, and hold ceremonies. It holds a remarkable significance."

"I can see why."

It was true. There was a peacefulness here that was hard to explain.

Kari said something in Norwegian, and Marit translated for her. "She said it feels like the earth and the heart are happy here," Marit said.

I stared at her because that was exactly how it felt. I nodded, struggling to find my voice. "That's how it feels for me too."

I could feel Paul watching me, and when I was brave enough to meet his gaze, he smiled. A soft, private smile that cemented something in me.

Yeah.

I wasn't leaving in two days.

I WAS GLAD TO GET BACK INTO CAMP. THE LATE AFTERNOON WAS warm and humid, the view of the valley below shimmered in the rising heat. Clouds rolled in again for a late afternoon shower, a sure sign that summer was on its way.

It wasn't in the distance this time. It was right over us.

I managed to get my mattress back into my tent before the storm hit. I had no intention of sleeping on it, but I didn't want it to get ruined. Marit, Kari, and Norah were all in their tents, waiting for the rain to hit.

I made a run for the communal kitchen as the skies opened up, getting myself drenched in the dash.

I laughed, my arms outstretched, water dripping off me,

my hair plastered down my forehead. "Holy shit. I feel like I walked out of the ocean."

Paul smirked and threw me a dishtowel to dry myself off with.

I shook my head like a dog and patted my face dry, and he was still looking at me, his eyes full of heat and desire.

"You should probably get out of those wet clothes," he said over the sound of the rain on the roof.

"Wanna help me with that?"

"Hell yes," he replied.

But a shriek of laughter came across the way and we turned to see Marit and Kari running into the rain, barefoot, still in their shorts and singlet tops. They laughed and danced, and then Norah pulled off her sandals and joined them.

I couldn't help but laugh, so I pulled off my shoes and socks. "Get your boots off," I said to Paul before I ran into the pouring rain. I was already wet, so it was no big deal.

But if I was ever going to have the chance to dance barefoot in the rain in the middle of Kakadu, I was going to take it.

I was surprised when Paul joined us. I didn't think he would. But he did. As barefoot and as soaking wet as the rest of us.

In the fading afternoon daylight, on the edge of the cliff overlooking the wetlands, we laughed and danced. Free, without a care in the world.

We probably looked mad, but it would be one of my fondest memories.

And afterward, when the rain cleared, we sat in the chairs overlooking the darkening world below us. Not talking, just taking it all in.

It had been a great day. One of the best days of my life, if I was being honest.

Because I'd made up my mind. I was staying here. I hadn't

told Paul that yet. I hadn't worked out the finer details yet, but I had a plan brewing.

I just had to get him on board with it.

And from the way I'd caught him smiling at me a few times, the way it sent a rush of warmth right through me, the spark between us ready to ignite, I got the feeling he wouldn't mind.

CHAPTER SEVEN

PAUL

I'D TOLD MYSELF AND I'D TOLD DEREK THAT WE NEEDED TO *ONLY* *talk*, knowing that falling back into bed, back into old habits, wouldn't be good for us.

But I was pretty sure I was going to blow that tonight.

Watching him laugh in the rain, the way his hair stuck to his forehead, around the nape of his neck, watching the happiness on his face . . .

There was no going back.

And we had talked. And we'd need to continue to communicate like we had been.

But tonight was going to end in orgasms.

I could feel it in my blood.

It had been a long day, full of long arduous hiking in warm and humid conditions, so I wasn't surprised when Norah called it a night early, and Marit and Kari soon followed.

Derek was washing up in the communal kitchen while I cleaned down the grill. I told him he didn't have to do that, but he just rolled his eyes and did it anyway. So I got busy scraping down the grill, and when I was done, I handed him the scraper to wash.

Everyone else was gone, the campsite dark. We were alone, and I risked a slow hand across his lower back.

"Thank you for helping me out today," I said.

He finished and pulled the plug. "You're welcome." He stayed where he was, turning his head. "Paul?"

"Yeah," I replied, standing close enough to feel his body heat.

"I'm not sleeping in my tent tonight," he whispered.

I smiled and dropped my forehead to his shoulder. "Good."

"And I know you said we should just talk, but—"

"I want you," I murmured. "Since I woke up next to you this morning. All day hiking. Seeing you at the rock art site, how you understood what the place meant. Then dancing in the rain. Derek—"

He turned then, his dark eyes pools of black fire. "Paul," he said, his voice rough. "Let's go."

He was gone so fast, I almost fell forward. But with a smile, I turned the kitchen light off and followed him into my cabin.

His shirt was already on the floor and he stopped with his shorts almost pulled down over his ass. His eyes caught mine. "Yes?"

"Fuck yes."

There was no stopping now. No reason or logic was going to convince my body to not do this. My blood was on fire, my balls were full and heavy, my cock already hard.

I hadn't had sex in so long.

I stood there, so mesmerised watching the magic of him undressing, that I forgot about my own clothes. When he was fully naked, his long, lean body pale in the darkness, he smiled. "See something you like?"

I nodded, words failing me.

He chuckled and strode over to me, unbuttoning my shirt. "Oh," I said, beginning to help him.

He left the shirt for me and unbuttoned my shorts, groaning as he found out how hard I was. "Fuck, I've missed this," he said, palming me.

I hissed. "It's been a long time," I said. "I've not . . . since you . . ."

His nose was almost touching mine, his gaze intense. "Me either." He licked his lips. "I know we should probably work our way into familiar territory, start slow," he whispered. "But I really want you to fuck me. I want to remember. I want you inside me, where you belong."

My knees almost buckled. Then I remembered. *Fuck.* "I don't have anything . . ."

I wasn't kidding when I said I hadn't even looked at anyone since him.

He smirked and went to his bag. He pulled out a bottle of lube and threw it on the bed. I was confused. "I thought you said you hadn't . . ."

He bit his bottom lip. "I haven't had sex with anyone, but I jerk off a lot." He gave himself a long, slow pull, twisting his hand over the head of his cock.

Warmth pooled low in my belly and my cock twitched. "Get on the bed."

He grinned and, one knee at a time, slowly went to the middle of my bed. I threw him a towel, which he spread out, then he took his pillow and put it under his hips as he lay down.

So familiar, like we'd just done this yesterday. Like five years hadn't passed.

He stretched his back like a cat, perching his arse high in the air, and he began to jerk off. "I imagined this a thousand times," he whined. "Remembered every time, the feel of you inside me. Made me come every time."

I let out a puff of breath. I think I'd stopped breathing there for a minute. "Christ, Derek," I murmured. "This is going to be over before it begins."

He lifted his arse higher and smiled into the mattress. "Then stop wasting time."

I pulled off my briefs and crawled onto the bed behind him, running my hand over his arse and lower back. He moaned at the touch, arching his back even more, the hand on his cock working faster.

God, I was so hard already. This really was going to be over before it began.

I poured the lube down his crack, smearing his hole with my thumb, slipping it inside him. Gentle at first, slow and delicate. Then deeper and then another finger, until he whined at me. "Paul, I'm not fucking kidding."

I chuckled.

He hadn't changed one bit.

Still a greedy lover. Demanding, bossy.

With a hand on his shoulder, I pulled him up, so his back was to my chest, my cock pressed against his arse. He gasped, trying to back onto me. I held his hips still. "Are you sure you want me bare?"

We'd had condomless sex a thousand times. But that was before.

His chest was heaving. "You said you haven't been with anyone."

"I haven't. Not since you."

He groaned. "Then yes. Fuck me. Come inside me."

My cock pulsed at his words and he smirked, so I pushed him back down, his face into the mattress. And then I pushed my cock against his hole and slowly slipped inside him.

Hot and slick and so fucking tight.

"Holy shit," I breathed.

He whined, his fists now clawing the bed covers. "Oh fuck, yes."

I pushed all the way in, up to my balls. And I stayed there, letting him get used to it. He tried to push back, tried to make me move, so with my hand on his hip, I pressed into him.

Deeper and harder to remind him who was in charge. He cried out, staying still then, breathing deep and measured.

After a few moments, when he was fully relaxed, he began to whine with each breath. Like he used to when he was truly ready for me to move.

We were so familiar, so in tune.

So I pulled out a little and slid back in a few times, and his hand went back to his cock. "Oh god, Paul. This is what I needed, so bad."

I put my hand on the bed by his shoulder and began to fuck him. Exactly how I knew he loved it, how he needed it.

He gasped with the change of angle, his hand moving fast, his hips rolling, and I was so deep inside him. He was so tight, taking me into his body like a glove. With his forehead pressed into the bed, he arched his back. "Paul, yes, right there, fuck," he groaned, his arse clenching tight around me as he came.

Milking me.

I thrust into him hard, once, twice, my cock rock hard and swollen, the coil of pleasure inside me winding tighter and tighter until it snapped.

My cock pulsed and spilled come deep inside him, and he gasped again, moaning as I filled him. The room spun, my world went white and fuzzy . . .

I'd never come so hard.

I'd never felt like this. Like all my wounds were healed, the pain of the past five years was gone. I collapsed on top of him, staying buried inside him, trying to catch my breath, to make sense of what my heart was trying to tell me.

I was home.

He was my home.

Eventually he moved, groaning as I rolled off him, but I quickly pulled him back into my arms. "Don't go too far," I murmured into the back of his head. "I'm not done with you yet."

He chuckled, sighing contentedly in my arms. Both of us dozed for a while, sleep swirling with happy thoughts and a happy heart.

Somewhere around 2:00 am, I woke him up with a sleepy trail of kisses over his chest. I rolled him onto his back, nestled myself between his legs, sucking on his nipples and flicking them with my tongue until he fisted my hair and wrapped his legs around me.

This time, I kissed him as I pushed into him. My tongue in his mouth with my cock in his arse, his legs around my waist, our fingers entwined. The slower I fucked him, the higher he lifted his legs, then his arms were around my neck, and we found our rhythm, like we always did.

Making love with Derek was so easy.

So right.

His eyes in the darkness, wide and vulnerable, pleading. All I could do was nod and kiss him deeper, giving him what he was silently asking for.

He whined and grunted, his head pushed back, neck corded, and his eyes rolled closed as I hit that magic spot inside him. He came with a silent scream, clawing at my back, and I followed him over the edge.

Coming inside him, making him mine all over again, was everything I needed.

When I cleaned him up, he could barely keep his eyes open, smiling and somewhat incoherent, like he was drunk on me. "Feel like yours again," he mumbled.

I grinned, my heart happy that he felt the same way. I tossed the washcloth toward my bathroom, wrapped my arms around him, then kissed the side of his head. "Because you are."

I closed my eyes, knowing morning would come all too soon.

He was only supposed to have one more day here, one more day with me.

We needed to change that.

We needed to discuss our futures. With him in my arms, it all seemed so simple. Yet I had to wonder what the morning light would bring.

He mumbled something into my chest that I didn't quite catch. "Mm, what did you say?"

"I don't want to go back," he murmured. "Stay here with you, forever."

I smiled into the dark, my arms tightening around him. It sounded so easy when he said it like that. "You make it sound so simple," I whispered, my heart thumping.

"'Cause it is. Now go to sleep. Busy day tomorrow."

I chuckled, rubbing his back.

Could it really be that simple?

CHAPTER EIGHT
DEREK

I woke up hot and sweaty until I realised I was clinging to Paul and he was the reason I was sweating before six o'clock in the morning.

I peeled my skin from his and rolled onto my back, earning myself a sharp ache in my arse. I smiled at the familiar reminder of what we'd done.

Sunlight was beginning to dawn outside, the last day of the tour. I was excited, sure. But more excited about my plan, about my future. And it had been a long time since I'd felt excited about anything.

I rolled out of bed and took a quick shower. I found myself grinning when I remembered the reason why my arse felt wet and slippery. The memory of Paul planting his seed in me burned in my chest, making my whole body tingle.

I couldn't remember feeling so alive.

I shut the water off, and as I grabbed for a towel, Paul walked in. "Morning," I said, still smiling.

He squinted one eye at me, his hair sticking up on one side. "Hm. You're awfully cheerful today."

"I have every reason to be."

Paul frowned. "It's your last day," he said.

I snorted. "No it's not." Then I looked down at his very naked body. Damn, he was so sexy. "Come on, hurry up and get showered, or I'll end up back in here with you, going for round three. I'll see if I can figure out the coffee."

I left him to it, getting dressed and going out to the communal kitchen. I had two brews made just as Paul joined me, right when the sun was coming up. I handed him his cup. "So," he began, eyeing me cautiously. "Want to explain the good mood?"

"I told you last night," I said, sipping my coffee. "Today's not my last day. I'm not leaving tomorrow. It's that simple." Then I shrugged. "I mean, there's more to it than that, and it's probably more complicated in the details, but the bottom line is I don't want to leave. I want to be with you. Not just living in Jabiru, like I thought could be a possibility." Jabiru was the closest town. It made sense, but it wasn't close enough. "But here, with you. At this camp. Helping you."

He stared at me.

"Come on, let's go sit out here," I said, walking to the chairs that faced the valley below.

I waited for him to join me.

"So that's your plan?" he asked.

I sighed contentedly, smiling as I sipped my coffee and taking in the glorious sunrise. "Yep."

"There are permit applications and some pretty strict rules that apply to working out here," he said. "It's not a simple procedure. It took weeks for mine to come through. They do background checks—"

"I'm fine with all that."

"They'll need valid reasons, economical reasons. My business does okay, Derek, but I don't know if it can sustain us both."

"I have a business plan," I said. "I can run additional astronomy tours. You can charge more. I can take them up to the ridge, or even just here. You can't tell me people wouldn't like that."

He opened his mouth, then he made a thoughtful face. "Um, maybe . . . ? I'd need to think on it. We'd need to run numbers and submit a changed business plan with the permit, and . . ." He shrugged and his eyes cut to mine. "It could work."

I grinned and settled back in the seat, gazing out across the wetlands as the sun rose. "If I get to do this during the day," I gestured out before us. "And you get to do me all night, then we will make this happen."

He chuckled, then sighed. "You're serious, yeah? You want this life? It's remote. It's new people every few days. It's tiring, it's subject to weather, and I've had some clients that are, how do I say it?"

"A pain in the arse."

"To put it mildly."

"I'm serious. I told you before, Paul. Whatever it takes. My place is here with you. Last night cemented that for me. I can't go back. My life in Darwin without you was killing me. I feel alive here."

"You said you'd thought about living in Jabiru?"

I nodded. Jabiru was a small town in Kakadu. There were houses, a fuel station, a fast-food place, and not much more. "I thought it could work, and if they knock back my application to work here with you, then I will look at Jabiru. Seeing you on weekends would be better than not at all."

Paul's eyes met mine, warm and filled with understanding. He got it now, just how serious I was.

"My place is with you," I said quietly. "When you strip away all the bullshit, it's really kinda simple. Whatever it takes."

He nodded. "We'll make it work."

"Yes, we will."

Norah's door opened and Paul stood up as she walked over. "Well, this looks nice," she said.

"Take a seat," Paul said. "I'll make a start on breakfast. Want a coffee?"

Then Marit and Kari joined us, and after breakfast, we loaded up the Cruiser and headed out. The last day was the biggest—a lot of hiking, a lot of driving—but it was by far the best day of the tour.

We were going to the Jim Jim Falls and finishing the tour with a sunset cruise on the Yellow River.

Getting to the waterfalls was an effort. A fair drive along the highway but then a very slow and bumpy drive along a dirt and sand road that ended at a carpark. From there we crossed a river on a punt, then hiked into the falls.

World famous, amazing, ancient, and breathtaking. They were worth the effort.

From the base of the falls, we hiked for a good ninety minutes through the gorge to the private billabongs, which were like plunge pools carved from ancient stone.

It wasn't an easy hike, and I could see Paul kept his eye on Norah, but she was an absolute trooper. She was sweating and red-faced and puffing and panting. But she never once complained. She was first to her feet when we paused for a drink, and she loved every step.

She swam in the water, she mothered Marit and Kari, and me a little, if I was being honest. At first it was a bit weird, but over the last few days she'd really grown on me.

I offered her my hand when she had to jump down a long step on the way back to the Cruiser. Which I also offered to Kari and Marit as well, and then as a joke, I offered my hand to Paul. Marit and Kari giggled, and from the way they looked between me and Paul, I was sure they knew something was going on between us.

It did make me wonder what we'd do, down the track, if

my business proposal became a reality and we ran these tours as a couple.

Would we keep sharing his cabin?

Would we even be a *couple* when we had clients?

I couldn't take a tent for myself, because then we'd be cutting into how many clients we could manage. But maybe some clients wouldn't want to be stuck out in the middle of nowhere with a gay couple.

"What are you quiet for?" Marit asked in the Cruiser on the way to the Yellow River cruise. It was now late afternoon, it'd been a long day already, and those hours of missed sleep were now catching up with me. Plus, my mind was running through a hundred scenarios. "You look worried."

I didn't miss the flash of Paul's eyes in the rear-view mirror. "I'm not worried," I said, offering a smile I didn't quite rightly feel.

"You don't want to leave tomorrow," she said. "We don't want to leave either. But we fly from Darwin tomorrow night."

"I'm not leaving tomorrow," I said, trying the words out for size. It felt good. All eyes turned to me, including Paul's in the rear-view. "I have a few extra days. Part of a new stargazer tour that Paul's trialling."

"Oh, with your telescope?" Marit asked excitedly. "Oh, so amazing."

"Is it new?" Norah asked. "I'd have liked to have gone on that."

I smiled at Paul in his reflection. "Yeah, it's only new. Still in the trial phase. But you all enjoyed the stargazing we did."

They all agreed with enthusiastic nods. "Very much," Kari said.

It was probably silly, being a very small test group of sorts. But it bolstered me to think my plan could actually work. The hope that seeded in my chest was growing into something more like determination. People travelled from all over to see the stars from Kakadu. My plan could actually work.

Would it be easy? No.

Would we need to work out how we lived, worked, and coexisted as a couple? Sure.

But it *was* possible.

———

THE SUNSET CRUISE WAS MAGICAL. BIRDS, CROCODILES, EVEN wild horses, and a sunset like only Kakadu could do made an excellent end to a great little tour.

It was the perfect end to four perfect days.

Four days that righted wrongs and gave me back my life.

When we got back to camp, I was almost sorry there was no late-night storm that made us take shelter in our tents. While part of me was bummed that I didn't get Paul to myself, part of me was happy to sit around on the camp chairs and talk.

Marit and Kari were flying back to Norway, and Norah had two days in Darwin before heading back to Sydney.

"So when do you go back to Darwin?" Norah asked me. "How long does your stargazing thing go for?"

"Unsure at this point," I said vaguely. "Hoping for it to be a permanent thing."

"It'd be an amazing experience," Norah said. "I feel very privileged to see what you showed me. Not many other people can say they saw Saturn from Kakadu."

It made me happy to hear her say that. "Should I get my telescope out?"

"Oh yes, please," she said. Marit and Kari also agreed.

So we spent another hour or two looking skyward. I showed them constellations and planets. The way Paul smiled at me made me proud.

And when it was too late and no one could withhold

yawns, we said goodnight. I went straight into Paul's cabin, kicked off my shoes, pulled off my shirt, and fell onto the bed.

It had been a long day.

"I'm tired," I murmured as Paul came in.

He pulled off his boots and sighed as he crawled onto the bed, over my body. He kissed up my stomach. "You were great today," he said, kissing a slow path up to my chest. "I could get used to having you here, helping me."

I carded my fingers through his short hair and pulled his head up so he was looking at me. "You'll have to get used to it. Because I'm not leaving."

"You'll have to go back at some point," he said. "To get your things, to finalise paperwork, your apartment."

"But not for long. A few days, at most." I sighed. "I was thinking today . . . How will it work? How will we be us and run your business? Will your clients know we're together? Will they boycott you because of that? Paul, I don't want to jeopardise what you've worked so hard for."

His eyes met mine. "Where did your confidence go? That adamant 'I'm not leaving' line you said half a minute ago?"

"I'm not leaving . . . I don't want to leave. But this is a reality question. It's a 'how do we move forward' question."

He smiled. "We'll work it out. I've never hidden who I am, and I don't expect to start now. We can just tell folks that this cabin has two single beds."

"But it doesn't."

"They don't know that." He kissed my lips. "But I like that you're thinking of these things. You're thinking about reality."

"I'm trying. I won't always get it right, Paul. But I'm trying."

"I know you are." He kissed my sternum, then kissed the tattoo over my heart. He stared at it, then rolled us onto our sides, collected me in his arms, and brushed my hair off my forehead. He searched my eyes and traced his finger down my lips, chin, to my chest, and back to the tattoo. "You said this nebula is like you. Because it decimates everything in its path."

I knew he'd bring that up eventually. I didn't really want to talk about it, but if I was going to learn how to be honest with him, it started now.

"It's how I felt when you left," I admitted. "That I'd taken your love and decimated it. I'd ruined everything good in my life. Everything that was pure and worth anything. Until there was nothing left, just a massive black hole."

He smiled sadly. "No, this nebula is like you because it's made up of a million beautiful moving parts just looking for peace."

Oh god.

"You search the sky every night looking for peace, but, Derek, it's not up there. It's right here," he said, his palm pressed over my heart. "The peace you need to look for is in here."

I nodded, because I knew that was true. It just hurt. "My peace starts here with you."

He smiled, tired and heavy lidded. He kissed me, soft and warm. "Too tired to get up," he mumbled.

Washing faces and brushing teeth could wait. I pulled him closer and rested my chin against the side of his face and smiled into the darkness.

My peace started here.

My peace had already started.

EPILOGUE
PAUL

EIGHTEEN MONTHS LATER

I jumped out of the Cruiser, handed one box of supplies to Derek, grabbed the other, and we dashed into the communal kitchen.

"He's on his way now," I said over the sound of the wind.

"He's insane," Derek said, looking out at the storm about to hit. "This one's gonna be a doozy."

I nodded. "Sure is." The air was already charged, thunder rolled overhead, and cracks of lightning lit up the too-dark afternoon sky. "Did you get the tie-downs done?"

"Yep. She's all secure as it can be." Derek was stacking the supplies into the fridge and cupboards. "Tent two stuck a bit. Thought I was gonna have to wait for you, but I got it in."

When storms like this hit, we needed to make sure our whole campsite was locked down and secure. We couldn't afford damaged tents or, worse still, someone getting injured.

Having Derek here was a godsend. In the beginning, I'd worried about how it'd all work, with money and getting his stargazing tours up and running, but it had been incredible. And he never stopped working. He was either mowing grass, clipping the trees around the campsite, making every-thing more client-friendly without losing any of the natural charm. He taught himself how to sew canvas patches on the eco canopies on the tents, he cooked meals, he cleaned up. He made my tours run more smoothly, taking half my work-load without complaint. And once a month, he ran his own night-time astronomy tours. Which were booked solid. We were considering maybe introducing more throughout the year.

It hadn't been all smooth sailing. We'd had some adjust-ment issues and a few arguments, but mostly it had been the best personal and professional decision I'd ever made.

But he, himself, the Derek I used to know—the moody and brooding Derek, the Derek that would sometimes let the darkness in—was gone. Sure, he was still a little moody sometimes, but taking him out of his old life, where his past was only ever a step behind him, had been good for him.

Being outdoors was good for him.

Being surrounded by this remote and rugged country was good for him.

Being able to watch and study the stars whenever he wanted was good for him.

Being here with me was good for him.

He was good for me too.

With the last of the supplies put away, I took his face in my hands and kissed him. "What was that for?" he asked with a smile.

"Thank you," I said. "For being here. For being great. I love you."

He grinned, his long hair tousled by the wind. "I love you too."

"You know what we should do?" I asked. The wind stopped as though it was listening to us and wanted to hear my answer. But then the rain dropped, fat and heavy drops in a deluge. A crack of thunder boomed right above us.

We both ducked on instinct and laughed. "Holy shit!" he yelled over the roar of the storm. "What should we do?"

Leaning in, I still had to yell so he could hear me. "We should fuck all afternoon."

He looked at me, wide eyed, and he laughed. "Oh really?"

I nodded and gestured to the empty tents. "No guests today."

Just then, the old Jeep pulled up. "What were you saying?" Derek asked.

I waved him off. "Tully doesn't count."

"Pretty sure he does."

Tully Larson was the storm chaser who would use our camp as a base intermittently during the height of the electrical storm season. He had another camp further up toward the coast, still in Kakadu, but access was tough going in the wet season. He'd arrive here, say hello, maybe stay a night or two to wait for the perfect storm, then disappear into the wilderness for days on end.

Only this time, he was bringing someone.

His guest was a meteorologist from Melbourne, apparently. A fulminologist, to be exact. If you'd ever heard of such a thing. Someone who studies lightning.

Tully ran into the communal kitchen area, unfazed by the rain, his grin wide. His blond shaggy hair stuck to his head, his shirt clung to his chest, but he didn't seem to care. He was a storm chaser after all. Rain was nothing to him.

"G'day fellas," he said, shaking my hand, then Derek's. "Real good to see ya's again."

Another man appeared then, just as wet but clearly more bothered. He was dripping water from his short dark hair, he had stunning dark blue eyes, and a frown. He was also wearing proper shorts and a button-down shirt and boots; his outfit screamed scientist on a field trip, but at least he wore boots.

God, he had the bluest eyes I'd ever seen.

"This is Jeremiah," Tully said. "Jeremiah, this is Paul and Derek. They run this place. And they live here."

"You live here?" Jeremiah asked. Stunned. Horrified. "All the way out here?"

I laughed and gestured to the wall of water that was rain just a few feet away. "Best address on the planet. But," I pointed to our cabin, "more specifically, that's our home right there. Tully will look after you tonight, but if there's an emergency, you come find us."

Then I clapped Tully on the shoulder. "I put you guys in tent one. Fridge is full. You know where everything is. We're gonna be busy for a few hours. If you need us for anything, you don't need us for anything." I winked. "If you know what I mean."

He grinned. "Loud and clear."

Derek and I made a quick run for our cabin. He locked the door, and I grabbed us a towel each before we stripped out of our wet clothes. "I can't believe you told him that," Derek said.

I laughed. "Remember when you thought me and the storm guy were a thing?"

Derek rolled his eyes as he dried himself. "That was before I ever met him. He's cute, in a Patrick Swayze from *Point Break* kinda way, but he's not your type. I know that now."

"Oh really? What's my type?"

He threw his towel onto the bed, standing before me stark naked. "Me. I'm your type."

"Yes, you are." I gave him a few strokes while I kissed down his neck, then I captured his mouth with mine. "Now get on the bed."

Thunder boomed overhead and lightning lit up the sky outside. The air between us crackled, charged with energy.

Derek smirked and did as I told him. As the summer storm wreaked havoc outside, we made slow love, over and over. Steamy and sweaty, our bodies joining in the most intimate of ways, the way our hearts already had.

As one, and forever.

OUTRUN THE RAIN

BOOK ONE

OUTRUN THE RAIN

CHAPTER ONE

TULLY

I sat in my old Jeep Wrangler, waiting for the plane from Darwin to come in. Jabiru Airport was no more than a one-building low-key airport, smack bang right in the middle of Kakadu National Park in the Top End of the Northern Territory.

It wasn't a thriving metropolis, lemme put it that way.

The brick terminal building was better than the tin shed it used to be, but still. Heathrow, this place was not.

Jabiru itself had a grand population of around one thousand people. Well, that many in the dry season, less in the wet season. The climate up here did funny things to folks, and most packed up and went south for a few months, before the heat and humidity and torrential rain set in.

That was when I got here.

Because with that heat and humidity came summer storms. Brutal, fierce, electrical storms that rolled in almost every afternoon, dumping monsoonal downpours, and setting the skies on fire with lightning.

Which was why I was waiting at Jabiru Airport.

A guy was coming up from the Bureau of Meteorology in Melbourne. Staying for a week or two to study lightning.

Well, he'd already studied it; he had some doctorate or some other fancy title. Well, he had *Atmospheric Sciences and Meteorology* after his name, followed by a whole bunch of letters. He was coming all this way to *observe* it. To run some fancy tests, or some scholarly thing I didn't understand.

Apparently, he'd put some feelers out in the Darwin scholarly meteorology circles about wanting to spend a week in the wilds of Kakadu National Park studying and observing all he could. I was surprised he didn't get laughed at, but someone mentioned me—a non-scholarly type who spent weeks chasing electrical storms—and a few phone calls later, he'd tracked me down.

I'd told him I wasn't like those university dicks. I just spent my summers chasing storms because it was fun and because I could. I explained it involved camping out in Kakadu National Park. That there was some hiking involved. That it would just be me and him in the middle of nowhere, and there would be a possibility that we saw no other human beings for his entire stay.

He said that was fine.

He'd offered me some ridiculous payment, some government study grant, and I told him to donate it to the Kakadu National Park. He did exactly that, and I was all out of excuses.

So, despite my best efforts to convince him otherwise, he was getting in today.

Doctor Jeremiah Overton.

With that name, he had to be eighty. I'd not spoken to him on the phone, only via email with his fancy doctorate signature, but even the way he wrote was very formal. Or maybe that was just the way super smart scientists wrote requests from their fancy science websites.

I had no clue.

But I was about to find out.

The small plane flew in, went careening down the runway,

and with a sigh, I climbed out of my Jeep and went inside. At least the terminal was air conditioned.

"Afternoon, Tully," Yasmin said from behind the check-in counter.

I gave her a smile. "Afternoon."

"What brings you in today? A person or cargo this time?"

"A person."

A person who I didn't know at all. Hell, I didn't even know what they looked like, didn't know what kind of time I was in for. *Why had I agreed to this?*

Regret ratcheted up a notch or two as the plane rolled to a stop and the door opened.

I had a bad feeling about this.

Me and some snobby old guy stuck out in the middle of the most remote scrublands, surrounded by deadly wildlife that he probably ain't ever seen before, while we chased electrical storms so he could probably stand out in the middle of a clearing holding a metal rod up to the sky . . .

I mean, what could possibly go wrong?

People climbed down the steps onto the tarmac and began to filter inside. Some of them already fanning their shirt collars against the heat and they hadn't even been here a minute.

I counted twelve people, about all that'd fit on that size plane. Some couples, which I scanned right past. A young mum with a kid on her hip. Definitely not. Two guys in suits, who I gave a hard pass. A young guy, who looked sexy in a nerdy kinda way, with his proper button-down shirt all tucked in and his navy shorts with hiking boots. *Nope, can't be him.*

Then I spotted a man. Seventy at least, wild and wiry grey hair under a bucket hat, dressed like Doctor Livingston from Jumanji or whatever fucking movie that was. He was the Jeremiah-ist looking man of the lot. So I made a beeline for him, grinned my fakest grin, and held out my hand.

"Tully Larson."

He looked at me, then at my hand, then back to my face and put his hand to his ear. "Whadya say, son? Gotta speak up. I'm deaf as a post."

Oh great.

I opened my mouth and took a deep breath so I could yell, just as the sexy shorts guy with his pretty button-down shirt and hiking boots interrupted me. "Tully Larson?" he asked. Christ, his eyes were like dark sapphires on steroids. So freaking blue.

"Ah, yeah?"

He held out his hand. "Doctor Jeremiah Overton."

Well, I'll be fucking damned.

"Some people call me Jeremy."

I grinned at him—my next week was now looking a whole lot brighter—and shook his hand. "Hey, Jeremiah. It's real nice to meetcha."

CHAPTER TWO

JEREMIAH

Jabiru Airport was a dirt strip in a dust bowl. The heat was suffocating, and getting off the plane and walking into the humidity was like having a hot bath, only somehow the water was dry.

Welcome to the Top End.

I wasn't sure what to think of my guide, if that's what I could call him. Tully Larson's reputation preceded him. The team at Darwin University had said he was a wild card. He had no meteorological academic credentials but had earned himself a reputation as a smart and savvy storm chaser.

A storm chaser.

He might have reported his findings and taken some readings and footage a few times for local weather channels and the bureau here, but he spent weeks at a time on the front line of monsoon storms for fun.

For *fun*.

He was handsome, no two ways about it. Undoubtedly well and truly out of my league. He looked like a surfer from the Sunshine Coast in Queensland, with his longish blond wavy hair, but after hearing him speak, it was clear he was very much a Territorian. He had a laid-back manner to the way he walked and the way he talked. He had a drawl and an easy smile that made him instantly likeable.

My first impression of him was that he was an easy-going, smiling type, and nothing fazed him. Including monsoonal electrical storms. Nothing seemed to be a problem.

Although calling me by my shortened name seemed somewhat difficult for him.

"So, Jeremiah," he said, lifting my heavy equipment crate into the back of his Jeep. He lifted it effortlessly, then relieved me of my duffle bag as well, sliding it in beside my crate. "How was your flight?"

"It was fine," I replied, getting into the front passenger seat, and looked up at the scorching sky. "Does your car not have a roof? A canopy, perhaps?"

The sun was blisteringly hot, the humidity making it worse. I went to put on my seatbelt and almost branded myself with the buckle. "Ow!"

Tully laughed. "Yeah, sorry about that. And yeah, there's a canopy somewhere. But it's cooler without it once we get goin'. You'll see."

That was hard to imagine.

"So, I thought we could swing past the store and grab some last-minute supplies. We won't be back this way for a while."

"Sure."

I didn't know what *supplies* we could get that wouldn't spoil in these hot and humid conditions, especially whilst camping. I was certainly too scared to ask. But he did this all the time apparently, so I'd need to trust him.

The store itself was more of a convenience outlet, with very few selections and exorbitant prices. "Wow," I mumbled, looking at the price of butter.

He smirked, slow and easy. "The prices? These aren't Melbourne prices. These are two-hours-from-a-supermarket prices out here."

He grabbed things like bottled water, flour and sugar, canned goods, beef jerky, and dried fruits and nuts. And a jumbo roll of toilet paper. "The most important essential." He chuckled at my embarrassment. "Would you rather I didn't get it?"

"Uh, no, it's fine. Thank you."

He snorted. "Now, when were you wormed last? If we're gonna eat wild pig . . ."

I stared at him. Horrified. "Uhhh, I'll eat beans. And grass, if I have to, before I eat worm-infested feral pig."

He burst out laughing. "I'm just messin' with ya." He pushed the trolley, then stopped and looked back at me, very serious. "There was one time I did eat goanna. And brolga is tough eating." He made a face. "Like eating a rubber pigeon."

He laughed at my expression. "Just kiddin'. About the brolga. I totally ate goanna once."

I added a few more cans of beans to the cart and ignored the way he laughed all the way to the checkout.

"Afternoon, Tully," the man behind the counter said. He was about fifty with greying hair, sun-weathered skin, and a tired smile. "You headin' out again?"

"Yeah, mate. Got company this time," he said, nodding to me. "But I'll be sure to keep an eye on this one and make sure he comes back. Not like the last one . . ." I stared at him again, wondering what on earth I'd got myself into, and he laughed again. "I'm kidding!"

I looked at the man behind the counter. "You don't happen to sell a sense of humour, do you? I think I'm going to need an upgrade."

He rumbled a laugh. "Don't let him fool ya," he said to me. "Tully here knows what he's doing, so you be sure to listen to him, ya hear? Unless you don't wanna come back, that is."

Tully grinned at me and handed over his credit card, then we loaded the gear into the back of his Jeep. He looked up at the darkening sky and pulled the canvas cover over the food and my gear, but the front seats were still without protection.

I almost branded myself with the seat buckle again, earning another smirk from Tully. I was already beginning to rethink my first impression of his smile. At first, I'd thought it made him likeable. Now I thought it made him insufferable.

Cute, but incredibly annoying.

Or was it annoying me because I thought it made him cute?

I sighed and pretended not to care.

With his annoying smile firmly in place, he reversed out of his parking spot without so much as a glance behind us, then sped out of the small town of Jabiru along the Arnhem Highway.

The wind whipped around us, and he was right. The air movement with the roof off did make it more bearable. The humidity was thick with the threat of rain, even though the sun still beat down on us. The passing scenery was spectacular—sub-tropical greenery sprouting new life with the start of the wet season.

"I was just joking back there," Tully said, yelling over the engine and the wind. "When I said I wouldn't lose ya out here. I ain't ever lost no one yet. I also haven't brought anyone out here. Which is a technicality, I know. But I didn't wantcha to worry."

"I take it the morbid sense of humour is a Northern Territory thing?" Yelling for conversation wasn't really my favourite way to communicate.

"Can't speak for everyone," he yelled back, that annoyingly cute smirk now a grin. "But it kinda helps to joke about life out here. Go crazy otherwise."

I wanted to ask him if he lived out here but thought I could save that conversation for when we weren't yelling across the car at each other.

An hour out of town, thoroughly windswept and probably sunburned, we turned off the highway onto a road that soon became a track. "Might wanna hold on to the oh-shit bar," he said.

Yes. The permanent smile was now *officially* annoying.

As was the way the wind tousled his hair, and how the way the sunlight made his eyes shine.

Get yourself together. Focus on why you're here.

A serious bump in the track had me reaching for the grab bar across the dash. "Oh shit!"

"Yep. That's how it got its name." Tully laughed. Then he pointed up ahead to another track we were about to pass by. It was a goat track in the scrub. "That's the way we'll go tomorrow."

More of this kind of road? Oh goodie.

"Does this road become impassable in the wet season?" I asked, bouncing around in my seat. I couldn't imagine it getting any worse.

"It's impassable now."

That damn grin.

It was no longer just annoying.

I was beginning to actively dislike it.

"Well, for tourists anyway. When we get down into the lowlands," he went on to say. "When she floods, *then* it's impassable."

"Are we expecting floods?"

"It is the wet season."

Like the skies were listening, it began to spit rain. Fat and heavy droplets at first, then it began to pelt us, but Tully didn't pull over to put the rooftop on. Hell, he didn't even slow down.

Looks like getting drenched was as natural as sitting in the sun to him.

"And how do we navigate through flooded terrain?"

"Just gotta be faster than the rising water." He patted the steering wheel. "She ain't ever let me down yet."

Oh great.

When they'd said he was a wild card, I hadn't realised they meant he was a cowboy with a death wish.

He laughed again and—thankfully—we rounded a bend and, after a small incline, arrived at our first campsite. He pulled up in an open car shelter, alongside a big Cruiser, behind what looked like an amenities block. From there being another vehicle, I could deduce there were other people here. Or *one* person at least.

He opened his door. "We'll come back for our gear when the rain stops," he said, then made a run for it into the camp. "Come on."

It took a few seconds for me to realise I was expected to follow him. I ran around the corner of the amenities, ducking under the roof and almost running into the back of Tully. He was there with two men, both looked to be in their thirties, both smiling. One of them had short brown hair, sun-kissed skin. The second man had longish black hair and stood back a little.

"This is Jeremiah," Tully said. I was going to correct the full-name thing and suggest they call me Jeremy but figured there was no point. I had a feeling I was going to be Jeremiah for the duration of my stay. Not that I minded. In fact, I probably preferred my full name. "Jeremiah, this is Paul and Derek. They run this place. And they live here."

They lived out here? In the wilderness? Down that road? "You live here?" I asked. "All the way out here?"

Paul laughed and gestured to the wall of water that was rain just a few feet away. "Best address on the planet. But . . ." Then he gestured to the closest cabin. "More specifically, that's our home right there. Tully will look after you tonight, but if there's an emergency, you come find us."

Then Paul clapped Tully on the shoulder. "I put you guys in tent number one. Fridge here is full. You know where everything is. We're gonna be busy for a few hours. If you need us for anything, you don't need us for anything, if you know what I mean."

I wasn't sure what he meant. If we needed him for anything, we didn't need him for anything? That made no sense. But Tully grinned, laughed almost. "Loud and clear."

Paul and Derek disappeared into the pouring rain and into the closest cabin.

Together.

Oh.

Oh wow.

Tully must have seen the look on my face when I connected the dots.

"They run this place," he said again. "Together. They're a couple. Is that a problem?"

I felt my cheeks redden. "No, not at all. Goodness, no. I don't mind. It's great."

Shut up.

For the love of god, shut up.

"Good," he said cheerfully, his smile back in place. "So this is the communal kitchen. We'll probably cook up a BBQ for dinner, I'd reckon. Paul's a pretty good cook."

"But not for a few hours," I mumbled, checking my watch. It was already four o'clock.

Tully laughed, almost louder than the rain on the tin roof.

"But when we're out on our own, we won't have a setup this nice."

I could see now that the camping site was more like a luxury eco-lodge of private tents. The fancy kind with the small wooden decks out front, no doubt nicer than my apartment back in Melbourne.

I hadn't been expecting that.

And when the rain eased up a little, I could see the view.

The rain was moving north, rolling right over us and heading towards the coast, revealing an entire wetland below us. It was a patchwork carpet of green grasses and forest, stitched together with silvery blue rivers.

"Oh wow."

"Glad you like it," Tully said. Then he pointed his chin to the horizon, where the clouds were now dark, where the storms were rumbling. "Because that's where we're going."

Sheets of lightning lit up the clouds, negative charges seeking positive, sheet lightning with crawlers, and cloud-to-ground lightning—an impressive display of nature and destruction.

It made my pulse quicken.

My eyes met Tully's, and I smiled.

CHAPTER THREE

TULLY

Dinner was a quiet affair, just the four of us sitting around the communal kitchen. Jeremiah gravitated toward Derek. Once Derek mentioned his telescopes and astronomy, Jeremiah was intrigued.

"Science-minded," Paul said, with an admiring nod toward them both. The sky was dark, the storm long passed, so Derek had his telescope near the edge of the campground, overlooking the wetlands, and he and Jeremiah had been in their own little world for about an hour.

"Does Derek have a limit to the number of questions he allows?" I asked. "Because I think Doctor Jeremiah has far exceeded it."

Paul laughed. "If it's questions about stars and planets, there's never a limit."

I sipped my water and watched them for a while.

"Are you really taking him for a full week?" Paul asked. "That's a long time out there."

I sighed. "Well, I said I normally go for a fortnight, and he asked if he could tag along. How long he lasts is the real question."

Paul smirked. "Should we take a bet?"

I chuckled. "Probably not."

"Storms are supposed to be bad this summer," he added. "The park has issued warnings, which I assume you know about."

I nodded. "And I explained that to him. He said that's why he's comin' here. Because it's supposed to be bad."

Paul squinted. "Is he sane?"

I snorted. "I'll letcha know in a week."

We watched them for another few moments. "He's kinda cute," Paul mused. "And it'll just be you two, alone?"

I shot him a glance. "Yeah, I know what you're implying, and that's not gonna happen."

He snorted. "Why not? What's a little harmless fun?"

"When is it ever just harmless fun?"

Paul's grin faded into something more serene, his eyes trained on Derek. "When it turns into the love of your life."

I ignored that.

I wasn't the fallin'-in-love kind.

"He's got the bluest eyes I think I've ever seen," Paul added quietly.

That made me look at him. "Right? They're so fuckin' blue. Like a weird dark blue. Could be coloured contacts."

"Doubt it. He doesn't seem the type. Normal contacts, sure. But coloured ones? Nope."

That was true. He didn't seem the type. Not that we knew him at all.

"And he studies lightning," Paul said, almost wistfully. "Like your hobby, but for a job."

He had that implying-tone again. "So?"

"Like a perfect match, dontcha think?"

"No, I don't think."

"Harmless fun, Tully," he said, smiling as he sipped his water.

"About as much harmless fun as getting struck by lightning."

Jeremiah looked back and directly at me, like he'd heard what I'd said. I hoped to god he hadn't heard the whole conversation.

Paul hummed a happy tune, smiling as he drained the last of his water. "Hmm. I think you're in for a whole lotta fun, Tully." He shrugged. "Harmless or not, that's up to you. But can I offer you a suggestion?"

I was certain I didn't want to hear this. "Sure."

"If you're not sure if he's interested and you don't know how to ask, the 'oh no, there's only one bed' thing totally works."

Oh god.

I winced. "We're staying at the bunker. There's only one bed."

Paul laughed. "Of course there is. Just don't pull any of that chivalry shit and take the floor."

I laughed. "Thanks. I'll keep that in mind." I absolutely would not be keeping that in mind. I had no intention of having any fun with Jeremiah, harmless or otherwise. Then something occurred to me . . . "Ah jeez. You didn't take one of the beds outta tent one, did ya?"

Paul grinned. "No. Would you like me to?"

"No thanks. Two is just great."

He sighed and got to his feet. "I'm off to bed. Breakfast's at seven. What time are ya's leaving?"

"We'll probably head out by eight."

"Sounds good."

He said goodnight to the two stargazers, and figuring they'd be studying the stars for a while yet, I left them to it and went into our tent.

It was real nice. One of those fancy glamping tents with white canvas walls and roof, two single beds, a small bathroom, and a little table and chairs. I'd thrown my single duffle bag onto the closest bed, and Jeremiah's bag and big black box were neatly placed at the foot of his bed.

He'd called it his equipment crate. It weighed enough, looked heavy-duty and waterproof, and I had to wonder just what kind of equipment a lightning scientist had. I also had to wonder how he was going to carry it around for his stay. The Jeep would get us most places, but there were some roads too impassable even for me.

It was the beginning of the wet season, after all.

I took a shower, changed into my sleep-boxers. Which were more professional than my sleep-briefs. Or my preference to sleep-naked.

I was pulling back the bedcovers when Jeremiah came in. He stopped when he saw me, averting his eyes away and blushing.

Well damn.

"Oh," he said. "Sorry. I should have knocked."

"It's fine. You should be grateful I put clothes on at all," I joked, but not really. His gaze cut to mine before he hurried to his duffle bag. "I normally wear my birthday suit to bed. Thought I'd dress up a bit for ya."

"Oh well," he said nervously. "I should be grateful. Thank you."

He still wouldn't look at me, so I got into bed and pulled only the sheet up. It was too hot for anything else. "Might wanna take full advantage of the proper shower," I suggested, folding my arms behind my head. "Be the last one for a while."

He gave a nod and took his toiletry bag into the bathroom. I was half asleep when he came back out. He was quiet in the dark as he slipped into his bed, wearing proper sleep shorts and a T-shirt that clung to his chest perfectly. He smelled good, too.

Shaking that thought out of my mind, I settled into sleep.

I absolutely did not dream of harmless fun. Though I did think a jerk off in the shower before breakfast was a good idea. I couldn't risk Jeremiah seeing me with a raging hard-on our first day.

Christ.

This was going to be a long week.

AFTER BREAKFAST, WE LOADED UP THE JEEP AND WENT ON OUR way. We had jerry cans of fuel, canisters of water, food supplies, emergency gear, and his equipment crate. The weather would be pretty good up until lunchtime when the humidity and storms would kick in, so we needed to be at our destination by then.

Jeremiah shook hands with Paul and Derek, and with an excited smile, he climbed in. "I'm looking forward to this," he said. He wore more sensible shorts and a looser T-shirt today. I couldn't tell if it was supposed to be expensive vintage or if it was just old, but I got the feeling the outfit he travelled in yesterday was his *good clothes*. I wasn't entirely sure why. His shoes, maybe. They were sensible hiking boots, but not the expensive kind that rich people bought to look the part. His were the kind that poorer people splurged good money on.

I didn't mean that in a bad way.

It's just the Jeremiah who got in my Jeep today seemed like a different Jeremiah to the one who got in yesterday.

The drive was slow going, the road accessible by four-wheel drive only. It was all narrow track, trees and ferns brushing the side of the Jeep, on uneven surfaces, and going very downhill.

"Ugh," he moaned, holding onto the oh-shit bar as we went over a particularly big bump. "You know how I said I was excited to get underway today?"

"Yep."

"I take that back."

"The road'll flatten out some when we get down the ridge," I said.

"Good."

"But then we have water over the roads."

He shot me a bewildered look and I grinned at him. "Excellent," he said, putting his hand flat on the dash to hold himself in his seat. "Do we come back this way? Please say no."

I chuckled. "Nope. We'll be further north by the end of the trip, and we'll come back from the east, near Arnhem Land. It's flatter out that way."

"You mean we could have gone out that way?" His knuckles were white on the grip bar. "Instead of on this goat track?"

"We could, but where would the fun in that be?" We hit a hole and both of us jolted in our seats. "Plus, this isn't a goat track. It's a wild pig track."

His sharp blue eyes cut to mine. "Your sense of humour is about as funny as this drive."

I grinned at him, but it was lost on him because he didn't look at me. Not until we were on much flatter ground anyway. His fingers uncurled from the grip bar and he finally exhaled. It was still a track, still crowded over by trees and ferns, but flatter.

I slowed the Jeep to a stop.

"Is everything all right?" he asked, alarmed.

"Sure." I pointed back up at the ridge now behind us. "See that gap in the trees on top of the ridgeline? That's Paul and Derek's camp."

"Oh wow."

"It's a hairy climb down," I admitted. "But I saved us a full day's drive."

Jeremiah gave an annoyed sniff but faced the front again. "Some warning would have been nice."

"I did warn you. I said it was impassable."

He turned slowly to face me. "Impassable would imply that the road is not drivable, meaning one is not supposed to drive on it because it's impassable."

"Impassable is not impossible." I grinned at him and, putting the car in first, began driving again. "Anyway, that's for tourists, not me."

His eyes lasered in on mine, and oooh boy, those dark blue eyes could hold some fire. It didn't help that I found it funny. It certainly didn't help that I found it sexy as hell.

Disgruntled but choosing silence, he pulled out a map, the kind you found in old service stations, and it was probably just as well. Not that we had phone service out there, but it also meant he wasn't looking at me, and it meant that sapphire gaze wasn't trying to burn holes into my head.

The track had evened out, but it didn't mean it was any less bumpy. The huge potholes were now filled with water, their depth—and subsequent amount of bouncing—hard to gauge. I took it slow, not wantin' to break my suspension.

Jeremiah only just seemed to notice. He looked up from his map to the narrow track ahead, then to me. "The fact you're driving with considerably less speed on this horizontal ground compared to the speed you drove down the vertical hillside makes me believe you actually weren't controlling the speed with which we were plummeting down the vertical hill."

I laughed. "Plummeting is a strong word."

"Plunging also works."

"I think expertly navigating is better."

He rolled his eyes. "I think I know where we are," he said, checking the map again. "We have no phone service out here."

"There ain't much of anything out here."

"I have a serious question. What happens if one of us is injured?"

"I have a first aid kit."

"No, seriously."

"I am serious."

"I meant seriously injured. Like a compound fracture. Or if one of us is bitten by . . . well, anything out here."

"Serious answer—the other one drives us out the long flat way. I have a satellite phone for emergencies. We call 000. You'd be surprised, we're about as remote out here as it gets, but there *are* people around. They'll come. And same goes for us. If we get a call from someone for help, we go to them. It's what you do out here."

He nodded, seemingly pleased with this. "Have you ever had an emergency before?"

"Nope. Don't intend to start now. Even though you probably wanna go holdin' metal rods at lightning bolts or somethin' like that."

He smiled. "Something like that."

We hit a particularly big divot in the road and both of us bounced in our seats. He grabbed the oh-shit bar again. "At risk of sounding like a small child, how much further?"

I laughed. "We got a ways to go. We haven't even crossed the river yet."

He stared at me, those blue eyes trying to determine if I was joking or not. "A river? Please tell me it has a bridge."

I snorted. "A bridge out here? You're funny."

He sat back in his seat. "I should start counting regrets and see how many it takes before I tap out."

I burst out laughing. "Regrets? How many are ya up to already?"

"One, coming down that bloody mountain. I'll let you know after the river, if we survive, if it earned a second regret."

I found myself smiling at him. "Well, with a bit of luck, the water won't be too high yet." I knew it wasn't, but I couldn't help playing with him just a little bit. "But if we do get into trouble, whatever you do, don't get out of the Jeep. And if you do end up in the drink, don't cling to any logs." I paused for effect. "Cause those logs are the bitin' kind."

Those blue eyes almost popped right out of his head. "There are crocodiles here?"

I laughed and shook my head. "Just kidding."

He paled and shrank back in his seat. "That was not funny."

I thought it was hilarious. "I mean, it was a little bit," I said as we jostled along.

He held up two fingers. "You. You just became my second regret."

THE RIVERBED WAS FILLING NICELY, BUT THE CAUSEWAY WAS STILL easily passable. It wouldn't be in a week or so. At all. I still took it slow across the causeway; jokes aside, there was no room for stupid mistakes out here.

Jeremiah's hand tightened on the door as he peered out.

"The river will start to come down now. Over the next two months, we'll get anything up to fifteen hundred millimetres of rain. This whole track'll be underwater for two months. All road access will have to come from the east. Choppers come from Darwin, which is due west from here. And I joked about the crocs before. There won't be any here yet, but when all this is water, this'll be full of them."

"But we don't come back this way," he said, almost to reassure himself.

"No. We don't. And the bunker, the spot where we're staying, is on a rise. Like a plateau. There are no waterways close by. Unless the rains get real bad."

I stopped short on saying anything else, because the rains were expected to get bad, and he knew this.

It was why he was here.

"But this is Kakadu," he said with a sigh. "The tropical Top End. There are crocodiles."

"True."

"And the place where we're staying," he said. "The bunker. You stay there often?"

"Yep. Once or twice a year."

"How did you find out about it?"

"I used to come out here as a kid. My dad would go hunting . . . well, what they'd call ethical culling. Pigs, buffalo, crocs. When colonies got diseases, or if they got too big or too close to humans. We'd ride in ATVs and helicopters. It was crazy fun." I smiled at the memories. "We got to know the guides and the rangers over the years, so even when Dad stopped coming, I kept coming back every summer. But not for hunting."

"Why did your dad stop?"

"They don't do the culling anymore. Not like they used to. They move them on now. To different parts of the park and whatnot."

He nodded. "That's probably a good thing."

"Yep. We know more now. About how the ecosystems work."

He was quiet for a while then, watching the scenery, smiling at the birds and the occasional lizard or wallaby.

"Bet it feels a million miles away from Melbourne," I said.

"I was just thinking this feels like Indonesia. Well, except for the wallabies back there."

"We're not far from the coast. About twenty kilometres as the crow flies. You're closer to Indonesia than Melbourne, that's for sure."

He nodded again, only grabbing the grip bar a few more times before the track began to make a noticeable rise, and sure enough, after a few more minutes through the trees and grasses, we entered a clearing and up ahead was our camp.

The *bunker*, as it was known, was no more than a brown

tin shed when it was all closed up, and I tried not to smile at the look on Jeremiah's face. "Behold, the Kakadu Hilton," I said, pulling up beside the building and cutting the engine. "Let's get it set up before you declare this to be regret number three."

I climbed out of the Jeep and went straight for the front door. Jeremiah got out slowly, taking in his surroundings. The bunker itself was nothing fancy. It was literally a shed made of steel and concrete, hence the name. But it was built in the '70s, had a concrete floor, a diesel generator for power, a small kitchenette, a pit toilet, and an outdoor shower. There was even a small solar panel for lights.

It was all I ever needed.

"What exactly needs setting up?" Jeremiah asked as I got the door open.

"Let me just check for any unwanted friends first."

Jeremiah froze, his eyes wide.

I flipped the light switch and the overhead light buzzed and clicked a few times before it lit the room up in a yellow-orange glow. A few bugs and insects scurried and scampered, but nothin' slithered.

Not yet, anyway.

I took the long-handled broom and poked and prodded, lifted lids, and then the thin mattress on the bed. I checked the exposed rafters, and I opened the few cupboards. The only thing that greeted me were spiders and dust bunnies. "All clear," I yelled as I walked back out.

Jeremiah hadn't moved an inch.

I withheld the laughter, but I did smile. "Come on, you can help me lift the sides."

"The what?"

"The sides," I said again. "They lift out and up, like wings." I pointed to the side walls where he could now see the bolts. I slid the first bolt out and he did the other end. Then from inside the shed, we pushed the side wall out and up. Metal poles on the ends came down and held the wall up like an awning.

Then we did the other side, and the breeze blew straight through.

"Now that's pretty cool," he said, clearly impressed. He inspected the giant hinges and the crude welding. It was as sturdy and strong as anything I'd ever seen.

"Made in the '70s, after Cyclone Tracy," I explained. "When they could do shit like this without ten years of red tape and building codes. No way something like this would pass today. But it's classed as an emergency shelter for cyclones, and after Tracy ripped through Darwin, they put a few of these up over the Top End."

"I can see why it's called the bunker." He was frowning up at the long fluorescent light. "Why is the light orange?"

"Well, it's technically yellow," I amended. "Bugs aren't attracted so much to it. If it was a bright white, we'd be swarmed."

When he didn't say anything, I looked over and, sure enough, he was now staring at the bed.

At the very much one and only bed.

"Put your pillow at one end, I'll put mine at the other," I said like it was no big deal. Because it wasn't a big deal. And if he was that opposed to sharing a double bed with a guy, he could damn well sleep on the floor.

"Here, help me lift this," I said, not giving him time to dwell on the bed situation. I took one end of the table, he took the other, and we moved it out under the new roof. "Rain tends to come from the north," I said. "So we can move our stuff to the lee side."

"And this stuff just gets left here?" he asked, looking around. "Unlocked?"

It really wasn't all that great. "Uh, sure. It's a shelter in case of emergencies." I shoved the bed with my boot. "I brought this mattress with me about three years ago. You should have seen the old one." I made a face. "There's a few carcinologists who stay here on the regular, but only after the wet season."

"Carcinologists? What crustaceans live here?"

I was surprised he knew what that was. Then, given he had a doctorate in somethin', I probably shouldn't have been surprised at all. "Not here, exactly. But in the mangroves north of here. They trek in, into the real swamps. The crabs in the mangroves do something special, I dunno what it is though. Something about carbon emissions and the cycle of life and helping with global warming." I shrugged. "They stop here on their way out. And then there's the dry-season folks. It's busier then, but I tend to avoid people so I don't know much about the folks who stay here in the dry season."

I moved the chairs out to the table, giving us some more room. "But the rule is you leave it as you find it. Don't break shit, and keep it clean."

"That works," he said, looking around. "It's actually a lot cleaner than I was expecting. Nothing a good dusting can't fix."

I handed him the broom. "Don't let me stop ya."

He made himself busy sweeping and brushing spiderwebs down, dusting, and then he decided to wash everything in the small kitchen with soapy water before we unpacked the Jeep. He didn't seem opposed to hard work, and I liked that about him. He just got stuck in and got shit done.

While he was doing all that, I checked the bathroom and the pit toilet, made sure the water tanks were all in good order and free of creepy crawlies and unwanted critters. I boiled some water on the gas stovetop for cooking and brushing our teeth. By mid-afternoon, we had our camp set up.

Exhausted, I flopped down on the bed, but Jeremiah pulled his equipment crate over and started pulling every-thing out, takin' inventory and checking it all over. He picked up one piece, a box of some type, then another. He laid it all out on the table, neat and methodical.

"Hey, Jeremiah," I said. "How'd you get into all this? I mean, why lightning?"

He stopped, sitting still for a long few seconds. "I've always been fascinated by it," he said quietly; a frown marred his brow, a flinch almost, and his demeanour changed. "For as long as I can remember."

What an odd reaction.

There was no way that was the whole truth. There was definitely more to the Jeremiah Overton story than he was letting on.

Hmm.

Interesting.

CHAPTER FOUR
JEREMIAH

I LIKED TULLY. PROBABLY MORE THAN I LIKED MOST PEOPLE. HE was a 'what you see is what you get' kind of guy, and I appreciated that. He had a wild sense of humour that I still didn't entirely understand, but he was bright and always smiling. Completely carefree.

If sunshine was a person, it would be Tully Larson.

Well, if sunshine with a side of unpredictable was a person.

But I didn't know him well enough, or at all, really, to be telling him the ins and outs of my life.

When he'd asked why I studied lightning, I told him the truth. It had fascinated me. My entire life. That wasn't a lie.

Thankfully he hadn't asked *why* it fascinated me.

He just took my answer as gospel and moved on. Maybe he didn't care either way. Maybe he was just making polite conversation. We were stuck out here alone together, in the middle of freaking nowhere, for a long time, after all.

"What's that thing for?" Tully asked, getting up off the bed and taking a seat at the table.

Oh dear.

I sighed. "And we were doing so well."

His eyes cut to mine. "What do you mean?"

"With the lack of questions. We were doing so well."

He laughed and picked up the deploy system and looked it over. "What does this thing do? It looks like a gas cylinder?"

I took it off him and put it back on the table. "It's a quick deploy system. It screws into the automated weather station, measures wind speeds, pressure, temperatures."

"Cool." He went to grab the small solar panel and I took it before he could. "Please don't touch. This equipment is expensive, and it's all I've got."

"I'm not gonna break it," he said, pouting like a child.

People rarely ever *mean* to break things. But things get dropped by accident, and good intentions can't fix broken equipment, and I certainly couldn't afford to replace anything.

I took out the laptop and opened it. "What are the chances of a decent signal here?"

Tully snorted and held up two fingers. "Buckley's and none."

I thought as much. "That's okay. I can still record data. And just hope nothing happens to the unit before I can send it to the cloud, that's all."

Tully shrugged. "We can drive out every morning if you need. Just a couple of miles to see if we can get a better signal. You can upload your data every day that way."

I smiled at him, regretting how I'd scolded him when he was just trying to be helpful. "That'd be great, thanks."

I fired the laptop up, entered in the location information, and in a few moments, the screen was full of a weather radar and changing stats.

"Oh, that's cool," Tully said. I shot him a look and he put his hands up. "I'm not gonna touch it. Show me what it does."

"It's from the geostationary op satellite," I explained. "There are satellites each equipped with GLM, which is Geostationary Lightning Maps, that detects the light emissions from both cloud-to-ground and inter-cloud lightning which escape the cloud and make it to space. This technology helps severe weather forecasters identify rapidly intensifying thunderstorms so they can issue accurate and timely severe thunderstorm, and cyclone warnings, for example."

He snorted. "And what's the dumb version?"

"The satellites read data and track electrical storms."

"Right. Why didn't you just say that?"

"I did."

"I can assure you, you did not."

I sighed. "The bureau radars," I said, changing topics and changing tabs on the computer, bringing up a different radar, "are different. It's just reading data fed from local weather stations in Darwin and Warruwi." I looked at the numbers. "Well, it's trying to. It's searching, lagging, mostly."

"But the radar? Is that current?"

"No. It's lagging too." I went through the equipment crate and pulled out a booster. It looked like an antenna. I hooked it up to the converter, then plugged it into the laptop. "I need to find somewhere . . ."

He groaned. "Gaaah, why didn't you say you had a booster? I can put it on the roof for ya," Tully said, grinning. "Would that help?"

"Well, it would, actually. Very much."

His face lit up, as if being helpful was his favourite thing to do. He went out and looked up at the roof, and I followed. God, the sun had some bite, and the humidity was stifling. The bunker was surprisingly cool. "What about up there," he said, pointing to the highest pitch of the roof. "Lemme grab the ladder."

He found a ladder around the side of the bunker and I held it as he climbed, not at all looking at his muscular legs as he went up. "I'm very glad to see there are lightning rods installed," I said, seeing the metal diversion rods installed along the ridgeline.

"Yeah, they didn't muck around when they built this thing," he said, getting to the top. "Holy shit this roof's hot," he mumbled, but I held up the booster and he grinned as he took it from me. "Go and look on the screen and tell me when the signal's better."

"The cord isn't very long. I'll have to move the table. Sorry!" I tried to hurry because I didn't want him to burn himself on the hot tin roof, but it did give him more cord. He moved the booster and I checked the screen.

"How about now?" he called out.

It was better but still not great. "No."

The cord pulled up some more and I could hear him move further along the roof. "How about n—"

"Stop there! That's good!" I went back out so I could see him. "It's good now, thank you."

"We'll run the cord down the corner so we can close up the walls if we need, and I'll have to rig up a bracket or a brace," he said. "As soon as the wind and storms start, it's not gonna stay put."

He began to climb back down the ladder, and I was very much aware of how remote and isolated we were out here. "Please be careful," I said, again deliberately not looking at his legs as he came down.

He got to ground level and was grinning at me, like he could tell I was making an effort to divert my eyes. "You all good there?"

"Yes, I just didn't want you to fall," I said, ignoring the innuendo in his tone. "You may be fine in a medical emergency if I'm the injured one, but if it's you that's injured and you're depending on me to be cool, calm, and collected, you're bound to be disappointed. And in a lot of pain."

He laughed and clapped my shoulder. "You'd be fine." But then he went about scavenging up some wood and the lid of an old plastic container in a row of discarded materials on the ground at the end of the bunker. He found what he was after, somehow made it work, zip-tied it all together to make a little raft-looking device, shoved some more zip ties in his mouth and went back up the ladder.

I stood out in the sun to try and see what he was doing but the direct heat got too much for me. There were a few bangs, some mumbles, and some colourful cursing, then a victorious grin. "Pass me up my phone."

I found it on the bed and passed it up to him. This time, when he climbed down, his grin was even wider. "Just call me MacGyver," he said, showing me the photos he'd just taken.

There, zip-tied to the metal ridging on the roof, was a little wooden raft with my booster zip-tied to it. It made me laugh. "Good job, MacGyver." Then I noticed how sweaty he was. "Come in and have a drink of cold water."

"Yeah, it's gettin' hot out there. It's gettin' dark over the north-west too. I'd reckon the storm this arvo's gonna be a doozy."

I checked the radar on the laptop—seeing it was now in real-time—and turned it so he could see the band of yellow and red moving across the map. "I think you're right."

He clapped his hands together. "Hell yes."

It was rare to meet someone who shared my enthusiasm, and I found myself smiling at him. "I need to get my gear organised."

"I could help," he said, hopeful. "If I was allowed to touch anything."

I rolled my eyes but relented. "Fine."

That wild grin was back. "Awesome. I'll be the best fulminologist assistant to ever fulminology assist."

I sighed, pretending to be annoyed.

It was actually kind of sweet and fun to be doing this with someone else. I'd been working alone for so long, I wasn't used to having company in the field.

Tully picked up the small metal box. "Okay, so what does this thing do?"

I sighed again, for real this time, and tried to be patient with his inquisitiveness. It could have been worse. He could have been a real jerk, or a horrible person. But he wasn't. He was kind and curious.

And cute.

"It's the housing unit for the data logger, power supply and modem for the auto-station. Waterproof, of course."

He pointed to something else, having learned not to touch it. "And this?"

"It's the solar radiation sensor."

"What's this camera for?"

"It's a secondary unit," I explained. "The automatic weather station has a limited scope, so I like to focus a second camera on the unit itself so we can see the effect the storm is having from both perspectives."

He looked at it in complete wonder, excited. "That is all so freakin' cool."

I found myself smiling at him again. "Yeah. It is."

***

The storm hit at four fifteen, and even though it hit hard, it was a relief. Humidity sat over 90% for almost an hour before it broke, sweat was running down my back and dripping down my face. It was almost unbearable.

When Tully pulled his shirt off, I was going to complain but then thought better of it. It wasn't hurting anyone, and it was for his comfort, after all.

At least that's what I told myself.

It had nothing to do with his ripped physique, broad shoulders, defined pecs and abs, tanned skin, or the hair on his chest.

It had nothing to do with that at all.

Keep telling yourself that.

We lowered the walls a little, not all the way, but just so the rain wouldn't come in. The design of this shed was so simple yet genius, it was hard not to be impressed. It withstood the storm as if it were no more than a gentle breeze, let alone the thirty millimetres of water it dumped in the sixty-kilometre winds.

Thunder boomed and cracked, lightning lit up the sky in jagged cracks and bolts. It was a decent display and I managed some recordings, but it wasn't anything extraordinary.

The electrical readings weren't as high as I'd liked—it was mostly sheet lightning, intra-cloud, with little cloud-to-ground activity—but it was a good test for a first run.

A good taste of what was to come, perhaps.

And it was good to see how Tully reacted. He was so interested in the radar and the readings, and what both cameras recorded. The thunder clapped overhead a few times, loud enough to ring in my ears. The clouds were low, and the electrical charge readings were constant, which meant we were right in the thick of it.

"Is that high?" he yelled over the sound of the rain.

I see-sawed my hand. "No. It means we're close, but it's not bad or threatening at all," I explained. "It's pretty tame."

He nodded, but his grin was still there. I was pretty sure he just liked storms. He didn't care about the science behind it, he just liked the wildness of it.

When the storm had passed and the rain cleared, we opened up the walls again, letting the breeze through. It was much cooler now.

"Listen to that noise," Tully said, staring into the trees.

I didn't need to perk my ears at all. The sounds of the forest were almost deafening. Cicadas, frogs, birds sang a cacophony of song.

"It's a good sign, right?" I asked.

"Yep. Did you know birds sing a different sound after rain than what it is before the rain?"

"No, I didn't know that."

"It's pretty cool." He shrugged. "If you know what to listen for. One of the old guys that used to go huntin' with my dad told us that. He could tell the difference in birdsong. I can't. But he also said if you don't hear any birds before a bad storm,"—he gestured to the trees—"you know it's time to bail out."

"Yes, I've heard that," I admitted. "I did a study in South America a few years ago now. The field guides said the same thing. Listen to the forest."

He was clearly surprised. "South America, huh? Where else have you been storm chasing?"

Storm chasing . . .

"I don't chase storms," I said. I knew he meant no harm, but still . . . the demeaning generalisation stung. "I study fulminology."

Tully shrugged. "So where else have you studied the science of fulminology?"

Now I felt petulant.

"Just two places. Indonesia and South America. Venezuela to be exact. There's a place called Catatumbo—"

"Ah, the House of Thunder," Tully said, his smile back in place. "I've heard it's amazing."

I don't know why it surprised me that he knew of it. He was a storm chaser, after all.

"Yes, the lightning display is amazing. It's an atmospheric phenomenon that really has to be seen to be believed."

"When did you go there?"

"For my final thesis, I did a study there."

Tully sighed. "Must be amazing getting to travel the world to see all the different storms."

"I certainly couldn't afford to go on my own." I didn't know why I was telling him this. "Same with this expedition; I obtained a grant through the bureau. I was very lucky . . ."

"Still exciting though."

I gave a nod. "Yes, it is."

"And your work at the bureau? What do you do there?"

"High impact weather, aviation hazards, radar science and nowcasting, forecast systems, statistical post-processing, forecast verification. Those kinds of things. There is also a cross-data interaction with climate change and variability, with projections and predictions."

"Sounds . . . boring."

I almost smiled. "To some."

"Ah, come on, you gotta admit field trips are always more fun than theory, right?"

"I never hated the theory lessons."

"Of course you didn't." When I glanced his way, he was smiling at me. I resisted sighing, barely. His annoying grin widened. "Soooo," he said, "what are you actually hoping to find in this study? Is it just lightning in general? Or is there a specific theory you want to test?"

"I have . . ." I tried again. "The causation of strikes and the predictability; a study which would increase the ability to predict where lightning will strike, and perhaps the ability to direct the strike to a more favourable location, amongst other things. Not just for preventative measures, but also a better understanding of lightning activity from all around the world enables policy makers, government agencies, and meteorology departments to make more informed decisions related to weather and climate." That well-rehearsed line sounded flat, even to my ears. "Though mostly they choose to ignore anything climate related."

His brow creased and confusion crossed in his eyes.

"Don't they do that already? Not the ignoring climate data. We know that. But the predictions, with the metal rods on buildings, like this one." He pointed to the ceiling. "They don't offer protection, as such, but channel the strike to a point and divert the current to the ground."

I should have known I couldn't fool him.

"Well, yes. That's correct. But I'm not talking about diverting strikes away from one building. I'm talking about densely populated areas in general."

"Well, that's cool. But what do you really want to study lightning for?" He grinned, charming and cute. "Not the spiel you just gave me that probably smoothed over your faculty grant application admin. What are you *really* studying? What drives you to travel the world chasing lightning?"

My gaze shot to his, and the truth just rolled right off my tongue.

"I want to study the effects a lightning strike has on the human body. The causation, the predictability, the reason . . ." I stopped short and made myself breathe, regroup. "By studying lightning, I can better understand the basic principles of who, what, why, and where of future strikes."

He stared at me, somewhat bewildered. Then he scoffed and shook his head. "Please tell me you're not gonna wrap yourself up in foil and go stand out in the middle of the clearing hopin' to get struck," he said with a laugh.

"No, of course not," I mumbled. "I'm not going to wrap myself in foil."

He chuckled but then his smile slowly died. "But you're not going to try and get yourself electrocuted, are you? Foil or no foil."

I shook my head and concentrated on the laptop. "That's absurd." I ignored how he was staring at me. "I need to fill in my report."

"Jeremiah?" His tone was curt with warning. "I didn't bring you out here on a suicide mission."

I looked up from the screen and turned to face him. "Good. Because I don't intend to die."

"But you do intend to use yourself as an experiment."

And that was a possibility I couldn't deny.

CHAPTER FIVE

TULLY

Jeremiah Overton was in-fucking-sane.

He went about fillin' in his reports and doing statistics and numbers while I tried to get my head around what he'd just said.

He wanted to study the effects of lightning strikes on a human body, and when I'd questioned if he intended to use himself as a test bunny, he hadn't denied it.

The more I thought about it, the more it bothered me. "Isn't that morbid curiosity?" I asked. "Wanting to know what it does to the human body?"

"It's a medical science. Keraunomedicine is the medical study of lightning casualties." He shrugged.

"So why didn't you become the other kind of doctor and do that kera-nom-whatever you called it medicine?"

"Because I'd have to understand lightning first. Which is why I do this." He made a face, then gave me another well-practiced spiel. "To best predict lightning strikes and possibly save lives, first we have to understand it, right?"

Hmm. "True."

I guess.

"Why do you love storms so much?" he asked, turning the conversation on me as if it was proving that I, too, was morbidly curious.

"I told ya before. I love the ferocity of them, being completely at the mercy of nature. It's terrifying and magnificent. And it's one helluva adrenaline rush."

He raised one eyebrow as if that did prove his point, and I dunno . . . maybe it did.

"Couldn't you just go skydiving for that thrill?" he countered.

"I could." I thought about it for a while. "And being out here reminds me of my childhood, hangin' out with my dad, doing wild-boy shit. That's what my mum used to call it."

He frowned then and paused with his mouth open, as if he was trying to find the right words. But in the end, he decided on saying nothing at all.

Maybe he wasn't sure how to ask such personal questions.

"My mum still calls it wild-boy shit," I added, hoping it would make it easier for him. "Every year when I come out here, she shakes her head at me."

He packed up some of his gear, clearing away half the table, and he stayed silent so long I wondered if he'd heard me at all. But then he asked, "Do you have any brothers and sisters?"

"I'm the youngest of four. Two brothers, Rowan and Ellis. They're ten and four years older than me. And my sister, Zoe. She's seven years older than me. I'm closest with Ellis. The oldest two got lumped with the parental expectations to take over the family business," I said with a laugh. "Just kidding. We all work for the family company. But I'm the youngest, the most spoilt, and clearly the favourite. Also the best looking, and the funniest."

He smirked, thankfully understanding that I was joking. "And the most modest, I see."

I grinned at him. "Modesty is not a family trait, sorry. What about your family? Are you all geniuses? Or did you get all the brains *and* looks in your family too?"

His smile faltered and he turned back to his gear, a small black box in his hand seemingly forgotten. "It's just been me and my dad since I can remember. He . . . he, uh . . ." he put the box back in the crate. "He doesn't understand why I do what I do. He says if I'm so smart, I should have become a 'real' doctor." He used air quotes and then rolled his eyes. "God, could you imagine? One, I hate blood. And two, I don't like people. Why on earth would I want to help them?"

That made me laugh. I was glad his sullen mood didn't last long.

"So you *do* work?" he asked. "You're not just some lucky guy who doesn't have to work who gets to be a full-time storm chaser?"

I snorted out a laugh. "I wish. Yeah, I work. I do have flexibility. Like I said, it's the family business, so I can take time when I want. As long as I've earned it. I'm not an actual freeloader. I tried to be, but they wouldn't let me."

That earned me half a smile. "What is the family business?"

"Shipping. Imports, exports."

"Oh. Nice."

Something about his tone told me he didn't think that was nice at all, and I wasn't sure what to say about that. I decided a change of topic was in order.

"So, if your interest is in people getting struck by lightning, why don't you go to where the most occur? Like Africa."

"You seem to have the preconceived idea and highly deluded notion that there is money in academia that would allow such travels."

I snorted.

"We know *why* lightning happens," he added. "Abundant moisture and the mountainous terrain help initiate thunderstorms. That's why places like Africa, Central America, Asia, and Brunei experience the highest densities of strikes per square kilometre. Global patterns follow the equatorial band, more or less. Tropical storms, with high temperatures, high humidity; it makes sense. But lightning is still largely an unknown entity. We think we understand it, and we can grapple with the physics of lightning, but it's unpredictable and dangerous, and—"

"And that's why you love it."

His gaze cut to mine. "I don't love it. Far from it. I just want to understand it." His voice was quiet, so final, there was nothing I could add. He made himself busy looking at data readouts, so I lit up the citronella candles and plugged in the vibration poles at the four corners of the shed.

"What are they?" Jeremiah asked, watching me.

"Critter deterrents," I replied. "Snakes, mostly. The poles go into the ground like a tent peg and emit a low frequency vibration pulse. It keeps snakes away, but also goannas and other uninvited friendlies. Spiders don't like it much either."

"Good," he said, looking suspiciously up at the ceiling rafters, then his eyes drifted back to the bed. "And the netting thing?"

"We roll it down of a night. The mozzies are big enough to carry you outta here."

He made a face. "Oh great."

I put a can of bug repellent spray on the table. "This is your friend. It stinks but it works." I left him to it and made a start on dinner. "I hope you like beef and rice," I said. "Because we'll be eating it a lot."

"Oh yeah, that sounds great, actually."

I'd mastered the one-pot rice and beef in my time camping. I'd throw in some veggies or beans, and when I was sick of it, I'd add in different flavours and spices. I'd never much cared for cuisine. I'd just needed to feed myself enough of something to sustain me; I never needed anything fancy. Jeremiah didn't seem to be the fancy type, but after a week of eating the same thing, he might not be so thankful.

When I handed him a bowl, he took it with a smile. "Oh, wow. Thank you." He shovelled in the first few mouthfuls like he was starving. "This is really good!"

I chuckled. "We'll see if you're saying that at the end of the week."

He demolished his dinner, and it surprised me just how much he could put away. "I'll wash up," he said, taking my empty bowl. "Fair's fair."

I watched him at the makeshift sink for a while, with the pump faucet and having to boil water on the gas stove, letting him figure how to use it. He managed just fine. "How was the data you collected?" I asked.

"It was okay." He wiped his brow with his shirtsleeve. "Jeez, it's hot. The humidity is brutal."

I smirked at him. "Yeah. You get used to it."

"Have you lived in Darwin your whole life?"

"Yep. Where the only two seasons we have are hot and really fucking hot."

He finished washing up, then lifted the hem of his shirt up to wipe his face, giving me a great view of his waist. Trim, muscular even, which I did *not* expect, and a trail of dark hair from his navel down to his . . .

He cleared his throat.

I shrugged, not one bit sorry. "If you're hot, take your shirt off. Hell, get around in your undies. I don't care."

He made a face. "I might take a shower," he mumbled, quickly taking his toiletries and towel with him.

"Okay," I replied, even though he didn't appear to hear me.

I heard him mumble to himself, then I heard the water . . .

And then a scream that had me up and off the chair, racing for the door. Jeremiah burst out of the bathroom stall, grappling with a towel barely wrapped around his waist. He was pale and panting, now standing beside the bed, as far as he could get from the bathroom.

"What is it?" I asked, reaching for the broom.

He shook his head.

I poked my head in, gingerly peeking into the shower cubicle, expecting to see a snake . . . only to find a rather large green tree frog up near the water tank.

I went back out. Jeremiah had fixed the towel around his waist, which was disappointing, to say the least. He was still pale, his eyes wide. "The frog?"

His nostrils flared, his jaw clenched. "They have. Suction cups. For feet!"

I would have laughed if he didn't look like he was about to puke.

"Please get rid of it," he said quickly. "I don't care how or what you do with it. Just please get rid of it."

"Okay," I said, leaning the broom against the wall. I picked up the frog, and walking out into the clearing, I let him go. "Go find somewhere else to call home, little buddy."

When I went back into the shed, Jeremiah hadn't moved. He shuffled from one foot to the other. "Can you please check the shower? Actually, you know what? Never mind. I'll wait until tomorrow. In the daylight. Or maybe I just won't shower at all for the entire duration of our stay. I can stand in the rain tomorrow. It's fine."

I had to chew on my bottom lip to stop from smiling. "I checked the water tank earlier," I said. "There were no frogs in it. He must have just joined you."

He shuddered.

"Let me get your things," I said, collecting his toiletries and clothes, and walked over to him.

He swallowed hard as he took them. "Thank you." Then

he lifted his chin, proud and defiant. "I'm sure you have a joke or something you'd like to say. Maybe sing the 'Jeremiah was a Bullfrog' line. It wouldn't be the first time I've heard it."

I gave his shoulder a squeeze, ignoring the fact that he was very naked under that towel. "There ain't nothing funny about phobias," I said.

His eyes searched mine, and maybe he was looking for the punchline. He wouldn't find one.

"Thank you," he whispered, clutching his clothes.

"Gotta say, though," I said brightly, waving him up and down. "You're more ripped than I assumed a scientist would be."

He scowled at me then pulled his shirt back on. "Do you make inappropriate comments to all your visitors?"

"Only the really hot ones."

He stared at me.

It made me laugh. "Just kidding. I told ya before, I ain't ever brought anyone out here."

He grumbled under his breath, then pulled his shorts on under his towel, then finally pulled it free. He was still scowling at me but he sighed. "Well . . . thank you for getting rid of the . . ." He waved his hand in the direction of the bathroom.

"No problem. I'll try and rig up something for ya tomorrow," I said. "To stop any uninviteds from tryin' to catch a lucky peek at ya."

He clearly chose not to reply to that. "Well, if you don't mind, I'll have to brush my teeth out here."

"That's fine. Take a cup of the water I boiled earlier and spit it outside."

"Oh." He made a visible effort to compose himself. "Good idea."

I decided to take a quick shower, absent any frogs, and I came out wearing just my boxer shorts. If my shirtlessness bothered him, he'd have to get used to it. It was freaking hot.

He was unrolling the fly net above the bed and he stalled when he saw me. He checked me out, like he did the night before when I wore just boxers to bed and like he did when I took my shirt off in the afternoon.

He could deny it all he liked, but I knew what I saw.

His eyes on me when he thought I weren't looking. Raking over my chest, my back. I weren't blind, and I weren't stupid.

I knew appreciation when I saw it.

"Here," I said, standing on the other side of the bed. I reached for the rolled-up netting. "Let me get this side."

He was quiet and didn't speak much as we got ready for bed. He made sure his pillow was as far over as it could be, our sleeping spaces as separate as the bed allowed. He sat on the furthest edge he possibly could.

"I can sleep in the Jeep if you'd prefer," I offered. I switched on my LED lantern and turned off the overhead light.

"No, it's fine. You'd have no mosquito protection and . . ." He swallowed hard. "I think I'd prefer you in here. If I wake up to a freaking monitor lizard going through our camp, I'll need you close by."

I chuckled as I lay down. "Nice to know I'm good for somethin'."

He slowly lay down, stiff and trying not to take up too much space.

"Ever shared a bed with a man before?" I asked.

He turned his head so fast to look at me, his blue eyes stark in the darkness. "What's that supposed to mean?"

I snorted and put my arms behind my head. "Just askin'. You look petrified, like you think I'm about to jump ya bones or something."

"I am not." He turned back to stare at the ceiling, huffing

indignantly. "And for your information, I have shared a bed with . . . none of your business."

I chuckled. I knew it. I knew from the way he'd been looking at me that he was inclined, or curious at the very least.

"Good to know. And for the record, so we're even," I said. "I've shared a bed with a man before too."

I noticed his hands curl into fists by his side. "Well, that's . . . good for you and none of my business."

He was so easy to rattle. I shuffled onto my side so I could look at him, one arm tucked up under my head. "Okay, so super important question time," I said.

He was silent and stock-still, waiting . . .

"What's your favourite dinosaur?"

He stared at the ceiling, then blinked, then looked at me. "What?"

"Your favourite dinosaur," I repeated. "Everyone has one, they just don't talk about it."

"Umm," he hesitated, shaking his head. "I don't know. I haven't thought about it."

"Not even when you were a kid? Everyone has a favourite dinosaur when they're a kid. Mine's the Supersaurus. The biggest dinosaur to ever live. Most people say the T-Rex or a raptor or something, because they're cool. But the Supersaurus is so overlooked. They're huge. Like fuckin' massive. And gentle, and herbivores. And you know, T-Rex's and raptors are cool in a screeching violent-rampage kinda way, I guess. But the good ol' gentle giants are where it's at. Imagine being as big as a football field and not choosing violence."

When I turned to look at him, he was smiling. But he didn't say anything. Maybe he thought it was stupid or childish . . . whatever.

I sighed and closed my eyes.

Jeremiah was quiet and I was drifting off to sleep when he spoke. "The Quetzalcoatlus. It was a pterosaur, a flying dinosaur. As tall as a giraffe with wings like a bat and a long needle-like beak as long as a car."

I stared at him. "Jesus Christ. That's not fucking terrifying at all."

He laughed, more relaxed now, and I smiled as I drifted off to sleep.

CHAPTER SIX

JEREMIAH

Tully spent the entire morning rigging up some kind of netting over the shower stall and the water tank that fed the shower. His concern over my phobia of frogs was a nice change to the usual ridicule I received, and it was poor judgement on my behalf to assume he would have laughed at me.

Tully wasn't like the others.

He wasn't like anyone I'd ever met.

He learned of my phobia and fixed the problem. When he knew my aerial booster would need to go on the roof, he made a bracket for it and MacGyvered it to the roof. He just scooted himself up on to the roof, banged and clanged, swore a bit, sang off key at one point, but he fixed my problems.

No requests, no point to be made, no accolades.

He was incredibly easy to be around.

And him asking me about my favourite dinosaur? It was so unexpected and purely an exercise in helping me relax. I hadn't expected to be sharing a bed with my guide on this trip, and him asking me if I'd shared a bed with a man before was purely him scoping for information. I'd clearly not been as stealthy in appreciating his shirtless torso as I'd thought I'd been.

He'd noticed me staring, obviously. And he wanted to know what that meant, because . . .

Well, I wasn't sure why.

Because he'd shared a bed with men before. And he wasn't talking about camping, that much was clear. No, he'd asked because he'd wanted to know if I was gay or bi or . . . if I'd be so inclined?

Or if I'd be interested?

Hm.

He was definitely not my usual type. I'd always found myself in the company of fellow academics, those who I'd met and talked science with, and sometimes took to my bed, or me to theirs. It was never anything more than a calculated exchange.

But Tully was different. Wild, carefree, kind, and funny. Gorgeous.

And sleeping next to him had been disconcerting.

He'd fallen asleep long before I had, and I'd found myself watching him. The way the night illuminated his features— the waves of his hair, the rise of his cheekbone, the purse of his lips.

He'd even smiled when he dreamed.

So yes, this was presenting a rather peculiar problem. Because if he wanted to know if I was interested, I wasn't certain if I could lie and say no.

My mind was running all kinds of diagnostics on that scenario.

"Somethin' wrong with the laptop?"

His voice startled me. "Oh, uh . . ."

I put the pen down on the table—I wasn't even aware I was holding it—and tapped the space bar on the keyboard. I'd zoned out for so long it had shut down. "No, it's fine. Have you finished already?"

"Yep," he said, sipping his water. He was already sweating.

Already shirtless.

The way his chest glistened . . .

When his smirk became a grin, I knew I'd been caught staring again.

Dammit.

He smiled as he lifted his bottle to his lips. "The netting is over the water tank that feeds the shower. That water comes off the roof and the gutter guards should help, but frogs are pesky little buggers. I also added some dish soap to the tank to keep the mozzies out. The larvae can make you sick, so just be sure to only drink boiled water."

I nodded. "Yes, thank you. And thank you for putting the netting up. I really do appreciate that."

"No problem." He nodded toward the bathroom. "You can have a shower now. Amphibian-free, I promise."

I grimaced at the memory from last night. The big green slimy thing had been ready to jump . . .

But a shower did sound good.

I took my toiletries and towel and after a thorough inspection of the shower cubicle—before stripping this time—I showered.

There was no hot water. It wasn't required. The water was lukewarm at room temperature, but it felt good to scrub the sweat and dirt off, and I felt more awake afterwards. I pulled on the same shorts with a fresh T-shirt and hung my towel over the back of a chair.

I was ready to focus now and not get side-tracked by a certain shirtless man who was now lazing on the middle of the bed, reading something on his phone. "The network gods are shining on us. We have one bar." He turned his phone around to show me the radar on his screen. "From your esteemed colleagues at the Bureau of Meteorology, this afternoon's storm shall hit around half three. Not much activity where we are, though, unless you wanna head up north a bit. Just for the storm."

I checked the laptop and, sure enough, the precipitable satellite information relayed similar information. "How's the road north of here?" I asked.

He rolled onto his side, propped himself up on one elbow, and shot that grin at me that told me the road was hellish.

So I rephrased my question. "Is it worse than the pig track we came down the mountain on?"

"Nah. It's flat, mostly. About ten k's from here we meet the South Alligator River."

"Alligators?"

"There ain't no alligators here. The folks who made the white man maps way back when couldn't tell the difference between gators and crocs."

"But there's crocs," I mumbled. Because of course there would be.

"We'll follow the river along and she winds north, and that's about as far as we can go. Without a boat."

I made a face. I wasn't a fan of boats.

But I did trust Tully. Sure, he was a bit wild, but he'd been coming out here for years. He wouldn't do anything needlessly reckless.

"Okay, let's do it."

He jumped up off the bed and clapped his hands together, that ridiculous smile now a grin.

I was beginning to like his smile again, and if my brain had a weather warning siren like my equipment did, it'd be blaring at full volume, red lights flashing.

Because his smile was contagious, and the spark in his eyes did absurd things to my belly. And the logical part of my brain knew I was heading for trouble, but my heart didn't seem to care.

WHEN TULLY SAID THE ROAD NORTH WAS MOSTLY FLAT, HE WAS partly right. Gradationally speaking, yes. But flat as in smooth, no.

The road was another track, and while we didn't climb anymore hills or ridgelines, it was filled with holes, divots, and gullies—all filled with varying depths of mud and water. He handled them expertly while I bounced around, tethered to the Jeep only by my white-knuckled grip on the oh-shit bar.

We bounced, slid, and sped our way north to the river just as he'd said. It was surprisingly pretty and moving faster than I thought it would be.

"She's not normally this full," he said. "In the dry season, we could drive across here. And by the end of the wet season, where we are right now, we'd be two metres under water."

Jesus.

Then he pointed to the river ahead of us. "See that?"

See what?

I searched the water, not knowing what to even look for. Having a fair idea what he was going to say and dreading it just the same . . . and then I saw a crocodile slither from the bank into the water, just thirty metres in front of us.

"Oh my god."

He grinned. "Those are the logs that bite. You don't wanna go touchin' those."

I rolled my eyes and tried to exhale. My hands were now numb from holding on so tight. I wanted to ask what we'd do if we broke down here, but I didn't trust my voice to speak.

And I was pretty sure I didn't want to know.

"You'll be fine," he said, his grin not such a comfort now.

He followed the river along, heading north, which meant given I was on the left side of the Jeep, I was closest to the river the whole way. I saw a few more crocodiles, mostly just ripples in the river and suspicious looking logs that sank slowly below the surface as we drove past. But there was also an array of bird life that swarmed the trees and flew over-head. So as terrifying as the crocodiles were, the wet season also brought with it renewed life.

It was all very beautiful.

Soon enough the river began to deviate northwest, heading to the ocean no doubt, and the track we were on swung northeast. The further we went, the further we were away from the crocodiles, but also the better the road condition.

"How's this road for ya?" Tully asked over the sound of the engine.

"Much better," I replied. "It doesn't make me want to vomit."

He laughed, because of course he did.

Then he slowed right down and took a turn that led through thick brush growth with swampy brackish water either side of the track which, thankfully, came to its natural end in a large clearing. He cut the engine and jumped out. "Okay, this is us."

"Here?"

He looked around. "Sure. I'd reckon from your super-duper map, this'll put us right in the path of your storm."

The area itself was almost as big as a football field, and it certainly couldn't have been cleared naturally. "What is this place?"

"Pretty sure it was a mining test site," he said, pulling gear out of the Jeep.

It rankled with me that they'd allow such things in national parks, but perhaps that was a conversation for a different time.

"Yeah, I know," Tully added, putting my equipment crate on the ground. "Don't get me started on it. Mining corp money speaks a different language, apparently."

I mustn't have been able to hide my annoyance as much as I thought, but I was glad we held similar opinions. "Hm, yes, well." I huffed, wiping the sweat from my brow. "Jeesh, it's sweltering today."

"The humidity's a killer." Tully threw a bottle of water to me. "Keep hydrated."

He had a shirt on now, probably to save his skin from the direct sun, and it clung to him in the best of ways . . . until I realised mine was clinging to me as well. I fanned the hem, trying to get some air moving.

"You can take it off," Tully said, nodding to my chest. "Your shirt. I won't mind."

I sniffed and wiped my face with the bottom half of my shirt instead. "No thanks. I'm not a prude. I'm just prone to sunburn and I'd rather not make myself ill."

His smirk was sly and filthy. "I can apply sunscreen all over. It's my duty as your guide, you know. To make sure you don't burn."

"I'm fine, thank you," I said, ignoring the thrill his offer gave me.

Was he flirting?

God, I think he's flirting.

He walked over to me, studying my face. "Are you burned already? Looking a bit red in the cheeks, there."

That wasn't flirting. That was patronising.

I glowered at him. "I'm hot and bothered, that's all."

He grinned. "I can help with that too."

Jesus.

I picked up the portable weather station tripod and shoved it in his hands. "Please take that."

"Where to?"

"The furthest end of the clearing."

He snorted. "Are you trying to get rid of me?"

"Yes."

"I was just being helpful."

"You'd be a whole lot more helpful if you stuck that in the ground—" I pointed to the far end of the field. "—over there."

He walked off with a pout—which was just as cute as his smirk—and when he was out of earshot, I let out a sigh.

What had gotten into him?

He was full of innuendos and insinuations. He'd asked me if I'd slept in the same bed as a man before. He wanted me to take my shirt off. He wanted to rub sunscreen on my body . . .

Oh god. Was he actually flirting?

For real?

I watched him walking off to the far end of the field. His broad shoulders, his longish blondish-brown hair, his muscular legs.

No, he wasn't my usual type.

But damn, he could be . . .

"Is this far enough?" he yelled.

He'd gone about 75% of the distance but it didn't matter. I only needed a moment without him near me to try and clear my head. I gave him a thumbs-up and got busy setting up my laptop. The satellite radar was lagging, blinking in and out. "Dammit."

"Oh, I can tell ya when it'll hit and how big she'll be," Tully said, walking back. That annoying not-annoying annoying grin in place.

I squinted at him. "What?"

"The storm," he said. Then he pointed skyward, over the line of trees in the direction we'd come. "Don't need no radar for that. Can't you feel the drop in pressure?"

I took stock of myself. "I, uh . . . I was busy."

I was busy thinking about you.

Tully reached into the back of the Jeep. "Help me pull the canopy on."

I closed the laptop and helped him lift the roof on and clamp it into place, which he did with considerably more ease than me. By the time I was done, he'd packed up my crate and put it in the back. "Come on, we'll drive up to the other end so we can watch her come in. She's blowin' in from the east, pushed back by the warm air from the ocean up north. And you know what that means . . . ?"

"Well, I know what it means when cold air meets warm air in a low-pressure front," I said. "But in relation to your directional points of east and north, given I'm not from here, I'm not too familiar."

He laughed, and after we passed the tripod he'd stuck into the ground, he pulled the Jeep to a stop. "Storms from the east tend to get a little wild."

A thrill buzzed through me. Not just from his stupid smile and the spark in his eyes, but from the mention of a wild storm.

Just then the wind picked up, making us both turn in the direction we'd come. And sure enough, above the tree line, due east, was a front of clouds. Dark, bubbling, and brewing, with gentle intra-cloud sparkles of lightning, as if someone had filled a jar with black cotton balls and fairy lights.

"It's beautiful," I said.

The skies replied with a crack of thunder so loud, so close, it felt like a physical blow.

"Jesus!" Tully cried, ducking down.

I laughed and got out of the Jeep to set the camera up.

Hell yes. This is what I was here for. This—the thrill of a storm, the rush, the elements so close you could almost touch them.

I could definitely smell it. I could taste the ozone, the copper on my tongue.

It was so close.

More thunder boomed and lightning crackled along veins in the clouds, and I hurried to make sure he'd anchored the tripod properly, to make sure the camera was facing the right way.

The anemometer was spinning faster now, the wind tousling my hair. "Open my laptop," I yelled out to Tully. But I looked back to see he already had it open on the dash of the

Jeep. I liked that he knew what to do, that he was as into this as me . . .

Lightning cracked with a boom of thunder right at the front of the clearing.

"Holy shit! Did you get that?"

"Yes!" I wasn't sure how, given the thrill, the pure adrenaline rush, was making my hands shake.

The skies were dark as the storm rolled toward us, a curtain front of rain marching through the clearing like an armoured battalion.

Another crack of lightning split the sky.

"Get in the fucking car!" Tully yelled. "Jeremiah, now!"

Like it was all the warning I needed, I made it into the passenger seat just before the wall of water rolled across us. Wind howled, tousling everything around us. Thunder rumbled constantly, low and threatening, with the occasional booms for emphasis. Lightning danced above us, around us, in an amazing display of power. Intra-cloud, cloud-to-ground, sheet lightning illuminating the otherwise darkened sky.

Tully peered out over the steering wheel, looking up and out. The flashes of lightning a strobe effect in the Jeep, showing me flashes of his face, of his smile, of the look of wonder. How he laughed every time lightning jittered through the clouds, through the sky.

It made my heart race for a whole other reason.

Maybe it was the storm. Maybe it was the thrill, the adrenaline, the power of it all, and maybe it was because I was experiencing it with him . . .

I was beginning to think I didn't need an internal warning system to know I could be in trouble.

I think I already knew.

CHAPTER SEVEN
TULLY

IT WAS GETTING ON DARK BY THE TIME WE GOT BACK TO CAMP. Jeremiah went straight to work, plugging in his laptop and seeing what data he'd collected.

The storm had been a good one, and I was glad we'd made the effort to go stand in its path.

But something was different about Jeremiah. During the storm and after it.

Getting to sit with him in the Jeep, in such a confined space, while the storm put on a helluva show was insightful to say the least. Something about him changed when there was lightning. It wasn't excitement or exhilaration like I'd have thought. It wasn't some studious don't-miss-any-data attitude either.

There was a calmness to him. Serenity, almost. Like he was tryin' to drink it in through his skin.

He checked his smart watch, writing down all kinds of things in a notebook, separate from his laptop data. I'd noticed him doing that after last night's storm too but hadn't thought much of it.

"Whatcha writing down?"

He glanced up at me, the pen in his hand forgotten. "Oh,

this . . . this is just for me. It's not really work, as such."

I looked at his watch. "Do you measure your vitals during a storm?"

He opened his mouth, then closed it and raised his chin. "It's just for me. My data, not for the bureau or for any public record. I'm just interested to know, as a side note. That's all."

"That's totally cool," I said, unsure as to why he was so guarded about it. "You said before you were interested to know what it did to the human body. Writing that shit down isn't a big surprise."

"Yes, well," he said, putting his pen down and closing his notebook. "Some people think it's stupid and that it undermines our actual research."

Ah. Clearly a co-worker or colleague with a superiority complex.

"Oh, fuck whoever said that," I said. "There are no rules to what you find fascinating. Only gatekeepers."

His gaze darted to mine. So fucking blue.

"Well, yes. Gatekeepers who keep me on the payroll."

"Oh. *Those* kind of gatekeepers."

He chuckled. "Yes, the one and the same."

"Well, stuck-up bosses aside, what you research on your own time has nothing to do with them. It's just very convenient, and maybe a little coincidental, that you can collate your personal data at the same time you collate theirs."

His smile lingered and died, the same way a sunset fades; beautiful and slow, the light giving way to the dark.

"I'm not particularly popular at work," he said quietly. "They all think I'm a little . . . weird. I believe creepy was the word used in an evaluation once."

"Creepy? What the fuck? You're not creepy."

His eyebrow flicked upward in a telling sign that he didn't agree with me. Or that others wouldn't, at least. "I learned a valuable lesson though," he said. "Not to disclose my personal interests in our field of study, and not to disclose sexual orientation in our field of study. I've been without a field partner ever since. So, what I learned is basically just do the work they pay me to do and shut up."

I frowned and sat on the bed with a heavy sigh. "Well, I'm sorry that happened. And also, fuck them. On both counts. Your reasons for studying meteorology and lightning are your own. Everyone has different reasons for doing whatever they do. And about the other thing . . . well, it ain't anyone's business who you take home." Then, for a joke, I added, "Unless you were banging someone in the office on company time."

I laughed, because it *was* a joke, but then he shot me a look that said . . .

"Oh shit, no way!" I barked out a laugh. "You banged someone in the office?"

His cheeks went red and he mumbled something to his notebook.

"What was that?" I asked. "I didn't quite catch it."

"It wasn't at work," he said indignantly. "It was someone at a meteorology convention, which was technically work time." The corner of his mouth pulled down. "At the convention, in a bathroom stall in the men's room."

I laughed for a solid two minutes. "Holy shit, Jeremiah, you sly dog! That's awesome." I studied him, his nerdy, sexy self, with the ripped body and giant doctor brain. "I gotta say, I'm proud. And a little jealous."

His gaze shot to mine. "Jealous. Of whom?"

I snorted. Of whom? *Whooom*. Who the hell said whom?

"Jealous that you got your freak on at a work thing. In the bathroom stalls. Jealous that you've done that and I haven't." I shrugged without a skerrick of shame. "And jealous of the guy you were in there with. Because damn, Jeremiah, that's hot as fuck."

His cheeks turned an incredible pink, and so did the tips of his ears. He cleared his throat. "Yes well, my boss didn't think so. I managed to come out of the stall and come out of the closet all at the same time. My boss and two other state managers were at the sink, washing their hands."

I laughed again, holding my stomach. "That's the best story I've ever heard. Why didn'tcha have an exiting-the-stall strategy?"

He stared at me. "Strategy? We didn't even have an entering-the-stall strategy. We made eye contact at the bar, I needed to use the bathroom, he followed me. I'm still not sure how it happened."

I laughed again, this time clutching his pillow. "God, that makes it so much better."

"I fail to see how."

"Did you ever see him again?"

"Once, at the same convention the following year. I avoided all eye contact, should he assume it was another invitation. I didn't want to get fired."

"That's perfect."

He sighed and pushed his notebook closer to his laptop. "I received a disciplinary caution."

I laughed again. "Totally worth it."

And right there was the flicker of a smile. But he chose to say nothing.

After a moment of silence, I nodded to his notebook. "So, what do you write down? Just info from your watch, like heart rate and stuff?"

He paused, like he was weighing up whether or not to tell me. "Yes. It monitors heart rate, like most smart watches, I would guess. It's not the expensive kind, but I also have an app that goes further."

"Ooh, that's cool. Like what?"

"Electrical pulses," he answered, kinda cryptically. "But it's not calibrated, and I can't use it as actual theory because it's not certified. It's just my curiosity."

"The effects lightning has on the human body."

His blue eyes bore into mine. "Yes."

"We should get one of those things that athletes use. You know how they tie those bands around their chests? We could totally hook you up and run real tests. There has to be doctors that do this shit." Then I winced. "I mean, medical doctors." Then I winced harder. "Sorry."

He rolled his eyes. "There are."

"And?"

"They can't condone my experiments because of the risk."

"But you're a fulminologist," I countered. "The risk is implied. That'd be like a doctor not listening to a pilot about the effects of a pressurised cabin on long-haul flights."

He smiled. "I take the data anyway. For my own satisfaction."

"Well, I think that's cool as hell."

He smiled. A real smile this time. "Thank you."

"And I'm serious about the heart-monitor thing." Because that was interesting, and it was cool. "We should totally do that."

"I'd like to take blood tests," he added. "And I'd like to do an electrical pulse study on the brain while standing under a lightning storm."

Aaaand we took a little sideways step from cool into weird territory. "Um. Why?"

His face flinched, then smoothed out as he collected himself. His demeanour changed. He raised his chin. "To study the effects of lightning on the human body."

I shook my head. "No, why do you really want to do it? Not just a blanket response that you've practiced for your stuck-up colleagues. Why? The real reason."

"Because the human body runs on electrical impulses. The brain, the heart, every cell. It *has* to affect us more than we currently believe."

"But doctors have studied people who've been struck by lightning," I said. "They have heart problems, organ problems, blindness, deafness."

"I'm aware of that, yes."

"Do you think people gain superpowers?" I asked, joking. "Like Thor?"

He didn't think that was funny. He scowled at me.

I studied him, his guarded face. "What else are you looking for, Jeremiah? You gotta have something you think is there." Then it dawned on me. "You're looking for proof."

He flinched. "I'm not *looking* for proof. I *am* proof."

I turned his words over in my head.

I am proof.

Jesus Christ.

"You've been struck by lightning?"

Those blue eyes lasered into me, sapphire fire, before he looked away. "Indirectly. But yes."

God.

"When?"

"I was two years old."

"Oh my god. How . . . what the fuck? Jeremiah, my god, what happened?"

He was quiet for a long few seconds, the sounds of the night loud in the silence. Crickets, cicadas, birds, the wind, all urging him to speak.

"I was in a stroller," he murmured. "My mother was pushing me. It was a freak afternoon storm in the city. She was running for the tram in the rain when lightning struck the tram line. Her foot was on the track . . ."

Holy shit.

Holy fucking shit.

I could see the image in my head, and the footage, because I'd seen it. The whole country had. It was caught on a security camera in Collins Street, Melbourne. All those years ago. I remembered this story . . . I remembered how the lightning flashed, sparks flew out of the tram wires, and a woman on the road was struck, her body flung side to side as if she'd been shot, her stroller slowly rolling away.

That footage was still famous. It was still replayed, still used to propagate storm safety messages to this very day.

Christ all-fucking-Mighty.

"That was you?"

With his back to me now, his shoulders sagged, and he gave a nod.

"God, Jeremiah, I'm so sorry."

"They said I wasn't harmed because the stroller had rubber wheels," he said, his voice detached and quiet. "I was two. I can't possibly remember it, so perhaps it was the footage." He turned to me then. "Maybe seeing the footage over and over has implanted false memories in my mind, or my imagination. I don't know. It's weird because the footage is from a different angle to my memories, so I can't be sure. I assume you've seen it?"

I nodded. "On Collins Street."

"I can remember my mother's face when she was struck. Just a fleeting moment of surprise before she spun away." He shrugged. "In my memory, it's not raining. But in the footage, it's pouring. And in my memory, I'm facing her but in the footage I'm not. So I can only assume it's all just false memories. Put there by the photographs my father has, and that damn footage."

I went over to him and put my hand on his arm. "I'm really sorry."

"My entire life has been shaped by lightning."

"It's why you're so driven to understand it. That makes sense. I'd want to understand it too."

He inhaled deeply and let it out on a sigh. "The doctors said I was very lucky. The blowback and side-flash hit me, but I was unharmed. More or less. But what it did to my mother . . ."

I didn't remember any of the gruesome details. Maybe they were disclosed at the time but not later. In the footage, afterward, it just showed her body covered with a sheet.

"Jeremiah," I whispered, sliding my hand up to his shoulder and giving it a squeeze. "You don't need to explain anything to me. The dipshits you work with might think you're creepy for trying to learn more, but if anything, I think I understand you better now. How could you not want to know?"

His eyes searched mine, maybe looking for sincerity. I hoped he found it. I was dead serious. "If you want help trying to learn more, I'll help you," I offered. "It's fascinating as hell to me."

The corner of his mouth lifted just a fraction. "You don't think I'm crazy? The weirdo lightning guy?"

"If you're the weirdo lightning guy, then I'm the weirdo storm-chaser guy. Everyone I know thinks I've got some roos loose in the top paddock, if you know what I mean."

He smiled then. "Thanks."

"I mean, we have to be a little bit unhinged to do what we do," I relented. "But, on the bright side, the fact we know this is just a little insane proves we're not actually crazy, right?"

"Right."

"I mean, you don't want to actually wrap yourself in tin foil and go stand out in a lightning storm, so I think we're well ahead of the insanity crowd."

He chuckled and sighed. "If I ever get the urge, I'll let you know."

"Solid plan." I gave his shoulder a little shake. "Okay, so now we've got all that out of the way, tell me what you write in your little secret notebook. Let's look at your data."

CHAPTER EIGHT

JEREMIAH

Tully didn't ridicule me. In fact, he was interested in my findings and wanted further analysis. He made me help him cook dinner, and he asked all kinds of questions.

He knew about my mother and didn't ask me insensitive questions. In fact, he asked me no questions at all on that whole subject, and I was glad. He said he'd seen the footage—almost everyone on the planet had—and maybe that was all he needed to know.

It made me like him even more.

Not to mention that I'd openly discussed being caught having 'private interactions' with a male colleague, and he didn't even bat an eyelid. In fact, he'd found it hilarious. We'd skirted around the 'sleeping with a man in your bed before' conversation, which he'd freely admitted he had.

But I'd known Tully Larson for all of three days, and he knew my deepest, darkest secrets. No one in my real life knew these things about me after three days, some never at all. But it was so easy to talk to him.

Maybe because this was only temporary.

Maybe because when this was over and I went back to Melbourne, I'd never see him again.

Divulging secrets to strangers was so much easier.

I felt freer than I had in a long time. I was my true and honest self with him, and that told me more about my relationship with Tully than any analysis could.

I trusted him.

And I trusted very few people.

Even getting into bed with him was different this night. There was no awkwardness, no shyness. There was still shirtlessness, on his behalf, and I was still not opposed.

He was incredibly sexy.

And he was incredibly inquisitive. He hadn't stopped asking questions yet.

The lights were out, the netting on the bed was down, and I'd just laid down with the sheet up to my waist.

He was sat on the bed, legs half crossed, his knee almost touching me. He wore nothing but loose-fitting sleep shorts that revealed a little too much and nowhere near enough. "So, if we got one of those ECG reader things that the athletes wear around their chests," he said, "we can get better readings. Is there some kind of brain reader thing that's portable? I'll be the guinea pig if you want. Stick those circle pad things to my noggin and see what happens."

"You do remember that we're currently in the middle of nowhere, yes? Where do you propose we get such instruments?"

He made a face. "Well, I'm just thinkin' out loud. If you really wanted to, we could pack up and drive back to Darwin. It'd only take us a day or two and we could come back."

I smiled at his enthusiasm. "I think the heart rate data from my watch will suffice for now, but thanks."

"Well, next time you come out, we'll have the proper gear, and we can do it then."

"Next time?" As much as I liked the sound of that, it wasn't likely. "I highly doubt my department will approve another grant for me to come up here."

"You get holidays though, right? Like four weeks a year?"

"Well, yes, but . . ."

"But what?"

"But I don't exactly have the funds to do this again. I don't . . ." I sighed. "I don't earn a great wage."

He frowned, a sad pout, then he shrugged. "You'd just need the airfares. I got the rest. I'm coming out here anyway. It's no extra cost to have you here. The food, the fuel, the water, I gotta bring all that whether you're here or not."

I wasn't sure what to say to that. The offer, the invite, was very generous. Very kind, if not a little premature.

He laid down with a huff. "If you don't wanna, that's fine. It's just been kinda nice to have some company. Especially someone who likes storms as much as I do. I'm normally out here for a week or two on my own, which is how I've always liked it. I brought my brother once, and I wanted to kill him by day two. First and last time for that, lemme tell ya."

I snorted. "You could have thrown his body in the river with the crocs. No one would have ever known."

He nudged me with his elbow. "I told him that! But he didn't think it was funny and he made me drive him home. He told Mum and Dad what I said."

I laughed, and the warm rumble of his laughter filled something inside me. "I'd like to come back," I admitted. "It's not that I don't want to, it's just that . . . you know. Money."

"Hm." I felt him shrug. "'S okay."

"I'll be paying off my uni debts forever," I mumbled.

"You did a lot of years, right? To be a doctor?"

"To earn my doctorate," I amended gently. "Yes. I did get a partial scholarship for the first four years. There were bursaries and stuff later on, but it was hard. My dad never understood why I chose meteorology and fulminology. I mean, he knows why, obviously. But he didn't agree with it. He thinks I'm trying to bring my mother back or something.

Like what I'm studying will honour her memory, but that's not why I chose it. It's not why I do it."

"You do it because it changed your life. That day when you were two. It put you on a certain path."

I nodded, my heart blooming with the warmth that he understood. "Exactly. And we never had much money. Dad did what he could do, but his life changed forever that day too and certainly not for the better. I think he resents lightning. He hates it. And I understand that," I admitted. "He said if I'm so smart, I should have used my brains to be a real doctor or an engineer or something that earned a lot of money. He doesn't understand why I'd want to choose to be broke my whole life when I had the option not to be."

Tully rolled onto his side, his head propped up on his hand. He was close, we were sharing a small double bed after all, and his face looked a silvery blue in the dark. "Parents just want what they think is best for us. But that's not who you are," he said. "And you should be proud that you followed your heart. Not many have the courage to do that. They fall for the pressure to do what they're supposed to do. Like me, I work in a family business that I have no real interest in. But it's a cushy job and it pays well—well, they pay good money because I'm family. I'm good at my job, get shit done, produce the numbers that make people happy, and I'm told I'm very good at it. But I don't love my job. I don't live for it. My eldest brother and my sister, they love what they do. They live and breathe that shit, and it makes them happy, so good for them. But to me, it's just a job."

"A job that gives you time off during the storm season to camp out here for weeks on end."

He grinned, his teeth white in the dark. "Exactly."

Then something between us shifted. The air, the pressure, the electrical charge between us, and it had nothing to do with the weather.

He stared at me, and I couldn't look away. His gaze felt

like lasers burning everything in their wake. He licked his lips and I gasped, or moaned, or . . . leaned in. Or maybe it was him leaning in. The dark was disorienting, or maybe it was the fact I hadn't breathed in a minute or two . . .

Then he blinked and pulled back, shaking his head a little. "Oh wow, yeah, okay," he said, falling down onto his back with a huff. "That probably shouldn't happen." He turned his head to look at me. "Your eyes are really fucking blue and I feel like I'm falling into water or some shit."

I had to put my hand on my chest to try and calm my hammering heart. "Ah, yeah, I hear that a lot." I shook my head. "Not about the falling into water thing. That's new. But yes, blue."

"But they're a weird blue. Like freakishly blue. Is that from the lightning?"

I scoffed. "What?"

"Like a superpower from being struck by lightning. Are you secretly an X-Men member? Can you shoot laser beams out of your eyes?"

I sighed but was glad he was joking. I thought he might have been serious . . . "Pretty sure that's Cyclops, and no, I'm not him. Or any member of the X-Men."

"Shame."

"Yeah, not really."

He chuckled. "So I almost kissed you before," he said with a sigh, as if he was discussing something completely mundane. "Just in case you weren't aware."

My pulse was thumping, my heart in my throat. I had to swallow so I could speak. "Uh, I might have picked up on that."

"But it's not something we've discussed, and I personally happen to find consent extremely sexy."

My pulse was now staccato.

"Almost as sexy as you," he added, so very nonchalantly. He could have been discussing his favourite kind of toothpaste. He sighed again. "Almost. I mean, you do have a rockin' hot body under all that science nerd."

My watch beeped.

Traitorous piece of technology . . .

"What's that alarm for?" Tully asked, grabbing my wrist. I tried to pull my hand away, but he lifted it up so he could read the screen. "What does that mean?"

"Nothing," I blurted out.

"It says you should take a rest. But you're not doing anything."

"It must need resetting," I said, pulling my arm from his grasp. I fumbled with the watchband.

Tully laughed, rolling onto his side, somehow closer now. His chest touched my arm, his face so close to mine. Too close to mine. He smiled and pulled his bottom lip in between his teeth.

My watch beeped again before I managed to rip it off.

"Is your watch telling me something?" he asked.

"I hate your stupid smile," I said, dumping my watch onto the floor beside the bed.

Tully laughed, a warm, rumbly sound that was far too close. "If your heart rate's up, you're either excited or terrified. Which is it?"

Both.

"Neither."

He dragged his index finger up my chest, stopping at the base of my throat. "I don't believe you. But—" He rolled back onto his back with a huff. "—like I said, consent is my foreplay. No green light, no go."

My heart was knocking so hard against my ribs it hurt, and I had to pretend I could breathe normally. But I couldn't speak.

He rolled onto his other side, facing away. "Night, Jeremiah."

I wanted to tell him yes. I wanted to reach out and touch

him, bring him back to where he'd been when he was so close I could feel his body heat.

But I still couldn't form the words, and then I left it too long to say anything.

Not even goodnight.

TULLY WAS UP AND OUT OF BED WHEN I WOKE. I WASN'T surprised, but it did sting. I didn't want things to be awkward between us.

I didn't know what I wanted between us.

A quick fling? A sex-buddy for my stay?

It certainly wouldn't be hurting anyone.

Unless he had someone at home who would be hurt . . .

I sat up on the bed, my feet on the floor and scratched my head. Tully was walking back across the clearing, swatting away a fly. Shirtless, his skin radiant in the early morning sun with a sheen of sweat . . .

My cock certainly liked it, not helped by the fact I needed to pee. I made a dash for the bathroom before he got any closer so he couldn't see the tent in my boxers, but I didn't want him to think I was hiding from him.

"Morning," I called out before I closed the bathroom door.

"Oh, sleeping beauty has arisen," he said. "Want some breakfast?"

"Ah, sure."

Glad that things seemed to be normal between us, I took a real quick shower and brushed my teeth. And as I was drying off and pulled on my shorts, I had a thought.

I wanted him to know I was okay with what he'd said last night. And actually, I appreciated his asking. He could have just kissed me, and truthfully, I'd have let him. God, last night I'd have let him do whatever he wanted to me. But he wanted to ask first. He needed to know if I was on board, giving me full control.

And I liked that a lot.

I respected that.

It made me want to say yes. Which brought up a whole new set of problems because it was unlikely he'd ask a second time, so it was now up to me to make the first move.

If I wanted something to happen between us . . .

Which I did.

Well, my libido did. My dick was half-hard again at the thought of it; the cold shower clearly hadn't been cold enough.

So how the hell did I go about this?

With my shirt in my hand, I looked down at myself. He did say he wouldn't mind if I went shirtless, and it was hot today already . . .

So, before I lost my nerve, I walked out of the bathroom and tossed my shirt onto my bag.

Tully had a frypan of scrambled eggs in his hand, but he was stuck, staring at me with his mouth open.

I tried not to smile as I put my watch back on. "You're about to lose your eggs."

He snapped his mouth shut and righted the frypan. "Oh, I see the game you're playing, mister sexy science guy."

I looked down at my stomach and ran my hands over my abs and over my pec. "What? It's hot as hell today."

"It just got a whole lot hotter."

I snorted, secretly pleased at his reaction. "You don't wear a shirt, and you said I could do the same."

"I'd also tell you you don't have to wear shorts but I'm pretty sure I wouldn't handle that." He looked down to my crotch. "I mean, you're almost not wearing those as it is."

"What do you mean?"

"They're so low slung I know exactly where your happy trail goes."

I gasped and pulled my shorts up. "They're just old. The elastic isn't great."

And the material was a little thin now. Okay, perhaps a *lot* thin because Tully was still staring at them.

"Were you wearing those when that guy followed you into the bathroom stall? Because honestly, I can see why he couldn't resist."

I folded the waistband over to try and keep them up.

He put the fry pan down on the stove and stared at my crotch. "Jesus fucking Christ, are you goin' commando right now?"

I covered my dick with my hands. "What are you looking for?"

He spun around so he wasn't looking, his hands on his head. "Are you *trying* to kill me?"

"I don't like underwear," I said. "I never wore them much growing up, and I find they ride up . . ." I huffed. "If we could stop talking about my genitals, that'd be great."

He whipped his head around, his eyes shot to mine. "It ain't my fault you came out here naked."

"I'm not naked!"

"You might as well be."

"I can change my shorts to something more appropriate, if you'd prefer."

"I would *not* prefer that." He waved his hand up and down at me. "I prefer this, thank you very much. Just warn a guy next time."

I felt bad now and terribly self-conscious. My plan to perhaps entice him a little had well and truly overshot the runway. I went to my bag, picked up my shirt and quickly pulled it on.

"Aww," Tully cried. "You can't show me an unwrapped present then re-wrap it. That's not how this works. Leave the shirt off."

I shook my head and, hoping to move on from this embarrassing conversation, took two plates out. "Sorry. Want me to help serve the eggs? They look good."

He scowled at me. "T-shirt, one-star rating. Do not recommend." Then he looked down at my shorts. "Shorts, on the other hand, five stars. Highly recommended. Actually, the fact the shirt now hides the front of the shorts makes the shirt negative stars."

"Negative stars isn't a thing."

He raised one eyebrow, his gaze raking down to my crotch and back up to my eyes. "Oh, I assure you, it is."

I took the frypan from in front of him and dished up the eggs. "Thank you for cooking breakfast."

He pouted. "I'm still sad."

I rolled my eyes and laughed, glad that all awkwardness was gone. I cleaned up after breakfast, and we set about doing some work.

It was so unbearably hot and so humid, by two o'clock, I couldn't stand it. I pulled off my shirt and wiped the sweat off my face and chest with it. When I looked at Tully, he was grinning at me like a kid on Christmas morning.

"Shut up," I grumbled. "It's too bloody hot."

He ogled me, deliberately, from head to foot and back up again, stopping midway and shaking his head. "And it's getting hotter by the second." He shrugged with no shame. "I'm not joking, the temperature is actually rising." He turned the laptop to face me. "And the humidity's gonna get to a breaking point before the hour's out. This storm right here." He pointed to the large band of red and purple. "She's gonna be a good one."

I found myself smiling at him. "Excellent. I better get my gear set up." I went to my bag and rummaged around for the sunscreen and rubbed some into my face and chest. It might have been cruel and it was probably uncalled for, but I handed the tube to him and turned around, speaking to him over my shoulder. "Can you rub some in for me, please?"

He huffed with fake annoyance. Or maybe it was real, I wasn't sure. "If I have to. I mean, now you're givin' me an unwrapped present, you're lettin' me touch it," he said, smearing sunscreen across my shoulder and rubbing it in with strong, firm strokes. "But I still can't play with it."

My heart skidded and my belly swooped. Then my fucking watch beeped again, and he laughed. He was so close his breath was warm on my skin, his hands now rubbing sunscreen down my spine.

"You can pretend all you like," he whispered. "But your heart rate doesn't lie."

"The app must be glitching," I said, and maybe that would have been convincing if my voice hadn't come out all rough.

He chuckled behind me, his hands now running down my sides, fingertips digging in.

Not wearing underpants today had been a big mistake.

I cleared my throat and took a step forward, away from him. I half turned, not letting him see the tented commando issue I had going on at the front. "Thank you," I said, then walked out into the blistering sun and the suffocating humidity.

Thirty seconds of that torture and I no longer had a hard-on. Small mercies, I guess.

I checked the automatic weather station in the clearing, making sure everything was still intact and working, then looked up at the gathering clouds. There was a front coming in from the east again; a dark and foreboding wall of mother nature was coming our way.

It felt like the air would catch fire before it rained. As if one spark of lightning could light the whole sky up like a match to gasoline.

I went back to the shed, amazed at the difference in temperature inside. "How freaking hot is it out there? The tropics are brutal."

Tully didn't seem too fazed. "You get used to it." Then he nodded to my crotch and shrugged. "But you could take your shorts off if you get too hot."

I resisted rolling my eyes.

But then he was serious. He came over with a bottle of water and pressed it to my sternum. "Keep drinking water and take cool showers if you feel like you're over-heating." And then he was back to being Tully; he stared at my chest and abs and shook his head. "Damn, Jeremiah. How do you do it? What's your routine?"

"My routine for what?"

"In the gym."

"I don't go to the gym." I made a face. "Where there are other people, all sweaty and showing off. It's gross."

He gave me a crooked smile, and I was waiting for my watch to betray me, but thankfully it didn't. "So you work out at home?"

"I don't work out." Well, that wasn't exactly true. "I swim. For no other reason than it clears my head. And it's solitary. No one can speak to me while I do laps."

He laughed, his eyes alight with something I wasn't brave enough to name. "You crack me up."

"Glad I amuse you."

"Ah, don't be like that," he said, giving me a gentle nudge. "You are . . ." He met my gaze and shook his head. "Like no one I've ever met before."

"I can only assume that was because you don't frequent science conventions or libraries."

"Ouch."

I shrugged. It was true.

A bead of sweat chose that moment to run from my temple, down my jaw and neck, and of course he watched it, his eyes intense. So, meeting fire with fire, I opened the bottle of water, put it to my lips, and drank.

He watched my mouth and my throat as I swallowed, his

eyes dark, his lips parted.

I wiped the back of my hand across my mouth to hide my smile and offered him the bottle. "Some?"

His nostrils flared. "You're a cruel man."

I grinned at him. "I don't know what you're talking about. If you don't want the water, just say no."

He narrowed his eyes at me and snatched the bottle, then took a step back before he turned and walked away. "Christ, it's hot in here."

I pressed my lips together so as not to smile too wide. This was kinda fun. I knew how it would end; it was why I was doing it. I hadn't come here expecting any such thing—it was the last thing I expected, truthfully—but now it was a possibility?

Ending with a romp on that small double bed with a gorgeous man wouldn't be terrible. If he was willing . . .

And he *was* willing.

Then I remembered something. Before I took this any further . . .

I went to my laptop, tracking the storm, pretending to be grossly interested in it. "So," I hedged, trying for the nonchalance that he did so well. "Anyone in Darwin on your emergency contact list I should know about?"

He squinted at me, confused. "Emergency contact?" Then he came to see the radar. "Just how bad is this storm gonna get?"

"No, it's not that bad. I mean, it's a good one. There's a wind warning in conjunction with high precipitation falls and a flash flood warning for some parts. Decent lightning activity."

Tully looked at me then. "Why did you ask about my emergency contact? That's a random and totally weird thing to ask, not gonna lie."

"No, it's not that, it's just . . ." I shook my head and looked out at the darkening sky instead. "It's just good to know if something were to happen, who I should call, that's all. Like someone who would be upset if you were injured."

"Oh my god," he whispered. Aaaaand then he grinned. "Are you tryin' to ask me if I'm seeing someone back home?"

My eyes shot to his.

He laughed. "You totally are!"

Thunder rolled outside.

"You wanna know if I'm seein' someone. That's what this is all about. You taking your shirt off. Asking me to rub sunscreen on your back. Drinkin' water like a porn star."

"I did not drink that water like a porn star."

"You did fucking so."

"Just what kind of porn do you watch?"

"Don't try and change the subject."

I had an all too familiar taste hit my mouth and I licked my lips, tried to swallow it down. "I need some water."

Suddenly serious, he handed me the bottle. "Why do you do that? You did it the other day too. Like something tastes bad before it rains."

I sipped the water, swishing it in my mouth even though I knew it wouldn't help. "Not before it rains. Before the lightning."

His eyes met mine. "What?"

"I know when lightning is about to strike," I said. "Because I can taste it."

"You can taste it," he whispered, not a question, but this was usually when people thought I was weird. Like he was now. I could see it on his face.

"It's a metallic taste. Copper, to be exact." I tried to swallow down the taste on my tongue, as if the mention of it made it worse. "It's not pleasant. But it's common," I said. "In people who've been struck by lightning."

His eyes searched mine and a slow smile spread across his face. Okay, so maybe he didn't think I was weird. "That is soooo fucking cool!"

CHAPTER NINE

TULLY

Thunder clapped right above us, scaring the shit out of me. "Jesus!" I ducked on instinct.

Jeremiah didn't even flinch.

He could taste lightning.

Well, not *actual* lightning. But he could taste when it was close.

That was the coolest thing I'd ever heard.

He really was like no one I'd ever met before.

And he was being all kinds of weird all day. After last night, I probably couldn't blame him. I did almost kiss him. Hell, lying in bed with him so close, and so freaking sexy, kissing him wasn't all I wanted to do.

But he didn't answer when I asked him, and anything short of a direct yes is a no.

So I'd rolled over and gone to sleep, disappointed but not mad about it.

Then today, he woke up with an agenda, clearly.

Maybe it was his way of answering me with a yes?

Trying to be all seductive and shit. First, being shirtless. Then asking me to rub sunscreen in, which was as cliché as it was awesome. And the water bottle incident. Christ almighty.

He was playing a dangerous game.

And then—then!—he asked if I was seeing someone. Not outright, but that's what he was hinting at.

"I'm single," I said casually. "And considering I'm bisexual, you'd think I'd have double the options, but no. I'm doubly undatable, apparently."

He glanced up from his laptop, looked me up and down, and went back to the laptop. "I find that hard to believe."

"Why?"

He gestured to me, like that was his answer. "You look like the love child of Patrick Swayze and Chris Hemsworth."

I snorted. "I can't help that."

"Yes, because it would be so problematic." He rolled his eyes.

"What is problematic is that I spend my weekends camping out, and every holiday I get, I chase storms. I don't have commitment issues. I'm just committed to the wrong things. Apparently."

He smirked, still looking at the screen. "Sounds like you've heard that a few times."

"I have."

His blue eyes shot to mine. "Then you're dating the wrong people."

Oof.

Those eyes, and those words.

Damn.

"What about you? Seeing anyone? I probably should have asked you that before I almost kissed you last night. Though, broadly speaking, I did ask permission if I could kiss you so that covers that, right?"

His cheeks bloomed with blush. Or maybe it was the heat.

His watch beeped that warning sound. Ignoring it, he turned to his laptop instead. "Okay it's coming, we need to run the intra-cloud activity," he said.

"Is your watch working properly now? Or is it still glitching?"

He shot me a hard glare.

"Funny how it only glitches when I'm next to you," I said. "Almost like my presence makes your heart rate spike."

He stabbed some keys on his keyboard. "What's your reading?" he asked, ignoring my poke at him completely.

I looked at the screen, not sure what he wanted. I didn't know how to read any of this. "The amplitude pulses?"

"The spatiotemporal analysis of radiation field pulses," he mumbled, turning the screen to face him. His eyes scanned over the data and he nodded. "We should get some good readings." Then he did that mouth/tongue thing again, like something tasted bad.

And boom!

Thunder cracked right on top of us and lightning lit up the sky.

He really could taste it.

A huge gust of wind brought with it the smell of rain, and then the clouds opened up, bucketing thick, heavy drops.

"Shit," I said, racing to close the side wall down. "The wind's bringing it in." Some of our gear got wet, bags and clothes, but we'd have to deal with that later. Jeremiah helped with the other side and we got the wall lowered, to stop the rain coming in sideways at least.

The wind roared around the shed, rain pelted down, thunder was a constant rumble and bang, and lightning cracked all around us.

Jeremiah ran back to his recording gear, then leaned in, squinting at the screen. "Shit," he said. "The anemometer must be down on the station."

Then, like an idiot with zero thought for self-preservation, he ducked out under the other side wall and disappeared into the storm.

"Are you crazy?" I yelled out after him, but it was no use. He was halfway across the clearing.

Thunder clapped hard, right above us, and a bolt of lightning struck ahead of us. Maybe a hundred metres in the trees. But that sonofabitch never stopped running. He didn't even flinch. Surely, he saw it. It was right fucking there! He just kept running right toward it.

"Jeremiah! The fuck are you doing?"

There was no point. There was no way he could hear me over the rain and the thunder.

He reached the tripod station, skidding to a stop. He grabbed the arms with the small wind cups and fixed it.

Yes, please run out into a lightning storm to wrap your hands around the metal instrument in the middle of a clearing.

It was like sending lightning a freaking invitation to strike him down.

The man was fucking insane.

He came running back, the wind was wild, spraying rain in all directions. A sonic crack of thunder with lightning that felt like a direct hit, lit up our entire camp.

I expected Jeremiah to get knocked off his feet. I expected him to get blowback, or a side blast. I expected to see him take a direct fucking hit.

But he didn't. He just kept running toward me, his hair plastered to his face, his entire body soaked.

And grinning.

He ducked under the side wall like in the movies where they run for a closing roller door. Just like that. And he clambered to his feet, panting and dripping water, and then that fucker laughed.

He laughed.

Whereas I, on the other hand, was really fucking pissed.

I shoved his chest. "Are you insane?"

His smile died. "What?"

I pointed to the outside. "Do you know how close that was? Do you know how fuckin' close that was? I'm glad you got that on video so I could have shown the coroner that you died for being a fucking idiot."

His chest was heaving, he was drenched from head to foot. His eyes narrowed at me. He grabbed my face, hard and rough, and for a second I thought he was going to hit me, or shove me backwards for calling him an idiot . . . but he pulled me toward him and crushed his mouth to mine. He held my face and plunged his tongue into my mouth, totally dominating. Totally fucking hot.

I took his tongue willingly and gave him mine. He sucked on it, then pulled my bottom lip in between his, kissing me one last time before pulling back. My god, he could kiss.

He grinned, lips red and swollen, still drenched from head to foot. "That was a rush."

It took my brain a second to catch up but I couldn't put words together. My head was still spinning while he was already at the table checking his screens for data. I put my hand to my forehead and focused on what he'd said. "What was a rush? The storm? Or the kiss?"

"The storm." He gave me a look that said, 'what kiss?' like he hadn't just had his tongue down my throat.

Like he hadn't just given me the best kiss of my life.

Something on the table beeped and he picked it up, then went to his laptop, double checking something . . . I don't fucking know. I was too busy watching rivulets of water run down his back, how his wet shorts clung to him.

Without underwear.

"Holy fuck," I breathed.

He didn't look up. He just pointed to something out of his reach. "Pass me the sensor detector."

It took me a few seconds to move. I went and handed it to him, and he just continued to read and correlate data like nothing had just happened. "We've got upper negative and a lower positive charge," he said, reading three radar screens at the same time.

Did I imagine him kissing me?

My lips were still tingling, my whole body was tingling, my brain was still offline . . . oh yeah, he'd definitely kissed me. And now he stood there reading some machine, water puddling at his feet, dripping from his shorts . . . shorts that did nothing to hide the outline of his cock.

His long, half-hard and uncut cock.

Christ.

"Tully?"

My mind snapped back to reality, and I dragged my eyes up to meet his. "Huh?"

He smirked. That fucker smirked. "You zoned out on me. You okay?"

"Ah, not really," I said. "You kissed me. I had your tongue in my mouth not two minutes ago and now you're acting like nothing happened." I waved my hand at his body. "And those shorts, when wet, leave nothing to the imagination. Nothing. I don't know where you got them from, but they are absolutely a five-star purchase. Highly, *highly* recommended."

He stared at me.

"Are we not going to talk about you kissing me?" I asked.

He opened his mouth, then promptly shut it again, as if he was trying to remember if he'd kissed me or not. "I'm sorry. I was excited—I'd had a rush of adrenaline—and I apologise if it was out of line."

"Oh no," I said, shaking my head. "No apologies required. It was not out of line. It was very in of line. I don't know what the opposite of that is." I started again. "I was very okay with that. Where the fuck did you learn to kiss like that? Because Jesus, Mary, Joseph, and their freaking donkey, I ain't ever been kissed like that before. And I'd like to add, the only thing you should apologise for is if you don't do it again."

He chewed on his bottom lip so he didn't smile too big.

"I would say don't get smug about it," I added, "but honestly, you should be. Full credit where credit is due. It's worthy of the all-kissing accolades. If they gave Nobel prizes for kissing . . ."

He smiled then and ran his hand through his wet hair, brushing it up off his forehead, and damn if that didn't make him ten times hotter.

"I'm not seeing anyone," he said, as if I hadn't just rambled like an idiot. "Eternally single, I'm afraid. Too nerdy, too weird. Too focused on my work. Too . . ." He squinted. "I can't remember what else he said, but you get the picture."

"Then you're dating the wrong guy."

His gaze met mine, intense and searching, before he went back to his laptop. "Yes, well . . . and about the shorts. I should probably change. I'm dripping water—"

"Oh no. The shorts stay. You can't wear anything else for the duration of your stay." I put my hand to my chest. "As your official guide, I must insist. For safety reasons. It's very important."

His gaze locked with mine and his smile was interrupted by him biting his bottom lip. "I should go check the auto-station," he said quietly. He took a step backward, and of course my eyes went straight to his dick.

Yep. Still there. Still perfectly outlined. Still mouth-watering . . .

But then he turned and ducked under the awning, walking out into the clearing. The trees were blowing in the wind, but the rain was gone. He put his arms out. "How can it still be so hot?" he yelled.

I didn't realise just how big I was smiling as I watched him until he came back with the control panel and I had to school my features.

He set the control panel down. "We got some great readings," he said.

"Should we rewatch the video?" I asked. "And see just how close you were to getting zapped by lightning."

He stood at the table, facing me. His hands by his sides, his torso dry now, his shorts . . . damn, I couldn't stop staring. I tried to look away, but then his hand interrupted my view when he gave his dick a squeeze.

"Were you never told it's rude to stare," he murmured, his voice low and husky.

I made myself look up at his face, and his eyes were full of fire. Full of want.

Oh, hell fucking yes.

I went to him, gripped his chin in between my thumb and forefinger. "I want to suck your cock. Tell me yes or no."

He licked his lips and smiled as if he had all the time in the world. As if this was his game, he held all the cards, and I didn't even know the rules.

He was in charge, and I was 100% okay with that.

He leaned in, his lips against mine, his eyes dark and intense.

"Yes."

CHAPTER TEN

JEREMIAH

I wasn't normally so bossy when it came to sex. Well, not *this* bossy. But it felt good to be in control and Tully seemed to like it that way.

He went to his knees, slowly, kissing down my chest and stomach, below my navel. He slid my shorts down over my arse and they went surprisingly easy, given they were still wet. He hummed as he took me into his mouth. No preamble, no toying. Just instant wet heat, sucking me, tonguing and moaning.

"Oh god," I mumbled, trying to rein in the pleasure. I fisted his hair, but it only seemed to spur him on.

Of course, he likes his hair pulled.

Fuck.

His hands clawed the backs of my thighs and my arse as he took me into his throat, swallowing around me.

God, I hadn't had this in so long, and he was doing everything so, so right.

I pulled his head back by his hair, making him look up at me, the head of my cock still in his mouth.

"So good," I mumbled, the coil of my orgasm needing to unwind so badly.

Then he cupped my balls and took me back in, sucking hard and pumping the base of my shaft.

"Oh fuck. Tully, I'm gonna come."

He smiled around my cock and hummed, and that was all it took.

Pleasure so complete detonated in my belly, my cock surged, and I came. He moaned as he drank me down and the room spun and my vision swam.

Tully sat me in a seat from the table, my senses still obliterated. My body was heavy, my mind was floating.

He lifted my chin, a smug smile on his face. "You okay there?"

"Hmm."

He straddled my legs and adjusted his erection, right in front of my face. "Yes or no?"

I pulled him closer by the waistband of his shorts, unbuttoning them. "Hell yes," I said, smiling. I pulled out his cock, thick and cut, and licked my lips before licking his slit.

"Oh fuck, I'm not gonna last long," he breathed.

I took him into my mouth, swirling my tongue around his shaft, flicking his frenulum. He shuffled closer as I took him deeper, and he made a high keening sound, pained almost.

"Fuck, Jeremiah," he rasped out.

Then his fingers slid around my jaw, my neck, and I could tell he was trying hard not to thrust in. He was so hard, so ready. I took him into my throat and he grunted and groaned, his cock swelling and shooting come down my throat.

I held his arse, keeping him buried in my throat until his body stopped twitching, and when I let him out, I pulled up his shorts, led him to the bed, and pushed him back onto it.

He landed with a gruff laugh. "Fuck yes," he said. He had his eyes closed and his lips curled in a serene smile. "Christ, you have skills. Kissing. Sucking dick. God. Did you study that?"

I snorted out a laugh and fixed my shorts. Then, not

entirely sure what to do next, I grabbed my iPad. He raised his head off the bed. "Where are you going?"

"Nowhere." I came back to the bed and lay down beside him. "I'm gonna watch this."

I rewound the video and we lay there, both still shirtless, both now very sated, and we watched a replay of the storm. We could see the dark clouds rolling in, the wall of water as it came toward the bunker. I watched the sheet lightning light up the clouds like it was full of fireflies, mesmerised by how beautiful it could be.

Sparks of intra-cloud lightning shot across the clouds like spidery fingers, positive seeking out the closest source of negative charge. After a few minutes of raging winds, the auto-station fell over at the end of the clearing.

"Oh, here goes the crazy man," Tully said, "running out into a lightning storm to hold a metal rod."

Tully's voice in the video yelled at me too, and it was oddly comforting. That he should care enough to be concerned.

Just as I'd righted the anemometer, a bolt of lightning cracked into the trees behind me, and I hit pause on the screen.

"Can you see why I was pissed?" Tully said. He rolled onto his side, hooking his foot over mine, locking me in some wrestling leg-manoeuvre. He pointed to the screen. "Look at how close that is. Look!"

"I can see," I said.

"You didn't even flinch or duck," he said.

But I wasn't looking at how close the strike was. I was looking at the pure energy, the brilliance of light. The raw power.

"It's perfect."

Tully rolled onto his back, letting my leg go with an exasperated sigh. "Yes, it's amazing. But can you appreciate that you almost died? And just wait till you get to the part where you slide in under the wall like an action movie hero." He sighed again. "I'm beginning to think you have the whole Clark Kent vibe going on."

I looked at him. "Clark Kent?"

"Yeah, sexy nerd front, kickass superhero when no one's looking."

I scoffed.

"He also risked his life unnecessarily all the time, too. Stupidly put himself in harm's way, as if his book-smarts mean diddley freakin' squat in the real world." Then he shrugged. "But totally gets his freak on in the bedroom. Can we talk about where you learned to kiss like that? And suck dick? Because that's some Kryptonite bullshit right there. Jesus."

I stared at him, not entirely sure if he was being serious. "No one taught me."

He grinned. So he was joking . . . "So you learned by yourself."

"By myself?" I squinted at him. "How could I possibly kiss myself? And I certainly can't suck my . . . self."

Now he laughed. "Have you tried?"

"No!" I barked, the silence that followed was loud. Then, because I had to ask . . . "My god, have you?"

"I'm not flexible enough to even try. But I've seen it in porn. It's kinda weird. Now, I love sucking dick, but my own? I think that'd be too weird, even for me."

I took a deep breath. "How is this even a conversation we're having?"

He rolled onto his side again, facing me with that unlawful smirk. He hooked his foot over mine again. "Because of the Clark Kent thing," he said casually. "And now that we've crossed the line once, I'd like to discuss the possibility of crossing it many times. So if there are any preferences or hard limits you'd like to discuss . . ."

It was difficult to think clearly when he was playing footsies and lying so close, and looking at me like that. With his smiling eyes and his perfect face.

"I'm here to work," I said, trying to relinquish some of the control he had over me. "And—"

"And work we will," he said, taking my iPad. "Later."

I took it back, scowling at him. "Trying to distract me with your charm and roguish good looks with the promise of more sex won't help your argument for being able to get work done and engage in some kind of sexual relationship."

He took the iPad again, this time leaning right over me and laying it on the floor beside the bed. This, of course, meant he was now kneeling over me, looking down at me. "Did you say roguish good looks?"

I rolled my eyes. "Your smile is ridiculous."

Laughing, he took hold of my leg and pulled me into the middle of the bed. "Glad you like it."

"I never said I liked it."

He leaned down, his nose almost touching mine. "Oh, but I think you do."

For some reason, it was getting harder to breathe. "At first I thought it made you likeable. Then it was annoying. Then it made me irrationally angry."

He licked his lips, smirking. "And now?"

My watch beeped.

"I hate it."

"No you don't." He laughed and took my wrist. "It says so right here. Though it didn't beep before when I sucked your dick. Was that not good for you?"

We both knew the answer to that.

I pulled my hand free and clawed at the stupid watch, trying to take it off. "I told you it glitched."

"Uh-uh." He gripped both of my hands and held them to the mattress above my head, making the watch beep again. Grinning now, he whispered against my lips. "Leave it on. It will tell me when I do something you like."

Oh god. My brain scrambled, making it difficult to think, to speak. "Scientifically speaking, heart acceleration is also frequent during moments of rage and fear," I said, my voice barely a whisper.

He ghosted his lips over mine. "Are you scared?"

My breath hitched.

"Are you angry?"

My traitorous hips tried to meet his, desperate for friction.

He grinned and crushed his mouth to mine, forcing his tongue inside. He still had my hands pinned to the bed and pressed his full weight between my legs, holding me down, kissing me hard. It was everything I wanted.

There was a beeping noise somewhere near my head, distant and hazy in the desire coursing through me, until it got louder and louder and louder . . .

My watch.

I groaned and pulled my hands free, ripping my watch off and tossing it somewhere near the iPad. "They're gonna send a rescue chopper if it doesn't stop," I said, then pulled his face back to mine.

He laughed into the kiss and rolled his hips, his erection rubbing against mine.

How was I hard again? How was he? Was it the heat? Or was it just him?

I think it was him.

He was so sexy, and he wanted me. Me.

Miserable, lonely, weirdo me.

He broke the kiss and groaned, rubbing and thrusting against me. "Oh god. Fuck, Jeremiah."

I slid my hand between us, fumbling to get our shorts down, to wrap my hand round us both.

His eyes shot open and he bucked, pressing his forehead to mine. "Holy shit."

Our cocks slid together, slick with our precome, mine, his.

He grunted, the noise setting every cell in my body on fire, and then he kissed me again, our tongues colliding.

And he shuddered, bucking, and with a loud cry, he came in my hand. His cock pulsing against mine, tripping me over the edge . . .

When the world stopped spinning, I opened my eyes to find him staring at me. "Holy shit," he breathed. "That was so fucking hot."

I couldn't speak.

I was so tired, and my bones were heavy and spongy. He collapsed on top of me, smearing the mess between us, and it was hot and we were both sweaty, and I didn't even care.

His breath was warm on my neck, and normally that would bother me.

But not with him.

Instead, I surrendered to the world, slung my arm around him, and closed my eyes.

I TOOK A MOUTHFUL OF MY DINNER AND SCROLLED THE RADAR data. "Forecast for the next two days is good for lightning activity, but then two days of heavy precipitation. Up to one hundred millimetres."

Tully chewed thoughtfully and nodded. "We might have to pack up and leave before it hits."

My eyes shot to his, and I was struck by how much I didn't want that. "To higher ground? Or do you mean *leave* leave?"

He shoved in another forkful of rice and smiled as he chewed. "You sound disappointed."

"I am." I stabbed my rice, trying to play it cool. "I have four more days here. It's highly unlikely I'll get this opportunity again. I need to collect adequate data to justify to my department the cost of my being here."

He did more of that smirking that I absolutely hated. "It has nothin' to do with your amazing guide who gives you mind-blowin' orgasms and cooks incredible dinners."

I frowned at him, unwilling to respond to the first part of his statement. "This rice is actually very good." It was a Thai-style fried rice with vegetables, spices, and fried egg. "Where did you learn to cook this?"

"The cooks at work. We have a cafeteria type thing," he answered with a shrug. "Not what they cook for the workers, but what they cook for themselves. That's where the real food's at. Mostly leftovers, like day old rice, some chopped onions and capsicums and carrot, a bunch of sauces and a crack of chili. Add in a fried egg or two and you got yourself a whole meal."

I nodded as I took another bite. "Do you cook this at home?"

"Sometimes. What about you? What do you cook at home?"

"I don't. If I can avoid it. Just basic stuff." I shrugged. "Growing up, we had whatever was cheap and easy. Meat and veg, basically, because that was all my dad knew how to cook."

"He never remarried?"

I shook my head. "No. He . . . he was never the same after my mother died."

"It must have been hard."

I put my fork on my empty plate. "Yes. Given the public nature of it all. They never should have released the footage. They never asked my dad's permission, and he had to watch his wife die over and over again on every TV channel for weeks. Every time there's a documentary on the dangers of lightning . . ." I sighed. "And it never stops. Still, to this day. Just last year, there was a preview ad for one of those 'history of breaking news stories' shows on TV. Just out of the blue, there she was again, dying in front of him all over again in an ad on the television before he could change the channel."

"Jesus," Tully murmured. "I can't even imagine."

"He doesn't watch much TV now."

"I don't blame him." Tully stacked our plates. "And he doesn't understand why you do what you do?"

"Not at all."

He sighed sadly. "Does he . . . does he know you like men?"

"That I'm gay? Yes. It ranks about fourth on the list of disappointments."

"Only fourth?"

I counted on my fingers. "Number one disappointment is my chosen profession. Number two is that I support Essendon football. Number three is that I don't support Richmond. Number four is I'm gay."

Tully chuckled. "Football, huh?"

"Yes. The one and only thing he will watch on TV is the AFL. He goes to all the games, wears the guernsey and beanie, scarf, the whole thing." I shook my head. "I'm not even that much of a football fan to begin with, to be honest."

"Why Essendon and not Richmond like your dad?"

"When I was about fifteen, he made me go to a game. Essendon against Richmond. I didn't want to go, made a point of taking a book instead, scowled at everything and everyone, like a typical teen." I rolled my eyes at myself. "Of course we were right up close, by the locker room tunnel. And then I noticed the players."

He grinned at that. "Ohhh. You *noticed* the players."

"Oh yes. It was quite the sexual awakening, seeing them so up close in those tight uniforms, all sweaty and touching each other. One of the players smiled at me as he ran off after the game, and I almost expired on the spot. I've been a loyal Essendon fan ever since."

Tully laughed. "That's poetic."

"My father didn't think so." We stared at each other for a long second, both of us almost smiling. "Your parents know you're . . . bisexual?"

"Sure," he said, waving me off. "Being bisexual made no difference. I mean, out of four kids, they got three straighties and me. Statistically speaking, it was bound to happen. And like I told you already, I'm the baby; the spoiled one. I can do or be whatever and get away with it. Growing up, my eldest brother would get mad because 'oh, the spoiled baby can do whatever he wants' and I'd just laugh and be like 'hell yes, I can, sucks to be you.'" He shrugged with a laugh. "It's the card I was dealt. I use it all the time."

"You have no responsibilities at all?"

"Sure I do. I have bills and a home loan. I have a uni degree I'm still paying off, just like everyone else. I work full-time, and I'm good at what I do. I just choose to do this in my vacation time. You see me here, wearing shorts, no shirt or shoes, and think I live like this. But I don't." He leaned in a whispered like it was a national secret. "I even wear a suit to work."

That made me smile. "I can't imagine it."

Which was a lie because I was imagining it right now . . .

"Well, suit pants, shirt, and tie. It's too hot for a jacket. It's Darwin, after all." He winked. "But some days if I'm just at the office and don't actually have to see people, I can get away with some nice shorts and a company polo shirt. But this?" he gestured to his half naked body. "This is my preferred uniform."

"It suits you."

That cocky smirk was back. "What about you? Please tell me you wear a white lab coat to work."

I snorted. "Why would I wear one of those?"

"Just let me have the fantasy, okay? You would totally rock up in a white lab coat, looking all smart and sexy, studying your data under a microscope."

"I think you have a seriously misconstrued perception about what I actually do for a job."

He laughed. "Let me have the fantasy, Jeremiah. You're not playing the game properly."

I sighed. "Okay, yes. I wear a white lab coat and study data . . . under a micro . . . scope."

Tully laughed, his grin wide. "I'm totally picturing it now. Are you naked under the lab coat?"

"Absolutely not."

"Jeremiah."

"Okay, yes, I'm totally naked. Which would be a violation of almost every occupational health and safety code, but sure. Yes, let's pretend I'm naked."

His eyes did that shining thing when he smiled, which I didn't hate so much anymore. "This is fun. Is there a desk or workstation with computers and shit that you could fuck me on?"

I almost swallowed my tongue.

"Or I could fuck you on it," he added casually. "I don't mind either way. My door swings both ways. Actually, it's not that I don't mind both ways, it's that I prefer both ways. You know, variety is the spice of life. Or something like that."

I was still stuck on his words . . .

that you could fuck me on . . . or I could fuck you on it . . .

His tongue slipped out, wetting his bottom lip before he bit it. "You're picturing it right now, aren't you?"

I shook my head, trying futilely to turn the visuals in my head to mist. Of course that made him laugh. "You totally are. And I'm absolutely regretting not bringing any condoms or lube with me. I didn't think it would be that kind of trip. Unless you brought something with you . . ."

When I still hadn't said anything, he hooked his foot with mine, sliding his up my calf. It startled me out of my thoughts.

"Uh, no. I didn't. I didn't think this trip would be that kind either."

"Do you regret what we've done?" Tully was half-smiling, but his question was serious. He was just hiding it behind his humour.

"Not at all. Do you?"

"Hell no."

I swallowed hard, my mouth dry. "I, uh . . . your door, swinging both ways . . ."

"I just meant that I like to top and bottom."

"Yes, I understood the metaphor."

"Oh."

"I, uh . . ." I needed a sip of water so I could speak.

"I get total top vibes from you," he said, almost cheerfully. "You totally have that sexy in-charge vibe going on. Quiet, super-smart, do-as-I-say vibe. It's hot as fuck."

There he went again, scrambling my thoughts. "Oh."

"Am I right?"

"Well, yes."

"I knew it!"

"But I also like to . . ."

"Take a good dicking?"

I sighed. "Yes. On occasion. If it's with the right person and I can trust them to do it right."

He laughed. "So you gotta be in charge either way."

I scowled at him. "I do not. I'm not—"

"A control freak?"

I gasped, my mouth falling open. "I beg your pardon."

"It's not a bad thing. Like I said, it's hot as fuck. Honestly, I can't wait for you to fuck me. It's gonna be so good."

I blinked a few times, again completely stunned at his boldness. "You're awfully confident to assume that will happen."

He laughed like that was the most ridiculous thing he'd ever heard. Then he stood up, leaning right in close. "Because

I know you want to. Hell, it'd almost be worth me driving out of here for two days to find the nearest store that sells supplies." Then he whispered in my ear, his voice low and gruff. "And you want me to fuck you too."

Then he was abruptly gone, taking the plates to the sink, and I sat there too dumbstruck to speak. Hell, I couldn't even form a coherent thought.

Later that night when we climbed into bed, he pulled the sheet up over us, and I expected him to initiate some kind of sex or ask me more personal and embarrassing questions, but he didn't. He sighed into the dark.

"What's your favourite ice cream flavour?"

CHAPTER ELEVEN
TULLY

We had an easy morning. I made us a quick breakfast, Jeremiah made the coffee, then we sat around the table going over the data from yesterday and looking to see what was in store for today. The forecast hadn't changed. Storms today and tomorrow, then a shit-ton of rain.

And sure, it could ease up and the forecast could change. The cloud front and low pressure coming in from the Timor Sea could weaken, and maybe we wouldn't have to bunk out.

I didn't want to leave just yet.

I'd thought having some stranger in my space during this trip was going to be annoying, but that couldn't have been further from the truth.

I liked having someone here with me. Not like the time I'd mistakenly asked my brother Ellis to join me. But Jeremiah was like me; he loved the storms, the weather. And he was super smart and he understood the science of it. I was learning a lot and I was already making plans for when I got home to start buying the same gear he had.

It was so freakin' cool.

"So I was thinking," Jeremiah said, not even looking up from his screen.

"Uh oh. Good thinking or bad thinking?"

His eyes met mine then, his brow furrowed. "How is any thinking bad?"

"I'm sorry. What were you thinking?"

"Well, you mentioned the mangroves and the crabs before."

Oh god. I knew where this was going . . . This was bad thinking.

"I think I'd like to see it. During an electrical storm."

"Are you actually insane?"

"No."

"Then why?"

"Mangroves, in particular those with a crustacean colony, emit large quantities of methane and nitrogen, and I'm sure you know what lightning does to areas of ground with high positive charges."

"Yes. That's why I asked you if you were insane." The carcinologists had told me about that. It was why they came here but not normally in the storm season because it was too dangerous. "It's also the wet season. I don't know how accessible they'll be, and I'd need to check the tide chart. And we'd have to camp there overnight. It'd be too far to come back. We'd have to sleep in the Jeep because—"

Jeremiah stood up and closed his laptop. "Then I should start packing."

"—because of the crocodiles." Of course, he acted like he didn't hear me, so I said it again, louder this time. "Because of the crocodiles!"

He started to pack up his equipment crate. "I heard you the first time."

"Then why are you still packing?"

"Because if my time here is being cut short, I need to bring back information. What I have so far is fine, but it's not outstanding, and I need something extraordinary to justify my coming here."

"Okay, cool." I went and threw my bag on the bed, stuffing in a shirt, and did up the zipper. "Have you got your affairs in order?"

"My what?"

"Your affairs. Your papers, your last will and testament." I sprayed myself with insect repellent, and then I did it again. "Because if the lightning don't get ya, the crocs probably will. Or the mozzies." I stopped and looked at him then. "Had a malaria shot? Have you heard of Ross River Fever?"

He scowled at me; his piercing eyes looked like blue fire. "If you're trying to dissuade me, it won't work. It will just make me more determined to go. So if you won't join me, perhaps I can take your vehicle and drive myself."

I tossed the can of insect spray to him. "Oh great. So then I'd have to walk outta here to get you some help. Stellar idea, genius. Just out of curiosity, where would you like your body shipped to? If they find your body, that is. Usually a croc will just take ya into deeper waters and pummel you a bit, leave you stuffed under a log or something, till you're nice and tender. Bodies are rarely recovered. They just find finger marks dug into the riverbank and they stop looking. Call off the search parties right then and there."

He was staring at me now. "Are you finished?"

"Not even close." I sniffed. "Now, mangroves in particular have high concentrations of lightning strikes—"

He sighed loud enough to stop me. "Which is why I'm going. So, you can either come with me or I can go in alone."

I glared at him.

He glared right back at me.

And for the longest moment, neither one of us blinked. I caved first, snarling at him for good measure. "Did you major in stubbornness at university?"

"I have a doctorate."

"In stubbornness."

"Actually—"

"In *stubborn*ness."

Then he sighed and I felt like we were on a seesaw, where neither one of us would ever get the advantage.

He glowered. I huffed.

He mumbled under his breath while he packed up his own shit, I lowered the walls and closed the place up. We would likely be back, but it wasn't guaranteed, so I treated it like we were leaving for good.

We drove the Jeep out in silence.

"Are you driving recklessly on purpose?" he asked. The track was bad, and he was holding onto the oh-shit bar, giving me the stink eye every chance he got.

"Yes, I designed this track to have more craters than the moon, and I'm choosing to hit every single hole in hopes that I break the suspension so we get stranded out here because, honestly, getting taken by a croc and enduring one of the most painful deaths ever is preferable to whatever your fuckin' problem is."

He glowered at me even harder as we bounced through another bad part of the track. "And you think I'm stubborn."

"No, I think you're stupid. Incredibly intelligent, and really fuckin' stupid."

Aaaaand that earned me some more silence.

And then I felt bad.

But this *was* stupid. And he knew the risks and he still wanted to go. And I was stupid enough to be going with him.

Did that make me stupider?

Goddammit.

After a long stretch of silence and a lot of bumpy kilometres under the tyres, I knew I had to break the silence. "I'll need you to navigate," I said. "Can you see if you can get any signal for a map on your iPad?"

"Do you not know where we're going?"

"Not really. I've been out here once in the dry season. It looks a little different now."

He baulked then, schooling his reaction, quickly took out his iPad, and tapped the screen a few times. "Nothing."

"Shit."

"I have the paper map," he said, pulling it out of his bag. "I don't know how detailed it will be for these parts."

Not very, I thought. But I didn't say that.

He unfolded it and refolded it so he could see roughly where we were. "Our camp was here," he said, bouncing in his seat but not taking his eyes or finger off the map. "We took the north road out, turned off to go due east to the South Alligator River, about ten k's along . . ." He checked the scale of the map, then checked his watch. "Considering our distance over time, we should be approximately here." He held his finger to a certain point on the map. "Meaning we have about another five to eight kilometres to go."

It irked me that he used intelligence, reasoning, and common sense. "Thank you."

The forest around us had changed. No longer paperbarks and plum trees, it was now palms and mangroves, and the track was becoming more sandy. "I don't know how much further we'll be able to go by car," I said. "I won't risk getting us bogged in sand before high tide comes in. We'll have to park, then walk in for a bit."

He looked at me, then out the windscreen at the swampiness of our surroundings. And a look of 'shit, what have I done?' flashed in his eyes before he schooled that away too. He gave a nod. "Okay."

The track got sandier and sandier, and at the next part of the track with anything close to a turning area, I pulled us up to a slow stop. "Okay, this'll have to do us." Doing a quick three-point turn, I turned the Jeep around so we were facing the way we'd come.

"What are you doing?"

I pointed ahead to our escape route. "In case we need to leave in a hurry."

I didn't miss the way he swallowed, but with nothing else said, he got out of the Jeep and began arranging his gear.

"Take only what you can carry," I said, takin' his map and giving it a once over. He'd done a pretty good job of giving us an estimated location. These tracks off the main road weren't marked on any map, so I had to give credit where it was due. "You were pretty good with the map," I said, aiming for nonchalant. I wasn't goin' for friendly, but at least we were talking again. I turned the map over and scribbled out a quick note to leave in the Jeep, should someone come across it or if we didn't come back. At least the cops'd be able to tell the coroner our cause of death was stupidity.

Gone into mangroves on foot. Two men sat phone and water. One day at most.

I shoved it on the dash, then remembered to add the date at the bottom.

Realising Jeremiah hadn't replied, I looked over to see what he was doing . . . to find him emptying out my bag and adding his gear to it.

"What the hell do you think you're doing?"

He looked up, confused. "I'm taking as much as I can carry."

"That's my bag."

"Yes. I'm aware."

I got out and walked around to his side, grabbing his hand on my bag. "Don't touch my stuff."

His steely blue eyes met mine. "I was simply being efficient."

We were standing close, eye to eye. Well, he was a few inches taller than me, but still. My grip on his hand tightened. "You shoulda asked."

His nostrils flared and his jaw clenched. I would've found

that hot if he didn't piss me off so much. Hell, maybe he was hot *because* he pissed me off so much. He yanked his hand away. "Forget it. I'll carry it in the crate."

He leaned over to pull the crate closer, but I finished shoving his gear into my bag. "All you hadta do was ask," I said as I shoved in the spinning thing from the top of his auto-station. He'd dumped the first aid kit out of my bag so I picked it up. "And where the hell are ya goin' without this?"

"I was going to put it on top."

He absolutely was not.

I picked up the can of spray paint he'd ditched and glared at him.

Christ almighty.

He wiped the sweat from his brow and I noticed then just how much he was sweating. It was hot, and it was muggy as hell. I kept forgetting how he wasn't used to the tropics . . . "Here, drink some water," I said, handin' him a bottle. "Sip it. No gulping."

He gave me another glare for good measure, but he did drink some water.

When he was done packin' up his bags, he slung his back-pack on, then reached for my bag and slung the long strap over his head and one shoulder.

"What are you doing?" I asked.

"Taking as much as I can carry."

I took my bag off him, lifting the strap over his head. "I can carry this."

He looked at me as if he really wanted to say something, but he shut his mouth and looked away. "Fine. Whatever. Thanks, I guess. Sorry for being so stupid."

I put the bag over my head and one shoulder and let out a groan and handed him the tripod to carry. "Look, I'm sorry for the stupid comment. I shouldn't have said that. You're not stupid. You're the smartest person I know."

He looked away, petulantly, and I watched as a bead of

sweat ran down from his temple, along his jaw and down the column of his neck.

I shouldn't want to lick that . . .

I shook my head, getting back on track. "So, I'm sorry. I apologise. You're not stupid."

He pouted. "Fine. Thank you."

God, I wanted to strangle him. I also wanted to kiss him and do obscene things to his body, but mostly I wanted to strangle him. "But what you're *doing* is stupid. Just so we're clear."

He growled. Literally fucking growled at me.

My whole body reacted and I grunted, having to readjust myself. "Damn."

He squinted at me. "If we're discussing the measuring parameters of stupid."

"That was hot as fuck. Can you growl at me again?"

He rolled his eyes and stomped off, following the track.

"Jeremiah?" I called out.

He spun around. "What?"

Grinning, I pointed with my thumb into the scrub. "We gotta go this way."

I set off, not looking to see if he followed or not. The ground was wet sand and we had to climb over mangrove roots and branches. Our boots were sinking a little, nothing too bad yet, but it was definitely getting wetter the further we went.

I could hear Jeremiah behind me, his feet and the occasional grunt as he scaled a mangrove root. I was sweating now, so he had to be feelin' it. Taking the can of paint, I sprayed a pink stripe across a tree every ten metres or so.

"Is that your version of a Hansel and Gretel breadcrumb?"

"That's exactly what it is. So we can find our way outta here." I looked back. "Wanna stop for a bit?"

He glanced skyward. "No, not yet. Those clouds are coming in."

Awesome.

Can't wait.

"Don't look so thrilled," he said, brushing past me to take the lead.

"Okay, you go first," I said sarcastically. "Your turn to be on the lookout for all the things that can kill us."

"You're not funny."

I wasn't bein' funny, but okay. "Yep, I'm hilarious."

"These roots would make it impossible for crocs to navigate anyway," he said, like I was lying to him about it.

"Like this? Correct. But I'm tellin' ya, come high tide, we are back at the Jeep. Understood?"

He shot me a glance over his shoulder. I'm pretty sure he rolled his eyes.

We walked, climbed, and jumped over branches for a good while in silence. Our shoes were now sinking with each step, and all I could think about was our ability to get out of here once the water started coming in. Thankfully not too much further we came to a bit of a clearing in the mangroves.

I had my shirt off, dripping sweat. Jeremiah hung his backpack on a tree root, and liftin' his shirt up, he wiped his face with it. "Christ, how do people live here?" he griped.

"You get used to it. Drink more water."

He didn't need telling twice. He sipped his bottle and wiped his face again.

"Take your shirt off," I said.

"I think I'm better off with it on."

"I think the view is better with it off."

He glared.

I smiled.

"I'm immune to the smile now."

I let my head fall back. "Aww. It's my only party trick."

He ignored me, and extending the tripod legs, he sunk it into the sand. "Help me get this set up."

He went about setting all his contraptions up, checkin' to

see what readings he could get while I kept checking the water at our feet.

Dark storm clouds rumbled above us, expanding and rolling like living entities. Intra-cloud lightning sparked inside them and the wind picked up.

"Here, hold this," he said, handing me the display screen. He positioned the small radar at the top of the auto-station, and while it rotated, the screen beeped. "This is gonna be a good one," he said, excited.

For crying out loud.

"You know, I know this place is called Kakadu, but there's probably more Kaka-don'ts than there are Kaka-do's."

Jeremiah sighed, deflated, and he deadpanned a stare at me. "How long have you been waiting to use that joke?"

I laughed. "A while."

He rolled his eyes.

"But yeah, about the Kaka-don'ts," I continued, "I'd probably think standing in the middle of the mangroves with an electrical storm brewin' while holding a radar device up to the sky—*while standing in two inches of sandy water*—is high on that list."

"You knew the risks," he mumbled.

"What can I say," I said flatly. "I didn't want you to die alone."

"I don't plan on dying here today."

"Pretty sure no one plans to get struck by lightning."

His eyes cut to mine.

"Except for you," I added.

He went back to ignoring me, reading his machines, all while the winds picked up and the storm darkened.

"Why do I have a bad feeling about this?" I asked.

"Because you're a pessimist."

I gasped. "I am not."

Jeremiah raised one eyebrow. "You need to trust the science."

"I do trust science. But lightning is a great unknown. Unpredictable, dangerous. You can't harness it or control it. You can study it your whole damn life and still won't know all there is to know because you can't put it in a lab. You can try to recreate it, but it won't be the same."

He was staring at me. "So should I stop? Should I just never try because you think it's impossible?"

"No, I—"

"I could almost guarantee you that every scientist who did something great was told they were foolish for trying. Do you think the scientists who try to create cold fusion are wasting their time? They're so close to breakthroughs that could solve the world energy crisis, yet people dismiss it because they think it's impossible."

"No, that's not—"

His eyes met mine, cold and blue. "I don't know why I thought you were different." He snatched the RF antenna out of his bag, ignoring me.

I wasn't expectin' his bite to hurt so much. "Jeremiah," I murmured.

A clap of thunder cracked right above us, makin' me duck on instinct. Of course, Jeremiah didn't even flinch, with his back to me, his shirt blowing in the wind.

Jesus Christ.

I opened my mouth to tell him I was sorry just as the clouds opened up instead. Rain, fat drops, truckloads of them, heavy and drenching. It was falling so hard I could barely see Jeremiah just a few metres away.

"Well, that's fuckin' great," I yelled over the rain.

But then it got even greater.

Thunder and sheet lightning, the clouds so low and close it felt as if I could touch them. More intra-cloud lightning lit up around us like a strobe party and I had an eerie realisation.

We could *actually* die out here.

For real. No jokes, no snarky comebacks. For actual real.

"Jeremiah," I yelled again.

He turned to look at me then.

That fucker was grinning. "This is awesome!"

He trudged back to the screen like he was having the best experience of his life.

For fuck's sake. I was beginning to think he was legitimately insane.

He zipped up his backpack in the pouring rain, and taking the screen from me, he handed me the backpack. "Hold this!"

Thunder boomed again, so loud and so close that it shook us both. Cracking and rumbling, non-stop now, the clouds so dark that flashes of lightning were the only way I could see.

"This is crazy," I yelled.

Thunder ripped so loud it hurt my ears, and lightning struck about a hundred metres away. I must have jumped a metre in the air, my heart was hammerin' to the point of pain. That was far, far too close.

"Jeremiah!"

He held up two fingers. "Two more minutes!"

"Now!"

He shook his head.

I unzipped my bag and shoved the screen in it, then began pulling pieces off the station. We were done here. This was stupid and crazy, and he was in-fucking-sane if he thought we were staying in this. The anemometer was spinning so fast—the wind was in a frenzy, blowin' the rain in all directions, but I unhooked it anyway. We were leaving, whether he liked it or not.

The thunder was constant and the lightning all too frequent, and far too fuckin' close.

And if that wasn't bad enough, it was then I noticed his shoes. They were completely underwater. I looked at mine. The water was up to my ankles.

"Jeremiah, now!"

He turned then, his hair stuck to his forehead, water

pouring from his chin, and I don't know what he saw on my face but it made him pause. I pointed to his feet. "We have to go!"

He was clearly surprised to see his feet underwater. He nodded quickly, and we packed up, shoving everything into any bag. It didn't matter. He folded up the tripod and began for the return trip and stopped. "Which way?"

It was hard to tell now that everything looked different. Our footprints were all underwater and washed away, but there was a pink stripe on a tree to our left. "This way."

Going back was harder and slower. The rain was whipping us, and we were trudging through almost shin-deep water and waterlogged sand. We had to climb and hurdle branches, and I held my hand out for Jeremiah to hold as he swung his legs over one in particular.

Then something splashed in the water behind us.

I pulled Jeremiah in front of me. "Move," I yelled. "Go, go!"

Like the storm was keeping tempo with us, thunder rumbled and roared and lightning put on a light show around us. And we hightailed it as fast as we could. My heart was in my throat the whole freaking way. I had scratches up my legs and hands, but I didn't care.

High tide was comin' in way too fast with the storm.

We passed more trees with the paint spray, and the further we went, the more the water level dropped and the sand was firmer underfoot until Jeremiah stopped. He put his hand on a tree root, bent over, trying to catch his breath.

"What did you stop for? Keep going."

He pointed his chin further along where, through the mangroves, I could see the Jeep.

Oh, thank god.

I sighed, taking in gulping breaths of air.

The rain had eased up a bit, the storm clouds had mostly

passed over us, leaving behind the setting sun, humidity, and the sounds of birds and cicadas.

"We can stop when we're in the Jeep," I said, urging him to push on. "High tide's coming in faster than us."

With a nod, he collected himself, scaled the tree root, and walked the final distance to the embankment and up to the Jeep. He dumped his backpack, his hands on his hips, panting. "That was fun."

Fun. Did he just say . . .

"Fun?" I pointed to the way we'd come. "We almost died. Several times."

He smirked. "I got some good readings."

I threw my hands up. "Well, that makes dying all worth it then, doesn't it?"

He laughed, walked over to me, took hold of my face in his dirty hands, and kissed me. A big wet smacker on the lips. "Thank you."

He was giving me whiplash.

"What for?"

"For bringing me here. For doing this. For marking the trees. That was a really great idea."

"The crab people told me they do that," I mumbled. "They had cans of spray paint. I asked them what it was for."

He grinned and moved some hair from my forehead with his finger. So gently, sweetly. "And you put yourself between me and whatever that thing was that splashed in the water. I mean, it was probably just a fish or something, but still . . . It was sweet. Thank you."

"It probably wasn't a fish, just so you know. It was probably a croc or maybe a northern river shark, given the water wasn't very deep. But it's the smaller ones you gotta be careful of. The small crocs are the dangerous ones. They're fast and—"

He cupped my face and pulled me in for another kiss. It was deeper this time, open mouths and a little tongue, and a very effective way to shut me up, apparently. It also made all my anger melt away, and my desire to wring his neck was more desire to keep kissing him.

When he pulled back, he was smiling. "We should probably try and get cleaned up."

"Probably."

We were drenched, from our dripping hair to our sodden boots half-filled with sand, but by the time we managed to dry off and clean up a bit, it was getting on dusk and the water was right up to the embankment and I had the eerie feeling of being watched.

So, barefoot and with a decent spray of insect repellent, we got into the Jeep. We ate baked beans straight from the can, then put the front seats back as far as they'd go, which wasn't far, and looked out the windscreen as the clouds were replaced by a brilliant cover of stars.

"It's so easy to see why the First Nations people believe their gods come from the stars," Jeremiah said quietly. "It's so beautiful."

I turned to look at him, his face silver in the moonlight. Speaking of beautiful . . .

Then, ruining the serenity of that moment, he sat up in his seat. "I need to pee." He went to open the door and I grabbed his arm.

"No!" I barked. Then I turned on the headlights to show him why. A dozen sets of eyes glinted back at us, and five or so crocs slithered off the road as the light hit them.

He shrank back in his seat, bringing his arms in and legs up. He was now deathly pale.

"Still need to pee?"

He shook his head. "No."

I laughed and, reaching into the back, found him an empty water bottle. "If you get desperate, pee into that."

He shot me a wild look. "Ew."

Chuckling, I turned the headlights off and lay back down

in my seat. It was dark and quiet, but after a few minutes, I heard the rustle of clothes and then the sound of him pissing into the bottle. I laughed.

"I hate you," he mumbled.

I snorted. "No you don't."

When he was done, he tossed it out the window. "I'll pick it up tomorrow. Then we shall never talk about it again."

I smiled into the dark, and after a while, I reached for his arm and pulled his hand into mine. I threaded our fingers and closed my eyes.

"Jeremiah," I mumbled sleepily.

"Yes?"

"What's your favourite colour?"

CHAPTER TWELVE

JEREMIAH

I BARELY SLEPT, KNOWING THERE WERE CROCODILES OUTSIDE THE Jeep. I kept waiting to hear a thunk or scraping noises. Even though I knew, rationally, it wasn't likely that a crocodile would try to climb or attack a vehicle, it didn't stop my imagination from running wild.

Mangroves were noisy too. Birds and cicadas sang to us all night. And I totally did not lie there watching Tully as he slept, at how his eyelashes cast shadows on his cheeks, at the cupid's bow of his lips, at the three-day growth, the wisps of his wild and wavy hair. I longed to run my fingers through it, but of course I didn't.

He'd perhaps saved my life today.

In all likelihood, I'd have been caught by the rapidly rising tide—I hadn't realised just how fast it would come in. And the paint marks on the tree. I wouldn't have done that, and after being turned around and blinded by the storm, I'd have got lost for sure. Lost in a rapidly rising high tide in crocodile infested mangroves. And then, with the loud splash behind us in the water, he'd put himself in harm's way instead of me . . .

Not to mention the lightning.

The storm had been low and powerful. High energy, low barometric pressure, strong winds, and a lot of electrical activity, and I couldn't wait for sunrise to get back and run the data.

Even though it meant another day down meant one less day here. One less day with Tully.

I liked him.

He infuriated me, but he challenged me. I was mad that he'd not understood my reason for wanting to come to the mangroves, but I could see now that his concern was for our safety.

And he'd been right, of course.

But so had I.

I needed to prove to my colleagues in Melbourne that I was serious and not just the weirdo they all thought I was. I needed to bring back data they had neither the aptitude nor the balls to get.

And maybe I did that today.

I hoped so, anyway.

Daylight crept over the horizon, the skies a pastel palette of pinks and oranges. I was relieved to see the road was clear of crocodiles, and from my seat, it looked as if the water had receded, taking the crocodiles with it.

I still wasn't getting out of the Jeep until Tully gave me the all-clear. After all, it was never the crocs you could see that you should be worried about. It was always the ones you couldn't see . . .

I made a point of sitting up with a loud yawn and stretch, then righting my seat with a clunk, and it worked. Tully cracked one eye open, scrubbed his faced with his hands, then sat up. "Did we survive?"

"Yes. Thanks to you. Are all the crocodiles gone?"

He looked out the front windshield and down his side of the Jeep. "Looks like it. The water's low."

"Am I right to get out?"

He nodded, and when I'd opened my door an inch, he said, "Unless there's one under the Jeep."

I might have screamed and pulled the door shut, bringing my legs up onto my seat. I don't know why.

He laughed, and I shoved his arm. "That's not funny."

"Kinda was," he said, getting out of the Jeep without a care in the world. He stood up, stretched his hands above his head, and yawned.

I hated that he was so attractive the second he woke up.

And cheerful.

Jerk.

I got out with a huff, and seeing Tully peeing into the mangroves on his side of the Jeep, I did the same on my side. Then I remembered the bottle I'd thrown out the window during the night and went to find it . . .

"Oh my god," I said, trudging a few metres into the mangroves. The sand was dry, thankfully, and it was easy to walk on, given I was barefoot. The water bottle that I'd relieved myself in last night was now about five metres from the track, completely empty and crumpled flat with several large puncture marks.

I picked it up, horrified, and got my arse back to the Jeep as fast as I could. I held it up to show Tully. "Look at this."

His eyes widened as he realised what he was looking at. "Holy shit. Is that the bottle you pissed in?"

"It has to be," I said, looking around. There was no other litter anywhere, and it was the same brand. "Look at the teeth marks." I could stick my index finger through the holes.

Tully took the bottle, like it was the best thing he'd ever seen. "He drank your electrolytes . . ." Then he laughed. "Oh my god, it's Gatorade! Get it? Gator-ade. Except it's Croc-ade."

I sighed. "That's not funny."

He clearly thought it was hilarious. "I'm keeping this," he said.

"I urinated in it!"

He held it out and shook it. "There's no piss in it now. The croc drank it all."

I rolled my eyes, obviously not going to win here at all, and got in the Jeep. "Can we please go now?"

He took the roof off the Jeep so everything could dry out a little and we drove for a while, the track now noticeably different. The craters and holes were filled with water and it was slower going, and it wasn't until we got back on the larger track—I still wouldn't call it a road—that I could stop holding onto the grab bar long enough to rummage through our gear for some fruit.

I handed him an apple, which he took with a grin. "Thanks."

I ate half mine in just a few bites, not realising how hungry I was. "I'm really looking forward to a shower. I feel gross."

"You look just fine to me," he said, his hair tousled in the breeze, his carefree smile and kind eyes making my heart stutter. He ate the rest of his apple before tossing the core out of the Jeep. "What?" he asked at my questioning stare. "It'll feed the birds or plant a tree."

So I finished my apple and did the same, earning me a grin from Tully.

"You know," he said over the wind and the engine. "We should probably shower together. Conserve the water consumption."

"Given it's the wet season and it dumps a truckload of water every afternoon, I doubt the shower tank will run out of water."

He laughed. "Can't be too careful."

Back at the camp, we lifted the walls of the bunker to let some air in, then we unloaded the Jeep. Tully checked for any snakes or frogs, and I made us some coffee and set my gear up.

We made a good team.

Which was a first for me, because I rarely worked well with anyone else. Well, I liked it just fine. Usually it was the other person who didn't like working with me. I was too *pedantic* or a *control freak*. Which, as I'd told my boss when he'd requested a meeting with me to discuss this problem, was honestly them admitting their standards weren't high enough.

I wasn't looking forward to going back . . .

"What's up?" Tully asked. He sipped his coffee. "You just sighed twice in thirty seconds."

I made a third just for good measure. "Nothing. Just . . . I'm not looking forward to returning to my office in Melbourne."

He nodded to my gear on the table. "But you have all this new data."

"And it's good." I put my cup down. "Well, I'm hoping what we collected yesterday is great. I need . . ."

"You need to justify the expense of you coming here," he finished for me.

"Yes. But I also need to prove that I'm capable and that I do take the science of this very seriously. It's not just about me being fascinated by lightning because . . . because of what happened." I breathed in deep and let it out slowly. "I need to prove that I'm better than them. I *am* better than them. Just because I'm not in their little clique, and because I don't sit at the cool kid's table. I'm sick of that bullshit. I want to take this data back to them and say, 'hey, look at what you can actually do if you took your head out of your arse.'"

Tully laughed, his eyes wide in surprise. "I'd like to see that."

"I am serious about this. I want to further the field and understand what I can, in hopes of reducing the likelihood of strike fatalities. Of course, that's a priority. But there's more to it than that."

"It's personal to you," he said quietly. He reached over and took my hand. "They'll never understand that. They'll never understand you. So don't let them. And that cool club cliquey shit is high school all over again. Fuck that shit. And fuck them."

I snorted. "True." I studied his hand over mine, and when he went to pull it away, I quickly threaded our fingers. "Thank you."

He gave me a shy smile, then he took my hand and examined my knuckles, then my fingernails. He stood up and pulled me to my feet. "You need a shower. And I need to inspect you do a thorough job."

I would have objected, but he stripped me naked and pushed me into the shower, sliding himself up against me, using his talented hands to scrub me clean, and his mouth . . . my god, the way he used his mouth . . .

I returned the favour, eagerly going to my knees for him like he had for me.

And afterwards, he took a nap on the bed while I downloaded all the data from the day before. Though I kept looking over at Tully. He looked so peaceful, so comfortable, I wanted nothing more than to forget work for a moment and join him.

So I did.

I lay down beside him and he immediately rolled over and threw his arm and leg over me. I smiled into his chest. He pressed a soft kiss to my forehead. I closed my eyes, smiling, probably happier in that moment than I'd ever been.

And we slept.

"Shit," Tully said. "Wake up, wake up."

I sat up, dazed and confused. I'd been so sound asleep, it took me a second to even remember where I was.

Then I noticed the radar beeping and the wind outside.

Shit.

Storm, incoming.

"Help me get the side down," he said, running to the far end of the shed. "It's coming in from the east. It's gonna be a good one."

I raced to my end of the shed and we got the wall down, the wind fighting us the whole way. Once it was locked down, we lowered the other side halfway, then ducked under it to take a look at the sky.

Dark, foreboding, and as Tully said, coming in from the wrong direction. The trees were whipped around in a fury, and thunder began to roll.

He clapped my back. "Let's get your gear set up."

I followed him, both of us racing back inside. He took the auto-station, and without me asking him to, he raced it to the far end of the clearing to set it up. I gave him a thumbs up when I got the first readings, and he raced back, quickly checking the camera screens as soon as he came in, while I opened the radars.

"How does it look?" he asked.

"It's a wide front," I replied. "About ten kilometres from our location but heading straight toward us. It's moving pretty fast." I pointed to the band of clouds with multiple white dots. "High electrical activity and hail."

"Excellent."

"I know—"

It was only when I looked at his face that I could tell he was being sarcastic.

"Yeah okay," I mumbled.

He walked back toward the door. "Help me throw the tarp over the Jeep."

It was a heavy sheet of army green canvas, and it took both of us to secure it with the wind. By the time we got it done, the rain had started.

It was thin and needle-like in the wind, and I was glad when Tully pulled me inside and shut the door behind us. "Whoo," he said on a breath. "It's gonna be a good'n."

He went to check the radar and the readouts, excited as I was, and it thrilled me that he loved this part as much as me.

The build-up, the anticipation before the storm hit. The way the air grew thick and dense, ripening the atmosphere for lightning.

Thunder rolled and a crack boomed not far from us. Maybe five kilometres away, and my excitement grew even more.

"I can't believe we slept that long," Tully said.

Neither could I. We'd napped for hours. "I didn't wake once," I admitted. "As soon as you put your arm over me, it was lights out for me."

He tried to rein in his smile. "I didn't expect you to join me."

"I barely slept at all last night. Kept waiting for a crocodile to open the door or climb onto the Jeep and fall through the canopy top."

He laughed, just as a boom of thunder shook the shed and lightning lit up the darkened sky outside. The radar warning started to beep on my laptop, and we flew into action.

"Jesus, it looks wild out there," Tully said, his eyes glued to the camera screen. "I'm gonna put the other wall down to the ground."

I nodded. "Good idea."

The footage outside showed the trees being whipped in all directions, the cloud cover was low and heavy, swelling and rolling. Lightning sent its spidery fingers through the clouds, cracking and hissing, sending forks to the ground in the forest around us. Rain pummelled the bunker, the wind was roaring, rattling the shed, and I couldn't hear anything over the furore of it all.

I saw the automatic station get ripped from the ground, and a second later, the wind data cut.

Dammit.

Tully grabbed my arm and he had to yell so I could hear him. "Leave it. It's too dangerous. There are trees down out there."

I looked at the footage screen and saw a small branch shoot across the clearing.

I nodded, because even I knew that it was too dangerous to go out in.

And then the water canister flew across the clearing.

Jesus.

It was deafening, but somehow the bunker remained unscathed. Oh, it rattled and protested, but it held . . .

Then a familiar and dreadful taste filled my mouth. It was cloying and strong. It was going to be close.

Shit.

"Lightning!" I yelled.

Tully spun to face me, confused, just as thunder boomed so close, so loud, it almost knocked us off our feet. And with a flash of bright light outside, a massive crack ripped through the bunker. Deafening.

Frightening.

The power board exploded, sparks flying.

Tully lunged for me, grabbing me, pulling me close and wrapping his arms around me, ducking my head to his chest. My ears popped, and for one moment, all I could hear was his heart, his pulse. Or maybe it was mine. Our panting breaths, one arm around my back, the other holding my head.

He was protecting me.

After a few heart-thumping minutes, the sound of the rain and wind died off, whether the storm had lessened any or if it was just my hearing, I couldn't be sure.

But he held me until our chests stopped heaving. When he slowly pulled me back, I saw the look of fear on his face. He was a shade paler, his eyes wide. There was the pungent smell of smoke, but thankfully no fire. The power board was still smouldering.

"Did we just get struck by lightning?"

I swallowed thickly, the acrid copper taste lingering in my mouth. "The bunker, yes." The lightning rods on the roof worked.

When he let go of me, I noticed his hands were shaking. I quickly grabbed one hand and held it, squeezing. "Are you okay?"

He ran his other hand through his hair, looked around the room, bewildered. He went over to the power board and pulled it from the power socket. "Uh, yeah. I think so."

I needed a drink. My tongue felt putrid. I guzzled half a bottle. It didn't make it much better.

"You knew we were about to get hit," Tully said, stating the obvious.

I shot him a look. "Yes. I can still taste it."

He put his hand on my back. "Do you feel okay?"

"I'm fine. Physically. And you?"

He half shrugged, then grabbed my wrist and looked at my watch. "Heart rate's up."

"I bet yours is too."

I nodded toward my gear on the table—no lights were flashing anymore. "We've lost power."

"Video's still recording," he said, going over for a closer look. "The one that you run separately. Looks like the worst of the storm has passed us."

It was still raining, and the wind was still toying with the trees and there was debris, branches and leaves, strewn across the clearing, but it was nowhere near as strong.

"We should check your Jeep," I said, given it was our transport out.

"And your auto-station," he said. "It's probably wrapped around a tree." Then he pointed to the ceiling. "I'll need to check your booster. Maybe it got blown over."

"Or fried."

He grimaced, then let out a long sigh. "I can't believe we got hit by lightning. That shit is scary as fuck."

"Thank god whoever built this put lightning rods on the roof. Or you and I would both be dead, more than likely."

His eyes met mine, solemn and grim with the confirmation of just how close we came, and he nodded.

"Okay, help me get the walls up." He stopped before he touched the crank handle and pulled his arm back. "Uh, is this safe to touch?"

"Yes. Lightning rods have metal tracks to the ground that divert the power. Once it earths, it's fine."

He still wasn't too keen to put his hand on it, so I took the water bottle and threw a spray of water against it. Nothing sizzled or sparked. "Phew," he said, gingerly touching the handle with the back of his hand. "Okay, it's fine."

Once we got the walls up, the rain had eased to a gentle drizzle and the wind had died down too. We stepped outside and took stock of the damage.

The Jeep had a branch on it, but thankfully the windscreen and windows were intact. It was pretty much soaked, but otherwise unscathed. The water canister was at the tree line on the side of the clearing. Tully set off to collect it, and I headed to the far end to look for my automatic weather station.

It wasn't in the clearing, so I headed to the tree line at the top end. I picked up some smaller branches that were strewn and tossed them into the trees so they wouldn't become a missile in the next storm.

Then I trekked into the trees a little, and sure enough, noticed the tripod about twenty metres in. It was on its head, broken, and half wrapped around a tree. The screen was smashed, the anemometer arms and the sensors were broken.

Goddammit.

I inspected it, not hopeful it could be repaired. But the equipment box looked mostly undamaged. Hopefully I could salvage some data . . .

I headed back to the shed, only to find Tully climbing up onto the roof.

Because he hadn't almost died enough times in the last twenty-four hours.

"Please be careful," I yelled.

He waved and carefully trod across the ridgeline, where he stopped at what I could now see was the booster, which he'd MacGyvered for me on our first day. He picked it up—clearly it was no longer secured—and I could see why we'd lost our signal.

It was a lump of black melted goo.

"Ah," he said, tossing it onto the grass below. "Don't touch it. It's still kinda hot."

I went to inspect it and, yeah, it was almost unrecognisable.

Tully climbed down, dusting his hands off as he came to stand beside me. "RIP that thing," he said. "Was that what the lightning hit? Or did it just get fried for being so close to the rod?"

I used the broken tripod to turn the melted booster over on the grass. "Hard to tell. But just fried from being so close, I'd think. If it was a direct hit, it'd be blown to smithereens."

He took the tripod, and when he held it up, it bent in the middle. "Jeez, this is shot too."

I nodded, unable to hide my disappointment. "Yeah."

He looked at me, studying my face for a few seconds. "You know what I think? I think this gear is replaceable." He poked me in the chest. "You, are not."

I half shrugged. I knew what he said was true, but damn . . .

"I know," I whispered. "It's just . . . it's not replaceable. Not for me anyway."

I unfastened the data box and threw the broken tripod by the door, with all the other scrap material, and went inside. I closed my laptop—there was no point in staring at a black screen. And I watched Tully on the camera screen. He was standing right where I'd left him outside. He ran his hand through his hair and went toward the door. He disappeared off the screen as he walked inside.

I threw myself on the bed with a sigh and slung my arm over my eyes.

A few moments later, Tully knelt over me and peeled my arm away. "Hey," he said. "Talk to me."

I was being petulant. I knew I was. But still . . . I couldn't help the way I felt.

"My gear isn't replaceable because I have no money, and now that I have no gear, I can't do anything. I'm leaving in two days and now I have to go back without my instruments, without any data," I gestured to the table, "because it's probably all fried, and it just feels like a failure. The way they all expected me to fail. As if I'm proving those arseholes right. And all I wanted was to go back and prove to them I was worthy. Now I don't want to go back at all."

Well, that came out a lot easier than I expected. I surprised myself by how easy it was to tell him this. How easy it was to talk to him.

I tried to pull my arm free so I could cover my face, cover my shame, but he tightened his grip and pinned me to the bed. His eyes bored into mine. "Hey. You listen to me. You're not a failure. You lived through two electrical storms in two days. Closer to lightning than we had any right to be. I bet those pen-pushin' nerds you work with ain't ever been that close to any storm in their miserable lives. You got good data.

Data you can analyse for months. Data that will give you new information, new findings. And then those arseholes will know just how good you are." He straddled me, sitting his full weight on me, and he let go of my arms. "Now about your gear, don't worry about that. I can get you new stuff."

"You don't have to do—"

"Yeah, I do. Because I'm pretty sure the way I MacGyvered your booster thing is what blew it out." He shrugged. "So it's technically my fault."

"No you didn't. You used no metal. Just wood and zip ties."

He leaned down and kissed me. "Shh. It was my fault."

"Tully—"

He pinned my hands above my head this time. "I said shh," he said with a sultry smile. "All your equipment is off, it's raining outside. There is nothing for me to do . . . except you."

I would have objected—I fully intended to object—but he ground down on me, rubbing himself, and my hips rolled involuntarily. Smirking, he put his knees between my legs and drove my legs apart.

I gasped, and my watch started beeping like crazy . . .

He laughed and I rolled my eyes, but then he kissed me, deep and filthy, until nothing else existed. No money problems, no work problems, no almost-dying twice in twenty-four hours, no leaving this place, and not my stupid watch that only stopped beeping when Tully pulled it off my wrist.

Nothing but him and the obscenely good things he did to my body.

CHAPTER THIRTEEN
TULLY

Somethin' was different with Jeremiah after that last storm. I understood about his gear and not havin' the money to replace it. And I understood that he needed to prove to his jerk colleagues back in Melbourne that he was more than a guy just obsessed with lightning.

He was a scientist. He was intelligent, and he had guts. He was determined and driven.

All he wanted was to be taken seriously and to be credited with his work.

And maybe he was extra bummed about not being able to read any of his data because his booster was a melted pile of metal and plastic. Or maybe he lost the data. We wouldn't know until he could get a look at it. And that was deflating.

But it wasn't just that.

That last storm had shaken him.

"You sure you're okay?" I asked.

We were sitting cross-legged on the bed with bowls of rice in our laps. He'd barely touched his dinner. Even after the mind-blowin' afternoon we'd spent in bed, his mood hung heavy around him like the clouds outside.

"Yeah," he answered, more of a hum than a word.

"We have to leave tomorrow," I said, not for the first time. I pointed to the sound of rain on the roof. "This is the real beginning of the rainy season. They've predicted two days of heavy falls and that means all roads in and out will be underwater. Unless you wanna get choppered out, or if you wanna stay here for three or four months . . ."

His eyes cut to mine, and I realised I'd said the magic words.

He didn't just not want to go back to Melbourne and back to work. He didn't want to go back at all.

"I'd like to stay here," he said quietly. "I know it's not possible or feasible, at all. We'd be out of food in a few days, and I don't fancy eating crocodile."

"It's not so much the eatin' crocs that's questionable," I said, trying to lighten the mood. "It's the catchin' of the croc that's problematic."

He shrugged. "If we get enough rain, I could just go and stand out in the clearing as bait."

"That's not funny."

He smirked. "It kinda was."

I smiled and finished the last mouthful of my rice. At least he'd almost smiled; it was a start.

He sighed and stirred his rice a bit before pushing it away in disgust.

"Sick of my cooking already?"

I was aiming for funny, but he blinked, wide eyed. "Oh no, not at all. I'm just not that hungry. Sorry."

"It's okay. There's only so many days you can eat spicy rice."

"I actually really like this," he said. Then he frowned. "I wish I didn't have to leave. I wish I could stay here. Just us two." Then he cringed. "Or just me, if that sounded a bit presumptuous. I just . . ." He sighed. "It's just being here with you, with no responsibility, no outside world. Just chasing the storms, doing what we want when we want, and . . ."

"And having great sex," I finished for him.

He blushed, his smile shy. "It's been the best time of my life," he admitted, his blue eyes deep as the ocean. "That probably sounds lame to you, but this?" He gestured to the bunker, then to me. "This doesn't happen to guys like me."

"What do you mean guys like you?"

"Nerd. Loner. Weirdo. Freak. I believe there's a list."

"You mean smart and sexy, with cojones the size of basketballs."

He gawped, then felt his crotch. "What?"

"Not literally." I chuckled. "Metaphorically speaking. You have balls of steel. Fearless."

His smiled twisted and he frowned. "I was scared today. And yesterday," he whispered. "For you. I was scared for you. That I'd put you in danger, and I'm sorry I did that."

"You didn't make me do anything."

"Actually, I kinda did. I said I would just take your Jeep and go to the mangroves without you if you didn't want to come."

I chuckled. "I already added stubborn to the smart and sexy list."

He chewed on the inside of his lip for a few moments. "Thank you for bringing me out here," he said, meeting my gaze once more. "I know I cut into your time off, and having to babysit me mustn't have been your idea of fun."

"Are you kidding? I've had the best time! You're forgettin' that this is what I do. I'd be here regardless, if you were with me or not. Storm chaser, remember? And the company's been great. I've really enjoyed having you here. Plus, the sex has been amazing."

He blushed again and played with his fingers. "I just want you to know I'm grateful, that's all."

"You're welcome. Maybe next time you come out here, one of us will remember condoms so we settle that 'who's a top' argument once and for all."

He laughed then. "I'll try to remember."

"I won't forget, believe me."

He scooted off the bed, collected the bowls, and took them to the sink. "Thank you again for dinner."

I watched him as he began to wash up, then I walked over and leaned against the counter. "So, about tomorrow."

"What about it?"

"We should pack up tonight, so in the morning we'll have breakfast, load up the Jeep and we can go."

He nodded solemnly. "Sounds good."

I took the tea towel and began to dry. "So, where are you staying in Darwin?"

He glanced at me, confused. "I'm not."

"Oh, it's just that given we're leaving here two days early," I said. "I wondered if you had somewhere to stay. When's your flight?"

He baulked. "Oh. I hadn't thought of that." He shook his head, mad at himself. "I'll see if the airline can amend my booking. I'm sure I have a flexible ticket." He grimaced. "I hope it is, at least."

"You can stay with me," I offered, aiming for casual, feeling anything but. "I'm still off work so I'm not expected to be anywhere. I can play tour guide in Darwin instead of here, if you want. My place is big enough. I have a spare room if you're sick of sharing with me, and—" I waggled my eyebrows at him. "I have a decent supply of condoms and lube."

His whole face went red, not even the tops of his ears were safe. He stared at the bubbles in the sink. "Oh, uh . . ."

He was considering it, I could tell. He didn't want to say no, he just wasn't sure if he should say yes. I had to strike while the iron was hot.

"And we should take your gear to the bureau office in Darwin."

That made him look at me. "What for?"

"To check the data box and run your laptop, see if it survived the power surge. They'll have the equipment to download your information. So you know what you've got before you get back to Melbourne." I had no idea if that was what meteorologists in the field did, but it sounded good to me. "I dunno," I added. "Is that what smart and sexy science guys do?"

He fought a smile. "Are you asking me to stay with you until my scheduled flight?"

He was absolutely staying.

"Damn right I am. More storms, more science-y stuff, and more sex. What's not to like?"

He grinned then. "Okay."

Packin' up the Jeep and locking up the bunker felt really final. Like we were leavin' something behind. Not any physical thing, but maybe a part of myself.

I'd never brought anyone special to the bunker before, and now I wasn't sure I ever wanted to come back alone.

Now that I knew how good it could be to share it with someone.

I emptied the last of the jerry can of petrol into the Jeep and jumped in behind the driver's seat. The rain was still coming down steadily and I had to shake my hair like a dog, just for good measure.

Jeremiah gave me a shove. "Ugh."

He wiped his face melodramatically as I started the engine. "You ready?"

"Not really. How bad will these roads be?"

"Drivable," I answered. "But if we leave it any longer, we'd need a hovercraft."

He sighed. "You said every road we've been on was

drivable. I can assure you, we have differing opinions on what is drivable."

"It won't be so bad," I said, trying to help him relax. "We just gotta outrun the rain."

I grinned and began the slow drive out. The road out was wet and slippery, and I didn't want to risk putting us in a ditch. The rain was constant and heavy, dangerous even. We probably should have left yesterday after the storm.

"I guess I should be grateful you put the roof on," he said, one hand on the oh-shit bar as we bounced down into one particularly rough part.

"You hate it now," I said. "But you'll miss this."

He shot me a glare that was half 'I absolutely will not' and half 'shut up I know I will.'

At the fork in the track, this time we turned right. We'd gone left to the mangroves and we could see now that all that area to the west was now *very* swampy.

"Oh god. Is that where we were?"

I nodded. "Ten kilometres further into that."

"Jesus," he whispered. "I'd have died out here for sure."

I laughed. "That's why you have me. So maybe next time when I say, 'hey, it's not a good idea to go into the mangroves at this time of year,' you might listen. Because when it comes to being out here, I'm the expert."

I just then happened to hit a very large, very deep, very wet pothole, and we bounced so hard we both almost hit our heads on the roof.

He held on with two hands and shot me a harrowed look. "You were saying?"

It still rained, but the further southeast we went, the better the track became until we turned onto an actual road. And the sadder it made me. I didn't want my time with him to be over, and every mile we drove, it felt like we were leaving our time together behind us.

Sure, he'd agreed to another two days in Darwin. But being out here at the bunker with him had been special, and it was only when we were leaving that I truly realised that.

When we'd reached a tarred road, the rain had eased, and Jeremiah asked me to pull the Jeep over. "Why?"

"I want to roll the top back," he said with a grin. "If I have two more days of freedom, I want to feel it."

So we rolled the roof back, and as we drove back toward civilisation, through the ancient green forests of Kakadu, the wind tousled our hair and Jeremiah put his hands up into the wind and laughed.

Yeah. I was going to miss him so fucking much.

CHAPTER FOURTEEN
JEREMIAH

We refuelled in Jabiru, and I met Tully at the counter of the service station. "You two made it out before the rains," the man behind the counter said. "Was wondering how you were gettin' on out there."

"Sad to cut it short this trip," Tully said.

I was quick to add a bottle of Coke and some snacks to Tully's fuel total and he grinned at me. "Anything else?"

I shook my head. "Unless you want something."

He looked at the lollies and Pringles. "I'm having half of that."

I rolled my eyes, took my stash, and the man serving us laughed. "See you boys again soon."

Yes, well, as much I wished otherwise, that wasn't likely. I nodded all the same and went back to the Jeep. I understood now why all the cool kids would drive with the tops down on their cars. The feel of the wind in my hair felt like freedom. Sitting next to Tully, having him laugh and wear that damn grin, aiming it right at me . . . it was the closest to real happiness I'd ever felt in my life. Carefree, all while being the real me.

I'd never shared the real me with anyone before. Just him. And that time was slowly ticking down to an end.

As we got closer to Darwin, as the traffic filled in around us, as the greenery became farms and then houses, I couldn't help feeling a little sad.

"Have you been to Darwin before?" Tully asked.

"Just the airport, for one hour, then I flew into Jabiru and met you."

"I'll show you around," he said, leaning over and taking my hand. He brought it to his thigh, leaving it there, smiling at my surprise. He kept his hand on mine, unless he had to change gears, but he was quick to grab it again, squeezing, slipping his fingers through mine.

It both thrilled me and made my heart ache.

Why couldn't I find this in my real life?

Why did something so perfect have to end?

I tried to push those intrusive thoughts away, until we were in the centre of Darwin and I realised, stupidly late, that the streets we drove down were very nice. Huge houses, new and perfectly neat and tidy, expensive cars and palm trees, and . . .

And he slowed down at a driveway, the automatic gate to the property sliding open. He drove in, the garage door opened, and he parked next to a very expensive Range Rover.

He opened his door, got out, and stretched his arms up high with a loud yawn. "Are you getting out?"

I wasn't sure if I should.

"Is this . . . do you live here?"

He looked around, confused. "Ah yeah? This is my house. Well, mine and the bank's."

It had white rendered walls, and even the garage was spotlessly clean. And the car . . . "Uh, is this yours too?" I pointed my chin at the Range Rover.

"Yep. The company leases them. I get a new one every two years."

Must be nice.

"Cool."

He shrugged, like it was no big deal. "Let's unpack the Jeep first. Get all the shit out and dump our bags straight into the laundry." He opened the tailgate and pulled out my crate of equipment, gently placing it by the door that I assumed went into the house. He carried the box of left-over food. I grabbed both our bags and followed him inside.

We entered in through what I quickly realised was a laundry room. Except it was almost the size of my entire apartment. The floor was dark, the cabinetry all gloss white, a full counter top and cupboards.

"Just throw 'em in here," he said, indicating to our bags. "We'll need to wash everything."

I propped them by the washing machine and followed him into the rest of the house. It was massive, open plan, double storey. The walls were white, the floor a dark grey marble, the furniture was straight from a designer, and the kitchen was ridiculously luxurious. There was white glossy cabinetry and a dark grey stone benchtop that opened out to the lounge room with a sofa setting that looked as comfortable as it looked expensive. But none of that was even the best part. Because there were glass doors that led out to a balcony and, sure enough, it looked straight out over the ocean.

Was he kidding me right now?

He slid the box onto the countertop and opened one cupboard door—which I realised was a built-in fridge. Jeez.

He unloaded the canned goods into his butler's pantry and put the box on the floor. "Come on, I'll give you a tour."

"There's more?"

He laughed and led the way upstairs. "Spare room," he said, pointing at one door. "Another spare room. Bathroom through there. And this," he said, opening a door at the end of the hall, "is my room."

It was huge, and it had its own balcony. Everything was

huge. The room, the bed, the walk-in wardrobe, the ensuite, and for a second I had a hard time marrying this house to the guy I'd just spent days with roughing it in the tropical jungle, staying in a tin shed, and driving an old beaten-up Jeep. I wasn't sure how they could be the same person . . .

But then I noticed the framed photographs on the wall. I mean, they too looked like they belonged in a museum, black frames all artfully displayed. But they were black and white photos of storms.

Rain clouds and lightning.

He stood beside me. "I took those photos," he said quietly, and we both studied each image.

I got closer to one, pointing to it. "That's the bunker."

"Sure is." He slung his arm over my shoulder, effectively tucking me under his arm, and pointed up to another photo. "And that one. And this one. Can't see the shed at all, but that's the clearing looking east. It's a few years old so the trees look a bit different."

"I love these pictures," I whispered. "I was beginning to think this wasn't your house."

He pulled back so he could look into my eyes. "What do you mean?"

I shrugged. "This is all very extravagant and luxurious, and the you I know just spent a week running around in the jungle without a shirt or shoes in a banged-up Jeep."

He smiled and took my hand, bringing my palm to his cheek, and he closed his eyes. "That's who I am," he murmured. His brown eyes met mine. "Out there, where I have no expectations or obligations. Here?" he said, looking around the room. "You think this is all glamour, but it's not really. I mean, it is. I know I'm privileged to have this. I know that. So yeah, this is also me, but this me is where real life takes the shine off who I am." He dropped my hand and frowned. "Don't get me wrong. I'm not cryin' poor little rich boy, but who I was with you this last week was the me no one else gets to see."

Oh wow. Okay, I wasn't expecting such heartfelt honesty. And I wasn't expecting him to echo my thoughts so completely.

I put my hand to his chest. "Who I was this last week with you was the real me too. The me that no one else understands. Or likes."

The corner of his mouth pulled up in a half-smile, and he put his finger to my chin, bringing me in for a soft kiss. "I like you."

CHAPTER FIFTEEN
TULY

I gave Jeremiah some shorts and a shirt from my wardrobe and handed him a clean towel. "Come downstairs when you're done."

"Oh, I need my shaving kit."

I rubbed my thumb along his scruffy jaw and hummed. "Or you could leave it."

I wanted nothin' more than to get into the shower with him, and I almost did, but getting cleaned up after a week of camping was a solitary thing. Sure, the shower at the bunker was adequate, but here he had proper hot water, shower gel, and a flushing toilet.

I left him to it and went downstairs. I upended my bag of dirty clothes into the washing machine and put in a quick grocery order for some essentials, and I'd just finished ordering some pizza when Jeremiah came down the stairs.

"Hm," I said appreciatively. "I like you in my clothes. Did you notice that I didn't give you any underwear?"

He rolled his eyes but he did smile. "That was the best shower I've ever had."

"Which is why I didn't join you," I said. His mouth fell open and I shrugged. "I thought about it. I almost did. I *really* wanted to. But that first shower when you get back . . ." I held his chin. "And you left the scruff."

"Yes, well, I didn't have a razor."

My eyes fell to his lips, his very kissable lips, and god, he smelled so good. I groaned and took a step back. "I want to do unholy things to you right now, but I need to get myself cleaned up first." I headed for the stairs. "The AC's on. I've ordered pizza. Help yourself to anything in the fridge."

I took the stairs two at a time to put some distance between us. I wanted to drag him to bed, but god, considering how good and clean he smelled, I must have stunk like a sweaty horse. Takin' him to bed like this would be gross and insulting. I intended to have the quickest shower of my life until I felt the hot water on my skin. I scrubbed my hair, lathered up soap over every inch of my body, then did it all again.

I felt decidedly more human when I went downstairs, and excited. We'd talked about having sex when we got here, now that we had condoms and lube, and I was keen to know if that was still on the table. I found the glass doors open and Jeremiah was taking in the view.

"You like it?" I asked.

He turned when I spoke and smiled. "I've never seen the Timor Sea before."

"Technically this is Beagle Gulf, and the Timor Sea is a bit further out," I said.

"Can we go for a swim at the beach?" He asked. "Because it's hot as hell."

I made a face. He'd said before he liked to swim. "Uh, well, you can," I said. "But it's not exactly recommended. We get the occasional crocodile, and the Irukandji jellyfish—"

He put his hand up. "I'm sorry I asked."

"But it is about twenty degrees cooler inside if you'd prefer to look at the pretty, unswimmable water from the other side of the glass door. You know, where there is air conditioning."

He smiled, squinting one eye at the sun. "You can't really get the whole Top End 'baked and steamed at the same time' experience from inside though."

"Baked *and* steamed, huh?"

"I feel like a dumpling."

I laughed and went to the door, waiting for him to walk in first. "They call it the silly season here," I explained. "This weather, the oven and sauna effect, it makes people do silly things."

"Like choose to live here?"

I went to the fridge, took out two beers, and handed him one. "You get used to it."

He looked at the beer, then looked at me. "I generally don't drink a great deal, so unless you're getting me drunk to take advantage of me."

I grinned at him. "I was hoping you'd bring that up because—"

The intercom buzzed.

"Goddammit," I said, putting my beer down. "That'll be the pizza."

I took the delivery and put the pizzas on the coffee table. "Let's eat here," I said, collecting my beer and waiting for him to join me on the couch.

"This is the biggest couch I've ever seen." He sat down. "And the softest."

It was big. I bought it because it was deep and pillowy. "So easy to fall asleep on this thing. I'll be watching TV and then the next thing I know, it's 3:00 am."

He chuckled but made a face. "Is it okay to eat on here?"

"Hell yeah. Why wouldn't it be?"

"Because it's . . ."

"It's my house. I eat all my meals here, or standin' at the kitchen counter. I spilled nachos on this couch *the day* I got it." I opened the pizza box and handed him the first slice. "I'm not the pretentious fancy type."

He smiled, but it soon became a grimace. "Sorry. I don't mean to judge. I've just never been in a house this nice before. I wasn't sure what I should touch."

"Touch anything you want. Including me." I took a bite of my pizza. Then, like the uncouth monster I was, I spoke with my mouth full. "Hope you like supreme."

He laughed and, like a gentleman, chewed and swallowed before he spoke. "It's great, thanks."

I waited until I'd swallowed before I spoke again. "I get it, though. Honestly, my eldest brother and sister are the pretentious type. They're the real serious ones, serious about the business. It's all about the money to them. They name-drop and do the snobby pouty faces when something's beneath them. Which is weird because my parents aren't like that. They earned their money, and they were normal before they got rich. My brother and sister grew up rich and feel entitled, or something, I dunno." Then I felt bad for saying that. "Well, that's not true, really. They work hard and they shoulder a lot of the responsibility. But they look down at me because I chase storms for fun when their idea of time off is to read *Business Insider*. Know what I mean? We're just very different. So yeah, people who live like this can be pretentious and think they're better than others. Rowan and Zoe are proof of that."

Jeremiah made a face. "I'm sorry. I didn't mean to assume. This is just . . . it's not a world I'm familiar with." He sipped his beer. "When I say I grew up poor, I mean it. Some days we ate, some days we didn't. My dad worked very hard."

Oh man.

"I'm sorry," I said. "And more often than not, the degree to which someone works is not indicative of their pay grade. Half the CEOs of the world couldn't do what their employees do. They wouldn't last half a day doin' manual labour, and it's those workers who make the world turn." I took another bite of pizza. "That's why you find me with the cooks and ground staff at our docks. I'm more comfortable with them than I am at those fancy dinners my brother and sister go to. But if the bosses need to know what's really going on or what needs to be done, or what's not being done properly, or what issues the workers are havin' at the ground level, they come to me." I shook my head, unsure why I was telling him this. "Sorry. I just don't want you to think I'm like them."

His eyes met mine, kind and warm. "I don't. And I like that you understand." We ate some more pizza, and he took another mouthful of beer, almost drainin' his bottle. "Now, this may be the beer talking, because I haven't drunk alcohol in over a year, but about that offer to touch anything I want."

I grinned at him, downed the rest of my beer, took his hand, and led him upstairs.

And we'd hinted and joked about which of us would top, but there was never any doubt. He pulled my shirt off and tossed it, his eyes dark, and he licked his lips. "Get on the bed."

That look, those words, almost set my blood on fire.

I quickly complied, scooting into the middle, my head on the pillows. I pointed to the bedside table. "Top drawer."

He found the condoms and lube, throwing them onto the bed beside me, then pulled off his shirt and knelt on the mattress, crawlin' over to me. He planted himself between my legs and slid his hands up my thighs, over my hips to the waistband of my shorts. He smirked as he pulled them down, like this was the victory he'd wanted.

He leaned forward so he could kiss me, soft, open lips, and the hint of tongue. "I want to kiss you," he murmured. Those blue eyes were like fucking fire. "Then I'm going to suck your cock and eat your arse before I fuck you."

My body felt hot all over, my brain short circuited. I think I groaned. "Fuck."

Who was this guy?

"When I said you gave me top vibes, I didn't expect this."

He sucked my bottom lip in between his. "Want me to take it easy on you?"

I grinned at him, trying to get his shorts off. "Hell no."

He took my wrists in his hands and pinned them beside my head. "Can I ask you something?"

I was almost panting with need. "Yes."

"Have you ever had a prostate orgasm?"

Jesus fucking Christ.

It took me a second to think, to breathe. "No," I whispered.

He grinned. "You will tonight."

I don't know why I was so stunned. Thinkin' back to what we'd done in the bunker, and the way he'd pulled my hair, how he'd held my face when he slid his cock into my throat, I should have known.

This quiet science nerd had a freaky side.

Hell fucking yes.

He kissed me then, tanglin' his tongue with mine until I forgot my own name. He moulded me with his mouth, with his hands, the perfect combination of gentle and rough, and his body against mine until I was pliable and desperate.

Then he flipped me over, massaged my back, kissed up my spine, and bit my shoulder; an ebb and flow of pleasure and pain. He rid me of my shorts and splayed me open, delving his tongue inside me.

I gripped my bed covers and lifted my hips for him, and he worked me harder. First with his tongue, then with his fingers and lube, fingering me and stretching. Feeling . . .

Until he found his prize.

"Holy shit," I gasped, coming up on all fours.

"Hm," he purred. "There it is."

With his fingers still inside me, he pushed my head back down with his other hand so my arse was in the air. And he pressed against my prostate again and again, sparking a pleasure inside me like nothin' I'd ever felt before.

"God, right there, don't stop," I mumbled. It was so intense I could have cried. I was prepared to beg for this to never end. Then he wrapped his hand around my cock and began to stroke, and it was too much pleasure. It was sensory overload and obliterated every synapse in my body, and I needed him to make it end but also to please, never stop. "Fuck, Jeremiah," I cried, almost a sob. "Please."

Please, what? I wasn't sure.

Finish me, make me come, please please, never stop, I need this forever, I can't take anymore, god please . . .

Pleasure was overwhelming, so consuming, it bordered on pain, until the build-up was too much. An orgasm so powerful it felt like I exploded and imploded at the same time. I screamed into my mattress, my voice hoarse, my hands were claws in the bedding.

I was shaking and groaning, the ultimate fucking high . . . until I collapsed in a heap.

I'd been obliterated.

It took a few minutes for my senses to come back to me. I was still shaking, my body trembling, muscles convulsing.

Jeremiah pulled the cover over me and kissed the side of my head. "Are you okay?"

I wanted to say no and yes, but it came out as a laugh.

"The fuck did you do to me?" I managed to say. My voice sounded weird. "Imma need you to do it again."

He chuckled and I focused on him then. He looked so happy, so sexy, my god, so sexy . . . but he still had shorts on —and I could see his erection confined in them. "You didn't . . ."

His smile became a grin. "I haven't finished with you yet."

I shivered and another tremor racked through me. My words came out in a groan. "Oh god."

He laughed as he rolled off the bed. He went into the bathroom and used mouthwash, came back out with a cloth to clean me up, and he did let me recover. Somewhat.

For about an hour, he massaged me, skimmin' my body with his hands as if he was mappin' me out. He peppered soft kisses all over me, rubbing me down, and I was so relaxed by the time he rolled a condom on, all I could do was smile into my pillow.

Face down, arse up, he knelt behind me, added more lube, and slowly pressed into me. "Oh fuck," I groaned into my pillow.

He was slow and thorough, pushing in to the hilt, then pressing his weight onto my back. He kissed my spine, my nape, his breaths short and sharp, shaking with his restraint.

So I moved my hips, pushing back on his cock, and he took it as permission to move.

He pulled back and pushed back in, slow and deep. He slid his hands over mine, threading our fingers, his breaths and grunts hot on the back of my neck and in my ear. "You feel so good," he moaned.

I pressed my forehead into the pillow, trying to stretch my back, my hips pinned to the bed. Then he pulled out of me and flipped me over, bringing my legs over his thighs, he bent me in half and sunk back into me as he sunk his tongue into my mouth.

Oh dear god.

He whined, a low guttural sound, and his grip on my hips tightened. He thrust harder and deeper until he gasped and cried out as he came.

I held his face and watched as those blue eyes melted, liquid sapphires lost to his own pleasure.

It was fucking beautiful.

My god, this man . . .

How was I ever going to let him leave the day after tomorrow?

I traced patterns on his back until he could lift his own head. He plonked his cheek onto his palm with a goofy, sleepy smile, and he looked kinda drunk. It made me laugh.

"Yeah, so," I said. "About you leavin' in two days. How are you going to do the prostate thing once a week when you're in Melbourne and I'm here?"

He raised one eyebrow. "Just once a week?"

"Pretty sure that's all I could handle."

He smiled, kissed me one more time, then rolled out of bed. We played clean up and got redressed and went in search of our now-cold pizza.

Jeremiah stopped at the glass doors. "Oh wow," he said, looking out at the horizon.

I chuckled. It was a brilliant array of orange, reds, yellows, all reflecting off pillows of dark clouds. "Ah, the famous Darwin sunset. Pretty, huh?"

"There's a warm updraft rolling in. There'll be lightning for sure."

I took the pizza and opened the sliding door. "Then let's go watch the show."

It was hot outside, even as the sun was setting, but the sheen of sweat on Jeremiah's skin made it worthwhile. The colours of the sunset and the threatening storm made him look even more beautiful.

"Want another beer?" I asked.

"Uh, sure," he replied, just as his phone beeped. He'd had a few messages, which he'd groaned at and ignored, but this time he sighed. "It's my boss. Telling me to ignore the earlier messages because they've just realised that I'm not in the office. After a week, mind you." His eyes met mine. "Can we go back to the middle of nowhere where there's no phone service? Or should I just lob this into the ocean?" He held his phone as if about to throw it.

I grabbed his hand and put it around my waist, leaning against him and giving him a soft kiss. "So don't go back."

He rolled his eyes. "While that sounds all good and well, I believe reality beckons."

I lifted his chin, brushing my nose against his. "What

awaits you in Melbourne?" I kissed his lips, down his jaw. "A job you hate."

"A job I love, work colleagues I hate." His breath caught when I bit his earlobe. "My father."

That made me pause. I sighed and pulled away. "Yeah, sorry. I forgot. I just . . . I just don't want our time together to end just yet."

He studied my eyes, searching for something. "I'm trying to decide if you're pranking me. My dating history would tell me yes, but then you seem so sincere. I'd like to think you're different . . ."

I sighed, reining in my temper because his knee-jerk reaction to being ridiculed wasn't about me.

"Jeremiah," I murmured. "I am sincere. And clearly I am different to the arseholes you've dated before. I'm sorry they made you doubt me."

"It's not you," he said apologetically.

"I know."

"But . . ." He ran his hand through his hair, then used it to wave me up and down. "But you're perfect. Gorgeous, rich, successful. And I'm . . ."

"You're what?"

"Me."

"You," I said, pointing my finger and lightly jabbing him in the chest with every point I made. "You who earned a doctorate probably a decade sooner than any of the pricks you work with. You, who shows absolutely zero fear. You, with the bluest blue eyes that give me butterflies. And you, who earlier ate my arse and gave me the best orgasm of my life. That same you?"

He almost smiled, clearly not very adept at taking compliments. "The best orgasm, huh?"

"Uncontested." I ran my hand over his heart, up to his jaw, and made him look at me. "What you did to me earlier? It's no wonder I want you to stay. Honestly, if you do go back to Melbourne, I might have to come visit a few times a year just so you can do it again."

He chuckled, his eyes warm. Then licked his lips, wincing, and turned to the ocean. "Lightning."

And sure enough, the clouds over the bay lit up. A deafening crack of thunder ripped through the sky, and while most normal people would have run for cover, Jeremiah turned to face it. Several bolts of lightning hit the water, less than a kilometre away. Furious and frightening, the storm broke and rain poured.

Jeremiah smiled.

CHAPTER SIXTEEN

JEREMIAH

"Hɪ, Dᴀᴅ. Iᴛ's ᴍᴇ," I sᴀɪᴅ, ᴍʏ ᴘʜᴏɴᴇ ᴛᴏ ᴍʏ ᴇᴀʀ. I ᴡᴀs standing at the glass doors overlooking the ocean, only from inside where it was air conditioned, because this Darwin heat was no joke. Even at 8:00 am. I'd left Tully in the shower upstairs, and I could hear him singing from where I was. Maybe the hand job after breakfast made him too happy . . .

"I was wondering when I'd hear from you. How's your trip?"

"Yeah, it's great. Back in Darwin now. Had no phone service all week, sorry."

"You get what you were after?"

I thought about my gear, how the recording unit was probably fried, how this whole trip was probably for naught, and I considered launching into an explanation my father wouldn't care about . . . but then Tully began a very loud rendition of 'Sex on Fire' and I smiled. "Yeah. I think so, Dad. I'm heading into the Darwin office this morning."

"Okay. You back tomorrow, right?"

I withheld a sigh, because going back to my shitty life in Melbourne was the last thing I wanted to do. "Yeah. I'll call you when I get in."

"Right then. I better get back to work. You're in a different time zone to me, ya know."

"Yeah, Dad. I know."

The line went quiet in my ear, just as Tully came skipping down the stairs. He was grinning until he saw me. "Oh, what's up?"

"Nothing. Just spoke to my dad."

"Everything okay?"

Not really. "Yep. Same as always."

Tully watched me for a second and thankfully dropped it. "You ready to go?"

"Yep. My equipment crate is in the garage. I'm ready to see if it's all completely fried and all my work is gone."

He slung his arm over my shoulder and led me toward the garage. "It'll be fine, just you wait and see."

I envied his optimism.

In the garage, I lifted the crate and carried it to the back of the Jeep, but Tully opened the back of the Range Rover instead. "Today we go in style."

I frowned. "Uh, the Jeep is more my style."

He laughed and helped me slide the crate into his new car and I already had to wipe my brow. "I have two words for you," he said. "Air. Conditioning." Then he walked to the passenger door and opened it for me. "Your chariot, sire."

I rolled my eyes but got in, and yes, the newer car was amazing and very fancy, and I'd have been perfectly happy in the Jeep, but yes, the air conditioning was very much appreciated.

He drove me along the shoreline, pointing out things of interest. "This whole marina is new," he said. "There's cafés and restaurants. We can have dinner there tonight if you want. All the trees have lights and it's really pretty."

I nodded, trying not to think that it'd be our last night together. "Sounds good."

He pointed out more landmarks as he drove us out of the

city centre, through some back streets, until we eventually got to our destination. The Darwin meteorology station was a small blond brick building sitting in the middle of a large dirt block, fenced off and not inviting at all. Built in the 1970s, by the looks of it, and not updated since.

But the gate was open and a motorbike with a sidecar was parked under the shelter at the side of the building.

I'd had very limited dealings with this Darwin office—this was the station, not the admin office—and I really had no idea of who or what to expect.

"Have you met Doreen before?" Tully asked.

"Uh, no. Have you?"

"I had to pick up some gear a time or two and take it out to the Jabiru Airport. Someone told her I was headed out there." He grinned at me. "She's a bit different."

"I have no issue with different." Before I could ask if the motorbike was hers, a figure came through the front door with a baseball bat. Big and tall, shaved head, black jeans and a black singlet top with 'Vagitarian: I eat pussy' written in pink across the front. She was late sixties, maybe seventies. Big boobs, menacing snarl.

"You got no business here," she said, pointing the baseball bat at us.

"Oh my god," I hissed, clutching at my seatbelt. "Tully, turn the car around!"

Tully laughed and got out. "Calm down, woman. Jesus Christ," he said with his disarming grin. "Love your shirt."

Oh my god! He did not just call her *woman*!

We were both about to die . . .

She lowered the bat and relented a smile. "Tully. Whatcha hidin' that good-looking head of yours in those tinted windows for? Dumbass, I almost took m'bat to your fancy car."

Tully gave me a nod, silently telling me to get my arse out of the car. "Brought someone to see ya."

He shut his door and walked over to her, turned, and waited for me to get out, which I did. Still unsure if we were about to die . . .

"Doreen, this is Doctor Jeremiah Overton. From the Melbourne office."

She eyed me. "Who's your boss?"

"Brian Carling."

She gave a nod. "Got your ID card on ya?"

In a panic, I fumbled my wallet, barely managing to hand her the card. She studied it, then me. "Doctor, huh?"

"Yes."

A slow smile spread across her hardened face. "Why didn't ya say that?" she said, grabbing my hand and shaking it, almost rattling the teeth in my head. "Come on inside."

I wasn't led in so much as accosted through the door, and I was too terrified to not comply. There was a small entry hall with a plastic plant, and a door that led through to a dark room where one wall was lined with radar, sonars, screens, and flashing lights, the other wall was lined with shelves full of gear. Old anemometers, a tripod, a machine that looked like a hygrometer from the '60s; boxes of gear that belonged in a museum.

Jesus. How old was this place?

"Here's the bridge," she said, as if this was some ship that needed steering. Every single panel was something from the '90s. Oh my god, it was older than me. Doreen must have noticed my face.

"Bet it's nothin' fancy like you're used to. She's old, but she ain't ever stopped."

The old air conditioning unit rattled and clunked, scaring me, and Doreen walked over to it and walloped it with the heel of her hand, which scared me even more. I was surprised it stayed on the wall, let alone kicked into gear.

Then something yipped and I almost jumped out of my

skin until Doreen scooped up a small poodle-looking thing off the one and only seat in the entire room.

"This is Bruce," she said. "Not scared of a little dog, are ya?"

Before I could answer—words were failing me right at that minute—Tully was behind me, holding my crate. "He ain't scared of anything," he said with a smirk. He put my crate down. "Well, maybe an amphibian or two, but a fifty-thousand-volt lightning strike don't faze him at all."

I was beginning to think I'd walked into a time warp. How was this station still operational?

"I gotta say," Doreen said. "I'm surprised to see ya. I didn't think anyone was ever comin'."

I was still trying to get my head around any single thing that had happened in the last three minutes.

"Uh, my automatic weather station was taken out in a storm two days ago, and a power surge took out my hard drive," I said. "I was hoping I could use your system to see if anything's retrievable. I'd hate to think all my data is lost." I looked at the console unit, doubting anything was compatible for me to use. Not without a time machine.

Doreen fished her keys from her pocket, and putting Bruce back on the seat, she unthreaded some keys and handed them to me. "I don't give one fuck what you do, kid."

Uh . . .

Um . . .

"P-p-pardon?"

"You're my replacement, right?" she picked up a pink biker helmet and put it on, then nodded to the keys in the palm of my hand. "Keys. There's only two. Front door, front gate. Lock 'em both when you leave."

I shook my head, confused. Bewildered. "What?"

She picked Bruce up. "I retired six months ago, been waitin' on my replacement for-fucking-ever. Arsehats in Sydney kept tellin' me there was no one. Guess it was

Melbourne who come through for me. Always did like Melbourne, though that Brian's a bit of a knob."

I shook my head and held out the keys she'd handed me. "No, no, there's been some kind of mistake," I tried.

"Air con's been dying for five years," she said. "A good kick in the ribs usually gets it goin'."

"Doreen, there seems—"

"I'll leave ya the bat by the door," she said. "Sometimes the local kids think they need an antenna off the roof. Whatever's in the fridge is yours. I'm outta here. I've been here since Tracy."

I looked at Tully, bewildered. *Who the hell was Tracy?*

"Cyclone Tracy," he murmured.

Oh.

Panic was starting to bubble in my chest. "I just wanted to calibrate—"

Doreen clapped me on the shoulder so hard I fell into Tully. "Congrats on the job," she said. "Hope you don't like co-workers or budgets, cause you ain't got either."

And with that, she was gone. The door banged as she left, a second later her motorbike rumbled to life and by the time I thought to chase after her, all we got was a wave as she took off out the gate, Bruce sitting up in the sidecar with dog-goggles on.

And I stood there with my mouth hanging open and a set of keys in my hand.

I turned to Tully, dumbfounded. "Wh-what the hell . . ." I held the keys on the palm of my hand as if they'd just landed from outer space. "What just happened?"

Tully pressed his lips together so he didn't smile too hard, but his eyes were full of humour. "I think you just got a promotion?"

I shook my head, my mind reeling. "That's not . . . I can't . . . what the . . ."

"Yeah, look," he said with a shrug. "I ain't mad about it. There's a saying about gift horses or something."

"Tully! I live and work in Melbourne!"

He made a face, glanced pointedly at the keys, and clicked his tongue. "Well, I'm thinkin' that's not exactly true." Then he winced. "Anymore."

A beeping noise began blaring inside. "What the hell is that?"

We raced inside. One of the small warning lights was flashing yellow.

"I dunno," Tully said. "This gear is your domain."

"This gear is older than me," I said. "I don't know how any of this works."

"Flip some switches," he said, flipping the old metal switches that did god-only knows what. "Make the noise stop."

"You can't just flip—"

The beeping stopped.

Jesus H Christ.

I looked at the screen. It was a radar, and there was a mass of orange and purple blinking in and out of view. It was old, yes, but I knew what that meant. "Storm front moving in from the north. I think it's a low-pressure warning system. It's gonna be decent."

Tully looked at me, grinning.

"Don't smile at me," I said, taking my phone out and calling my boss. I held my phone to my ear and began to check the other equipment. "Come on, answer your damn phone—"

"Overton," he said, grumpily. "You finally replying to the messages I left for you."

"How long was it until you realised I was on annual leave?"

Silence.

Maybe he still hadn't realised.

He grumbled something I couldn't hear. "What do you want? This better be good."

I scoffed. "I'll give you good. I've just been handed the keys to the Darwin station. The woman that gave them to me quit, or finally retired, I don't even know. The equipment here is from the '90s. Hell, there's an anemometer so old I think it came off the Endeavour. Do you hear what I'm saying? I can't work here. I never agreed to work here. I came here this morning to see if I could use the in house system to recalibrate my gear and maybe save some of the data I collected that got fried from when we got *struck by lightning* in the middle of the damn jungle, but I can now see that was an exercise in futility because the computer system here is straight out of a time machine, and you'll have to excuse my language but it's so fucking damn hot here my brain is melting!"

There was a long beat of silence. "What the hell are you talking about, Overton?"

"Brian, listen to me," I said through clenched teeth. "What you're gonna do is find out what the fuck is going on. Call Sydney, call Canberra. Call the fucking prime minister if you have to. Get Doreen back here, today, and find out who the hell is the replacement officer up here."

"Who's Doreen?"

"She's the six-foot woman with a shaved head and a base-ball bat that just gave me her keys to the Darwin station, that's who! Now get off your arse and start making phone calls!"

I disconnected the call, my chest heaving. "The incompetence," I muttered.

Tully took my hand, grinning. "You're awesome, you know that?"

My head was swimming and my vision blurred. Tully put me in Bruce's seat and patted my cheek. "You okay?"

I shook my head. "I just wanted to check my data."

"I know," he said.

Fucker was still smiling.

"Glad you find this whole situation amusing."

He laughed, now on his knees before me, and cupped my face. "Are you okay?"

I shook my head and shrugged. I had no clue what I was.

"You bein' all kickass to your boss just now was really hot."

I sagged, burying my face in my hands. "I'm so fired."

Just then, the radar began to beep again. With a heavy sigh, I began to look at the instruments, the equipment. "I feel like I'm in a movie, you know when a modern-day pilot has to fly a plane from the 1940s or something and the whole dash is full of buttons that don't make sense." I shook my head, starting to think a little clearer. "That's an early Doppler and this is a RAPIC, I think. I've seen them in pictures."

Tully squeezed my shoulder. "See? You're getting it already."

I flipped the switches back on that he'd shut off earlier. I wheeled my chair over to the right. "And this is one of the first time-lapse sequencers. My god, did we *go* back in time?"

"Kinda feels like it."

"Can you please do me a favour and see if there's a manual or instruction booklet on the shelves or in a cupboard, or—" I looked around. "—something, somewhere. A filing cabinet, maybe. Google won't help me here."

Tully went straight to the shelves and started lifting things and rummaging through boxes. I turned back once to see that he'd found a helmet with a torchlight strapped to it. It was now on his head. By the time I'd read the old printed labels underneath some metal flip switches and correlated it to its function on the dash, Tully let out a loud, "Ta-da!" while wielding a book over his helmet.

"Printed in 1992," he said, handing it over.

It was, indeed, a manual to the instrument dash. From 1992.

"Oh god," I said, taking the book. I dusted it off and skimmed through the first pages. The radar beeped again, and at least I knew which switch to flip. The storm was still moving in, and I could only guess by the gauges on the radar that it was a few hours away. "Who the hell am I supposed to notify about the warning?"

Tully grimaced and shrugged in an 'I have no clue' kind of way, just as my phone rang. I saw it was my boss and answered halfway through the first ring.

"Tell me you have good news," I said. I probably could have started with hello . . .

"I got good news and bad news," he said. "Good news is you're the temporary replacement officer. Starting today."

What?

What?

"What?!"

"I'd call it being in the right place at the right time," he said. "You get to be the boss. Isn't that what you always wanted?"

I rubbed my temple, feeling my blood pressure rise by the second. "Temporary. You said temporary. How long until they find the full-time replacement officer?"

Brian sighed. "Well, that's the bad news."

Oh no . . .

"You see, Doreen Boyle, the lady who left today? She's been waiting on a replacement for a while."

"She said she'd technically retired six months ago. Are you saying I'll be here six months?"

Tully's eyes and smile widened, excited.

"Wellllllll," Brian said. "She technically applied for a replacement back in 2004."

I slow blinked.

"Two thousand and what?"

"Yeah, just don't hold your breath, Overton," Brian said. He sounded far too happy to be getting rid of me. "I sent all your employment data to HR to transfer you over to the Northern Territory bureau."

Already? He hadn't even spoken to me . . .

"I have an apartment in Melbourne, I, uh," I whispered lamely. Stupidly. My brain wasn't working.

"The bureau will cover all moving costs," he said quickly. "They'll pack your place up and send it up to you if you want."

I wasn't sure what to say.

I wasn't sure what was left to say.

"You know what you can do with my transfer papers," I said, just as the air conditioning unit began to buzz and whirr until it conked out. I stood up. "You can take the form, fold it up nicely into a neat little square." I closed my fist and punched the side of the air conditioner. It coughed back to life. "And shove it up your arse!" I disconnected the call and tossed my phone onto the instrument dash. "Argh!"

Tully stood there, wide eyed, slack-jawed but somehow grinning. "Did you just tell your boss to . . . ?"

"He's no longer my boss," I said. "Apparently I work here now." I sagged back onto the chair and held up my hand. "I think I broke it."

Laughing, Tully knelt before me and inspected my knuckles. "You have a pretty mean right hook." He gently manipulated my fingers, checking that everything still moved. "I think you'll be okay."

I nodded, fighting tears. "I'm sure everyone at the office will be pleased. They'll probably have a party in my honour right this second, to celebrate the fact I'm gone."

Tully pulled me to my feet, spun me around, and we began to do some slow, crazy waltz. He was still grinning. "No tears allowed, because this is the best day ever." I looked at him as if he'd lost his mind, and he spun me out and made me do a twirl before he pulled me back into his arms. "Now you can eat my arse and do that prostate thing all the time."

I laughed despite the emotional whirlwind and mindfuck of the last ten minutes.

Tully pulled me flush against him, our dance now a slow sway, his eyes focused on mine. "Seriously, Jeremiah," he murmured. "I'm glad you're staying. I know this wasn't exactly what you wanted, but I think you'll love it here. If you just give it a chance." He pouted. "If you give me a chance."

I sighed. There was no way I could be mad when he was holding me like this, looking at me like that.

"I'll need to look for a place," I said. "God, I have so much to organise. I need to call my dad . . ."

My mind was beginning to swim again.

Tully held my face, grounding me. He kissed me softly. "You're stayin' with me. Take a spare room if you want. But you're still eating my arse and doing the prostate thing."

I snorted just as the radar began to beep again. That low-pressure system rolling in from the north wasn't slowing down. "There's a storm coming," I murmured.

"I know." He grinned that annoying grin that I was beginning to love. "Isn't it wonderful?"

~Fin

INTO THE TEMPEST

BOOK TWO

INTO THE TEMPEST

BLURB

Jeremiah Overton is now in charge of Darwin's Bureau of Meteorology, and his storm chaser boyfriend, Tully Larson, couldn't be happier. For Tully, it means watching summer storms with the love of his life, but for Jeremiah, it means relearning everything on equipment that's older than he is.

But summer storms also mean it's cyclone season. While Tully's no stranger to tropical storms and the occasional cyclone, for Jeremiah, it's a first.

As Tropical Cyclone Hazer bears down on the city, Jeremiah and Tully prepare to stay behind. Jeremiah knows what to expect, theoretically, but living through it is a different story.

If they live through it at all.

CHAPTER ONE

TULLY

I was nervous waiting for Jeremiah's plane to land.

Two weeks after being at the Darwin Bureau of Meteorology, he'd made a quick trip back to Melbourne to collect some of his personal belongings, pack up his apartment, and clear out his desk at work.

One night.

He'd been gone for one night and I missed him like crazy. How he'd turned my life upside down in a matter of just a few weeks I'd never know. The first week at the bunker in Kakadu had been awesome, and the two weeks helping him get his new office into some kind of workable space had been fun. But gettin' to watch afternoon storms with him, havin' him in my home, and in my bed had been the very best two weeks of my life.

I was besotted with this man, and I was nervous as hell waiting for him. Nervous that he'd get off the plane and tell me he wasn't staying, that he'd be goin' back to his old life in Melbourne. That his life was there and not here with me.

I was nervous that he wouldn't get off the plane at all.

I'd spoken to him this mornin' when he was on his way to the airport, but a lot coulda happened between then and now, and maybe he'd realised that this was all too much too soon. Maybe he didn't want to pack up his entire life and move five thousand kilometres away.

Maybe he didn't feel the same about me as I felt about him.

I was just about ready to puke by the time his flight landed. I noticed a few familiar faces in the terminal and a guy I knew from the bank made an attempt at small talk as he waited for someone to deplane as well.

"Everything okay?" he asked, glancing from me to where people were coming in through the Arrivals door.

"Oh, yeah," I mumbled distractedly. "Sure, just waitin' . . ."

Waitin' for him not to show. Waitin' for him to break my heart.

He'd nodded and, thankfully, said nothing else. His person arrived, and they left smilin' and as happy as could be. Everyone else came in greeting their familiar faces, their loved ones, their people. All smiles and hugs and laughter.

And no Jeremiah.

The doors closed and people wheeled out their luggage, leaving my stomach in knots, my heart thumping and heavy. My chest felt all too tight, and that nervousness from before was quickly becoming a sinking realisation that Jeremiah hadn't got on his flight.

He didn't want me. He didn't love me . . .

"Please be careful with that," a familiar voice said as airport staff wheeled through a cart with two large black crates. Jeremiah was ushering alongside them, frantic and frazzled.

And fucking gorgeous.

The tight band around my chest let up and, just like that, I could breathe.

"Hey," I yelled, making them stop, and in a few quick

strides, I collected Jeremiah in a crushing hug, surprising him and the man pushin' the cart.

"Oh," Jeremiah squeaked, red faced and flustered, now for a whole other reason. "Tully, what are you . . . ?"

"I missed you," I blurted out, squeezin' him tight. "And I didn't see you get off the plane. I thought you mighta decided not to come back. I'm so happy to see you."

He pulled back, seemingly confused by this. "I told you I was coming back just this morning. Actually, my employer insisted I take this job. I wasn't allowed to *not* come back here; I believe that was the term they used."

Laughing, I cupped his face and pulled him in for a quick kiss. His magnificent blue eyes widened.

"Tully," he hissed.

I just grinned at him. I didn't give a fuck what people thought. I wanted to kiss him, so I did. "Need help with your gear?"

With his hand to his forehead, still flustered, he blinked a few times. "Ummm."

"You okay?"

"You befuddled me."

"Befuddled?" I threw my head back and laughed. "God, I missed you."

He scowled at me, then gestured absently to his crates and to the guy who'd been pushin' the cart, who was now looking at anyone but us. "This should be fine, but if you could take one of my suitcases . . ."

He glanced uncomfortably over at the few straggling travellers, some who were now watching us.

I got the feeling they'd never seen two men kiss before, so I grinned at them too as I collected Jeremiah's luggage. "Come on, *babe*, let's go home," I said, extra loud for our audience's benefit.

Jeremiah rolled his eyes and grumbled as we walked out. "Did you need to be so obvious?"

Yes, I did.

So, for good fuckin' measure, I pushed him up against the side of my Range Rover and kissed him properly. He resisted for half a second . . . until he didn't. He groaned as I sucked on his tongue.

I pulled back, leaving him dazed and flushed, then booped him on the nose with my finger. "I missed you."

"Don't be ridiculous," he mumbled, trying not to smile. "I've been gone one day."

"Thirty-five hours, to be exact." Not that I was counting.

The blush on his cheeks deepened, and he chewed on his bottom lip. "Should we go home then?"

Hell yes, we should.

I loaded his gear into my car, cranked up the air conditioning, and we headed out of the carpark.

"I very quickly forgot how hot it is here," he said, wiping his brow with the back of his hand. "The humidity, jeez."

"Did you get everything sorted?"

He nodded. "Brian had already boxed up my desk, so that took exactly one minute. There was no love lost there, I can assure you. They're as glad to see the back of me as I am to see theirs."

"I'm sorry."

"I'm not."

I reached over and took his hand. "It's their loss."

"My parting words were something similar."

I laughed but then asked something more serious. "And your dad?"

"He was fine," he said with a shrug. "Wished me luck. I took him out for dinner last night, like a farewell, I suppose. He said it was a waste of money."

Oh man.

I squeezed his hand. "I'm sorry."

"He appreciated the fridge and lounge I gave him though.

Mine were newer than his by a decade or two." He tried to smile but it didn't quite work.

I lifted his hand to my lips and kissed his knuckles. I hated that no one in his Melbourne life was happy for him. "I'm glad you're here."

He watched me for a long moment. "I'm glad I'm here too. Did I miss a great storm last night?"

I grinned at him. "It was kinda lame. Or maybe that was just because I didn't get to watch it with you."

He rolled his eyes and looked out his window, but I could tell by his cheeks that he was smiling. "Oh," he said, as if he'd just remembered. "The heart-rate monitor you suggested? The chest strap that sports people wear?"

I think I liked where this was going . . . "Yeah?"

He cleared his throat. "I may have bought one."

I grinned. "Oh hell yes. Now we just need one of those brain monitor things, so next time you try and get struck by lightning, we can get some proper readings."

He sighed. "I don't *try* to get struck—" He stopped talking and shook his head, not even bothering to finish that sentence. "I also inquired about helmets that perform non-invasive medical imaging of the brain, because I did some research while I was stuck in traffic. There is a relatively new device that employs near-infrared light to determine the relative concentration of haemoglobin in the brain, via differences in the light absorption patterns. Because, well, most non-invasive brain scanning systems use continuous-wave spectroscopy, where the tissue is irradiated by a constant stream of photons. However, these systems cannot differentiate between scattered and absorbed photons. But this new one—"

"Okay, I'm just gonna stop you right there," I said, putting my hand up. "And remind you who you're talkin' to. You're really gonna have to dumb all that down for me." I gave him the smile he liked best. "Or just say it's one of those helmet thingies with the white sticky pads."

He kinda winced. "Well, it doesn't have white sticky pads . . . Anyway, they're incredibly expensive, so unless I can obtain some kind of study grant, which is highly unlikely given the nature of the experiment, it's not likely I'll be purchasing one any time soon."

I reached over and squeezed his hand. "But you got the proper heart-rate monitor thingy?"

He smiled. "Yes."

My phone rang, Bluetooth putting it through the stereo system. My brother's name came on the dash screen.

I hit Answer. "Hey, butt nugget."

"Hey, nut sac."

Jeremiah's eyes widened and I laughed. "You're on speaker, and Jeremiah's in the car."

"Ah, the mystery man who's been keeping you busy."

Jeremiah's eyes almost bugged out of his head, and with a grin, I squeezed his hand. "What do you want, Ellis? We're heading home."

"Well, I'm glad you're in the car. It'll save you a trip."

"What for?"

"I need you to come to the office."

"Can't it wait till tomorrow? I'm back in the office tomorrow at eight."

"Nope. You need to sign off on the Goyer account. Shipment leaves at twenty-two hundred today."

I groaned.

"Quit your bitching," he said. "You're already in the car so you're, what? Five minutes away?"

"Hey, Ellis," I said flatly.

"If you're gonna tell me to eat a bag of dicks, I'll leave that up to you."

I snorted. "Believe me, if they sold 'em in bags, I would."

He laughed. "You're so gross."

"You started it."

"See ya when you get here. Oh, and Jeremiah," Ellis said. I could hear the smile in his voice. "Tell me, does Tully—"

I hit End Call so damn fast I hurt my finger. "Sorry about that," I said. "Whatever he was about to say was going to be embarrassing and more than likely rude."

He smiled at me. "Would you really eat dicks from a bag?"

Laughing, I changed lanes and headed toward the depot. It really wasn't far, and now that it was about to happen, the idea of Jeremiah meeting Ellis kinda gave me a thrill. We'd been so busy at his new office, and in the bedroom, everythin' else just kinda got ignored.

"This won't take more than a minute or two," I said, pulling into the depot yard. I lowered my window and slowed down at the gate, waved through when the security guard saw it was me.

Jeremiah stared at the cargo ships and the shipping containers, and at the famous knight logo. Then he turned to me, stunned. "This is you?"

"Nope, this is my mum and dad's business. I just work here."

"But this is . . . you never said you were one of Australia's major freighting companies."

I snorted. "It's just work to me." I drove up to the admin building and into my parking spot, then shut off the engine. "Come on inside. It won't take a minute."

He looked horrified. "You want me to come in with you?"

"Sure. I know you've been travellin' all day, but you can meet Ellis, and then you can confirm, once and for all, that I'm by far the better-looking brother." I grinned for good measure. "If you could say that to his face, that'd be great. If you don't mind, that is."

I got out and went to his side of the car and opened his door for him. "Come on, he won't bite. He'll be on his best behaviour, I promise." I waited for him to get out of the car, closed the door, and slung my arm over his shoulders as we walked toward the main building. "If he's not, I'll kick his arse."

"You wish you could kick my arse."

I stopped in my tracks and pulled Jeremiah to a stop with me, my arm around his shoulders falling to his waist . . .

Because there, now standin' in a neat little welcoming line at the front of the building, was Ellis—wearing a shit-eating grin.

And my parents.

I was gonna kill my brother.

CHAPTER TWO

JEREMIAH

WHEN TULLY STOPPED WALKING, I KNEW SOMETHING WAS wrong. He'd stopped dead, his arm fell from my shoulders, and his fingers gripped my waist.

There were three people waiting for us, it would seem. The reason Tully froze.

One man, maybe early thirties, who looked a great deal like Tully. Only he was wearing suit pants and a shirt, and his blond hair was short.

But his grin was exactly the same.

And an older couple. Maybe fifties or sixties, well-dressed, and smiling. She was pretty, with blonde hair tied up in a twist, wearing a pantsuit. And he was a tall, solid man, with silver hair but very familiar brown eyes, and that grin . . .

Oh.

Oh boy.

"Mum," Tully said. "Dad. I wasn't expecting you . . ." Then his voice dropped. "Ellis. You scheming, festy ball sac."

Ellis laughed and leaped onto Tully in a tackle and they wrestled like teenagers. Tully's father laughed, and his mother sighed loudly. She ignored them and aimed right for me.

"Hello, dear," she said, walking toward me. "Please ignore the heathens. I tried to raise them right." She held out her hand. "I'm Brielle, Tully's mother."

Oh my god.

So this was happening.

I remembered my manners and shook her hand. "Hello. It's very nice to meet you, if somewhat unexpected. Please excuse my clothes. I've been travelling all day. If I'd have known I'd be meeting you—"

Tully was back beside me, his arm firmly around my waist again. "Mum, this is Doctor Jeremiah Overton. Jeremiah, this is my mum."

She blinked in surprise at my title. "How lovely to meet you."

Then Tully turned me to face his father. "This is my dad, Ken." And his brother, whose shirt now looked decidedly dishevelled. Had Tully ripped the collar? "And the walking, talking nut sac, Ellis."

His dad shook my hand. "Ignore them. It's nice to meet you."

Ellis gave Tully another shove and shook my hand too. "So you do exist. I thought for sure he'd made you up."

Oh, goodness.

"I do exist, yes."

"And you spent time out in the cell block with him?"

"The cell block . . ."

"He means the bunker," Tully explained.

"Oh, right. Yes. I loved it. I'd actually like to spend more time there."

"Oh, so you're as batshit crazy as he is," Ellis said, trying to touch Tully's face. Tully wrestled with him again until their mother spoke.

"Boys!"

They stopped immediately, but Mrs Larson took my arm.

"Come inside out of this dreadful heat," she said, ushering me in toward the door.

I turned back to see Tully's father give them both a clip behind the ears. It didn't help that he was smiling when he did it.

"Holy shit, he's got the bluest eyes I've ever seen," Ellis said. I think it may have been an attempt to whisper but we all heard it.

"Shut the fuck up," Tully said, putting him in another headlock.

"Forgive those two," his mother said as we entered the building. "They get like that when they haven't seen each other for a while."

It was an easy twenty degrees cooler inside, and I almost sagged with relief.

"We'll go through to the cafeteria," she said. "Can I offer you a drink? Did you say you'd been travelling?"

"Ah, yes. I've come back from Melbourne."

"Oh, you must have been up early," she said, frowning. "Help yourself to whatever food you want."

"I'm fine," I tried. But wow. It was an actual cafeteria, and there were some guys in blue overalls at one table. I assumed them to be dock workers.

"We offer all our workers meals around the clock," Mrs Larson explained, clearly reading my curiosity for what it was. She led me to the beginning of the cafeteria line, slid a tray over, and loaded up a plate of sandwiches, some cut fruit, and two coffees. She took the tray to a table and sat down, and seeing Tully was in the line with his brother and father—and not really knowing what else to do—I sat opposite Mrs Larson.

She took one of the coffees and put the food in front of me. "Please, eat," she said. "Travelling is a beast, and airport food is terrible. These are made fresh all day long."

I wasn't sure what to say. "Uh, thank you." I picked up a

small triangle of ham, cheese, and tomato sandwich and bit into it. It was really very good.

"So," Mrs Larson said. "You're a doctor?"

Oh great.

By the time I'd finished chewing and swallowing, Tully had plonked himself down next to me. "He has a PhD in meteorological sciences," he said, with his mouth half full of what was possibly chocolate cake.

"Not a medical doctor," I added. "Much to my father's disdain."

I hadn't meant that to sound so bitter, but anyway, there it was.

"Don't let him fool ya," Tully said. "He's humble and self-deprecating, but he's a genius, and at least ten years ahead of his colleagues."

I looked at Tully then, because that was such a weird thing to say . . . and he smirked at me with a hint of daring in his eyes. And something that looked like pride?

I wasn't sure. I wasn't familiar with it. My face flamed, nonetheless. "Uh, I think genius is a stretch."

Tully laughed and, to my utter horror, put his hand to my jaw and thumbed my cheek. His brown eyes, kind and warm. "Whatcha blushing for?"

Oh.

My.

God.

I went so red and my cheeks burned so hot I was sure it could only be measured in kelvin. I could even feel it in my hairline. I pulled his hand away, giving him a 'your parents are right there' look, and what did he do?

He laughed.

His hand fell to my thigh, and he kept it there, giving my leg a squeeze. My throat was suddenly feeling a little tight, so I sipped my coffee and dared to glance at Tully's parents and brother.

They were all looking at Tully. His dad was smiling at him, though clearly surprised. His brother was staring at him as if he'd sprouted a second head, and his mother was looking at him fondly.

At least they weren't looking at me. I ate more sandwich and pretended this whole encounter wasn't mortifying.

"So, Jeremiah's now in charge of the Darwin office," Tully said, still singing my praises, which I wasn't used to—at all. "He's staying with me."

Oh my days.

He just told them we were cohabitating. Not even that I was staying at his house, but rather that I was staying *with him*.

As in, not leaving. Not returning to Melbourne. I was *with him*.

I let out a long, slow, somewhat shaky breath. "Well, the position was thrust upon me."

Oh . . .

Did I just use the words position and thrust upon me in one sentence?

To his parents? And his brother?

I wanted to die.

Was it possible for the floor to open up and swallow me whole? Maybe I could choke on a grape.

I tried. No luck.

Tully chuckled beside me, his face far too close to mine. "You okay there?" he whispered.

"No. Is a sinkhole not too much to ask for?"

He laughed and kissed my shoulder, then pulled me to my feet. "Okay, we're gonna get going."

"Oh, did you sign whatever needed signing?" I asked. I hadn't noticed him doing that, but this had all been such a whirlwind.

"No." Tully glared at his brother. "Ellis was bullshitting me. This was an ambush."

Ellis grinned. "Just wanted to see if you actually existed, sorry. And to embarrass Tully. Given Mum and Dad were both in the office, it was perfect timing."

"Oh."

All right then.

Tully grumbled. "After travellin' ten thousand kilometres in two days, he had to pack up his apartment, maybe grab a few hours' sleep to make it back to the airport in time this morning, fly for half a day, only to get here and meet my family without any warning." He put his arm around me. "Jeremiah has every right to be pissed at you, Ellis."

Oh my . . . "Uh, no, it's fine," I said quickly.

Tully nudged me. "No, be pissed at him."

I shook my head. "No, no. It's fine."

Ellis stood up. "I'm sorry."

I shrank back into Tully and gave him pleading eyes. "I said it's fine."

"Why won't you yell at him," Tully urged. "Lay on the guilt. Make him suffer."

Oh god.

This was all a ploy to chide his brother.

I smiled at Mr and Mrs Larson. "Thank you for the food and coffee. It was very nice to meet you." And then Ellis. "And you, as well. But yes, I should get going. I need to check in at the office this evening."

Tully slung his arm over my shoulders, not before giving his brother the bird, and led me to the door. "Why didn't you rip him a new one?" he asked. "I set it up perfectly."

"Because he looks too much like you!"

Obviously, I said that too loud because Ellis laughed before the cafeteria door could shut, and Tully gave him another bird before leading me out and into the car.

I sat in the seat, and Tully closed my door. I couldn't believe what had just happened. I couldn't get my thoughts together. Apparently, all I could do was stammer at Tully as he got in behind the wheel.

"Wh-wh-what the . . . I just . . . just met . . . oh my god. Those were your parents!"

Tully's annoyingly breathtaking grin lit up his whole stupidly handsome face. "Okay, first up, I had no idea. That was all Ellis' doing. So, I'm sorry for blindsiding you. Not my intention at all." He sat back in his seat, still smiling, far too pleased with himself. "But ya know what? I ain't mad about it."

"I can see that."

"I thought it went well."

"I said the words *position* and *thrust upon* in the same sentence, Tully. To their faces."

He laughed. "Pretty sure they like you."

"I've never met anyone's parents before!"

He shot me a look. "Well, fair's fair. I've never introduced anyone to my parents before."

I stared at him. "I'm the first? Because that bestows a whole lot of added pressure I didn't need right now. Oh my god, Tully, they must think I'm . . . ." I gestured to my been-travelling-all-day clothes and hair. "I look like a homeless man."

"You look perfect."

I sighed, my hand to my forehead, unable to process . . .

"Hey, Jeremiah. Look at me," he murmured softly. I did, and his smile softened as he studied my face for a long second. "I'm glad it was you."

"Pardon?"

"I'm glad you were the first to meet my folks. As my boyfriend."

Boyfr . . .

Boyfriend . . .

I squeaked. "What?"

He chuckled, leaned right across me, and pulled my seatbelt. Our faces were an inch apart, his eyes alight. "Boyfriend." He buckled me in, the click loud in the silence, and I started. "Well, we *are* living together, so . . ."

I was feeling lightheaded. "Do you . . . is that . . . maybe we . . ."

He grinned. "Nope. Boyfriends it is." He took my face in his hands, planted a soft, wet kiss on my lips, then sat back in his seat and started the engine. "Did you wanna go home first? Or straight to the office?"

My mind was a spinning wheel without the hamster. "Uh . . ."

He put the car in reverse and backed out. "Maybe we should go to the office first, because once I get you home, I don't see us leavin' for a while. If you know what I mean."

The next thing I knew we were on our way to my office. "I thought I was supposed to be the bossy one."

"You are. But you can't win all the time."

"So you can just declare us boyfriends without consulting with me?"

"Correct. What would you prefer I introduce you as?" He looked from the road to me. "Lover? Fuck buddy?"

"Oh my god, no."

"Meteorological cohabitator?"

I squinted at him.

He grinned, victorious. "See? Boyfriend it is."

I sighed, even though my heart was doing some weird palpitational dance and I was trying not to smile. "I've never had a boyfriend before."

"Me either. Or a girlfriend." Then he made a face. "Well, not really. There were some I hung out with a few times over the course of some weeks or months, but we were never . . ." He shifted in his seat. "We were never like us."

We were never like us . . .

"Like us?"

He shifted in his seat again and changed hands on the

steering wheel. "Yeah. Like we are. Living together and stuff."

I got the impression that wasn't what he wanted to say.

We pulled into the yard at my Bureau of Meteorology office, and when Tully stopped the car, he gave me a smile that didn't sit quite right. "Okay, here we are," he said quickly, and got out.

I wasn't sure what that was about, but Doreen's motorbike was under the carport and I didn't want to keep her waiting.

Quite frankly, she scared me.

Tully bounded up the steps to the office and hollered, "Hey, it's us," as he disappeared inside.

I followed, bumbling into the darkened office to find Tully standing next to Doreen. Bruce, the fluffy dog, was on the chair, watching me as if I had to report in to him. Tully was grinning, Doreen was glaring. Her shirt had the Rolling Stones' mouth and tongue on it with *Lick a Lesbian* written underneath.

Nice.

"Huh," she all but grunted at me. "Surprised to see you came back."

Why did everyone think that?

"I told you I'd return," I said. "Not entirely sure why the general consensus was that I'd quit. I'm yet to quit anything. If you believe I lack the intestinal fortitude—"

She threw her head back and laughed. "I can see you got plenty-a that, kid."

I frowned at her, unsure of how to take her. "Anyway, I'm very grateful you could fill in for me and watch the fort while I squared away my old life in Melbourne."

"Well, ya gave me two weeks off," she said. "Least I could do is fill in one day for ya. Just try not to make a habit of askin'. I'm still retired, just not dead yet."

I nodded, almost bowing to her. "Thank you."

She clapped me on the shoulder, hard enough to make me have to counter my weight. I really needed to learn how to brace myself better. Then she scooped up Bruce and moved to the door. She pointed to the Doppler radar. "Got a tropical low moving in from Malaysia. They've had heavy falls and localised flooding. But we also got a storm cluster moving in across the Philippines. If they meet in some perfect storm scenario bullshit and swing south, and it's lookin' likely they will, shit's gonna get real bad. I've been keepin' an eye on it. Suggest you do the same."

I looked at the screen. "This front's moving directly into it?"

She gave a solemn nod. "Mm."

Well, shit. That wasn't good. "Okay, thanks."

With a gruff goodbye, she left, and a few seconds later her motorbike roared to life, and she and Bruce drove away.

"She frightens me."

Tully laughed. "Which is why you looked her right in the eye and said, 'If you think I lack the intestinal fortitude.'" He shook his head. "If that's how you react to people who scare you, I'm not surprised walkin' into a lightning storm ain't a problem for you."

I had to think about what he said, what he meant. "Was I abrasive?"

Tully, still grinning, shook his head, and with his hands to my face, pulled me in for a kiss. "You're amazing, you know that?"

"I didn't mean to sound unappreciative to her. Perhaps I should—"

"You were fine," he murmured. "I think she likes you."

"I didn't want to have to ask her to come back, even for one day."

"I know you didn't. But she didn't mind. Pretty sure if she didn't want to help out, she'd tell you." I sighed, and he pulled me close, brushing his nose to mine. "I've missed you."

"I was only gone for one day—" I began, then when his

eyes met mine, I amended, "—thirty-five hours."

His smile was so serene, but then he looked around. "Well, do what you gotta do. I have plans for you tonight that don't involve bein' naked in your office. I'd rather see those plans unfold in bed and not here."

I rolled my eyes but set about getting my work done. Tully busied himself tidying up more of the shelves and packing all the old gear into boxes. He'd done most of it during my first two weeks here. He'd helped me every day, even spent his own money buying me new monitors, and he fixed a second chair he'd found in the corner.

But given there wasn't much for him to do, after only one hour, he was bored.

And horny.

He kept bothering me with sensual touches, slow neck massages, and back hugs with soft whispers in my ear.

"Please tell me we won't be here long," he murmured. "Unless you wanna do me on the control panel." He nodded toward the radars. "Not sure those switches would be too comfortable, but I'm willing to try. I don't want to wait anymore."

I could feel his excitement pressing against my arse, and when I didn't rebuke his idea, his smile became a smirk and he leaned his back against the panel board and pulled me with him.

"Where's the chest-strap monitor?" he asked, raking his hand down over my arse. "Is it in your bag in the car?"

"I'm not wearing it during sex."

He chuckled. "Oh, we absolutely *will* be using it during sex. We can take it in turns. I insist that we do." But then he pulled my hips to his and shoved his tongue in my mouth, so I couldn't argue.

I hated that it worked.

My god, he felt so good against me, and as I pushed my weight on him, he lifted one leg, hitching it around my arse. I held his face and kissed him, opening his mouth with mine, tilting our heads so I could give him more of my tongue.

He made a guttural sound that curled my insides, and he clawed at my back.

Was I really about to do this here?

At my work? On the control board?

God, I think I was . . .

How was this even my life now? Me . . . doing this, with a gorgeous man like Tully . . .

Something beeped, and he groaned. He tried to widen his legs and I pinned him against the panels, grinding against him like some horny teenager. My god, it was so unbidden. So wicked.

So hot.

Something beeped again, and he smiled against my mouth. "You're about to set me off," he said, then kissed me again, deeper, more frantic. "Gonna make me—"

It beeped again, and then again, and again, and again.

I tried to see what it was, not wanting to take my mouth from his, not wanting to stop . . .

"Is that your watch?" he asked. "Take it off."

But it wasn't my watch.

Then I saw what was beeping.

"Holy shit."

"Oh yeah," Tully breathed. "I need to get naked."

"No. Holy shit," I said, stepping back and letting him find his feet. I couldn't take my eyes off the screen. "Holy shit, Tully."

Whether he could see the seriousness in my eyes, or if it was my voice, I wasn't sure. But he followed my line of sight. "What is it?"

"That's an early detection warning."

The data reel began to spin, and more lights flashed.

"An early detection warning for what?"

I met his gaze, my heart hammering. "A cyclone."

CHAPTER THREE

TULLY

I stared at the radar. Jeremiah flipped some switches and made the beeping stop. "But that won't reach us, right? It's so far away."

Jeremiah didn't answer.

In the next few seconds, he had his phone pressed to his ear and he was searchin' on one radar while reading data on another.

I should have known then.

Nothing scared him.

But he looked kinda scared now.

I looked at the radar that had been beeping, the same one Doreen had signalled to. She'd been watching something on it, was concerned enough to mention it . . .

On the blinking radar, a massive cloud band was moving across Asia. It was sweeping southeast, carried on a warm tropical low. A massive spiral rainband, with intense rainfall extending outward from the centre. And it was now projecting a path to cross land over Darwin.

"Yes, an initial tropical cyclone alert . . . Yes, I'm aware," Jeremiah said. "If it continues to . . . That's correct, official cyclone watch . . . No, sir . . . Yes, that's correct, sir, I believe we'd be looking at a Category 5."

His eyes met mine, and I felt the blood drain from my face.

Category 5.

Jesus fucking Christ.

He ran his hand through his hair, nodded, and spoke into his phone. "I'll issue the CXML, but it'll take some time . . . because the instruments here belong in a goddamn museum."

He ended the call and tossed his phone onto the panel, then tapped the radar, his eyes meeting mine.

Grim.

"Category 5?"

He nodded. "If its trajectory doesn't change. There's nothing but warm air in its path and it's just going to gain strength."

Category 5.

He gestured to another screen. "It has perfect conditions. There's nothing between there and here to stop it."

"When?" I asked. "When will it be here?"

"Five days."

"Five? That's ages. Anything can happen between now and then. Why isn't it on that radar yet?" I pointed to another screen.

"Because it's out of Australian waters. This radar"—he pointed to the really old one—"is tracking. We share feeds with the International Committee . . ."

"But it might dissipate, right? It might lose momentum, change trajectory?"

His eyes caught mine, and I could see he was trying to understand why I didn't believe him.

"It might," he allowed. "And I really hope it does. But the probability that it will continue as projected is high. We have these measures in place for a good reason, Tully. It's now an official cyclone watch. If it stays on track and reaches

Australian waters, that will upgrade on day three to an alert. People need to know so they can make informed choices. Even if the cyclone downgrades, there will still be flood warnings, wind warnings, dangerous surf conditions. Severe storm warnings, rain, hail. If people want to evacuate, they can. Either way, people need to stock up on essentials and get prepared."

Again, the sincerity with which he spoke, the urgency underlined with fear, told me all I needed to know. Whatever was comin' was enough to put that edge of worry in his eyes.

I took out my phone, found the number I was after, and hit Call. "Tully," Dad answered cheerfully. "Your mother and I were just talking about you. What's up? Thought you'd be busy tonight with your new man. Gotta say, we were surprised to meet him. I know it was your brother's doing, but still, we've never met any—"

"Ah, Dad," I said. "Sorry to interrupt. I'm with Jeremiah right now. We called into his work before we went home. I know you have people who watch the weather and shit, but the bureau will be issuing an official cyclone watch. It's being sent out now."

"Is this that storm off the coast of Malaysia? Joseph's already monitoring it, and we've already changed shipping routes. You know this."

"Yeah, well, Jeremiah said it's heading our way. And I'm lookin' at a radar right now that's tellin' us Darwin will be a direct hit, Dad. And a possible Category 5 when it gets here."

There was a beat of silence and then the quiet tapping on a keyboard. "A Category 5, you said?"

Jeremiah nodded.

"Yeah, Dad. It's not good. We've got less than five days to get all the ships loaded and out of the harbour."

There was a familiar beeping of an incoming call. "That's Joseph calling me now. Christ almighty. Thanks for your call, Tull."

The line went dead, and Jeremiah gave my arm a squeeze. But then another radar started to beep, and the data screens were rolling information so fast they almost blurred.

Jeremiah was flippin' switches and reading screens like a madman. "Argh, why is everything so goddamned old?"

His phone rang again, and he was talking stats and data so fast to whoever that was, and about a minute later, a familiar motorbike came back into the yard. Doreen, with Bruce under her arm, came stomping back into the office. "I been gone for a hot minute and you issued a track map on a Cat 5? And I hear about it on the damn radio?"

He pointed to the radar screen and her face paled. "Fucking hell," she mumbled. Then she growled. "It wasn't that bad when I was in charge. What the hell are you doin' to the world?"

He shot her a glare and ignored the person he was talking to on the phone. "Like I did this," he said to her. "We need to run the CMXL."

I didn't know what that was, but she did what he asked, and then, like one single being with four arms, the two of them worked that panel together.

My hopes of takin' Jeremiah home for a night of smoking hot sex were dashed, but I didn't even mind too much. 'Cause it sure was amazing to see him at work.

Life-threatening Category 5 tropical cyclones, aside.

He was a pro. He was in charge, doing everything all at once. Takin' phone calls, makin' calls, directing information and data.

I helped where I could. I ordered them pizza for dinner. I played with Bruce. I took him out to see the storm roll in as the sun went down. And at about ten, everything had died down enough for them to stop.

"What do we do now?" I asked.

"Now we wait," Jeremiah said. "And we watch."

Doreen stretched her back. "Now we go home. You ain't

gonna be sleeping much this week. Get some shuteye tonight. See ya back at six."

"You don't need to come back," Jeremiah said, standing up. "I respect your decision to retire, and quite frankly you deserve a break. You've managed this place forever on your own, and I—"

"Son, you've gotta Cat 5 on your hands. I said I'll be here at six." She whacked him on the shoulder again and he fell onto the control panel. By the time he'd collected himself, Doreen and Bruce were gone out the door.

He rubbed his arm and made a face. "Right, then."

Chuckling, I cupped his face. "Let's get you home. You've had a big day."

He nodded with a sigh. "Yes, okay."

He did what he needed to do to the control panel, we locked everything up, and went home. He was quiet on the drive, though I noticed his blinks were getting longer and slower. "Almost home," I said, taking his hand.

"Thank you for today. For the pizza. For staying with me."

"You don't need to thank me. It's what boyfriends do."

He snorted and shook his head. "I forgot about that."

I gasped, faking my horror. "How could you forget?"

"Had a busy evening."

He sure had.

"Do you think it'll hit us?"

His eyes cut to mine and he gave a nod. "Unfortunately, it looks that way. There's just nothing to pull it up. In fact, the path it's on will only make it stronger."

"Then all we can do is be prepared," I said, trying to cheer him up. "You've sent out every alert you can, you're trackin' it, satellites are monitoring for every little thing." I squeezed his hand. "Darwin learned a lot after Cyclone Tracy. New constructions all have to comply to cyclone building standards. We'll fare much better this time."

"What about the remote communities?" The corner of his mouth turned down. "What about them?"

"There'll be evacuations and they'll be moved to safer locations." I gave his hand a bit of a shake. "Jeremiah, that's not your responsibility. You've issued the alerts as soon as you could. You gave them the most notice possible. That's your responsibility, and you've done it well."

"I've never . . ." He sighed, then started again. "I've never had to issue alerts for a cyclone before. I've never been in charge before."

I slowed down for my driveway and waited for the garage door to open. "Babe, you'll do great. You've already done great. And Doreen's stickin' around. She's been through this before. You two will be the best team for the job."

I drove in, and he still hadn't said anything, so I got out and walked around to his door. "Come on, let's get you to bed."

"My gear . . ."

"Can wait." I took his hand and helped him out of the car and led him straight up the stairs to my ensuite bathroom. "You need a steaming hot shower and sleep," I said, pulling his shirt over his head and giving his nipple a tweak just for fun.

He batted my hand away and rubbed his pec. "Ow."

"Sorry. It's what boyfriends do."

He rolled his eyes and pulled off his shoes and socks as I set the shower going for him. I wasn't gonna join him, but seein' him naked and wet, with his head back and his eyes closed . . .

I stripped off and walked in after him, my hands on his hips, my dick against his arse, my lips on the nape of his neck. He groaned under the stream of water, lettin' his head fall back onto my shoulder. I took the soap and began washing his chest, his arms.

"Is this what boyfriends do?" he murmured, his voice rough.

I turned him around and pushed him against the tiles, crushing my mouth to his, cupping his balls, and stroking his erection.

He groaned into my mouth and raked his hands down my back, to my arse, and finally to my cock. We brought each other to orgasm, a mix of soap and steam and sex. And when he slumped against me, I dried him off and took him to bed.

He rested his head on my chest and his breathing was deep and even and I wrapped him my arms around him tight. He snuggled in and mumbled something I didn't quite hear.

I kissed the top of his head. "What did you say?"

"'S what boyfriends do."

I chuckled and gave him another kiss, because yeah, apparently this—being close, being affectionate, and being so damn happy—was exactly what boyfriends did.

***

JEREMIAH WAS UP AND GONE BEFORE SIX. HE TOOK THE JEEP. Why he preferred it over the newer Rover I'd never know, but it somehow suited him. And with the house empty and the sun barely risen, I went to work early.

I'd had time off when I'd taken Jeremiah to the bunker and a few afternoons here and there over the last two weeks to help him get his office up to some kind of standard.

I knew there'd be a lot of catching up to do at the office, so heading in early was the least I could do. Plus, the imminent cyclone meant the shipping industry went into overdrive.

I'd replied to all my emails and had my first coffee by the time Dad arrived, pokin' his head through my door. "You're here early."

"Figured we'd be busy," I said.

He nodded. "Thanks for the heads-up last night. Perks of being a storm watcher, huh?"

"Well, we got to Jeremiah's office and the bureau radars started going off."

"Ah," he said. "Gotta love getting firsthand inside information." He stepped inside my office with an awkward look on his face and I knew he was about to say something about yesterday. "So, Jeremiah, huh? Your mother and I wondered why we hadn't seen much of you lately, and your brother told us you'd met someone."

I sighed, but stupidly couldn't help but smile at the mention of his name. "Yeah. Jeremiah. He's uh . . . He's kinda great."

"And he's staying with you?"

"He is. It was just supposed to be a temporary thing. Given he had no notice about takin' on the job here."

"But now it's not temporary?"

"I'd like it not to be," I admitted. "We haven't really talked about it. He just got back with some gear yesterday. We met you guys, then went straight to his office and got the cyclone warning. We didn't really have the chance to talk about much."

Had the chance to give mutual handjobs in the shower though . . .

"You really like him," Dad said. "It was good to see you happy with him yesterday. Your mum's over the moon. Finally getting to meet your . . . your . . ."

"Boyfriend."

He grinned at the confirmation.

Then, like a sudden pimple appearing, my brother Ellis walked in. "Oh, if it isn't little love-struck Tully-wully who couldn't keep his hands off his boyfriend's face yesterday."

I threw my stapler at his head. He deflected it with his arm and it hit the floor, separating into pieces. "Ow."

Dad huffed at him. "Pick that up."

He rubbed his forearm. "He threw it at me."

"You deserved it," Dad said.

Ellis sneered at me and I gave him the middle finger. He picked up the stapler and all the staples and dumped them in a pile on my desk.

Dad was back in boss mode. "Meeting at nine in the boardroom."

He left and Ellis sat down in the chair across from my desk. "So, cyclone, huh?"

I sighed. "Yeah. Jeremiah's pretty confident it'll cross land here. It might change. Hopefully it'll get downgraded."

He watched me for a second. "You really like this one, doncha."

It wasn't a question.

I nodded.

"I mean, you've had dates before, but I ain't ever seen you be all touchy-feely with 'em like you were with him."

"Shut the fuck up," I said jokingly.

He shook his head a little. "His eyes. They're so blue it's freaky."

"He's not freaky," I snapped. I wasn't joking this time. Sure, when I'd first met Jeremiah, I'd thought the same. But after getting to know him and knowing that people had called him freak and weird his whole life, I couldn't help but feel defensive.

Ellis put his hands up. "Okay, calm down." He watched me again, and if he was waiting for an apology, he wasn't getting one. "I get it. Sorry," he said. "You *really* do like this one."

"He's not a *this one*." I wasn't entirely sure if Jeremiah was *the one*, but hearing him bein' disrespected really fucking irked me. I picked up the stapler. "Unless you'd like to explain to the ER doctor how this got lodged up your arse, shut the fuck up."

Ellis grinned and sighed. "We're gonna be running double

time trying to get cargo offloaded so the ships can get back out to sea, away from the storm."

I was well-aware. "Yeah."

"Dad said you were at the bureau office when the alert went out. Must have been pretty cool."

I smiled at the memory of Jeremiah in his element, in charge. "It was, yeah."

CHAPTER FOUR

JEREMIAH

Cyclone Hazer.

When the approaching tropical storm's centre reached winds of over sixty-three kilometres per hour, it was given a name. In conjunction with the World Meteorological Organization's Regional Tropical Cyclone Committee, and given the cyclone had technically originated in Indonesia, it was named there.

Which meant I didn't get to allocate the name.

And for that, I was grateful.

I didn't want the responsibility of that. I felt bad enough that I'd been the one to initiate the warning alerts.

Sure, it was exciting and probably what most meteorologists dreamed of, but the danger was real. And knowing it was coming . . .

It wasn't so much excitement as it was dread.

The meteorological world was abuzz with the news, but I didn't want this.

I wanted lightning and thunder. I wanted light shows of fury and power. Not paths of death and destruction.

Knowing Doreen would be arriving at six, I made two

coffees and handed one to her as she walked through the door.

She sipped her coffee and studied the radar screens. "How's it shaping up?"

"Right on track," I said. "Cyclone Hazer."

"T-minus?"

"Still at five days."

She nodded as though she knew this already. "Shit."

"Yep."

We did what needed doing for an hour—comms with the World Cyclone Committee and confirming data with the bureau head office—until Doreen stood up and collected Bruce. "Well, we may as well take shifts for the next few days; no point in us both being here all the time. I'll be back at eight tonight for the graveyard shift, and you can start at six bells tomorrow. How does that sound?"

She didn't wait for me to answer. With another whack to my shoulder, she was gone.

"Sounds great, thanks," I said to the empty room.

Because it *was* a good idea. I was grateful for her being here at all. And while my name was now atop hers on the boss list, we both knew who was calling the shots.

I didn't mind.

It wasn't a power grab. This was an impending natural disaster. It wasn't time for a pissing contest. It was time for all hands on deck and teamwork.

Plus, I liked Doreen.

I liked that she was absolutely no nonsense, no bullshit. A very far cry from my old colleagues in Melbourne. And when this cyclone was over and she went back to retirement, I might even miss the company.

I thought I'd like being on my own. In Melbourne, I'd basically worked on my own anyway, and given this post was a one-person job, I was expecting to be solo.

But since I'd started, I'd had Tully with me almost every

day, sorting out the office, updating the two old box screens above the dash to flatscreen TV's, and getting familiar with the old dashboard itself. Then I'd had Doreen come to help, and . . . for the first time in my career, I'd actually had a co-worker that I liked, that I trusted. That I respected, and who respected me.

It was a nice change, and it reinforced that I'd made the right decision in being here.

Just after nine that morning, a white van pulled into the yard. At first I thought it was a storm-chasing van with the radar and aerials on top, but then I saw the small news logo on the door.

Great.

A woman with a terrible jacket and a microphone got out, followed by the driver who, as it turned out, was also the cameraman. I met them at the door, not knowing what to do or say and wishing to god Doreen was still here. Though the shirt she'd worn today— with a cute cat licking its paw and the words *I lick pussy* on it—would need blurring out on TV, but at least it wouldn't have been me . . .

"Can I help you?" I asked, coming down the steps to meet them.

"Lindsey Ashley, Channel 4," she said in that voice newsreaders used. "We'd like to speak to someone about the latest cyclone warning and perhaps what our viewers can expect over the next coming days."

"Ah . . ." Dear god. "Well, that'd be me, I guess. I'm the only one here."

"And you are?"

"Doctor Overton, meteorologist. However, I'm sure you can appreciate my time is best spent elsewhere." I gestured back to the door. "This office is run manually, and I have a lot going on right now."

"I won't keep you long," she said, as if I didn't have a choice in it.

The cameraman moved to get a better angle, which was apparently closer.

A lot closer.

"And we're rolling," he murmured.

"Doctor Overton joins us from the Darwin Bureau of Meteorology. We thank you for your time, I understand you're incredibly busy. We believe the initial warning alert came from this office."

The camera trained in on me.

I tried not to be a rabbit in headlights. I kept my eyes on her and not on the camera, cursing Doreen for not being here, with her crude shirt and yappy dog.

And her baseball bat.

"Ah, yes, that's correct," I said.

"What can you tell us about the approaching storm? Cyclone Tracy devastated Darwin in 1974, and the horrors of that are still fresh in the minds of many Darwinians. Will we see a repeat of Cyclone Tracy?"

Don't cause panic, don't cause panic. Just be factual.

"Tracy was a Category 4, and Hazer is shaping up to be a Category 5. The last Cat 5 we saw was Ita, which devastated parts of far north Queensland, though Ita crossed land as a Cat 4 in an unpopulated area and deflected. Hazer is expected to make direct contact with Darwin as a Category 5. We will see rainfalls of anywhere up to five hundred mils, which will cause flooding, and destructive winds of up to two hundred and twenty kilometres per hour. I'm assured there have been construction changes since the seventies to better withstand such destruction, however I would urge all residents to listen to emergency services and police. If you're issued an evacuation order, please heed those warnings. There will likely be disruptions to essential services, so be prepared; stock up on food and water, ensure the safety of any elderly folks in your life and any pets. And if you are able to leave, I would suggest you do so."

She stared at me before blinking a few times, seemingly to collect her thoughts. "That's a grim warning," she said.

I wasn't sure which parts of what I'd said she didn't understand. Was I supposed to sugar-coat it?

"Is there any chance the cyclone will change course?"

I resisted sighing and managed a nod instead. "As with any calculations regarding weather, there is always a chance, and I'll be very happy to be proven wrong in this case. But as it stands now, we can expect the storm to begin its approach with torrential rain and strong wind gusts. Hazer is on track to hit Darwin in the morning five days from today. Any changes will be updated as they happen, and the public will be notified as a priority."

A radar started to beep inside and I took that as my cue. "Thank you for your time," I said, making it up two steps before she stopped me.

"Doctor Overton," she said. "Can you tell us what to expect?"

I thought I already had.

"We've had other cyclone warnings in Darwin before," she said, "that never amounted to much, and there tends to be complacency—"

Out of patience, I looked straight at the camera. "This will be a *significant* weather event. Listen to emergency service announcements. If you don't need to be here, don't be here."

I turned then and went inside, locking the door behind me. I didn't have time to dwell on how badly that interview had gone because for the few next hours I had more data, more comms with other agencies, and no time to be concerned with second-rate reporting.

Another news van pulled into the yard, a man in a suit this time knocked on the door, and I ignored them.

And then my phone began to ring with unknown numbers. How they got my number, I'll never know. I could only assume they got my name from the interview I'd done earlier . . . The first few callers claimed to be with some news channels I'd not heard of—which I declined to comment for—and after a while, I switched my phone to silent.

After that, in my little dark office, doing a dozen things at once, I completely lost track of time. It wasn't until a familiar Range Rover pulled into the yard that I checked my watch. It was after six. But then a not-familiar man got out of the car.

I did a double take on the security camera.

I mean, he was familiar.

But oh boy, did he look different.

Tully took the steps two at a time and I dashed to unlock the door before he could try to open it. I swung the door inward and looked him up and down. "Uh, hello, stranger," I said. "While you *are* incredibly gorgeous, I won't be buying anything you're selling as I already have a boyfriend."

His smile quirked upward, confused. "What?"

I gestured to his suit pants, lace-up shoes, and crisp white button-down shirt, his hair pulled back into a small ponytail. "Who are you and where is the Tully who wears old clothes and no shoes?"

He rolled his eyes. "I told you I wear proper clothes to work. Do you not like it?"

I glanced down at how his shirt was tucked in at his narrow waist, how the column of his neck looked against the open collar. His hair . . . pulled back. "Oh yes. As I said, gorgeous. But I like the shorts with the rip in them and the threadbare shirt just as much."

He grinned, and his voice dropped to a sultry whisper. "And I like it when you turn down handsome strangers because you have a boyfriend."

He looked at my mouth and licked his lips, stepping in for a kiss.

I pulled him in, then closed and locked the door behind him. He leaned up against the wall and pulled me against him, his hand on my hip. "My sexy and smart boyfriend was all over the news today. On the TV and everything."

Well, that was a mood killer.

"Oh god." I sighed. "Was I terrible? I wasn't expecting an interview and I hadn't prepared anything, and she asked me stupid questions. Then I had more people turn up and so many phone calls I turned my phone off."

He took my hand and studied my fingers. "I know. I called several times. I was coming to see if you were okay. I was worried."

"I'm sorry," I whispered. I cupped his face and kissed him softly. "I've been so busy."

"I assumed that was the case, but still . . . I had to come and see if you were okay." He pulled me against him again, his back against the wall, his hand snaking up from my hip to my jaw, and he brought my face in for another kiss.

A deeper kiss, open mouths and a taste of his tongue.

Damn.

He made me forget where I was, what I was supposed to be doing. I almost forgot how to breathe.

Until my stomach growled so loud it made him laugh.

"Hungry for something?" he murmured, his lips wet and swollen.

"Yes," I breathed, touching my fingertip to his bottom lip. I went to kiss him some more, but then my stomach growled again, and he held my face, his smile now gone.

"What did you eat today?"

"Oh, I uh . . ." Uh oh. "I forgot. I was busy and I . . ."

He sighed and pinched my chin between his thumb and forefinger. "You need to look after yourself," he chastised warmly. "You have to remember to eat. I know you're busy and you're stressed but, Jeremiah, you'll be no good to anyone if you're sick."

I opened my mouth to argue, because I could damn well look after myself, just as something on the console started to beep. He sighed again and squeezed my hand. "I'll be back with some dinner." He went to open the door and found it locked, giving me a puzzled look.

"Reporters and . . . just people in general, really."

He chuckled as he let himself out. "I'll be back."

I didn't remember to say thank you until he'd already gone. I wasn't used to having someone look after me, and I made a mental note to make more of an effort.

I switched off the beeping noise and uploaded the latest data to the news feed. The fact I still had to do this manually was a testament to the age of this gear, and after this cyclone, if this building still stood, I'd officially be requesting a full upgrade.

When Tully came back with a bag of takeout, he sat in Doreen's chair and I reached over and squeezed his hand. "Thank you," I said. "I didn't mean to sound ungrateful before. I appreciate everything you do. I'm not used to having anyone look out for me, so my first knee-jerk reaction is to be defensive, and I want you to know that's not a reflection on you, but rather on myself."

He studied me for a quick second before he wheeled his chair over and gave me a quick kiss. "I know. But thank you for saying that."

"I'm very new to this, and I'm set in my ways. And I would never mean to offend you or take you for granted, so if you ever feel disrespected or unappreciated, please tell me. What might be glaringly obvious to other people is somewhat lost on me, and I just want you to know that." I cringed. "That you will probably have to tell me to stop every once in a while to remove my head from my arse."

"Oh, don't worry. I'll tell ya." He grinned at me. "But thank you. I know it ain't easy for you. I'm more of a let's-talk-about-our-feelings kinda guy, and the idea of doin' that makes you wanna die. I get it. There's nothin' wrong with it. It's just how we were raised."

I opened my mouth to argue that point, but everything he'd said was the truth.

He shrugged. "So I just hafta be extra mushy with you until you're used to it."

I snorted. "Excellent."

"But it did feel good to hear you call me your boyfriend." He gave me one of his killer smiles and handed me a takeout container. "Now eat something or I will get mad."

It smelled so good, and I only truly noticed then just how hungry I was. He'd bought us each a gyros snack pack, which was basically shaved gyros beef over fries with Greek yoghurt dressing and a mix of salad.

It was the best thing I'd ever eaten.

I was half done the first time I looked up to find him smiling at me. "You were starving."

"Mm," I hummed with a mouth full of food. "So good."

He laughed and stabbed some meat and fries with his fork. "So before, when I said you were on the news," he said. "I do mean on every local channel. And on the radio on my way to the kebab shop just now."

Ugh.

I rolled my eyes and groaned. "It's embarrassing. Though I've since mastered the 'I'm unavailable for comment at this time. Please stay tuned to the bureau's weather channel for updates' spiel. I didn't really think how official my comment would be. I'm not used to managing press releases."

His eyes softened. "You did great. You didn't mince your words at all."

I grimaced. "Was I too blunt? My forthrightness tends to land me in hot water." I shrugged. "But I don't see the point in sugar-coating anything, especially when talking about the severity of the storm that's coming. I know it's not my place to issue warnings in regard to evacuations and such, but she asked me what the residents of Darwin can expect. Rightfully, they should expect to evacuate."

Then I looked at him.

Oh.

"You should leave," I added with a lump of dread quickly solidifying in my belly. "You and your family. Do what you need to do with your shipping—"

"I'm not leaving."

"Tully, it's a reasonable response. There's no reason why you should stay behind. If you have the opportunity and the means to leave, you should."

His brown eyes met mine, curious and a little hurt. "Are you leaving?" he asked.

"No, I can't," I replied, gesturing to the control panels. "I have to stay."

"Then so do I." His eyes met mine, scrutinising and unblinking. "And I do have a reason to stay."

"Take your family with you—"

"Not my family, Jeremiah," he said brusquely. "You."

"I'm not worth it—"

"I beg your fuckin' pardon?!"

That stopped me so hard, I recoiled. "Pardon?"

"Don't sit there and tell me you're not worth it. Worth what, Jeremiah? What aren't you worth, exactly? What is your life not worth?"

Oh, wow.

He was actually mad at me.

"I didn't mean it like that," I mumbled, now looking at my half-eaten dinner, having lost all appetite. "I just meant . . ."

He put his container on the control panel desk, then took mine and put it there too. He took my hands and wheeled us so that our knees were touching. "Jeremiah, look at me."

My eyes met his, and where I'd expected to see anger, there was only sadness. "I'm sorry," I murmured quickly.

"You are worth staying for."

His eyes were full of sincerity. It was a little difficult for me to understand that he would want to stay for me.

"What I meant was that if you stay for me, if you stay behind *because of* me, and if something were to happen to you, I'd never forgive myself. Never."

He pulled my chair a little closer. "Then we need to make sure nothing happens to either of us."

"It's easy to say that, but Tully, this storm could be bad. And I mean *bad*."

He smirked. "I know. I watched your interview."

I rolled my eyes. "I mean it. I would be worried for you and your family. I've never been through a cyclone before. I know theoretically what to expect, but firsthand . . ." I shook my head.

"My parents have a cyclone-proof cellar, so they'll be fine. They'll take everyone in, including the old couple next door. They'll all be fine," he said. "I'll be here with you."

I stared at him. "No you won't." I looked around at the room. "Tully, this place is old, and god knows how it'll hold up."

"So why is it safe enough for you but not for me?"

"Because . . . well . . ." Damn. "That's not my point."

He laughed. "And you're forgetting one thing."

"What's that?"

"Storms are my thing. I love them."

"Yes, storms, Tully. Not cyclones."

"But I get to be here at ground zero with all the latest techn—" He glanced at the prehistoric radars. "Well, with all of last century's latest technology."

"My point exactly. It's crazy to expect you to be here."

"But I get to be here with you." His gaze met mine, all humour gone. "And maybe I am crazy. I know it sounds like it because we've known each other for just a few weeks, but, Jeremiah," he tapped my chest, "you're my kind of crazy."

His words made my heart knock against my ribs. His words, the way he looked at me, the way he always had to touch me. It made me shake my head. "I don't get it."

"Don't get what?"

"I see you and the way you look at me. I'm not stupid. I know you like me. I can see that." I ran my hand through my hair, embarrassed.

He snorted. "Yeah, of course. You're my boyfriend. I'm supposed to like you."

"But I don't get why," I whispered. "I'm waiting for the punchline or something. I don't know. I'm usually the butt of the jokes, and you're gorgeous and rich. You could have literally anyone you wanted."

He frowned at me, and from the hurt in his eyes, I knew I'd offended him. "Tully, I—"

"You know what," he said. "This is new to me too. This whole being in a relationship thing, having a boyfriend, it's all new to me. I ain't ever done this before and I feel so in over my head. I want to spend every second with you. I wanna touch you and kiss you all the fuckin' time. It gives me butterflies." He shook his head. "But if you don't feel the same . . . if I came on too strong or if you felt pressured because you got lumped here—"

I fisted his shirt, pulled him in, and kissed him, but when we broke apart, he still wouldn't look at me. God, I was going to have to say this stuff out loud. "You give me butterflies too," I whispered. "I don't know what I feel because I've never felt this before. The way you look at me, the way you hold me, it scares me because I've never . . ." I put my forehead to his chin. "It's all new to me too. But if you feel this—" I took his hand and placed it over my heart. "—then I feel the same as you."

His eyes met mine, an ocean of umber and honey. He leaned in and slowly pressed his lips to mine. "Thank you." He smiled so serenely. "I needed to hear that. And you think you can't be all mushy and shit. Look at you just now. Extra mush."

"I wasn't kidding about feeling my heart," I mumbled. "I actually feel lightheaded after saying that."

He laughed and a loud knock at the door startled us both. "I gave my key back, ya know," Doreen yelled.

I scrambled to let her in. "I'm so sorry. I didn't see you come in on the security camera."

She barged in with Bruce under one arm. "You two weren't testing the structural integrity of the control panel, were ya? Both look a little flustered."

"Uh, no," I began.

"I wanted to," Tully said cheerfully, "but he shot me down."

I was going to object, but she wasn't paying me any attention. She looked him up and down. "Jeez. You scrub up okay, doncha? Wouldn't have recognised ya if it weren't for your flash car out the front."

He grinned. "Love your shirt."

Her shirt tonight had three big Scrabble tiles across the front. *V*, *A*, and *G*.

Because of course it did. It was better than *pussy licker*, though.

Doreen laughed. "Thought I better wear a nice one in case anyone wants to interview me." Then she looked at me. "Not like Mr Significant Weather Event celebrity here."

I groaned. "Ugh. Don't remind me."

"It's the new catch phrase, apparently," Doreen said. She took her seat at the control panel. "Lock the gate on yer way out."

Okay then. That was our cue to leave.

I gave Doreen back her keys, we collected our half-eaten dinner, and Tully followed me home. I wasn't sure if we'd be continuing our conversation from before or if we'd said all that needed saying up to this point.

But he really did like me. He got butterflies because of me.

As I did because of him. When he smiled at me, when he put his arms around me, when he kissed me.

It was a powerful feeling, knowing someone liked me. That *he* liked me. That this incredible man—who was miles out of my league—felt the same way about me. I wasn't kidding when I said he could have anyone . . . but for some reason he chose me.

Walking into his house, he turned the TV on, then took two beers out of the fridge and handed me one. He nodded to the balcony.

He slipped his fingers through mine and led me outside. There was a storm on the horizon. I'd been watching the radars all day, so I knew it would be brief, but there was lightning activity over the ocean.

"Ah, perfect timing," he said.

We stood there, his arm around me, his chin on my shoulder, sipping our beers, and we watched as the intracloud light show lit up the skies above, as the wind whipped around us, the smell of rain filled the air. But when some negative charge bolts hit the ocean closer to us, he pulled me inside. "I'm not risking you today, sorry," he said.

A furious downpour of rain battered the balcony the second he closed the door behind us. "Ooh, that was close," he said with a laugh.

But then his eyes cut to the television behind me. "Look, it's you!"

I turned, and sure enough, there I was on some daily news update show, where the hosts talked about daily current affairs. I understood the cyclone was an important news update, and I was interested to hear what they said after my segment.

Did they take me seriously?

Had people started evacuation plans? Were they heading south already?

I sure hoped so. I wanted them to talk about it. I wanted

them to push the importance of listening to emergency services and to evacuate if possible.

I took a swig of my beer and waited to see what they discussed.

"All seriousness aside, and we will get to the crux of the report in a moment," one host said. "How blue are his eyes?"

"I know!" the other host said, almost coming out of her seat. "Like sooo blue."

"Freakishly blue."

Jesus fucking Christ.

My heart sank, and shame washed over me.

Tully turned the TV off, tossing the remote onto the couch and pulling me against the kitchen counter. He took my beer and sat them both on the sink, then cupped his hands to my face, his nose touching mine.

"I'm sorry," he murmured. "It's just a stupid talk show. Don't pay any attention to them. They don't know what they're talking about."

"I've heard it all my life," I mumbled. "I'm used to it. I should get contacts. Brown, like yours."

"No, baby," he whispered. "I love your eyes. They're beautiful, and they're part of you. People can fuck right off. You don't change a single thing, 'kay?"

I couldn't look at him. "I'll never be taken seriously. Not ever. I deliberately didn't give my full name, because you know what comes next." I pressed my forehead to his chest, to his neck. "I'm sure all the guys at my old job think it's hilarious."

Tully wrapped his arms around me, holding me tight, so tight it was a little hard to breathe.

It felt so good.

"Fuck them," he said. "Fuck all of them. When they come knockin' next time for information or updates, tell them to fuck off."

"I already stopped taking calls," I mumbled into his neck. "I just want to do my job."

He somehow held me tighter, and we stayed like that in his kitchen for a long while, just holding each other in the dark while the storm raged on outside. Rain pelted the windows, lightning strobed the room, flashes of light in the dark.

So very fitting.

He kept our hips flush but pulled back so he could see my face. He traced his finger down my cheekbone, then thumbed my bottom lip. "You're perfect," he whispered before he kissed me.

Soft and deep. God, the way he kissed me . . . perfect, plump lips and a tangle of tongues, he showed me what perhaps he thought his words couldn't convey.

He kissed me like maybe he loved me.

Then taking my hand, he took me to bed.

CHAPTER FIVE
TULLY

I woke up when Jeremiah slipped out of bed. The sun was comin' through the windows because I'd forgotten to close the blinds last night.

God, last night.

It'd sure been something . . .

I was gonna need more gold star stickers.

While Jeremiah showered, I made coffee and toast, so at least I knew he'd eat something before he got busy all day and forgot to eat again.

He came down the stairs, dressed for work, his hair wet and smellin' all kinds of lovely. "What are you doing up?"

I handed him a cup of coffee and pushed the plate of toast toward him. "For you."

He seemed genuinely perplexed, like he did whenever I did anything nice for him. "Oh. Did you get out of bed to do this for me?"

I nodded and bit into my toast. "I was going to suggest a repeat of what we did last night but didn't want you to be late to relieve Doreen. Breakfast was option number two."

He smiled as he sipped his coffee. "Yeah, I'd rather face a nest of news reporters than an irate Doreen."

I was hopin' he'd forgotten about that. "A nest, huh? Like vipers."

"Similar." He took his toast, kissed my cheek, then my temple. "Thank you for breakfast."

"Thank you for last night."

He blushed and tried to laugh it off. "You take half the credit."

"I do regret that we didn't try out the chest monitor."

His lips twisted in a thoughtful pout. "Maybe we could try it tonight. You know, purely for scientific purposes."

I grinned at him. "That's my kind of science."

He smiled as he got to the door and stopped. "You should probably wear another gold star on your shirt today."

I laughed, surprised that he'd even mention it. "Oh I will. You should wear one too. Want me to run upstairs to get you one?"

"No, it's fine."

"I'm makin' a mental note to leave an emergency sheet of gold stickers downstairs."

He smiled. "Have a good day."

"I'm already havin' a great day."

He blushed again and ducked his head as he left, and with a happy sigh, I took my coffee and went out to the balcony. It was hard to imagine, lookin' out at the peaceful ocean to the north and the clear skies, that a massive storm was on its way.

It was hard to imagine that I was standing out there wearing nothing but boxers, smilin' at the sunrise.

I'd never been this happy.

I'd never been in love before.

And that's what this was. Stupid, far too soon, but love all the same. I'd fallen headfirst, with my whole heart, for Jeremiah.

And maybe it was too soon to admit such things. I'd

already told him I liked him, that he made me feel all swoopy inside, and it made me happy to be with him.

He said he felt the same, pressing my hand above his heart. He'd finally admitted he had feelings for me, and it just did something to me.

It solidified something that I already knew.

I was so in love with him.

Not even just a little bit, but the whole way, in over my head, smiley-giddy-stupid love.

And I didn't care who knew or what anyone else thought.

I noticed my neighbour, old prudy Mrs Caddel, on her balcony in her expensive robe givin' me a scowl of disdain. Oh yes, how dare I stand on my own balcony in boxer shorts? She was lucky I was wearing anything at all.

I lifted my coffee in her direction. "Morning!"

She gave a curt nod and disappeared inside, and I snorted. I hoped she could see the scrape along my ribs to my nipple, the half hickey, half toothmark, where Jeremiah had latched onto me as he came.

A battle wound of the very best kind.

Aaaand my mind was back to everything he'd done to me last night.

Christ.

I downed my coffee and took a long, very handsy shower, wishin' it was Jeremiah—imagining it was his hand and not mine—and went to work in a very good mood.

Not even Ellis' shit-stirring digs at my smile could ruin this day.

Not even Rowan and Zoe's curious disdain.

I took my coffee and decided to answer emails and return some calls before spendin' the afternoon boarding up windows. That was the plan. I'd have to probably call into the supermarket at some point, I realised.

I probably should have done that before now.

I checked my watch. It was just on half eight. Hmm, maybe Ellis needed to go too. I picked up my desk phone and buzzed his office, but as I waited for him to pick up, my mobile phone rang.

It was Ellis, and I laughed as I answered, thinkin' he must be stuck on hold with some pain-in-the-arse customer on his desk phone. But before I could speak, he said, "Cafeteria, now."

There was no joke, no smart-arse comment. Clipped and serious.

I jumped to my feet and dashed for the cafeteria where several people—including my parents and siblings—were watchin' the TV on the wall. It was only ever on some morning show bullshit that I never had time for, but what I saw stopped me cold.

"It's all over the news," Ellis said.

It was Jeremiah's interview from yesterday. Half the screen was his face frozen, his blue eyes unmistakable. Then the other half of the screen played the very familiar footage of his mother on Collins Street, the tramline being struck by lightning, her doing that macabre dance, his stroller rolling away. Then it showed a policeman carrying a crying toddler, a small boy with dark hair and very, very blue eyes.

The screen froze, Jeremiah's face on both sides of the screen. From yesterday and from all those years ago.

Jesus fucking Christ.

What he'd said last night came back to me.

I never said my full name because you know what comes next.

He was exactly right. He knew. He *knew* this would happen.

"Those motherfuckers," I said, feeling a rage explode within me. An anger like I'd never known.

"Is that really him?" Ellis asked. "Was that his mother?"

I managed to look at him, at all the faces now watching

me. And despite how angry I was, I was hurt for Jeremiah so much more. This was going to kill him. "Yes, that's him. I need to go."

I turned and ran, only stopping to grab my keys and phone from my desk, and I raced to my car.

Fuck all those arseholes.

Christ.

When Jeremiah had said he has to relive his mother dying every time that footage was played, I never really understood . . .

Until now.

How dare they.

How fucking dare they.

I sped the whole way to his work. I was way past caring. And of course there were news vans parked at the gate, which was, thankfully, locked.

At least they weren't banging on his door.

I skidded the Rover to a stop, maybe a little too close to them, gaining the attention of every reporter and camera there. I got out and slammed my door, getting madder by the damn second.

They weren't here for emergency news updates. They were here for nothin' but gossip.

"You wanna be careful," one cameraman said, nodding his chin to my car.

I spun and pointed my finger at him. "And you might wanna watch your fuckin' mouth."

No, *now* I had their complete and undivided attention.

"You all come here for what?" I asked. "This office is trying to do a job, obtaining information that will save lives, and you're all here for fuckin' what? You wanna broadcast footage of a mother dying in front of her kid, for ratings, then expect him to, what? Come out for an interview? Every single one of you can fuck right off. You want news? Go back to your offices and wait for official bulletin releases. Or do what they suggested yesterday and leave Darwin—and just keep fucking drivin'."

I noticed a few of them look behind me, into the yard, their eyes widening. And when I glanced back, I saw why.

Doreen was coming across the yard, whistling a cheerful tune, and swingin' her baseball bat, just as two police cruisers arrived. "Right on time," Doreen said as she walked up, still swingin' her bat. "If any of you leeches had a fuckin' brain cell between ya's, you'd know blocking access to a government building is a *big* no-no."

The cops got out, and while they began to speak to the reporters, asking them to move along, Doreen opened the gate for me.

The reporters and cameramen slowly dispersed, but not before giving me a lengthy glare and getting in their vehicles.

"Thanks, Hewy," Doreeen said.

One of the cops, the oldest of them, gave her a nod. "No worries, Dori. You weren't actually gonna use that bat, were ya?"

"Nah." She winked. "Nice day for a home run, doncha reckon?"

He grinned and went back to the remaining reporters, and I looked up at Doreen. "How is he?"

She shrugged her reply, meaning not great.

So I ran across the yard and up the stairs. I pulled open the door and found him at the control panel. He'd surely been watching the security screen and seen it all. And all the anger I'd felt, that rage that had fuelled me, melted away.

"Hey," I said gently.

His eyes met mine.

"You okay?"

"I'm fine."

No, he wasn't.

I went over and spun his chair so I could kneel in front of him. "Jeremiah, baby, it's okay to not be okay."

He sagged and gave the slightest shake of his head. "I knew it would happen. It's like a shadow I won't ever be rid of."

I put my hand to his face. "I'm so sorry. I came as soon as I saw."

He closed his eyes. "Doreen went home, got a news flash on her phone, and came straight back," he murmured. "She thought it was just going to be the interview, so she watched it. She knew . . . she didn't think I should be here alone. She didn't have to come back . . ."

I knew I liked her for a reason.

"Thank god she did." With my hand at the back of his neck, I tugged him forward and all but lifted him to his feet so I could hug him properly. "I'm so fucking mad," I hissed. "I can't imagine how you feel."

"Just . . . sad."

I hugged him tighter and rubbed the back of his head. "I got you."

He nodded against my throat but didn't say anything for a few beats. "Thank you," he said, so softly. So sad. "I've never had anyone care before."

I pulled back and put my forehead to his. "I care. A whole fuckin' lot."

Doreen came through the door, stood the bat up in the small entryway, and Jeremiah immediately stepped away from me. I didn't care what Doreen thought, and I knew for a fact she wouldn't care. I kept my hand on his back so he'd know I wasn't going anywhere.

"Well, me and Bruce'll be off now," she said.

I hadn't even noticed the dog.

"Stay with him," she said to me, nodding to Jeremiah.

"I plan to. Thank you for coming back."

I also only just noticed that her fresh shirt had *read my lips* written on it with a somewhat artistic image of a vulva on it. Yeah, there was no way they were showing any footage of that on the news. Not without a lot of pixelating.

"Gonna grab some shuteye. I'll lock the gate on my way out, and I'll be back at eight tonight." She scooped up Bruce. "And Tully, I heard what you said to those leeches out the front. Good for you. If they come back, don't be scared to swing that bat around."

Oh. Yeah, I probably wouldn't do that. But then I remembered how angry I'd been. Maybe I would . . .

Then, on her way out, she peered closer to the radar. "Yeah, he ain't slowin' down any. If you're stickin' around, how about boardin' the place up a bit? There's some pieces cut to size from last time."

I nodded. "Sure. I'll be here."

"Good lad."

And with that, she was gone.

Jeremiah all but fell into his chair. "You don't have to stay," he mumbled.

I lifted his chin and leaned down to peck his lips. "I'm not leaving."

I pulled over Bruce's chair and parked my arse in it, then studied the radar screen and in particular the very large, somewhat circular cloud band moving in our direction. "Sooo," I said brightly. "This doesn't look good."

Jeremiah almost smiled. "Yeah. As Doreen said, it's not slowing down any. In fact, it's just gathering steam."

"Still on track for here?"

He nodded. "Dead on."

One of the other screens started to beep and he had to switch something over to something else and relay some data stream to another office, and for a guy who'd never seen a dash as old as this just a short while ago, he was all over it now.

"I should look and see what I can board your windows up with," I said, gettin' up. I went to move past him to the far end where all the ancient field equipment was—I was sure I'd seen planks of plyboard there at some point—and he grabbed my hand.

"Thank you," he murmured. "I didn't mean to sound ungrateful before."

I squeezed his hand. "You didn't."

He sighed. "I should probably call my dad."

My heart sank for him. "Okay. Want me to sit with you while you speak to him?"

He did smile then, somewhat sad but laced with gratitude. "No, it's fine."

"I'll be here, just showing off my handyman skills." I gently lifted his chin and kissed him. "I'm not leaving."

He nodded, a little happier now. "Thank you."

I left him to it. Albeit I couldn't go far; the office was tiny and there really wasn't anywhere *to* go. And the windows that needed boarding up were small. One in the toilet room and one long narrow one under the eaves. The office was basically a dark cave. But I found the plyboard Doreen had mentioned and a drill that was so old it needed to be plugged into a power outlet.

There was a steel ladder fixed to the back of the building, which was incredibly helpful, given all the aerials and satellites on the small roof area, though it was so hot in the Darwin sun, it almost seared straight through my hand when I grabbed it.

I went back in, grabbed Jeremiah's keys and moved the Jeep over, and stood on the hood instead.

He had his phone pressed to his ear when I went in, though he wasn't talking. I could hear the mumble of his father's voice, and Jeremiah was frowning.

I hated that he had to live with this.

It wasn't his fault. He'd done nothin' wrong. In fact, he'd

done the *right* thing by issuing a statement when asked of the dangers of the coming storm when that reporter had asked.

I guess he'd learned a lesson though, as the new boss of the Darwin office. To never give those arseholes anything. Issue all statements via bulletins and offer no interviews, ever. And if any of 'em ever needed anything—anything at all—it'd be a flat fucking no.

It took me a while to get the boards in place and fixed to the window frames. Doreen wasn't kidding when she said she thought the boards were the ones used last time. I wasn't sure when the last time was, but they were old and this would be their last use.

Everything at this office was outdated, like they'd been forgotten when every other Bureau of Meteorology office probably had state of the art gear.

I had to wonder how that made Jeremiah feel.

Had they shoved him in this post so he'd be forgotten too? Probably.

I hated them all.

I went back in, determined to try and brighten his day. Before I could ask him how the phone call with his father went, he nodded to my phone where I'd left it on the console.

"Your phone buzzed a lot," he said.

I gave his shoulder a squeeze. "How was your dad?" I sat down and picked up my phone.

His only reply was a shrug.

I had three missed calls from Ellis and a text message.

> Ah bro, you're in the shit now. Call back.

Then a few minutes after that, I had two missed calls from my father and one text. And he *never* texted.

> You need to call me. Now.

Shit.

"Well, this isn't good," I mumbled, showing Jeremiah the text, and hit Call. "Dad," I said. "It's me."

He sighed. Not a relieved sigh, but a disappointed one. "I take it you've seen the news?"

"Yeah, I did. That's why I came to see Jeremiah. I was with you in the cafeteria—"

"Not that news. The latest news."

Cold prickled at my scalp. "No. Why, what happened?"

"Just you, ranting and swearing at the news reporters at the bureau office?"

"That was on the news?" I didn't remember any of them filming.

"Yes, it was on the news," Dad hissed at me. "There was a lot of words beeped out, which I should probably be grateful for."

I made a disgusted sound. "You know what? Fuck them. They deserved everything I said, and I'm not sorry."

"You should be sorry!" he said, a little too loudly. It reminded me of when he'd get mad at us kids for doing something stupid. He hadn't yelled at me like that in years. *Shit, he is really mad.* "Tully, do me a favour and look down at the shirt you're wearing. And tell me what the *hell you were thinking!*"

I looked down at my shirt . . . at my work shirt, with our company logo across my left pec.

Oh no.

"Oh shit," I mumbled, covering it with my hand—what good it did now was anyone's guess. "Oh fu . . . Dad, I'm sorry. I didn't realise. I didn't think. I was just so freakin' mad at what they'd done, and then when I saw them all lined up at the gate like wolves at the door." My eyes met Jeremiah's. "I'll issue an apology on behalf of the company, or—"

"You'll do no such thing," my father said. He was definitely in boss mode now. "You'll not say another word. I don't care if they shove a camera in your face, you will keep your head down. Say no comment, or better yet, say nothing at all."

Hmm.

Yeah, I don't think so.

Anger flared in my belly, burning hot in my chest.

"You know what, Dad?" I said. "I fucked up and I'm sorry for that. But if those leeches come for Jeremiah again, I won't keep my head down, and I won't keep my mouth shut."

Jeremiah slid his hand onto my knee and shook his head, silently telling me no.

It only solidified my resolve. "What they did was wrong, Dad," I continued. "Where's their accountability? Where's their apology to him? And I won't apologise for what I said or how I said it because for that, I'm not fuckin' sorry."

"Tully—" he snapped, but my mother's softer tone cut him off.

"Tully," she said, "for what it's worth, personally, we agree with you. But professionally, we now have a media PR circus to deal with, on top of emergency shipping offloads, fast-tracking quarantine regs, clearing the docks, and battening down hatches."

I sighed, running my hand through my hair. I felt bad enough, but gawd, a mother's disappointment weighed too damn much.

"I'm sorry," I whispered.

"What time will you be home?" she asked.

"After eight," I replied. "I'm not leaving Jeremiah here by himself."

Jeremiah frowned at me. "I'll be okay, you can go if you need," he whispered, just as another alert came through that he had to switch the alarm off for.

"Then we'll be at your place after eight," Mum said. "We'll bring dinner."

I wasn't sure what to say. What could I say? Not that it mattered, because the line went dead. I tossed my phone onto the control panel. "Fuck."

"What happened?" Jeremiah asked. "I heard most of what your father said, sorry. He spoke rather loudly."

I sighed again. "My little tirade at those fuckers at the gate this morning made the news."

"Oh."

I pointed to the company logo on my chest. "With some prime-time advertising, apparently."

His eyes widened with realisation. "Oh no."

"Yeah. Anyway, my parents will be at my place when we get there. So that's gonna be a lot of fun. I mean, it's not the arse-reaming I had in mind for tonight. My father is pissed." Not sure what else I could do, I stood up and ran both hands through my hair. "Fuck!"

Jeremiah stood up and took my hand. "Hey," he breathed. "I'm sorry. I didn't—"

"It's not your fault. I lost my cool at those reporters. I was so fuckin' mad for what they did to you. While I was wearing my father's company name on my shirt."

His brow furrowed as we studied my knuckles. "It seems a day for both of us to disappoint our fathers."

Oh god. The phone call he had with his dad . . .

I sagged and pulled him into my arms. He slid against me easily, our arms holding each other like interlocking parts.

It felt so good.

His embrace, his touch, soothing away my pain and anger, was healing me in real time. I held him tighter, not wanting to let go.

Not now, not ever.

"Was your dad okay?"

He hummed a non-committal sound. "Same as always. He said it wasn't my fault while also implying I should know better."

"I'm sorry," I murmured.

He tried to pull back, but I kept him held fast. "Mm-mm," I mumbled. I wanted to help him forget the shitty morning we'd had, so keeping my arms around him, I sat myself down slowly on the console dash, leaning against it while holding onto him. It really was the perfect height . . .

"Hmm," I hummed against his neck. "You could fuck me on this." I lifted one leg as proof.

He chuckled and managed to pull back a little. His hips were still flush to mine, so I didn't object too much. "Maybe if we didn't have a life-threatening weather event aiming right at us."

"Ooh." I smiled. "That wasn't a no."

He gripped my other thigh and lifted it, pressing me hard against the controls. "No, it wasn't a no."

"Damn. Maybe we could see how many alarms we can set off and how many weather warnings we can issue across the Territory. We could keep a whiteboard with our different scores on it for each time."

He chuckled, and our attempt at joking our way out of our miseries seemed to have worked. Him pushing against all my best spots didn't hurt either. I didn't even mind the buttons and switches pressing into my back.

He rested his forehead on mine and gave me a soft kiss. "Thank you for being here."

I pecked his lips with a smile. "Don't thank me yet. We have to get through dinner with my folks first. If you still want to thank me after that, I'll take payment in sexual grati-*fuck*-ation."

He smirked. "I'm almost certain that's not how that word sounds."

"Pretty sure it is."

And of course, the data feed for something or other began to buzz, and after that it was a weather warning for the top east corner of the state with high precipitation forecast, and then it was an alert for cattle graziers in the bottom part of the Territory because of possible flash flooding in usually dry riverbeds.

It just never stopped. And it was for all of the Northern Territory, a land area twice the size of Texas. He had a lot to cover, and it wasn't just the monstrous cloud band swirling its way toward us that he had to work around. It was all kinds of weather.

Needless to say, it was a busy day for him.

I just got to sit there and watch him be awesome. I fed him and kept him watered, and I texted intermittently with my brother who just loved that I was the one in my parents' bad books for a change.

I was so not lookin' forward to tonight.

When Doreen arrived a bit before eight, I almost wanted to tell her that she could go home, that we'd stay instead . . . but I had to face the music, and quite frankly, Jeremiah needed some downtime. He needed some rest.

I just had to make sure he got that, and not a standoff between me and my parents.

I didn't see any reporters on my way home, and I was going to tell Jeremiah that I'd take a different route to him— because reporters couldn't follow us both—when I realised I didn't care if they saw us go home together.

In fact, I kinda hoped they would.

Yeah, clearly I was still in the pissed-off and defensive stage.

When we got to my house, it wasn't just my parents who were already there, but my two brothers' cars were there as well.

And that little seed of anger and defensiveness sprouted into a whopping tree of rage.

Was this a whole family meeting? Were they all going to

stare at me and give me the 'we're so disappointed' lectures? Because I wasn't about to cop that.

I got out of my car and held Jeremiah's door for him. He saw me glaring at the offending cars, and he nodded toward them before the roller door blocked them from view. "Who else is here?" he asked.

"Ellis," I replied. "And Rowan."

"Oh." He looked uncomfortable. "Your eldest brother's here too?"

The brother I wasn't particularly close to. "Yeah. Look, Jeremiah, if you want to hang out upstairs, that's fine with me. I'll face the firing squad and—"

"I'm not leaving you," he said, a hint of determination in those incredible eyes.

I couldn't help but smile. "Come on, let's get this over with."

I took his hand and led him in through the laundry to a scene I hadn't expected.

At all.

My mum was in the kitchen. She was cooking something that smelled great, but on the balcony . . . was my dad and two brothers boarding up the glass panels.

"Uh, what's going on?" I asked, surprised. Shocked, if I was being honest.

Mum looked up from the dishes of food and gave us a smile. "We figured you'd been so busy you wouldn't have had time to take care of your house. I used your spare key." She walked over, took Jeremiah's arm, and led him into the kitchen. "Tully, go help your brothers. And behave yourself. There's a drill and a nail gun involved, and quite frankly, I don't want to explain any intentional mishaps to the ER doctors."

Intentional mishaps.

I snorted, still shocked, and seeing Mum enlist Jeremiah into her duty list, I went out onto the balcony.

"Oh, look who it is," Ellis said. "Blister's here. Always shows up after the hard work is done."

"Ellis, hold it straight," Rowan grumbled.

"I am holding it straight," Ellis griped.

Rowan drilled the screw in, then stood back to look at the slightly crooked board. He tried to whack Ellis with the drill. "Shoulda went to Specsavers, dickhead."

"Tully, hold this," Dad said, lifting another board into place. I held it and Dad fired a nail into it. Thank god he had the nail gun and not the other two.

"Oh look, it's the only straight thing Tully's ever done in his life," Ellis said.

I tried to take the nail gun from Dad but he wouldn't give it to me. "For Christ's sake, boys," Dad said. "Ellis and Rowan, go upstairs and start on the bedroom windows."

Ellis, who now had the drill, gave it a few whirrs. "Not the only thing getting drilled in there, huh, Tull?"

I wrestled the nail gun off Dad, but by the time I got my hands on it, Ellis had already laughed his dumb arse up the stairs.

I considered going up after him but thought better of it. With a sigh, I gave it back to Dad. "I could make it look like an accident."

He rolled his eyes. "Get the next board."

I held the plyboard in place, realising that now Dad and I were alone, it was probably a good time to talk.

"Look," I started. "About today. I'm sorry I dragged the business into it. I'm sorry for the shitstorm I created. It negatively impacts you and Mum, and everyone, I guess. I just didn't think. I saw them and I was so freakin' pissed off, I wanted to strangle them. I didn't even think about the shirt I was wearing."

He nailed the board into place. "What's done is done. I accept your apology, and I do understand. Your mother explained it to me, and I get it. At first I was mad because it was reckless and unprofessional, but she told me what was really going on, and she asked me what I'd do if the media treated her like that, and I get it. Yes, it created a media stir, but it's nothing we can't handle. We have a legal team—"

"I'm sorry," I said. But I was also confused. "Mum explained what to you? What's really going on?"

Dad fired another nail into the next corner of the board and looked at me. "That you love him. You were protecting someone you love."

The world tilted a little and blood pounded in my ears.

What?

"Pardon?"

"I mean, we were all kinda shocked with how you behaved with him in front of us. We ain't ever seen you be like that with anyone, all cute and smiling, touchy-feely and whatever." His cheeks ran pink. "I guess I just thought it was . . . fun and exciting, or physical. Or whatever. But you're living together already, so . . ."

None of anything he was saying was making sense.

He studied me. "Ah jeez, Tully," he said. "Are you telling me you don't? Because your mother is a good gauge at these things. You know she said that Rowan would marry Diah from the second he saw her because of some look in his eyes. I dunno, I didn't see it. But she did. Same with Zoe. Said her and Chris'd be married within the year because of the way Zoe looked at him. Guess she saw it in you and the way you look at him. I dunno how these things work, but she hasn't been wrong yet."

I tried to swallow.

"How . . . how did I look at him?"

Dad sighed and gave my shoulder a squeeze. "Are you saying you don't have feelings for him?"

"Yeah, of course I do," I whispered. "I . . . I love him. I haven't told him that yet though, and I didn't expect to hear it from you. But I've never felt like this about anyone. He's . . .

he's amazing, and I want to be with him all the time. The idea of not being with him makes me feel sick. I could spend every minute of every day with him and it's still not enough. I . . . want to do everything I can to make him happy."

Dad smiled at me, a little proud, a little teary. "Sounds like love to me."

CHAPTER SIX

JEREMIAH

DINNER WITH TULLY'S PARENTS AND HIS TWO BROTHERS WAS NOT what I'd been expecting.

I'd been expecting them to rebuke him for the public tirade whilst wearing a company shirt thing. I had been expecting that because Tully had been.

Especially from his father and perhaps Rowan.

But it never came.

Instead, they boarded up all the glass doors and windows while his mother got dinner ready. She made me help, with which I was no help at all, I'm sure. But while we busied ourselves in the kitchen, she asked me about the office and the new job, and if I was happy to have left Melbourne.

She asked me how I was finding Darwin and the terrible heat. She asked me if I actually enjoyed my time at the bunker in the middle of Kakadu or if I was just saying that to make Tully happy.

She was horrified and somewhat dismayed when I told her I'd loved it. That I couldn't wait to go again. She'd sighed dramatically, and said it was no wonder Tully was so smitten with me.

I certainly hadn't been expecting that.

We ate dinner at the dining table, and while it was an informal dinner, I did feel a little scrutinised. Especially by Rowan. He was polite, of course, but he was also curious and asked me about my doctorate and dissertation, and even though it was general conversation, it somehow felt as if I was being interviewed.

To see if I was good enough for his brother.

Ellis had grinned, about to speak, until Tully—while making direct eye contact with Ellis—took the carving knife from the tray of roast chicken and put it beside his plate. A silent threat, but Ellis wisely chose not to make any jokes at our expense.

I didn't have any siblings, or a close family for that matter, so I never had this . . . feeling. Sure, there was antagonism and snarkiness between them, but it was clear they all loved each other very much.

I envied them.

I envied them a great deal.

Though something else I noticed over the course of the evening was Tully's behaviour toward me.

He sat with his hand on my thigh for most of dinner and I caught him looking at me, as if he was trying to figure out a complex equation in his head.

He was still very much himself, but something was different.

Maybe it was just that Rowan and Ellis were sitting oppo-site us, or that his parents were at either end of the table.

They never mentioned the media circus. Not to me, anyway. But I suspected his father had said something on the matter when they were fixing the glass panels on the balcony.

I was still grateful.

Then his father asked me when to expect Hazer's pre-show. He'd been a boy during Cyclone Tracy, apparently. "I remember it all too well," he said.

"As early as tomorrow evening," I said. "The frontal

system will bring the beginning of the storm. Rain, wind gusts, sea swells, as I'm sure with which you're familiar. Hazer will likely be a two-day event, from the first rainfall, beginning to end. The cyclone is expected to touch down at 7:00 am the day after tomorrow. It's difficult to predict its behavioural pattern once it crosses land, but we can make educated projections." They all stared at me, and I tried to lighten the mood. "It's not too late to leave. You'd only have to drive a hundred kilometres south, maybe two. I estimate Hazer will progress east once it hits land. The change of atmospheric pressure will cause the storm front to ride the warmer ocean winds, so effectively it will mow through the coastline toward the Gulf of Carpentaria. It should down-grade in intensity once it hits though, but if you do decide to leave, please take Tully with you. By force if necessary." I looked at Tully and grimaced. I never should have opened my mouth. "I don't believe it's deemed kidnapping if it endeavours to save your life."

Tully chuckled, his eyes warm, and his fingers slid over mine. On the table, in front of them all. "I'm not leaving you," he said simply. "I told you that. And I'm pretty sure kidnapping is still kidnapping."

I noticed Rowan's eyes draw down to our joined hands, and when he glanced up, his focus was solely on Tully. A fond smile softened his features for a moment until Ellis nudged his elbow. "Told ya. He's a goner."

Tully shot him a glare and Mr Larson quickly grabbed the carving knife out of Tully's reach. "So, Jeremiah," Mr Larson said. "Hazer. What kind of name is that?"

"It's an Arabic name, common in Malaysia and Indonesia," I explained. "It means to be prepared, be ready."

They were all staring at me again. "Well, if that's not an omen," Rowan said glumly. Then he sighed. "I should get going. I left Diah to do dinner and put the kids to bed."

"I appreciate you being here," Tully said. "Is your house boarded up?"

He nodded. "Yeah."

"I'll get Jeremiah to work tomorrow and come around to help whoever needs it," he said.

I wanted to argue that I didn't need him to escort me but thought that might be a conversation best left for when we were alone. And the truth was, I really had needed him today . . .

"We should all be going," Mrs Larson said. "Ellis, help me clean this—"

"Please leave it. I'll take care of it," I offered. "It's the least I can do."

She grimaced, as if she wanted to argue but didn't want to offend, and Tully laughed. "Mum, don't argue with him. He's feisty, and he knows really big words."

I levelled a glare at him but it waned with the smile he aimed right at me.

"Gawd," Ellis drawled as he stood up. "Someone save me. The sappiness is killing me."

"Eat shit, nut sac," Tully said.

"Boys," their mother chided. She stood and we all got to our feet as well; then they made their way to the door.

When they were leaving, his mother had given Tully a kiss on the cheek and led him toward their car for a private conversation, I deduced. So, giving them some privacy, I went back inside and began cleaning up dinner.

I was washing up the few things that wouldn't fit in the dishwasher when he came back in. "Everything okay?" I asked.

He leaned against the kitchen counter, took a tea towel, and began drying a tray. "Yeah, yeah." He nodded. "I apologise for Ellis. He's a pain in my arse."

"Your brothers are great. Both of them. I wasn't sure what

to expect of Rowan—I think you made him out to be this big bad guy—but he's very nice. He cares for you a great deal."

Tully seemed to mull that over before he nodded. "I know."

"I think he bears the responsibility of being the eldest child, the one on whose shoulders the company falls."

"I know. I never meant to give you the impression he was a bad guy, sorry." Tully put the tray down and picked up the next. "I was expecting them to rip me a new arsehole when I saw their cars here." He let out a sigh. "Guess maybe that was me knowing I would have deserved it."

"They didn't come to rip you a new one," I said gently. "They came to support you. To rally around you because you'd made a mistake. That just proves what an amazing family you have."

His eyes met mine. "I apologised to my father, and he said . . . some stuff."

"What kind of stuff?"

He looked down at the tray he was holding, and his cheeks tinted pink. "Just . . . stuff I didn't think I was ready to hear from him but I dunno, maybe I am."

"Like what?" I rinsed the bubbles off my hands and dried them on the tea towel he was holding. "About me?"

His eyes cut to mine. "What? Did my mother say something to you?"

So definitely about me then . . .

"Do they not like me?" I suddenly felt a little unwell. "I tried to stop talking at the end there, about the cyclone and maybe kidnapping you, but I was nervous because they were all looking at me—"

"What? No," he said with a laugh, taking my hand. "The opposite, actually. My mum thinks you're great."

"Oh." My stomach was on a seesaw. "Then what is it?"

He looked at our hands, his thumb sweeping nervously across my knuckles, and he smiled and shook his head. He whispered, "I don't know . . . I don't know if I'm ready to say just yet."

Outside, thunder rumbled and a crack of lightning echoed through the sky from a few kilometres away.

We both turned to the balcony, but the glass doors were all boarded up. "This place looks like a prison cell," he mumbled. Taking my hand, he pressed my palm to his lips and his eyes met mine, a different depth to them now. "Take me to bed, Jeremiah. Have your way with me. I want you inside me while the storm rages outside."

Oh.

Well, then.

I lifted his chin and kissed him softly. "Are you sure? After last night—"

Something fierce flickered in his eyes, and there was no doubt.

He was sure.

Still holding his hand, I led him toward the stairs. He hit the light switch on the way, and his room, with the windows all covered with plyboard, was pitch-black. I went to turn the lights on, but he grabbed my arm and pulled me close.

"Go by feel," he murmured.

Oh boy.

My body already on edge, I did what he wanted. I raked my hands up his chest, feeling along his neck so I could undo the top buttons on his polo shirt. I pulled it over his head, quickly cupping his jaw so I could line up a kiss.

I teased his tongue with mine, pulling him in close and skimming my hands down his back and over his arse and back up again. My hands explored and mapped out every inch while I sucked on his tongue.

He fumbled with the button on his pants, and I gripped his hands to stop him. "You said I could have my way," I murmured.

He made a sound that was more groan than gasp. My eyes

had adjusted to the complete darkness, enough that I could see the outline of the side of his face, his eyes, and . . .

And the way he was looking at me.

Not even the darkness could hide that.

I undid his pants and slid my hands under his briefs so I could push them down. He pulled at the buttons on my shirt and then tried for the button on my pants. I wound my fingers around his wrists and stopped him. "Get on the bed," I said.

He groaned again. "Fuck yes."

I stripped out of my clothes while he complied and had to rummage around blindly for the bedside table. "Ow," I said when I caught my finger on the edge of a foil wrapper. Tully chuckled, but it became a moan when I kneeled on the bed, finding one of his feet first and making my way up his leg.

I kissed up his thigh, getting close to his crotch. "Hmm," I hummed, inhaling his scent.

His fingers found my hair. "Don't torture me, please."

"I'm going by feel," I whispered, finding the base of his cock and nudging his balls with my nose. Then I licked a stripe up the underside of his shaft.

"Oh fuck."

Thunder boomed overhead and he pulled on my hair and arched his back. "Jeremiah," he whispered.

Pleading.

I found the lube where I'd thrown it on the bed, and spreading his legs wide, I smeared his hole and pressed a finger into him. He grunted, not a happy sound.

I stopped. "Tully?"

"I need more," he said. "Not your fingers. I need your cock inside me. I need you to fuck me, Jeremiah. No games tonight. I'm serious."

"Tully, I—"

He reached up, blindly grabbed at my face, my neck, and pulled me up to meet him. His legs wrapped around my waist. "What part of 'I need you to fuck me' didn't you understand?" He crushed his mouth to mine for a bruising kiss and rocked his hips up, searching for what he wanted.

What he needed.

With my tongue in his mouth, I lifted his left leg up, my cock sliding against his hole, and he whined. "Do it, just . . . please."

It would have been so easy to push inside him.

Condom . . .

Condom.

Jesus.

Panting, I pulled back and went to my knees. I put that condom on so damn fast I almost injured myself, and when an impatient, frustrated Tully realised what I was doing, he laughed . . .

Until I lifted his legs up to his chest and sank my cock inside him.

His eyes wide, he gasped out a cry and groaned on the exhale. He tried to arch his back but I pinned him with my hips and sank all the way in, sinking my tongue into his mouth at the same time.

He dug his fingernails into me, clawing at my back . . . until he fully surrendered. Then he pulled me closer and we found a rhythm, slow, long, and deep. He held my face, his eyes imploring, the colour of burned honey and forever.

"Jeremiah," he whispered before sucking on my bottom lip.

This was different than before. All the times we'd done this had been amazing, but this . . . this was more.

My heart was in this. Beating in time with his, joined in the most intimate of ways.

I thrust in deep, his body a glove of warmth taking me all the way in. I tried to get my arms underneath him so I could get closer, impossibly closer. He wrapped his arms around me as if he understood.

As if he felt it too.

This shift between us.

Closer, something unspoken exchanged between us. In his eyes, in the way he held me, the way he took me. I never wanted it to end. I never wanted this feeling to stop, as a storm we couldn't see raged outside. Here, in his bed, in his arms, this was euphoria, this was ecstasy.

This was making love.

I crushed my mouth to his, our tongues tangled, and when I tasted his tears, I pulled back. His eyes were wet and glassy. I cupped his face, my forehead to his, and I stopped thrusting, holding as still as I could. "Are you okay?"

He nodded quickly. "Please don't stop. God, Jeremiah, please."

I pulled out to the tip and pushed all the way back in, and he groaned my name, over and over. His eyes rolled back in his head, he pushed his head back, his neck corded, and his whole body went rigid in my arms. His cock, untouched and swollen, jerked and he cried out as his warmth spilled between us.

When his arms fell away and all resistance was gone, he gave me his body. I drove into him again and again, as deep as I could, until I couldn't hold back anymore. I came so hard, with my whole body, with my whole heart.

And when I came back to my senses, when the room stopped spinning, he was tracing circles on my back, kissing my neck, my collarbone, my shoulder.

I pulled out of him but rolled us onto our sides, quickly wrapping him up in my arms. "Are you okay?"

He nodded into the crook of my neck. "Was intense, that's all."

I lifted his chin and kissed him softly. "It was. Glad you felt the same."

His eyes scanned mine, the room still dark but we'd

adjusted to it now, enough to see his face close up, anyway. "You felt it too? Do you . . . feel the same?"

My heart rate kicked back up a gear. Okay wow, we were going to discuss this . . . "I feel . . . something I've never felt before," I said, laying my truth bare. "I'm not sure . . . I, uh . . . God."

He snorted out a laugh, his hand to my cheek. "I said somethin' similar to my dad tonight."

Wait, what?

"Uh, you did what?"

Tully sighed, his sleepy eyes heavy-lidded and dreamy. "My dad, he said somethin' to me tonight. Somethin' I didn't think I was ready to talk about, but who knows, maybe I am."

I brushed his long blond hair from his forehead. "And what's that?"

"I'm falling in love with you," he whispered. "But I've never . . . I mean, I know what love is, but what I feel for you is so much more. I dunno how to explain it. And I don't expect you to say anything back. That's not why I told you. Ellis thinks I'm a hopeless sap because none of my family have ever seen me be with anyone else the way I am with you. God, this is embarrassing." He laughed and tried to duck his face, but I made him look at me.

I planted a soft kiss on his lips. "Tully—"

"It's okay," he blurted. "I don't expect you to say anything. I just wanted you to know, because . . . well, I don't know why. Because you deserve to be loved. God, I fell so hard, so fast, it's crazy, but you . . . you're someone very special to me, Jeremiah. And if you wanna know the real reason my dad and brother didn't rip me a new arsehole, it's because my mother told them they couldn't. She said it was very obvious that I was in love with you and therefore it was off limits because she would expect my dad to do for her exactly what I did for you." He sighed. "When Dad said that—you know, the L-word—I almost died, but you know what? They're right. I do. I love you. I knew I was in love with you but just wasn't sure if I was ready to hear it." He traced his finger from my temple to my cheek. "Pretty sure I fell for you back at the bunker when you went out into the storm and almost got hit by lightning and you raced back and slid under the side wall like an action-movie star. Pretty sure my heart saw that and went, 'Yep, you know what? That's a done deal right there. That's your person, Tully.' And honestly, the pissing into the empty bottle and givin' it to the crocodiles to drink was just an added bonus."

I burst out laughing. "I didn't give it to the crocodiles to drink."

He chuckled, his eyes searching mine. Happy, serene.

In love.

I traced my thumb along his bottom lip, my heart two sizes too large for my chest, knocking against my ribs, urging me to say something . . .

"I feel it too," I whispered. "To be honest, it scares me because . . . well, because I don't know what love is. I have no experience in talking about emotions. Growing up with my dad, he was very closed off. I threw myself into my studies, and my only experience with men involved brief encounters—"

"In bathroom stalls."

"Exactly." I managed an embarrassed smile. "But I think it's . . . what you said. When I look at you . . . God, Tully, I can't talk about this because I've never talked about this stuff." I closed my eyes and laughed. "My god, you should feel my heart."

He laughed and put his palm to my chest. "Oh, where's your watch?"

"I took it off. It would have melted on my wrist if it measured what we just did."

He laughed, his eyes bright, his smile wide. "Such a

shame. I'd have loved for it to send out a health distress alert to the ambos. We could have given them a show."

I chuckled. "I'm sure paramedics have seen worse."

"Worse? God, they'd be strapped to see better, I can tell you that much. Christ, that was hot. Possibly the best sex of my life. You made me cry, and that's a first."

I kissed him. "Because it wasn't just sex."

His smile faded into something more serene, his eyes intense. "No, it wasn't."

"So are you just going to ignore the fact that I told you I felt the same?" I asked. "And how much it scares me? Is that something we're just going to gloss over? Because I've never said that to anyone in my entire life. Not even my father."

"Nothing scares you. I've seen you not even flinch when lightning hit the ground fifty metres from you."

I scanned his eyes. If only he knew how wrong he was. "You terrify me."

He breathed in deep and sighed happily. "You feel the same."

I nodded.

"But you struggle to say it because you were never shown love."

I swallowed, suddenly not feeling so blissful. "Well, yeah. I guess."

Tully cupped my face, making me look at him. "If you feel what I feel, then you feel love." I gave the smallest of nods and he smiled. "Your dad might not be able to show you he loves you or tell you, but I'm sure he loves you."

I shrugged. "We've never spoken about . . . any emotions. At all. Ever."

He kissed me. "I'm gonna show you so much love you won't know what to do with it."

"I already don't know what to do with it, to be honest."

He laughed. "Well, let's start with a shower. I need to get cleaned up because I'm sticky and lubed all over."

"Oh." I let him escape my arms, only really feeling the stickiness when he had to peel himself off me.

After almost blinding us both when I flipped the light switch on in the bathroom, I started the shower and pulled him under the spray, lathering up the sponge with shower gel and giving him a thorough washing. He had to wash his hair —not entirely sure how we got lube up there, but anyway—I made a point of taking care of him, looking after him with tender touches and soft kisses.

I might not be able to tell him with words, but I could do this for him.

He hummed and leaned into every touch, looking at me with puppy dog eyes. "You do love me," he murmured. I smiled and ducked my head, nowhere to hide under the bright lights and being completely naked. He laughed and booped me on the nose with a soapy finger. "I know you do."

I met his gaze and gave him an embarrassed, reluctant nod.

He did a little happy dance. "I will make you say it one day. You'll be able to say it as easy as talking about the weather. Which, for you, is easy-peasy." I rolled my eyes and he gave me a playful shove. "Now get out," he said. "I need to soak under this water jet a little longer. Unless you'd like to give me round two in here."

Chuckling, ridiculously happy, I stepped out of the shower and began to dry off. "Oh," Tully said, now a foggy, steamed-up glass panel between us. "And I think we need to talk about condoms. Or more to the point, about not using them. Because tonight, when you were . . . not wearing one, I was imagining what that might be like. Well, I think I'd like to try that. Having you come inside me would be so fucking hot—"

I opened the shower screen door. Steam billowed out and he was standing there with his head back, under the water.

With a sly smirk, he put his head forward and looked at me. "Like the sound of that?"

"I, uh . . . I don't . . . do you think . . . ?"

"Oh, I think, yes." He put his head back under the water, still smiling. "I think very much. After the cyclone, we can have all the necessary tests. Together, like a couple." He shot his head forward again, a new spark in his eyes. "Like boyfriends, because that's what we are now, remember? I mean, we live together, so technically we're more than that, but officially, if I was to introduce you to someone, I could say, 'Hey, this is my boyfriend, the very smart Doctor Jeremiah well-hung Overton,' and—" He shut the water off. "And you could be all, 'Yes, dear boyfriend, that's completely correct.'"

Oh dear god.

I handed him a towel. "I'm sure they'd appreciate the insight." I hung my towel up and left him to dry off.

"I gotta dry my hair," he called out. "No fallin' asleep without me."

I laughed, and finding my phone, I plugged it in to charge before I slid under the covers. The room was dark, the only light coming from the open bathroom door. Tully singing over the sound of the hairdryer was the only sound.

What a night.

What an admission.

He loved me.

And what he'd just said.

Could I have sex without a condom? Was that something I'd be comfortable doing?

I was in a relationship, I countered with myself. And I trusted Tully implicitly. So maybe it was something we could consider . . .

I certainly wouldn't mind trying. Seeing how it would feel to be inside him bare. To come, to give him my seed, to make him mine in that way . . .

Sweet Jesus.

I needed to *not* think about that. My balls already liked the idea.

I snatched up my phone, needing the distraction, and of course my home screen had news updates. And there, in a small thumbnail image, was Tully in his work shirt, pointing his finger at a reporter, mid-rant.

He looked incredibly mad.

I'd seen the whole thing unfold on the security cameras along with Doreen, but I hadn't heard what he'd said.

Did I even want to know?

Then I read the subheading.

Storm brewing at the weather station.

Good lord.

Who wrote that drivel?

I clicked on it, expecting to read the article, but the video clip auto-played.

"You wanna be careful," a reporter said.

Tully spun around and pointed his finger at him. He was seething mad, his jaw clenched and that vein down the side of his neck popped out. "And you might wanna watch your *beeeep* mouth."

Oh boy.

He really said that?

"You all come here for what?" he asked. "This office is trying to do a job, obtaining information that will save lives, and you're all here for *beeeeep* what? You wanna broadcast footage of a mother dying in front of her kid, for ratings, then expect him to, what? Come out for an interview?" He pointed his finger at all of them. "Every single one of you can *beep beep beep*. You want news? Go back to your offices and wait for official bulletin releases. Or do what they suggested yesterday and leave Darwin. Do us all a favour and just keep *beeeep* driving."

Oh my god.

He really said *all that*?

He defended me. He defended my work and told them how awful they were for showing that dreadful clip of my mother . . .

And then Doreen entered the screen. She was swinging her bat, her shirt was pixelated—not surprisingly—and almost every word she said was *beeeeeped* out.

Also not surprising.

But they did that for me.

No one had ever defended me before.

The bathroom light switched off and the silver outline of Tully's naked form crossed the room before he climbed into bed. My phone screen illuminated him when he snuggled into my side. "Whatcha watching?" Then he saw the screen. "Oh."

"I hadn't watched it until now."

"Yeah, I'm sorry. I kinda lost my shit. I'm sorry you saw that."

"I'm not." I switched my phone off and slid it onto the bedside table. The room was now completely dark, and I tightened my arm around him. "No one's ever defended me or my work before."

He sighed and manoeuvred his arm under my neck so he could hold me instead. "Get used to it from now on."

I settled in against him, his warmth and strength everything I needed. So much had happened today, it was hard for me to get my head around the gravity of it. From the footage on TV, the phone call with my dad, Tully dropping everything to be with me, his rant at the media, then dinner with his family.

Him telling me he loved me.

Yeah, it'd been a day, that was certain.

And tomorrow was day one. Tropical Cyclone Hazer would begin its descent into Australian waters tomorrow, and we'd begin to see rain, winds, sea swells, and rising waters by tomorrow night.

Then it'd be a full twenty-four hours of hell, probably.

As if his mind had taken him to similar places, Tully tightened his arm around me and kissed the side of my head. "Get some sleep. We're gonna need it."

CHAPTER SEVEN
TULLY

Jeremiah was in the shower early; it wasn't even five. He'd slept fitfully at best, tossing and turning most of the night.

I know this because I did too.

I went downstairs, flipped the light switch and sighed when I saw the view to the ocean was gone, boarded up.

The reason for the lack of sleep . . .

Hazer was coming.

I filled the water tank on the coffee machine and turned it on and set about makin' two coffees. And some eggs on toast. I knew there'd be little chance of Jeremiah eating today, so I had to put some food in his belly.

He came down the stairs just as I was plating it up. "Oh," he said, looking at the spread on the table. "You didn't have to do this."

"I wanted to," I said, putting our plates down. "For my boyfriend, the man I love."

He sputtered and blushed and sat down, speechless apparently.

"I told you I'll tell you all the time," I said, givin' him one of those grins I knew he secretly loved. "Eat up. You've got a big day."

"We all do," he said quietly. "It's not too late to leave, you know."

I ignored that and squirted tomato sauce over my eggs.

The utter silence from across the table made me look up. Jeremiah was gawping at my plate. Horrified.

It made me laugh. "He who has not tried it shall not judge."

"I'm trying very hard not to judge," he said flatly. "Though I'm beginning to question your taste."

"My taste also includes you."

"That's why I'm questioning it."

I laughed. "If I made some fancy tomato relish and gave it a fancy name, you'd think I was posh." I shovelled in a mouthful of eggs and sauce and bit into some toast for good measure, then spoke with my mouth half full. "But I ain't fancy."

He chuckled. "I can see that."

We ate in silence for a bit, then I nodded to the boarded-up view. "I hate not being able to see outside."

"Blue skies this morning until lunchtime," he said. "Top of thirty-five degrees, humidity is currently a moderate sixty percent, but that will climb until breaking point around six o'clock tonight when the storm rolls in."

I stared at him. "Are you a walking weather station?"

He gave a shrug as he sipped his coffee. "It's what I do."

I shovelled in the last of my eggs, stood up, and downed my coffee. I gave his shoulder a squeeze on my way to the sink with my plate. "I'm gonna have a quick shower; then I'll drive you. We'll take one car, and I'll drop you off. I wanna get some cameras set up," I explained. "Can I use your gear for that?"

He shot me a surprised look. "Yes, of course. I forgot about that. I've been so busy and distracted . . . I should have thought about that."

I went over and kissed the top of his head. "You've been a

tad busy, so it's understandable. Now, eat up. I won't be long."

I took the stairs two at a time, had the quickest shower ever, and trotted back down. He'd cleared away the table, set the dishwasher going, but was staring blank faced at his laptop screen.

No, not blank.

He was ashen, grim.

"What is it?" I asked, walking over to him. Part of me dreaded asking. "Jeremiah?"

He looked up at me, startled, clearly having not heard me. He shook his head. "Uhh, there's footage." He swallowed. "And photos, starting to come out of the islands. In Indonesia, the Alor Archipelago. And Timor-Leste . . ." He blinked a few times. "Those tiny islands. They're . . . they're just no longer there. Jesus Christ, Tully. Look."

He turned the screen toward me and it was . . . devastation.

The foundations of buildings left exposed, the buildings nowhere in sight. Palm trees and greenery, whole damn islands, looked like a giant lawn mower had decimated everything in its path.

Debris, destruction, flooded streets, vehicles sprinkled about like toys.

"Is there . . . is there a death toll?"

"Not yet, nothing official." He put his hand to his mouth, his fingers trembling. "These poor people."

"Hey," I said, closing his laptop. "You're not responsible for those places."

"No. But I'm responsible for here, for the people here, Tully. And Cyclone Hazer that did that." He pushed his laptop away. "It's coming. Tonight. It starts tonight."

I pulled him to his feet and wrapped him up in a hug as tight as I could. "You're not responsible for the people, Jeremiah. You're responsible for providing information and data, numerical facts, nothing more. What the authorities and emergency services do with that information is out of your hands. You did your part. When they asked you, you told them in no uncertain terms what to expect, and you told them to leave."

"If they could leave," he mumbled. "A lot of people don't have the means. No transport, no money. All those Indigenous communities in remote areas. Their homes aren't built—"

I pulled back and took hold of his face. "Stop. Stop, Jeremiah. Those who were at greatest risk have been evacuated. Those who choose to stay make that choice for themselves."

"Like you. You shouldn't be staying."

I tried not to sigh. "I told you, I'm not leaving you."

He pouted. "Tully."

I squished his cheeks together and kissed his pouty lips. "Stop arguing with me, Doctor, and come and help me pack a bag."

"Pack a bag?" His eyes scanned mine, panicked. "So you *are* leaving?"

As much as he said he wanted me to leave, he absolutely did *not* want me to go.

I rolled my eyes, and with the mother of all sighs, I took his hand and led him upstairs. "No. This is a ready bag. Clothes, towels, first aid, lube. You know, the essentials."

He was quiet as we stuffed a duffel bag full.

"What's wrong?" I asked.

"I should have thought of this." He stopped, put his hand to his forehead, and sighed. "I didn't even think about the cameras, and now this. I'm so unprepared."

I squeezed his arm. "No you're not. Your mind's focused on other things."

"It shouldn't be. It should be focused on exactly this." He stuffed a towel into the bag. "On you. I should have considered what you need and how to make sure you're—"

"Jeremiah," I said, my tone sharp and serious. His gaze shot to mine. "Stop overthinking it. This is your first cyclone."

"Have you been through one before?"

"Well, no. We've had some come close, and most downgrade before they get here. None like this."

"Exactly."

"I've lived in the tropics my whole life. We get crazy shit every wet season. Extremes are the norm here."

"Well, by definition, that makes no sense. If those extremes are normal, then they're no longer extremes but the norm—"

Yeah, okay, he was freaking out.

I took his arm and made him face me. "Stop. We need to pack a bag, then get you to work. You don't wanna be late today. Hazer will be the least of your concerns with a pissed-off Doreen comin' at you." I peered into his eyes. "It's okay to be stressed. It's completely understandable to be concerned right now. Where's that unfazed scientist who walked us into the crocodile infested mangroves?"

"There were no crocodiles when we walked in," he mumbled. Then his eyes met mine. "I didn't have you then. I didn't have these feelings then. I mean, maybe I did, but this is different."

I put my hand to his cheek. "We'll be okay. And you did have me back then. You had me long before then." I gave him a quick kiss, then looked around the room. "Is there anything you want to bring with you? Any personal items you don't want to lose in case my house isn't here tomorrow?"

He blinked a few times, and I could see him grappling with the urge to freak out again, but he managed to fight it. He fisted my shirt. "Just you."

My smile was immediate and the thump of my heart almost painful against my ribs. "And you think you can't say you love me."

I was expecting him to smile or roll his eyes, but he didn't. His hold on my shirt was now with white knuckles. He tried to talk—perhaps he was trying to tell me he loved me—but in the end just nodded.

I put my forehead to his. "I know," I whispered. "I know."

He swallowed hard and nodded before he let me go, and I ran my hand down his chest and ribs . . . until I felt something that shouldn't have been there. "Are you . . . are you wearing a bra?"

His eyes went wide. "What? No, of course not." He blushed and shook his head. "I'm not wearing a bra."

I pulled up his shirt and he sighed, resigned. There, strapped around his chest was the heart-rate chest strap. I raised an eyebrow and my smile widened. "Clearly you're not as unprepared as you think you are."

He rolled his eyes. "We should get going. Or Doreen will take her bat to me."

"If she does, at least the paramedics will know your ECG stats."

He ignored that, took one last look around my room, at the photos on the wall, and I went to close the door, but Jeremiah stopped me.

"Wait," he said. He went to the photos I'd taken and took one frame off the wall. It was the black and white photo of a younger me at the bunker. He held it to his chest. "Okay, now I'm good."

I pulled the door closed with a smile.

He was quiet on the drive to his work. He was taking in all the boarded-up houses, all the sandbags. It was a comfort to know people were prepared, and I hoped he felt the same. "See? People are ready."

He gave me a tight smile and a nod. "I hope so."

I remembered the pictures of the islands north of us, how decimated they were, and how it was now coming for us. "I hope so too."

We were a little late, getting to the bureau a fraction after six, but Doreen didn't even seem to mind. She was more worried about what the radars showed and updating alerts now that daylight was breaking.

Though she did look at Jeremiah as he put the ready bag down, and how he stuffed the photo frame into the bag. "Clear skies up until around zero nine hundred," she said. "Then we'll start to see this band move in." She pointed to the massive circular cloud mass heading straight toward us.

"Did you see the images out of Timor-Leste?" Jeremiah asked.

She nodded, her expression grim. "Yeah. I saw." Then she whacked him on the arm, almost knocking him over. "Keep your chin up. There's shit to get done today. I'll be back around four. I'm guessin' you'll be keepin' me company tonight."

He nodded.

"Me too," I said. "I'll be here."

"He won't leave," Jeremiah said. "Doreen, if you could perhaps talk some sense into him."

She grinned at me and gave me a shoulder whack to match Jeremiah's. "Good lad."

Jeremiah sighed. "That's the opposite of helpful, thank you."

She collected Bruce, and with a slam of the door, she was gone.

I wasn't about to get into another argument with him. Instead, I looked around at the old gear along the back shelves. "Can I use some of these?"

"You can take whatever you want." He shrugged. "I don't know of how much use any of it will be."

Something on the control panel started to click and he sat himself down and began flipping switches and pressing buttons, which I was sure he'd be doing all day long. Then the phone started ringing, and he was talking to the Oceanic Administration, so I took what gear I needed, planted a kiss on the top of his head, whispered I'd be back soon, and left him to it.

I went back home and collected my storm gear from the garage and some of Jeremiah's and began rigging up a camera housing unit. I screwed it into the wall on my balcony and faced the camera toward the ocean. I set up the old wind sensor and the analogue output barometer from the bureau, hoping they would be able to give us any kinds of readings—if they survived. I hooked it all up, made sure all feeds were recording, and locked up my balcony again.

In the garden that fronted the ocean, I installed the automatic weather station from the bureau. It was circa 1970s, I was sure, probably left behind after Cyclone Tracy. It was nothin' like Jeremiah's, the one that had been damaged at the bunker, but I anchored it the best I could with the pegs and a hammer. I'd already looked into buying him a new one, so if this one didn't survive—and it wasn't likely it would—it wasn't the end of the world.

Jeremiah always had to be cautious with money, and I knew he'd worked hard to budget for all his equipment. But he was with me now, and I'd make damn sure he didn't have to worry about money again. If he needed a new weather station, I'd get him the best that money could buy.

If we made it through this.

No. Don't think like that. Everything's gonna be fine.

Because, damn, the idea of anything happening to Jeremiah made my stomach sour.

I needed to focus.

Setting it all up took longer than I'd hoped, and I didn't really have time to do much else. All my potted plants were inside, everything was as secure as it could be. If the windows exploded in or the roof came off, there was nothing I could do to stop it.

If my house was still standing at the end of this, I'd consider myself very lucky.

But at the end of the day, it wasn't the house that was important.

Next stop was my parents' house. Dad and Ellis were doin' one final check of the docking yard and the offices so they weren't there, but everyone else was. Zoe and her family, Rowan and his, and Mum, of course, was the epitome of grace under fire.

Rowan helped me install the old anemometer from the bureau at Mum and Dad's. It was so old it measured in knots and miles. If it survived, I'd give it to a damn museum. He was clearly worried, and I was sure he appreciated the distraction. He'd never been one to show outward emotion, but he breathed an audible sigh of relief when Dad and Ellis got back.

Then the focus was all about keepin' the kids entertained and getting the elderly neighbours organised, plus their one small dog and a cat in a cage, which was my cue to leave.

"I should get back," I said.

"You sure you won't stay?" Ellis asked me quietly. There was no joking, no name-calling. Just a concerned older brother.

I shook my head. "I can't. Jeremiah can't leave. He needs to man the station, and I need to be wherever he is."

Mum gave me a hug. "We understand."

Ellis nodded. "Yeah, okay. Stay in touch though."

"Yeah, of course. The storm tonight won't be so bad until morning."

Rowan gave a hard nod. "They're saying the mobile phone network will probably go down, so don't panic if you can't reach us."

"I know," I said, trying for more confidence than I felt. "Keep watching the bureau's weather radar and listen to the radio if you can. All emergency alerts will be broadcast." I looked at each of their faces. "Hazer is expected to make land-fall tomorrow morning around nine o'clock. You'll all need to be downstairs in the cellar by six. The eye will pass over around midday, and it should last for an hour or two. It doesn't mean it's over. The backend of the cyclone is almost always more powerful, and it'll be blowin' from the opposite direction. Don't go outside. Don't leave the house—"

Dad gave me a hug. "We know. You take care now. Be in touch as soon as you can."

Mum came out with a bag of food in takeout containers. "Take this. You be safe, you hear? And take care of him."

I gave her a long hug. "I will, Mum. Thank you."

She pulled back and gently tapped my face. "Stay in touch. Let us know you're both okay."

I nodded, refusing to let my emotions get the best of me, but the way she included Jeremiah really struck something in me.

"I will, Mum. You all take care of each other."

I waved them off and jumped into the Jeep. It felt strange to be leaving them. Knowin' my entire family would be together without me was a new and abnormal feeling.

But then I thought about Jeremiah and my need to be with him.

And that felt right.

Being with him was where I was supposed to be.

I drove past a servo, which didn't have too much of a waiting line, so I filled the Jeep and the jerry can with fuel, just in case. I grabbed some last-minute snacks and some more price-gouged bottles of water and checked the time before I got back on the road.

It was eight minutes past three.

The sky was dark to the north—far too dark for the afternoon. A wall of cloud was on its way like an ominous blanket about to cover us all.

What kind of havoc it would bring, only time would tell.

The images of those islands stripped bare ran through my mind, and I drove a little faster to get to Jeremiah.

The gate was now chained open, so I drove straight in.

It was crazy how still everything felt. How quiet it all was.

I took the food and water inside. Jeremiah was on the phone, sounding all kinds of official, and he smiled when he saw me.

Knowin' he was busy, I took the jerry can of fuel and filled the generator that was bolted to the back of the building. I was fixing the canopy of the Jeep when Jeremiah came out. "Hey," he said warmly. He looked like he'd had a helluva day already.

I clipped the last side down and shut the door. "Hey, you." I climbed the steps and ran my hand up his arm. "You okay?"

He nodded. "Better now you're here. I was worried."

"Worried that I'd done what you've been trying to get me to do and bail on you?"

He glowered. "No. Worried that you were . . . I don't know. Just worried."

I laughed and threw my arms around him, pushing him back inside. "Mum packed us food. I'm assuming you haven't eaten, because I haven't either. I'm starving. I was also robbed blind at the service station for snacks and water. The prices they charged were outrageous. When this is over, I'm gonna pay those jerks a little visit."

He rolled his eyes. "It's the day before a cyclone. What did you expect?"

Now the control panel was mostly flashing red and yellow lights.

Warning, warning, warning.

Jeez.

"I don't expect to be extorted or racketeered," I said, figurin' the distraction would be good for him. I began taking out the food Mum had packed. "I mean, I can afford it. That's not my issue. What about the people who can't? What about those who can barely afford normal prices and then, in an emergency such as this, they can't get essentials like water? We need to do better.

As a society. I probably should have thought about runnin' some kind of food drop to those who are gonna really struggle—"

Jeremiah was smiling at me.

"What?"

He shook his head. "You're a good one."

I sighed. "Well, I threatened physical violence on-camera, remember? So you might wanna hold off the sainthood." I handed him one container with a fork.

"Your mum gave you all this?"

I nodded. "With strict instructions to keep you safe. And fed. But mostly safe."

His smile softened and he looked at the food in his lap. "Tell her I said thank you."

"You can tell her yourself. There were also strict instructions to stay in touch. There'll be phone calls and probably FaceTimes. They're all stuck together in the cyclone cellar, so by tomorrow mornin', if you see Ellis hogtied with duct tape in the background, no, you didn't."

Jeremiah chuckled and ate some lunch. Then he frowned as he chewed. "Do you wish you were with them?"

I knocked my knee against his. "We're not doing that."

"It's a fair question."

"I wish maybe we were both with them. Together. But that can't happen, so no. I wish to be with you." I waved my fork toward the floor. "*I am here* because I wish to be *here*. Maybe you could stop asking me or I might get a complex for real that you actually don't want me around."

He froze, and I'd like to have said that I was joking, but I wasn't.

He shook his head, a little panicked. "I-I'm-I'm glad you're here," he whispered. "I don't mean to sound ungrateful. I really appreciate you choosing to be here with me. I'm sorry if I made it sound otherwise. I just worry . . . I don't want to be the reason that you're separated from them."

I knocked my knee to his again, and this time, I hooked my foot around his as well. "You're not. I'm the reason. Because stupid-me went and fell in love with a guy who has a pretty important job to do."

He went from pouting, to frowning, to smiling, to blushing all in the space of about three seconds. "The food is very good," he said.

I groaned. "I tell you I love you and you say mmm, the food's delicious." I pretended to stab myself in the heart with my fork. "My poor heart."

He made a cute, scowly smiling face at me, then he pretended to stab me with his fork. "You know what I mean. You know I can't talk about this stuff. God." He pouted and handed me back the container of food. "We should keep some. Ration it out."

I took it from him and put the lid back on. I nodded. "Yeah, okay."

"Tully," he murmured. "I'm sorry."

I should have found some comfort in the fact that he was blushing, and he *did* look sorry. "It's fine. Have you been busy today?"

He nodded. "Non-stop. It's been good, in a way. Otherwise I'd have gone mad. I didn't realise the time until I saw you drive in."

"The skies are dark to the north. Hazer's on his way."

Jeremiah nodded, then pointed his chin to the radar by my shoulder. "And he's not slowing down. Gathering speed, if anything."

I sighed. "Joy."

"Yeah, not really."

I tried to brighten the mood. "It'll all be over, mostly, by this time tomorrow."

He nodded. "Just one day."

"It'll almost be as bad as that time you went back to

Melbourne and left me for a day. Worst thirty-five hours of my life."

He chuckled. "Almost."

Then we noticed a truck on the security camera. A tow truck, more specifically. And it came into the yard.

What the hell?

"I'll go," I said, putting the food containers down and heading toward the door. I picked up the baseball bat and went out. The driver was a huge man, and I wasn't sure if holdin' the bat was a good or bad decision.

Until Doreen and a smaller woman jumped out of the truck. "Thanks, mate. Be safe," Doreen said with a wave to the tow truck driver.

The woman she was with, who I could see now was holding Bruce, blew the truck driver a kiss. Doreen laughed, slung a bag over her shoulder, and she turned to see me.

Holding her bat.

She grinned. "I knew I liked you, Tully."

I snorted. "Thanks. Something wrong with your bike?"

"Nah. Just thought I'd leave it at home. Safer there."

Yeah, of course. "Good idea."

Doreen threw her thumb toward the now-leaving tow truck. "That's my baby brother." Then she slung her arm around the woman. "And this is my Suri."

Suri was a small woman with long black hair, Indonesian or Malaysian, if I had to guess. She was maybe fifty years old, tucked right into Doreen's side like she was made for it, and had a beautiful smile. "Hello," she said brightly.

"Nice to meet you," I said, holding the door for them. "I do believe we're in for a spot of weather. Might want to come inside."

Doreen snorted. "Figured we'd get in before the rain started. No point in getting wet," she said, letting Suri walk in first.

I grinned at her and she rolled her eyes as she walked in.

"Oyyy," she said, seeing the screens and flashing buttons on the console dash. "Jiminy Crickets, you a bit busy or something?" she said, immediately taking her seat and helping Jeremiah. "Saw the gate was chained open," she said after a few seconds. She glanced back at me and gave a nod. "Smart thinkin'."

I shrugged. "Don't look at me. It was Jeremiah."

Jeremiah stood up and went to the data feed screen, which was now rolling like a poker machine. "I just thought it would be safer, should we need to leave in a hurry, or if debris should be forced against the fence, it could block us in. I didn't think we'd get any unwanted visitors today."

He went back to his seat and only then seemed to notice the other person in the room. "Oh, my goodness, I'm sorry," he said, getting back to his feet.

"Jeremiah," I said. "This is Suri, Doreen's better half."

"*Much* better half," Suri said.

"Hey," Doreen grumbled.

Suri winked, and then she nodded to the screens up the top, showing different views of the storm. "Oh, look. Some screens that work."

Jeremiah held his hand out for Suri to shake. "Nice to meet you. And Tully replaced those screens. And he fixed the old chair."

Well, the screens hadn't cost much, and I'd paid for them because it was unlikely that Jeremiah would get much funding out of the head office. The chair was a necessity, especially with all the time I'd spent here with him in his first week. It was bad enough that his office was straight out of the time warp, and I wanted him to stay. I tried to make it as comfortable for him as I could.

"Nice," Suri said, looking around. "It's actually a lot cleaner in here now too."

"Heyyyy," Doreen grumbled again.

I chuckled. "Well, I cleared out some of the old gear today.

I set up the camera on my balcony. It faces the ocean, so we should get a front view of Hazer comin' straight at us. And that old anemometer that was on the shelf, I set it up at my mum and dad's place. Oh, as well as the camera feed, I have one of those video doorbells. We should take a look."

I grabbed my bag and took out my laptop. It took a little while to get it all up and running, but soon enough we had a video feed from my balcony, lookin' directly out toward the gulf and Timor Sea, and the doorbell's street view from the front of the house.

The view lookin' out to the ocean was dark and foreboding, while the view at the front of the house looked like a beautiful sunny day. It looked like two different locations, worlds apart.

Suri moved a few things in the office, creating a safer place for her and me to sit against the wall and to make objects less of a missile should we lose windows or worse, the roof.

Then she plugged in some power boards and made sure everyone's phones and my laptop were charging. "We don't know how long we could lose power for," she said, pulling out two power banks to charge as well. "Fingers crossed we don't need them."

"You sound like you've been through this before," I said.

She shrugged. "I grew up with monsoons. But I'm from Banda Aceh."

Banda Aceh . . .

Oh my god.

Oh my fucking god.

The entire province in Indonesia had been almost wiped off the planet back in '04. I'd been only a little kid at the time, but people *still* talked about that tsunami. It had killed over 160,000 people in Banda Aceh alone . . .

Jeremiah turned his chair around so he could stare at her, his mouth open.

Yeah, he knew of it too, which wasn't at all surprising

given it was one of the most violent weather events of our time.

She smiled when she saw the recognition on our faces. "I moved here after that."

I couldn't even imagine . . .

"Jesus. And now you're facing another natural disaster."

She nodded with a long sigh. "What else can we do, huh? We just have to do our best."

"Have you been through a cyclone before?" I asked.

Suri nodded. "Yes, but smaller. Not as big as this one."

That didn't instil much confidence in me. But the truth was, not many Cat 5s had ever touched down in Australia, and until they'd changed the rating system, there had been *no* bigger cyclones than Hazer.

And Doreen had lived through Cyclone Tracey. Together they had some experience and neither one seemed the type to panic, so maybe Jeremiah and I were in great company.

The video feed looked ominous though.

"Okay, here it comes," I said, turning my laptop around so they could see the screen. "Here's the rain."

And sure enough, like any beast of that size, dark clouds crept slowly toward my balcony. Wind and a wall of rain marched right at us. Widespread and low, the sheer size of the front of it . . .

Jeremiah's eyes met mine, solemn and sorry. "Hazer's here."

I gave Suri's arm a squeeze. "You okay?"

She gave me a grim nod. "It's not so much the rain that falls that scares me," she said. "But the water that rises."

Christ.

I couldn't even imagine.

"Let's take one last look at daylight," Suri said, getting to her feet and pulling Doreen to hers. "Come on, Dori. God knows when we'll see blue sky again."

I stood up and held my hand out to Jeremiah. "Come on.

You too." He winced at the dash panel, so I took his arm and pulled him up. "Ten seconds won't hurt."

I dragged him to the front porch where Doreen and Suri already stood. They were looking back out over the carport, to the north. The clouds were almost above us, encroaching on the blue sky like smoke.

We were only a few kilometres from my house, so it wouldn't take long to reach us. But the winds came first. The trees in the street began to jostle, and the world was eerily quiet.

"Can you hear that?" I asked. "No birds. No noise at all, actually."

It was eery and unnatural, and it felt like the whole world was holding its breath.

Doreen put her arm around Suri, as if the silence of the birds was something she'd lived through before, spoken about before.

Before the tsunami.

I put my arm around Jeremiah's waist and rested my chin on his shoulder, and we watched as the first drops of rain began to spatter their way toward us.

Then it began to hammer down.

And the rain just didn't stop.

CHAPTER EIGHT

JEREMIAH

Over the next few hours, Doreen and I issued alert after alert for severe thunderstorms, dangerous hail, heavy falls of rain, rising flood waters, dangerous surf, and sea swells. The list seemed endless.

Right across the top end of the Northern Territory.

I was relieved that Suri was here because she kept Tully company. They set up camp on the floor in the corner, watching the video feeds on his laptop, playing cards, playing with Bruce, telling jokes, and having a great time while the skies turned dark and the storm raged.

By ten o'clock we'd all eaten, and Tully had had a few phone calls with his family, and one FaceTime in which his mother had made a point of asking me, very loudly, if Tully had made sure I'd eaten.

I'd waved awkwardly to her from my seat. "He did, thank you very much for the food."

"Anytime, dear," she'd said.

I'd turned back to face my console. Sure, it was busy, and every screen and button was flashing, but mostly so she couldn't see me blush.

Having a mum fuss over me was strangely comforting. Or

having any parent fuss over me was, if I was being honest. But a mother, in particular . . .

"Isn't he just the cutest?" Tully had asked his entire family watching the screen.

"Oh, Tully, you look after him, he's working so hard," his mum had said. We'd all heard it. Tully had the volume up over the sound of the rain, clearly not needing to hide anything from anyone. Not anyone in his family. Not anyone in this room.

I, on the other hand, was still not used to such outward affection. I ducked my head, and Doreen laughed beside me and shoved my shoulder. "Didn't think you'd be the shy type."

"Leave him alone," Suri chided her.

Tully laughed. "Okay, guys," he said to the screen. "We're gonna log off and try and catch some zeds. You do the same, and we'll talk again in the morning."

"Okay, love. Sleep tight."

It made my chest burn to hear them speak with such affection. A mix of embarrassment and longing.

"Remember, be downstairs early," Tully said.

There were murmurs of goodnights and good lucks, and he ended the video call. The live feeds all showed the same: heavy rainfall, slanted in strong winds that changed direction on a whim. It was gusty, no discernible pattern yet, only mayhem. A mere taste of what was to come.

"Suppose we should take shifts," Doreen said.

I nodded. "Yes, that would be best. Why don't you sleep first," I suggested.

With a nod, Doreen got up and stretched, groaning loudly, her hands almost touching the ceiling. "Okay, Tully, get up," she said brusquely. "You're in my spot."

With a grin, he got up, taking his laptop with him, and gestured to the floor next to Suri. "All yours."

As soon as Doreen was lying down, Bruce jumped on her,

and Suri curled under her arm, like it was exactly how the three of them slept every night.

It was kinda sweet.

Tully fell into Doreen's chair and slowly wheeled himself over to me. "You know," he said. "I deliberately didn't pack condoms in our bag, but there is lube."

"Still not asleep down here," Doreen said from the corner.

I gasped. "Oh my god."

Tully laughed, then pretended to whisper, "You know, I deliberately didn't pack condoms in our bag . . ."

Suri laughed and I wanted to die.

I pushed his chair away from mine. "Be quiet, they're trying to sleep."

Tully chuckled and opened his laptop again to check the live video feed. We had satellite radars and some footage cameras but the one he had was perfect. It was looking out to sea, directly into the face of the cyclone.

All we could see right now was squalls of rain for a few feet into the dark, but if it held out until daybreak, the footage would be spectacular.

If it held up. If the camera stayed intact.

If his house was still standing . . .

And through every minute and every hour that ticked by, the rain never stopped, the winds were a yo-yo of blustery to gale force. I sent out alerts for large hail and some lightning activity, more heavy rainfall, and more wind warnings.

Across the top end, all of Darwin, Kakadu, and Arnhem Land.

Tully fell asleep in his chair around one thirty, and I let him sleep. He needed the rest, and if I was being completely honest, I liked watching him sleep.

God, he was so handsome.

He had his arms crossed, his chin on his chest, legs outstretched. His longish hair was pulled back in that cute little sprout ponytail, and the lights on the control panel were painting his profile in orange, green, and flashing red.

But around three o'clock in the morning, a massive crack of thunder shook the building. Tully shot up out of his chair, and Doreen sat bolt upright, Suri still tucked under her arm, still half asleep. Bruce began to bark at the walls.

"Jesus Christ," Doreen said, picking Bruce up. "That was close."

"We've got an electrical storm," I said, stating the obvious. More thunder rumbled and a crack of lightning ripped through the night, right above us.

Tully ducked. "Holy shit. That's too close."

"What time is it?" Doreen asked.

"Zero three hundred."

"Three . . . ? I told you to wake me, boy," she said, getting up. "Split shift is supposed to be split. You shoulda woken me an hour ago."

"Well, considering you don't even have to technically be here at all, I thought I'd shoulder most of the time."

She sighed and jerked her thumb at me. "Outta the chair." Then she aimed it at Tully. "You too."

He didn't need telling twice, and given she was clearly not a morning person, I didn't either.

"I'll make some coffee," Suri said, disappearing into the small kitchen. The light from the open doorway allowed me to see where I could lie down, and even though I doubted I'd be sleeping at all, I knew resting my body was a good idea.

Tully took a quick look at the laptop, and his illuminated face showed shock and disbelief. He turned the screen around so I could see, and despite it being pitch-black and rain slanting into the balcony, lightning lit up the harbour like a horror strobe light.

It showed how truly big the storm was, how dark the clouds were, how tumultuous the water was already. And the rain on the wind . . . God help us.

He closed the laptop and pushed it over near the wall, then manoeuvred my arm so I was his pillow, and he sighed against me.

Suri turned the light off, though I could smell the coffee she'd made. The sounds of the storm were loud, and the booms of thunder crashed in time with the flashes on the screens above the control panel. There was zero time differential, meaning the storm, the lightning, was directly on us.

The city of Darwin was getting a light show so constant and severe it almost made it look like daylight.

But the weight of Tully on my arm, his body against mine, his warmth, were like a weighted blanket, and the sound of heavy rain, thunder and lightning, were oddly comforting. And, by some miracle, or a testament to how exhausted I was, my eyelids closed.

I could have sworn I only blinked.

But soon Suri was gently shaking my shoulder. "I'm sorry, sweet boys," she said. She glanced back at the control panel, at the radar showing the cyclone had finally crawled the final inch home. "It's game time."

Tully was now facing me, his face buried in my chest, his hair messed up. I think he'd drooled down my armpit.

Ugh.

I unwound my arm from around him and he rolled onto his back with a groan. I sat up and realised what I was hearing . . .

The wind and rain. Howling so constantly it sounded like brown noise.

"Holy shit," I said, almost having to yell. "It's loud."

"Creeps up on ya, don't it?" Doreen said. "Until you get so used to hearin' it you don't even hear it no more."

Suri reappeared with two fresh coffees. I stood up and took one, and she handed the other to Tully, who was still sitting on the floor, trying to come to terms with the world. "'S time?" he asked.

"Six o'clock," Suri answered.

I sat in my seat and took in the dash, the radars, the data, the warnings, the alerts, the non-stop beeping and flashing lights. How had I managed to sleep at all?

The darkness of our boarded-up office was deceiving because daylight had broken. I looked up at the screens above the panel. One was from the top of the news station building. It was looking pretty wild out there.

Seeing the radars and knowing what those numbers meant was quite different to seeing the live feed.

Palm trees were leaning at angles, fronds strung taut in the wind, small debris and rubbish swept along flooded waterlogged streets. Water from the bay was ebbing onto the road, the shores and sand no longer visible.

The foreshore and CBD were close to going under as the tide came in.

And the cyclone hadn't even started yet.

The low-lying areas to the east, into Kakadu and Arnhem Land, were flooding. Heavy falls continued to batter them.

Tully opened his laptop and went straight to the breakfast news channel. He turned up the volume.

"All eyes in the country are on Darwin this morning as daylight breaks and we can begin to see the size, the monstrosity of what is yet to come as Cyclone Hazer bears down on an already battered city."

There was a news reporter standing out in the street, like an idiot. She looked vaguely familiar as one of the reporters who Tully had told to take a hike. She wore a yellow raincoat, spoke to the camera, having to yell to be heard over the noise. She was being spattered by rain, the view behind her was of the street fronting the foreshore, barely recognisable.

I sighed. "She's an idiot for standing out there."

"They make them do it," Doreen said.

"Well, any producer who makes their reporters stand in harm's way for good ratings should be fired." I shook my head. "The ratings will be awesome when she's speared with flying debris live on morning television. Great family viewing."

Doreen snorted, and Tully sipped his coffee. "I think she's the one I gave an earful to the other day."

"We've had non-stop reports coming in from the weather bureau overnight," the reporter said on the screen. "Now, we know that station has to be controlled manually, so I'd like to give a shout out to the hardworking team that gives us the information to keep us safe."

"Woo-hoo!" Doreen hollered and whacked my shoulder. "She made us out to be heroes."

I rolled my eyes. "I still don't like her, and she's still an idiot for standing out there like that."

Tully shrugged. "Well, at least she's not here, annoying us."

That was true. "Fair point."

"Gonna call my fam," he said, quickly hitting the Face-Time app. In just a few seconds, the screen filled with a bunch of faces. "Hey, guys," he said.

"Morning, Tully," his dad said. Others chorused in as well. Including Ellis. "Hey, dick bag."

Then Rowan and two women I'd never seen before—maybe Zoe and Rowan's wife—shoved him out of the screen, admonishing his language in front of the kids.

Tully thought it was funny. "There's duct tape in the drawers. If you hogtie him, you *have* to send me pictures."

His mum sighed. "So how're you holding up?"

He had to kind of yell over the storm. "Yeah, we're fine here, Mum. How about you guys?"

His dad nodded. "We're all fine. It's nice and cosy right now. The noise above us is crazy, but we've got food and water, and everyone's safe."

"Good, good. And yeah, it's loud here too. Probably a good thing we can't see outside, though the video feeds are lookin' pretty wild." Tully's smile faltered for a brief second, and it hurt to know a part of him, even the smallest part, wished he was there with them and that I was the reason he wasn't.

"So," he said. "Things are gonna get rough for the next couple of hours. Jeremiah, what's the status?"

I didn't want to say specifics because I didn't want to sound pessimistic or scare them. I could only nod and repeat what he said. "Yeah. Things are going to get rough for the next couple of hours."

My eyes caught his, and he nodded. Then Tully smiled back at the screen. "Okay. We'll talk again soon, okay?"

They all nodded. "Love you," his dad said, and my heart burned. Hearing their affection and love for one another made my relationship with my own father feel so . . . sad.

I busied myself with the console, reading some incredible data. Wind speeds I'd never seen before, lows of 980 hPa and rainfall in excess of 200 ml in just a matter of hours. It was all Doreen and I could do to keep the alerts up to date with the data coming in. But my mind kept wandering . . .

Until Doreen's big hand gripped my shoulder. Gentle but firm. "You okay there, doc?"

Startled, I nodded quickly. I hadn't realised I'd zoned out. "Ah, yeah, of course."

Tully came over and parked himself on my lap. "Tully, I can't see—"

He held my phone. "Call your dad."

"I'm kinda busy."

He pressed the phone into my chest in hopes I'd take it. "While we still have mobile phone towers. While you still can."

"Tully—"

He sighed, then held my phone up to my face to unlock the screen. He scrolled for a second, pressed some buttons, then held the phone to my ear. My father's voice was faint. "Hello."

Goddammit.

"Hi, Dad, it's me. You're gonna have to speak up. I can't hear you."

"Jeremiah? Can you hear me now?"

It sounded like he was yelling but I could still barely hear him. "Yeah, now I can. It's pretty loud here."

"I've been watching the news," he said. "Wondered how you were getting on."

"All good at the moment. The frontal wall is just on us now. Things are gonna get busy for a while."

He was quiet for a second. "Right, yes. I suppose they will."

Then I was quiet, because I had no clue what to say. We were never good with talking. "Okay, Dad. I have to go."

Another beat of silence. "Well, thanks for calling. I would have been worried."

Would have?

It sounded like he was already, but maybe not.

"I'll call you when I can. They're saying we might lose the phone towers and power, so don't worry too much if I can't reach you."

"Oh, sure. Okay, I'll let you go."

"Bye, Dad."

"Okay. Be good."

And the line went dead.

Tully took the phone from my ear. He gave the back of my neck a squeeze. "You okay?"

I nodded. "Yes. Thank you." I met his gaze. "Thank you."

He kissed the top of my head. "You're welcome."

"Okay, we've got two hundred and twenty kilometre per hour winds coming," Doreen said.

Christ.

The roar outside was almost deafening as it was. The

building shook with the force of the wind, the roof rattled consistently. We could hear the equipment on the roof resisting, the antennas, the ariels, and satellite dishes protesting, the metal all creaking and groaning.

But it felt as if it'd hold.

I was beginning to think this building was another bunker, second to the one in Kakadu. Built in the days when things were made to last. Granted, the bureau wasn't built on the waterfront where Hazer was hitting first . . .

I glanced up at the screens showing live footage from the newsroom. The screen looked broken, only showing grey staticky images, but no. It was just all we could see. Shuddering views of horizontal rain and glimpses out to the ocean that looked like a void.

It was as incredible as it was frightening.

But the noise. I couldn't believe how loud it was.

I had to wonder how Tully's house was and if it was still standing. It fronted the water and would possibly be a direct hit.

"Tully, how's your camera holding up?" I glanced back to find him and Suri sitting against the wall, close together, his arm around her shoulder. She was clearly scared, visibly shaking, and knowing she'd survived the Banda Aceh disaster, I wasn't surprised.

Me looking back at them caused Doreen to look as well, and she froze. "Suri," she murmured as she stood, just as the sound of metal ripping screeched in the furore above us. One of the dash screens went black.

"We've lost the pressure sensor," I said.

But Doreen didn't care. The console panel was forgotten, the work, the cyclone, everything else forgotten as she quickly sat beside Suri and scooped her up, Bruce included.

"Jeremiah," Tully yelled, ducking his head at the noise. He patted the floor next to him. "Come and sit here."

More torn metal screeched above us, and I looked at the

console just in time to see another screen blink out. "The satellite's gone," I said.

Not that they could hear me.

The building was shaking so much now, rattling and groaning. I looked up at the ceiling, expecting it to peel back or rip away at any second . . . yet somehow it held.

Tully's hand on my arm startled me. He pulled me over to the corner with them, his hand in a death grip on mine. And I realised then—a little too late, like I usually did—that it wasn't for my comfort, but his.

He needed me.

So I put my arm around him and held his hands with my other. "It's okay," I yelled so he could hear. "We'll be okay."

I wanted to check his laptop, to see the view from his balcony, but thought better of it.

There was a good chance the camera would be out, and he didn't need to worry about if that meant his house was gone with it.

"I should have taken the job in the Antarctic," I yelled, holding Tully a little tighter. "They don't have cyclones there, and how bad could a snowstorm be?"

He looked up at me, and when he saw that I was joking, he almost smiled. "I'm from the tropics," he yelled back. "We can't move to anywhere it snows."

I laughed and kissed the side of his head, holding him tighter. I love that he included the *we* part to that.

That we'd be a *we* to factor in all our decisions.

Was it probably far too early in our relationship for that kind of thinking?

Maybe.

In the middle of a cyclone in a building that felt as if it was seconds from crumbling around us, did I give one fuck about what anyone else thought?

No.

This man who loved me, who sat huddled in my arms,

trembling and shying from every sudden noise, every bang, every creak and groan of bricks and mortar and steel. At the sound of hell being unleashed outside.

In the face of uncertainty, priorities are made clear.

If this was our last day on Earth, I wanted it to be with him. And if it wasn't our last, I wanted many more with him.

So I held him a little tighter, cradled him closer.

I knew, theoretically, what to expect from enduring a cyclone. I'd read data reports and heard accounts of people who had lived through them. I'd seen the footage of the after-math, and I knew the power of nature it took to amass that kind of destruction.

What I had grossly underestimated was the noise. Or perhaps one had to experience it firsthand to really grasp what the sound of a cyclone was like. It sounded like a plane was landing in the room. Or a train. Or both.

But the strangest thing for me was time.

Time felt wrong.

Every second was a minute, every minute was an hour.

I could see the radar from where I sat. I could see it still moving in real time, but everything else was in slow motion in almost three-hundred-kilometre-an-hour winds.

It made everything feel surreal.

And I realised then that I was having a moment of disas-sociation. That perhaps this level of fear had made my brain disconnect the emotional reasoning, and I started to assess the storm clinically, methodically. As if it were happening to someone else and I was simply analysing the data.

Winds up to 280 km per hour.

Low down to 925 hectopascals.

Another 100 ml of rain.

And those numbers, those statistics, meant high level destruction. That meant buildings would be gone.

People.

There would be a death toll. A fact those numbers couldn't deny.

And I'd warned people. I'd tried to tell them when that news reporter asked me.

Had they listened?

Tully didn't. His family didn't. Apparently they had a *cyclone-proof cellar*, but the more I looked at those numbers, and given their house was fully exposed, fronting the ocean . . . I had to wonder how *anything* would survive.

Like the islands that had been mowed off the map.

I glanced up at the screens.

The camera on the news building was gone, now just a screen of fuzzy white snow. And then I looked at the security camera out the front of the building we were huddled in . . .

A sheet of something had been swept into the yard. It looked like roofing iron. And there was rubbish and debris stuck in the fence, and something dark on the landing at the steps.

Something . . . an odd shape. A moving odd shape . . .

"What's that?" I said. I tapped Tully's shoulder to get him to loosen his grip so I could get up. I went to the screen to get a better look.

It looked like a . . .

Something alive.

"I'll be right back," I said, doubting they could hear me. I went into the foyer area and grabbed the door. It wouldn't budge at first, as if it were locked or suction-cupped shut, and I had to pull it with all my strength until it budged, and then the wind got it and it flew inward, almost knocking me off my feet.

The wind . . .

My god.

And the rain, and the noise. So much louder than I could have imagined. Something flew through the air past the building. A garden chair? Part of a house?

But there, huddled against the wall and utterly defeated, was a bird. Drenched, and the sorriest thing I'd ever seen. I wasn't even sure it was still alive, but I stepped outside, trying to keep my body mass as low as possible, almost getting blown off the landing. I grabbed the bird as the wind tried to take me, and I almost lost my footing . . . until an arm grabbed me.

Tully, holding the door with one hand, holding me with his other, a wild look of fear and anger on his face. He pulled me inside, the door slamming shut behind me. I think he'd kicked it.

The whole building shook.

"Are you in-fucking-sane?" he screamed at me.

The pot plant was knocked over, the baseball bat across the other side of the foyer. Tully's face was pale, his eyes wild. "Are you trying to get us all killed? Opening the fucking door could have blown the windows out or the goddamn roof off. What were you thinking?" He tapped the side of his head.

I shook my head, his anger at me was not expected, and my adrenaline was starting to crash. I tried to speak but couldn't find the words, so I held up the bird instead. It was the size of a magpie or pigeon, but it was hard to tell what it was because it was so wet and ruffled. Soaked to its fragile, hollow bones.

It was limp, but it was trembling.

Or maybe that was me.

I was drenched, I realised, dripping water, and I was shaking. I held the bird to my chest and Tully gripped my arm, none too gently, and pulled me back into the control room.

He all but shoved me to the floor where we'd been sitting before. Doreen's glare could have cut glass, as she was still cradling Suri and Bruce. "Not real bright, are ya?"

"S-s-sorry," I said.

Tully was back with a towel and he ran it over my face and through my hair. He was rough and frantic—my god, he was so mad at me—and he patted down my shoulders and arms, but his hands were shaking and his jaw was clenched so tight I wondered if he'd crack his teeth.

Then his eyes met mine and he sagged, falling back on his arse, the towel forgotten. He took a few deep breaths and he shook his head at me. "That was . . . that was not good. Christ, Jeremiah."

Doreen looked as if she wanted to kill me, but the disappointment in Tully's eyes hit me hard. "I'm sorry. I'm sorry," I said. Kept saying, over and over.

I took the towel and wrapped the bird up, tucking its wings in and covering its head to keep it safe. Tully watched me for a bit, though I still couldn't meet his gaze. He slid back over to sit next to me. "I'm still mad at you," he said.

"I'm sorry," I said. "I didn't think."

He looked at me with *no fucking shit* written all over his face. "For a bird. That's probably gonna die of shock anyway."

I held the bundle of towel more protectively. "No he won't."

Tully rolled his eyes, took the bundle of towel, and holding it to his chest, he sidled in under my arm. He held my arm over his shoulder, looking at my watch. It was flashing, though the beeps weren't loud enough to hear over the wind.

He knew what it meant.

My heart rate was high, and he knew then just how scared I was.

His eyes cut to mine and he held my arm tighter. "I'm still mad at you," he said, before snuggling into me and putting his head into the crook of my neck.

And then the lights went out and the dashboard went dark.

Suri let out a cry, and Doreen soothed her. "It's okay, the generator will kick in."

We waited and waited . . .

Nothing.

The generator had either been disconnected, or maybe it was no longer there at all.

I scrambled for my phone and hit the torch button. It lit up the small, dark room enough that Suri breathed a little better.

And we stayed like that for what felt like an age, until time didn't mean anything anymore, until the winds got quieter. I only really noticed because I could hear over the roar of the wind again. I kissed the top of Tully's head and lifted him off me so I could stand up.

I began flipping switches, trying to get anything to work. The only operational screen was the old Doppler radar.

It showed Hazer directly above us, rotating and not slowing down at all.

But within the span of maybe five minutes, the wind outside had stopped altogether. Like someone had switched the cyclone off, yet on the screen it was still very much there.

And that could only mean one thing.

We were in the eye of the cyclone.

CHAPTER NINE
TULLY

Jeremiah Overton was a genius. Super smart, graduated early, earned his doctorate well before any of his peers. An undeniably incredibly smart man.

He was also really fuckin' stupid.

Stupid for openin' the door.

Stupid for goin' outside.

Stupid, stupid, stupid.

If it had been for a human, I could understand.

But a bird?

An already half-dead bird, at that.

How the building we were in still had a roof, I didn't know.

I didn't want to question it or jinx it.

My heart didn't stop hammering for longer than was probably good for me, and as much as I wanted to wring his neck, I wanted to hug him even more. His watch told me how his heart was pounding too, and despite his outward calm, I knew he was as scared as me. I wanted to hold him and make sure he was okay, make sure he was still in one piece.

I also wanted to pummel the shit out of him for scarin' me like that.

And then the lights went out. He got up and went to the control dash, flipping a few switches and checkin' the data reel. All of the screens were now black bar one, and I could guess the antennas or satellite that had been on the roof were now a few suburbs over.

It had taken me a second to realise the noise was dying down, like I'd stood next to heavy duty machinery or a jet engine, and even though the noise was gone, my ears still rang with the sound of it.

"He's tracking east too fast," Jeremiah said. "Once he touched land, he pinballed east." He glanced back at Doreen like that wasn't good news.

She got up and basically handed Suri over to me.

Poor Suri.

She looked unwell, stressed, and scared.

"You okay?" I asked her.

She nodded quickly. "I wasn't prepared . . . I thought I was . . ."

I rubbed her arm. "You did good."

She cradled Bruce and scrubbed a tear from her cheek.

"This has gotta be the eye, right?" I asked. Jeremiah gave me a nod, and I rubbed Suri's arm again. "We're halfway done. Just another half to go and it'll all be over."

I was still holding the towel with the bird in it—which was probably dead already; I wasn't game to look—so I got up and found a box on the shelf. I tipped the contents out and gently put the towel in it and closed the lid. I put it down by Suri and she nodded.

"I'll go out and see if I can fix the generator. Maybe it got disconnected from the mains," I said.

Jeremiah was checking his phone. "No mobile service. Towers must be down."

Fuck.

No power, no phone service.

"Can you try email?" Doreen asked.

Jeremiah quickly thumbed his phone screen, then looked up. "Cannot be sent."

Jesus.

No internet meant major infrastructural damage.

Because Darwin wasn't already isolated enough, we'd just lost all communication with the outside world.

I went to the door, almost hesitant to open it, but the silence on the other side gave me false hope.

I was expecting the wind to grab the door and I gripped it hard . . . only to find the world outside was calm and quiet. Hell, there was even a peek of blue sky.

"What the fuck," I said.

It didn't seem possible. Like I'd opened the door and walked on to the wrong movie set.

If it weren't for the state of the yard, the water, the mud, the debris, branches, part of someone's roof, I'd think maybe we imagined the whole terrifying thing.

I peered around the balcony, surprised to see the Jeep still there. The canopy was torn and hanging by two clips, there was a branch in it, and it looked like it had been towed out of a swamp, but it was still there.

I went down the steps, past the Jeep, and around to the back of the building. There was more debris at the rear of the yard, more roofing iron, a tarp, the plastic parts to a child's playhouse. The kind Zoe's kids had . . .

And the small concrete slab against the back wall by the ladder was still there, where the generator used to be.

The generator was just gone.

A rusted metal bolt stuck out of the concrete, bent and stripped bare.

Jesus.

I climbed a few rungs of the ladder, which was more rickety than it had been yesterday. I got up high enough to see the roof and didn't need to see anymore. All the ariels and antennas, gone. The satellite was twisted on its side, the bracket that once fastened it, now bent with screws facing up.

But by some miracle, the roofing iron looked secure. Nothing lifted or bent, nothing likely to become a liability once the second half of the storm hit.

I jumped back down, squelching into the mud as I trudged around the other side of the building. All the window boards I'd put up looked to be holding, and as I got to the front of the building, I noticed someone across the street standing out the front of their house. An elderly man, lookin' a little lost.

I walked toward him, talking through the fence. "You okay? How you holdin' up?"

He gave a shaky nod and gestured around. "House's okay, I think. Is it all over?"

"No. This is just the eye. Still got the backend to go yet. You should go back inside."

He grimaced. "Better go check on Jean and Michael," he said, going towards the house next door.

"Don't stay out long," I said, but he didn't say anything, just kept walkin'.

I trudged through the mud, back up the stairs, and inside. Jeremiah's phone torch was the only source of light and it took my eyes a second to adjust. "The generator's gone," I said.

Doreen's eyes flashed in the dark as she stood up straight. "What do you mean gone?"

"I mean no longer there. Just one bent and rusted bolt stickin' up where it used to be."

She grunted. "Fuck."

"And the roof," I said. "Antennas are all out. Satellite's still there, but it's blown over and hanging on by a screw or two."

Both Jeremiah and Doreen turned to the one and only

working radar. "This old thing is still working," Jeremiah said. "That means there's one radio tower still operational."

"It bounces off the Coastal Radio Service," Doreen said. "But it's east of here." Jeremiah's gaze cut to hers, like that was bad news, and she gave a nod. "We won't have it for long."

"I'll try and fix the satellite," I offered, going to the shelf where I'd put the drill . . . the drill that needed power.

Fuck.

"Is there a screwdriver anywhere?" I asked.

Doreen dropped her head back with a groan. "It don't matter at this point. It's all over." She gestured to the black screens. "We got nothin' and we can't communicate with no one." She let out a deep, resigned sigh. "This happened after Tracy. We lost all comms. The whole city was cut off."

I wanted to say those were different times, that technology was different . . . but this bureau was so freaking old.

"We need to let people know," Jeremiah said, shaking his head. "It's imperative that people know."

I was almost afraid to ask. "Know what?"

"Hazer. He's tracking due east along the coast, much faster than we anticipated. He's pinballed, and he's not slowing down."

"Okay," I said, not really understanding his urgency. "We knew that was a possibility. Those people along the eastern—"

He put his hand through his hair. "It means the time in the eye is significantly shorter. We estimated a ninety-minute window in the eye, but that's now not going to happen."

"How much time do we have?"

His eyes cut to mine. "Twenty minutes, maybe."

Fuck.

Suri, still sitting on the floor with Bruce, drew her knees up. "Doreen," I said calmly, "why don't you take them outside for fresh air. I'm sure Bruce needs to pee. And the old guy across the street was going next door to check on his neighbours. I told him not to be long, but I don't know if he heard me."

Doreen took the hint and led Suri outside, leaving me with Jeremiah. "I'll have to drive to the police station," he said. "Maybe I can let them know. Oh god, is the Jeep still even here?"

"You're not drivin' into the city," I said. "You said yourself we've got twenty minutes." That wasn't enough time to get there and back, and god only knew what condition the roads would be in, if there were power lines down, or if he could get through at all.

He pulled at his hair and stared at the console. "Think, think, think."

"What about the battery from the Jeep," I suggested. "Could we rig that up to this console somehow?"

He was staring at the one radar that was still working. It stood to fucking reason that the one instrument still working was as old as time itself. Granted, nothing in here was very new. But this radar was *old*.

"Christ. Noah's Ark had newer technology." I sighed. "And people can still see this radar? This one and only image is the only thing communicating out of this office?" I looked closer at it. "I mean, they know it's us because it says Darwin in the corner."

Jeremiah, who was still staring at the screen, began to smile and grabbed my arm. "Tully, you're a genius."

Well, I absolutely wasn't, because I had no clue what he was talkin' about. But he was frantically searchin' for something on the shelves. "Can you shine a light here please," he asked.

"Uh, sure." I held my phone up for him.

He snatched up the user manual that he'd read, tryin' to learn how all the old equipment worked, and he began flippin' through pages. "Here," he said, flattening the booklet.

"Light, please."

I shone my light for him and he began reading, draggin' his finger down each page faster than I could keep up. "There's a key," he said. "A master key." He looked back at the door. "Doreen? I need you! There's a master key for this console to change the settings. Where is it?"

She came back in, looking confused. "A key?"

He turned to me. "That old keyboard that was here, please tell me you didn't throw it out."

"No, I packed it up," I mumbled, goin' to the shelf I'd put it on. To be honest, I'd nearly tossed it out—it was prehistoric and obsolete, or so I thought—but for some unknown reason, I hadn't.

After a quick search, I held up the keyboard. It was that beige colour old computers used to be, heavy as a brick, and the keys were huge and clunky. The cord attached had an old phone jack on the end of it, for Christ's sake. "This thing?"

Jeremiah grinned. "Yes."

Doreen was now going through the old lockbox, rifling through old keys and whatnot. She held up a key that didn't look like a key at all. The metal key part was small and circular, but Jeremiah grinned when he saw it.

"Yes, that's it!" He grabbed it and dropped to the floor. "I need a light, please."

I shone the light up under the dash and he shoved the key in and turned it, then with a strength I didn't know he had, he ripped off the under section of the panel.

"What the hell are you doing?" Doreen asked.

"The only way to change the official site ID text in the top righthand corner of the screen," he said, "is to do it manually with a keyboard. They would have entered in this information when they installed it."

He plugged the keyboard in, getting on his knees to check the radar screen. And lo and behold . . .

A cursor began to blink on the screen.

Doreen gave him a solid shake. "Jeremiah, you smart sonofabitch."

He backspaced through the four lines of authentication information where it stated Darwin Bureau details, and he began to type.

Darwin Bureau no comms.
Hazer tracking sharp east.
Eye less than twenty mins.
Seek shelter now.

And then we stood there, watching and waiting. The only sound in the room was our breathing.

We had no way of knowing if the message was received. No way of knowing if anyone in Darwin had anyway to see the message at all. It wasn't likely, given everything and everyone was so high tech these days, and this was so old.

"How will they know?" I asked.

"Other Bureaus will see this," Jeremiah said. "I think. And they should realise what we're trying to do. No comms means we can't run alerts; we've lost all signal. The international office will see this for sure. They'll be watching, they'll have guessed by now that we're down. Melbourne too, because Brian will be waiting to see if I fail. They'll issue the emergency warning for us." He swallowed hard and nodded. "I hope."

And we stood there. Waiting. Watching.

Then, after another beat of silence, in the distance, a familiar and very welcome sound.

The cyclone warning siren.

Doreen launched at him, pulling him in for a crushing hug. Jesus, I thought she was gonna break him. "They got it, Doc. You fucking did it!"

When she let him go, he ran his hand through his hair

before he braced his hands on his knees to catch his breath. "Oh wow. What a rush."

I ran my hand up his arm, along his shoulder, and gave his neck a squeeze. "You did good," I said. My heart was hammering, adrenaline pumping. Doreen went back out to find Suri, and I pulled Jeremiah in for a hug. "You did real good."

"It was your idea," he mumbled.

"I can assure you, it wasn't." I gave him a quick kiss. "Come on, you could use some air. While we can."

I pulled him out the front doors and he squinted at the sunlight, and when he looked around, I could tell he found the quietness as weird as I did. It was cloudier now, becoming dark again, but not raining, no wind.

No cyclone.

"Did that old guy come back out?" I asked.

Suri shook her head. "I'll go check on him," Doreen said. "It's old Arty. He knows me."

Doreen went down the yard, slip-sliding a bit in the mud, and I gave Suri's arm a rub. She was holding Bruce pretty tight, though he had muddy feet, so I assumed he'd been for a pee at least. "How you feeling, Suri?"

She gave us a weak smile. "Better. I'm sorry I freaked out before."

"No need to apologise," I said. "I freaked out too."

Then I remembered . . .

I turned to Jeremiah. "We need to talk about the bird ordeal. You runnin' out into the *cyclone*," I said, like that word didn't mean a damn thing. "Almost gettin' us all killed. If the wind hadda come through these doors, it could've taken the roof off and killed us all. You do know that, right? And yes, the typing of the message was genius and you get all the gold stars for that, but I'm still pissed about the bird."

He opened his mouth, then shut it again. "I didn't think. I'm sorry."

"You scared the shit outta me."

His eyes searched mine, filled with sincerity. "I'm sorry. I just . . . felt like my brain detached. I can't explain it. Like it wasn't real. I'm sorry."

I grabbed hold of his shirt and pulled him close enough that I could put my forehead on his shoulder. "No more doin' shit that almost kills you, okay? You gotta start thinkin' of me now, you hear?"

Doreen came out of Jean and Michael's house and pointed to Arty's house. "Just gonna grab his cat."

Ah, jeez.

I noticed then, further down the street, two kids were out on the road. They must have been five and three years old. Unfortunately for them, Jeremiah saw them at the same time. "You two," he yelled, pointing at them and walking down to the gate. "Get home. Go home now. Where's your grown-ups? You need to be inside. The big storm's not over."

Did they listen? No. Did they go back inside? No. They ran up toward us. They were all smiles and very excited, so I didn't think anything was immediately wrong.

"Big wind," the younger one said excitedly, putting their arms up. They wore a T-shirt and a nappy, they had bed hair and had clearly had an exciting day. "Big noise. I cover my ears."

They were at the gate now. Jeremiah stood with his hands on his hips. "You must go home. Which is your house?"

Doreen came out of Arty's with a cat carrier. "They live three doors down," she said. "Come on, kids, come with me. You can't be out here. Where's your dad? Is he okay?"

"He was fixing the roof," the older child said. "It was banging."

Ah, dammit.

Jeremiah began walking back toward us. He put his hand to his forehead. "What don't people understand about cyclones? Can they not hear the sirens?"

I sighed. People skills really weren't his strong suit. "Sounds like their dad's just trying to save the roof, to save his house, most likely. Kids will be kids, Jeremiah. They will come out to see people."

Doreen came back across the road, sans cat and kids.

"Are they okay?" I yelled.

"Yeah, yeah." She waved her hand like she did this every day. "He thought it might be better to stick together. Arty's eighty-seven, and Jean and Michael are in their seventies. Arty shouldn'ta been on his own to begin with."

As Doreen was walking up, a white van drove up and pulled into the driveway. Not just any white van.

Channel 4 News.

Jeremiah growled beside me. Actually fucking growled. Before I could ask him to do it again, he set off down the stairs.

Oh no.

"You have to be kidding me. What the hell do you think you're doing?" he yelled at them before the woman could get out of the van. "If you didn't hear the latest update, take a look at the sky." He gestured to the very dark sky coming toward us. "You have ten minutes to be back in whatever hellmouth you crawled out of."

Doreen snorted, and I sighed.

He was going to be on the news again for all the wrong reasons. I went down after him in some futile attempt to calm him.

"You shouldn't be here," I said to the van but taking Jeremiah's arm. "Come on, we have work to do."

The woman saw my attempt at distracting him as her moment to strike. She came out from behind her passenger door. "Doctor Overton, your message on the radar map, can you explain—"

He shot her a filthy glare. "So you know about the warning, yet you are still here? You admit to being fully aware of the risk, you know you had only twenty minutes when you left your newsroom, you can hear the sirens as we speak, and yet you are *still here*." He looked at the sky, at the wind that was now picking up, at the dark clouds coming from the west now. "You no longer have twenty minutes. You don't even have five. You need to leave. Now."

I noticed then Jeremiah licked his lips, doing that tasting thing he did. And he turned to look at me with fear in his eyes.

But then there was the sound of laughter.

Children's laughter.

The two kids were back, near the gate again, but they were stopped, laughing and pointing at each other's hair. It was sticking up, full of static . . .

Oh no.

"Get inside!" Jeremiah yelled, as he took off running straight for the kids.

Doreen flew down the steps and dragged me, the newswoman, and cameraman up the steps and undercover. Suri went inside with Bruce, and I knew I should have gone with her.

But I couldn't leave Jeremiah.

I couldn't take my eyes off him.

He sprinted through the mud and slid to a stop near the kids. He had to put his hand to the ground to stop himself from falling over. Then, all in the one motion, he scooped them up, one with each arm, and began runnin' back toward us.

I didn't dare breathe.

I couldn't.

He came up the steps to me, the kids were crying, and by god, the fear in Jeremiah's eyes . . . Then, in the next second, the whole sky went white and silent before a boom of thunder cracked so loud it shook us all, and a massive bolt of lightning hit the metal gate.

It was blinding, loud, and far too fuckin' close. The entire metal fence sparked with a loud bang, smoke pluming out in all directions.

Jeremiah was still holding the kids, his back to the fence, sheltering them the best he could. I had Jeremiah's shirt collar in my fist, not even realising I'd grabbed him. I didn't know if I was going to punch him or kiss him. My brain hadn't decided. "Jesus fucking Christ."

The kids were crying, but Jeremiah wasn't letting them go.

I think he was kinda frozen with fear, so I slid my hand up his neck, to his head, feeling for injuries. "Are you okay?"

He blinked back to reality and nodded. "Uh, y-yes. I-I think so."

"Hey," a man yelled out, running up the street. "Girls? Girls?"

Oh great.

He came into the yard, up the steps, barefoot, muddy, and pale as hell. He snatched his kids from Jeremiah, holding them tight. "I saw. I saw." He nodded, tears now running down his face. They clung to him, their little arms around his neck, and he looked up at Jeremiah. "You saved them."

And then, as if all of this was merely the encore, the wind and rain started for the main show.

There was no easing into it.

It hit us, and it hit us hard.

"Inside," Doreen barked. "Now!"

The dad and two kids, and the news woman and the cameraman, all filed inside. And for one second, in the last remaining moment of daylight, I looked at Jeremiah.

His hands were covered in mud, as were his shoes, and his knee from where he'd slid. He was pale, his stark blue eyes filled with unshed tears. With my hand to his jaw, I pulled him in for a quick, hard kiss to let him know he was okay.

Then we went inside.

THE ROOM WAS SMALL ENOUGH TO BEGIN WITH, SMALLER NOW when it was filled with so many people. There were two phones on the floor, shining light up in the room. Doreen sat with Suri where they'd sat before. The dad and his two girls sat by them, where we'd sat earlier. The news crew were sitting with their backs to the opposite wall.

No one was speaking.

I pulled Jeremiah down to sit in his chair. "I'll get somethin' to wash your hands," I said, ducking into the bathroom. I wet wads of hand towel and came back out. He pulled his beeping watch off and dropped it to the floor, then he lifted his shirt and ripped off the chest strap—I'd forgotten he was wearing it—and it joined his watch on the floor.

I took his hands and began gently wiping them clean.

He let me do it without complaint, and his hands were trembling, so I knew he was rattled. "You okay?" I murmured. The wind was loud outside, but I knew he heard me.

His eyes met mine, and even in the dark I could see how troubled he was. "I could taste it."

"I know. I saw." I got a bottle of water, twisted the cap off, and gave it to him. "Here, drink some."

He sipped it and I wiped a smear of mud from his temple before dumping all the dirty paper towels into the bin.

Jeremiah looked over to where the dad was still clutching his two girls. They weren't crying now, but they were still clinging to their dad. "I didn't mean to frighten them," Jeremiah said.

The dad was watching us, very obviously seeing me tend to Jeremiah, the soft words and gentle touches. I wasn't sure if he didn't like seeing two men together or if he was just in shock in general. "It's fine," he said. "You saved them. Thank you. I can't thank you enough. Scared yourself too, I bet."

Jeremiah nodded. "You could say that."

I gave his shoulder a squeeze. "He has a habit of running into dangerous situations with little regard for his own safety."

He glanced up at me and I gave him a smile to let him know I wasn't mad. "Saving people's fine, remember?"

That reminded me . . . the bird.

I stepped over Doreen's legs to near where the dad was sitting and picked up the box with the bird in it. But then I also saw the snacks and food I'd brought. I gave the box to Jeremiah, then handed some bottles of water to the dad and a bag of crisps for his kids. "You guys hungry?"

I gave some water to Doreen and Suri, and taking another bottle, I considered *not* giving it to the news pair, but begrudgingly gave one to them. They could damn well share it.

"Thank you," the cameraman said.

"Yes, thank you," the newswoman echoed.

I didn't reply. I just gave them a look of disdain and went back to Jeremiah. He was now sitting on the floor, so I sat down next to him.

"My name's Jeff," the dad volunteered. "And this is Casey and Presley." Both girls were still lying on Jeff, but they were eating some crisps, so they were going to be okay.

"Doreen, and this is Suri," Doreen said. "And our baby, Bruce."

"He rides the motorbike with goggles on," Casey, the eldest girl, said.

"That's right," Doreen said. "He does."

A clap of thunder and an immediate boom of lightning shook the building, and both little girls screamed.

The wind was back to roaring, the rain was hammering with a constant rumble of thunder. Or maybe the whole sky was roaring. I couldn't tell it apart anymore.

"I'm Jeremiah," Jeremiah said. He had to almost yell because of the noise outside.

"Tully," I said, looking at Jeff. I was pretending the news pair weren't even there.

They said their names, Shane and Lindy or Lindsey or whatever the hell her name was. I didn't care. I still didn't acknowledge them.

"You, uh, Jeremiah," Jeff said. "You knew there was lightning."

"Yes," he answered.

"The girls' hair," I added quickly. I wasn't giving loose-lips-Lindsey one more detail of Jeremiah's life for her to make a story out of. "Their hair was sticking up with static. It's indicative of an imminent strike."

Jeff instinctively patted both girls' hair down. "I was trying to fix my roof. Some of the iron had lifted. I told them to stay inside." He shook his head. "It would have got them. It was right where they were standing . . ." His voice got shaky. "Thank you."

Everyone was quiet for a bit as the storm raged. The sound of it, my god. It was deafening. There was no point in talking now.

Jeremiah opened the box and carefully lifted the bundle of towel out. I almost didn't want him to open it. If the bird was dead, letting the young girls see wouldn't be good.

He pulled the towel back and the bird just lay there. Not soaking wet anymore, but it looked lifeless. Jeremiah stroked the feathers down its neck and its beak opened. Dear god, it was still alive.

I smiled at Jeremiah, and he smiled at me before he began gently rubbing the bird over with the towel. But before it got more stressed, he bundled it back up and popped it back in the box.

Then we all sat there in silence, each huddled to our

person, as the cyclone battered us. A constant roar, incessant banging, howling, the sounds of metal and steel straining.

I expected the roof to rip off at any second. Or the walls to break apart, or something to slam into us. Every cell in my body was laced in fear, prepared, locked in fight or flight mode; the adrenaline was exhausting.

Jeremiah and I had our arms around each other, holding on tight. The girls were crying, screaming at every loud bang. Doreen cradled Suri's head to her chest, and even Lindsey covered her ears.

Then, after an age, the radar, the last remaining light on the dashboard, blinked off and back on. Our one last hope at communication.

I could feel Jeremiah hold his breath as he waited for the inevitable.

His head went to my shoulder, I rested my head against his, and no one spoke.

Just scared eyes and flinches every time something banged, or thunder clapped, or lightning boomed.

Then the radar blinked again, off and on, then off again, only this time didn't come back on.

"Radio tower's down," Jeremiah said.

Christ.

Time slowed down to a crawl.

Every minute felt hellishly long.

The tail end of the cyclone was so much worse. Jeremiah had said it would be, and he wasn't wrong.

The noise. The roar. The sound of hell unleashed.

For as long as I lived—if I lived through this day—I would never forget how loud it was.

It started to mess with my head. Like I couldn't hear anything else but the deafening roar, and then like I couldn't hear it at all.

Like I'd gotten used to it. Complacent. Like the utter horror outside wasn't happening at all.

Even the girls had stopped crying some time ago and now just stared blankly into the room. I think I preferred them crying.

Suri was sitting up now, still tucked into Doreen's side, still clutching Bruce. With just a hollow look of defeat.

It felt surreal.

Like the worst possible thing to happen wasn't happening at all.

I wondered how my family was.

If they were okay.

Did the cyclone-proof cellar hold?

Were they hurt?

My heart was thumping so hard it was painful.

"You okay?" Jeremiah asked.

I nodded, making myself let go of his shirt. I hadn't realised I was even holding it, but my hands hurt from clenching them. My whole body ached from being so tense.

He took my hands in his and rubbed where my fingernails had bitten into my palm. "They'll be okay," he said, somehow knowing where my mind had gone.

Maybe he was thinking about his dad back in Melbourne.

I nodded again. "I wish I knew for sure."

Then something occurred to me . . .

I looked over at Shane and Lindsey. "You drove here from the newsroom?"

Lindsey still had her hands over her ears, but Shane nodded.

"What was the damage like?"

Shane gave a small shake of his head, as if tellin' me not to ask.

"What was the damage?" I asked again, yelling this time. "The foreshore? The city centre?"

Shane glanced at Doreen and Suri, then at Jeff and his girls, and finally back to me. "Trees down, roofs gone. Flooding. Smashed windows. Some houses were ripped open. Some houses were flattened."

"Where?" I asked.

He took too long to answer.

"Houses gone, where? Which suburbs?"

Jeremiah put his hand up, like he was telling Shane not to answer. He pulled me back against him and kept his arm around me.

"Everywhere," Shane yelled. "Houses everywhere." He gestured to the air, to the cyclone outside. "And this half is worse than the first."

His words hit me like the storm itself.

I sagged back and Jeremiah's hold on me tightened.

Houses everywhere.

I shouldn't have asked.

Because knowing was worse.

It was so much worse.

And time dragged on slower then. The surreal time warp went on and on.

Until the bangs got fewer and farther in between, the roar was a mere ringin' in my ears, and all that was left was the sound of rain.

"I think it's over," Jeremiah said.

Everyone sat in silence, listening now, instead of tryin' to not hear.

He got to his feet and pulled me up with him.

God, my whole body hurt.

"I think it's over," he said again, going to the door. He put his hand on the handle and paused, looking at me.

The rain got quieter still, so he opened the door and we walked out. Seeing the outside world for the first time in what felt like years. Seeing sunlight trying to break through storm clouds and gentle spatters of rain.

And utter carnage.

CHAPTER TEN

JEREMIAH

It was hard to process what we were seeing.

The carport at the side of the building now had no roof. The Jeep was a few metres away and now facing toward us. The news van was on its side against the now-broken fence.

Arty's house was missing some roofing iron and it looked like some windows were smashed.

Jean and Michael's house seemed to be okay. Further down, there was a car on its roof out on the street, debris everywhere. Jeff, still holding his two girls, started for his house, made it a few steps, and stopped. It was missing half its roof, and I couldn't see what else.

Doreen went past him and raced across the street toward Jean's house.

My god, I hoped they were all okay . . .

People started walking out onto the street. Someone further down started running for Jeff's house. "Jeff?" they called out.

"Up here," he yelled back. He put Casey down and waved.

They stopped and sagged with relief when they saw him. It was a couple, a man and woman, and they began to walk up. Jeff glanced back at us, nodded, and taking Casey's hand, walked to the end of the yard.

"Oh my god, we were so worried," the woman said. "We saw your roof go. You were up here?"

Jeff was still staring at his house. Or what was left of it. "Ah, yeah," he said. He looked back to us and nodded again. "Yeah . . . the girls . . . Lucky we weren't home by the looks of it."

They walked back toward their house just as Doreen came out. She was helping Arty walk. He was holding the cat carrier, and he looked okay. Suri went to meet them.

Shane and Lindsey were over by their van; he had his hands on his head. They'd be needing a tow truck for sure.

And now the sun was out.

It was hard to get your head around. Like the cyclone hadn't happened.

But we'd made it through.

The office was useless—no power, no antennas, no satellites—but it had held strong and protected us.

I put my hand to Tully's chest. "You okay?"

He nodded woodenly. "Yeah. But I need to go . . . I need to check on my folks, my family."

"Okay," I agreed.

I hoped . . . I just hoped with everything that I was, that they were all okay.

"Let's go," I said. "The Jeep looks okay. You grab your stuff. I'll go tell Doreen."

He tried to swallow. "Okay."

I gave his arm a squeeze before ducking down the steps and slip-sliding across the muddy yard. "Doreen," I called out. She came out onto the veranda. "Is everyone okay?"

Doreen nodded. "He's a bit shaken up. Jean and Michael are okay. Arty's got some water damage to his livin' room, missin' a window or two, but he'll be fine."

"Good, that's good. Tully and I need to leave. He needs to

find his family. Jeff and the girls have gone to check his place. It doesn't look too good."

Doreen came over and collected me in a horrifying bear hug. "You did good today." Then she dropped me back to the ground and whacked my shoulder. "I'll lock the office. Clean-up can wait till tomorrow."

I nodded. "Sounds good. First thing."

She glanced back to the Jeep where Tully was throwing his bag in and carrying the box with the bird in it, and gave me a solemn nod. "I'll keep my fingers crossed."

God, same.

I didn't know what else to say. "Hope your house is okay."

I walked back across the street, seeing more people out now, and went into the yard.

Shane met me at the gate. "Are you leaving?"

"Yes."

"Can we get a lift?"

I nodded. "Sure."

Tully wouldn't be happy, but this was not the time for pettiness.

Tully climbed in and turned the key, and sure enough, the trusty old Jeep started. "She hasn't let me down yet," he said, patting the steering wheel.

I opened the passenger door, took the box holding the bird off the front seat, and pulled my seat forward.

Lindsey climbed up and Tully rolled his eyes. I knew he didn't like them, but he wouldn't say no. People needed help, and he was the helping kind. Even if he'd threatened to punch them the day before. Shane climbed in with his camera. I pulled the seat back into place and got in.

The canopy was long gone, the inside of the Jeep was as wet and muddy as the ground, but it was working and that's all that mattered.

We began the slow drive out.

There were trees down on the road, branches everywhere, clumps of hail against fences, debris in all shapes and sizes . . .

Some people were out, assessing the damage, checking on neighbours. Some houses were torn apart, some looked like a construction zone, some were gone altogether.

"Jesus Christ," Tully said.

There were cars on their sides, some had crashed into each other like tenpins. People were standing, looking at the carnage in shock, walking around in a daze. Most of them were crying.

Powerlines were down, no traffic lights were working, water covered most parts of the roads. Businesses and shops were a mess, signs and roofs were torn off or missing completely. The entire city looked like it had been through an industrial washing machine.

I hadn't noticed that Shane was filming as we drove. The Jeep had no roof on it, so he was getting an unimpeded view, and I didn't even mind. This footage should be seen. The level of destruction, the damage.

If he had any way of getting this footage to the outside world, that was.

Speaking of which, I found my phone and tapped the screen. No service. No internet.

That wasn't good.

And neither was Tully's grip on the steering wheel. I reached over and took his arm, pulling it free so I could hold his hand. He gave me a fraught smile, and I knew it wasn't just his family he was worried about.

This was his city.

This was his hometown. His community, his people, his friends.

And I didn't know if he forgot that Shane and Lindsey were in the back seat, because I'd assumed he'd drop them off at the news station, but he turned off before we got into the city centre.

We were going straight to his parents' house by the look of it, through residential streets of huge, brand-new homes strewn with more debris. He had to drive around boards and chairs and roofing iron, tree trunks snapped like matchsticks covering half the road. The once expensive estate now looked like a war zone.

"Holy shit," Tully whispered. "Oh my fucking god."

Up ahead, there were people standing on the road, shocked and distraught. The adjoining street was something out of a disaster movie.

It was . . . gone.

As if a giant plough had upturned one single stretch of earth.

There wasn't one house left standing. Just piles of debris and construction materials where houses once were.

Tully took his hand back, gripped the steering wheel, and floored it. Driving too fast by the debris, by the dazed people. He swung the Jeep around the corner, took one intersection way too fast, going straight past his street. I only caught a glimpse, but Tully's house looked okay as we sped past—the front was still standing, if that was some indication—though he just kept driving by and up and over the crest.

Shane was now kneeling on the seat, filming behind us, I realised, across the elevated view of Darwin. The entirety of the damage was indescribable.

There just weren't the words.

The huge houses in this street were still standing, unscathed, like the gaps between the giant ploughs had spared it. Tully drove up the gutter and slammed on the brakes.

He was out of the Jeep and running to the front of the house. "Mum! Dad!"

Oh god.

The front door was open and his father stepped outside, and Tully ran into his arms like he hit a wall. Then his mum was hugging him too, right in the front yard. "Oh, thank god," his mum cried.

"Ellis," Tully said frantically. "Where's Ellis? Is he here? Tell me he's here."

Rowan appeared, holding one of his kids, and Ellis came out from behind him.

As soon as Tully saw him, he sucked back a breath and finally exhaled, his hands on his knees, relief almost knocking him over. "Thank fuck," Tully cried, then collected his brother in a fierce hug.

Ellis was as shocked as the rest of them, and Tully pulled back, taking his brother's face in his hands. "Your house. Your whole street, Ellis." He shook his head. "It's gone. I thought you mighta been there. I was so fucking scared." He pushed against his stomach with the heel of his hand, as if the knots that had been there were beginning to unravel. He was still breathing hard.

Ellis shook his head, eyes wide. "What do you mean, gone?"

Tully held him by the shoulders. "I mean it's gone." Then he looked at his parents, at Rowan and then Zoe, who was standing in the door with a small child on her hip. "So much is gone. The damage. From the bureau to here." He shook his head and his voice trembled, teary-eyed. "The damage . . ."

I went to him then and pulled him against me. His hands came up slowly to fist my shirt and he sobbed, the relief that his family was safe, that Ellis was safe, finally bubbled over.

His dad came over and rubbed his back, then his mum went to Ellis. Her sad eyes met mine. "You're both okay, and we're all okay, and that's all that matters." Then she took Ellis' face in her hands. "Houses can be rebuilt. Things can be replaced. People can't."

He nodded and wiped a tear from his cheek, then he came

over and literally peeled Tully away from me to hug him. His mum took my arm. "We were so worried about you both. We came up when the eye passed over, but then the sirens went off so fast, so we all went back down."

Tully cry-laughed, wiping his tears. "Well, I got a story about that," he said. Then his eyes met mine. And if I could read him at all, perhaps his eyes acknowledged that my message on the radar screen had saved his family . . . "But the story can wait." He looked around at everyone. "We're all okay. That's all we can ask for." Then he looked at Ellis. "Come on, let's go take a look at your place before the cops close it off."

I grabbed Tully's arm and nodded to Shane, who was still filming the street, and to Lindsey, who was standing there like she was barely held together. "We should ask them where we can take them."

Tully's mother noticed Lindsey then and went to her, bringing her over. "Are you okay, dear?"

Lindsey scrubbed a tear from her cheek and recomposed herself, though she was far from her newsreader put-together appearance. She nodded. "Oh, we're fine," she said. "Well, I mean, first up Doctor Overton saved us from being struck by lightning, then we sheltered in the bureau office with them and with another family he saved from being struck by lightning, and our van was tipped over, so then they drove us back —" She sucked back a breath and started to cry. "I'm fine."

Yeah. She was not fine.

Tully's mother looked at me. Everyone looked at me. "I didn't save anyone, really," I said. "I just prevented—"

"Yeah, he did," Shane interrupted. "Saved those two little kids, one hundred percent. I got it on tape too."

"Oh good," Tully said, sourly. "Gonna run it before or after the footage of his mother's death this time? Which is worth more ratings?"

Oh boy.

"Tully," his father chided.

"No," he said flatly. He glared at both Shane and Lindsey. "I won't ever be quiet about it. Jeremiah can save your life, the life of those kids, and every person in this whole fuckin' city, like he damn well did today, and you'd still use him for ratings. Remember what I said about eating a whole bag of dicks—"

I pulled his arm, dragged him over to the Jeep, and pushed him so his back was against the door. He opened his mouth, another rant about to pour forth, no doubt, so I shut him up the only way I could think of.

I took his face in my hands and kissed him.

In front of everyone, and they were all watching, but I didn't care.

He grunted in surprise but slowly and surely the tension and the anger left his body. When I was sure he wasn't so mad anymore, I put my forehead to his. "It's been a helluva day, Tully. It's not over yet. Your brother needs you."

Tully's face crumpled a little, more tears fell, and he nodded, his forehead to my chin. He let out a shaky breath and regrouped. "Okay. Thank you."

"You're welcome."

Tully scrubbed his face, ignored the news crew, then looked over at Ellis. "Come on. I'll drive you."

They were all looking at us. I had just kissed Tully in front of them, so it wasn't surprising. Embarrassing still, none-theless.

"We'll be there shortly," his mum said.

Ellis opened the passenger door to the Jeep. "Get in the back," Tully said. "That's Jeremiah's seat. Learn your place."

"I gotta open the door to get in." He climbed through and sat down on the very wet seat. "Christ, did you park it in the sea?"

Tully started the engine. "We were in a fucking cyclone, Ellis."

I lifted the box carefully and took my seat in the front. Tully and Ellis were still bickering, and their mother was giving Rowan instructions about using the BBQ to feed people, while their dad was showing Shane and Lindsey to his car.

When he got to the top of the crest, Tully stopped the Jeep so we could see the view over Darwin.

It was hard to put into words. We could see where the cyclone had touched down, its trail of destruction like jagged wounds gouged open.

Ellis' jaw dropped, his eyes wide and teary.

When Tully saw his brother's face in the rear-vision mirror, he began the drive down. Slower this time. We drove past Tully's street, just able to see that his house looked intact. We wouldn't know for sure until we went inside, but there was no debris and it all looked decidedly calm.

Unlike just a few streets over.

There were more people out on the street now, clearly in shock and distraught, and Tully slowed the Jeep to a crawl as he drove into Ellis' street.

These were once huge luxury houses. Like Tully's, like his parents' house.

Now they looked like they'd been through a woodchipper.

Tully pulled up to one particular pile, getting off the street the best he could. The road was a minefield as it was, but the sound of sirens was getting louder and louder, and there was a good chance emergency vehicles would be arriving soon.

We got out, and Tully pulled his seat forward for Ellis.

He was pale and dismayed, and as he stood there looking at where his house once stood, his chin wobbled, and his hand shook as he ran it through his hair.

Tully put his arm around his shoulders, and for a while, no one spoke.

Then Ellis turned around to look at his neighbours' houses. "The Bakshis were in Perth, I think. Mrs Mahoney left to be with her daughter. John and Rayna went south." He pointed to a house down the road. "But the Lims were staying. God, so were the Wards . . ."

He began walking down there. Then he began to run.

"Ellis, wait," Tully said, running after him.

I began to follow too, but as Ellis got to the next house down, an older man came out with his arm around a woman, and Ellis stopped running. "Mr Lim! Winnie, are you okay?"

I stopped as well and let them talk in private.

I was glad they were okay, but my god . . . this whole street . . . I wanted to do something. I wanted to help. But I didn't know where to start. I was so tired and saddened, and I was so sorry that this had happened.

It wasn't my fault, I knew that. But still, there was a shadow of responsibility that hung over me.

There was no way to predict which street exactly would get wiped off the map, but any of these waterfront homes were a risk. Sure, we knew the warmer air over land would affect the trajectory of the cyclone, coming from the cooler air over water. We knew the science behind it.

But Mother Nature was an unpredictable beast.

There were always likelihoods and probables.

Behind Ellis' house was a nature reserve, by the looks of it, that fronted the bay. The cyclone hit land right here. Not a few streets over, not Tully's house. Not a few streets over from that. Not his parents' house where they'd all sheltered.

Thank god.

Having them all seek shelter in one place had been frightening, and in hindsight, probably foolish. If it had been their home that was hit, if they didn't have a cyclone-proof cellar,

Tully could have lost his entire family in one fell swoop. Every single one of them.

Does he know how close he came?

How would one salvage the wreckage from that?

How did we salvage anything from this?

Looking at Ellis' house, I wasn't sure what was left to salvage at all.

I walked into the mess of what was left. It was sodden and strewn everywhere. There was half a wall to the right still standing, nothing on the left, and there was no roof at all. Plasterboard was everywhere, half a couch upended, clothes, papers, a broken table. The kitchen island bench was still there, but the fridge was now laying a few metres outside.

I wasn't sure what I could tread on, so I didn't go far. It was unsafe, and the last thing the hospital needed right now was me being injured for being stupid.

"Jeremiah?" Tully called out from where he was standing with Ellis. "What are you doing?"

They were at the front of the house. I gave him a sad smile. "I know. I just . . ." My foot slipped a little, and I looked down to see I was standing on what was a piece of kitchen cabinet or a dresser of some kind. But I spotted something else, half hidden.

It was a clock.

It was silver and art deco, or some other style I wasn't familiar with. It looked old and maybe it meant something to him. I had to lift a piece of plywood off it, but I picked it up, surprised by its weight, and brushed it off. I walked out with it, stepping over everything, and Tully held his hand out to help me over the last part.

I handed the clock to Ellis.

He took it with a teary smile, wiping the crystal face.

"Granddad's desk clock," Tully said.

Ellis nodded and wiped a tear from his cheek. "It was upstairs," he said.

Christ. This house used to be double storey?

Tully pulled his brother in for another hug as their parents arrived, clearly shocked by what they saw.

"Oh, good heavens," his mother whispered, her hand to her mouth.

Their dad put a hand on each son. "Thank god you weren't here, Ellis."

A fire truck turned into the street, lights flashing, and they cut the siren. They stopped at the first house.

"Let's see what we can find," his dad said. "Before they kick us out."

"Dad, stop," Ellis said, grabbing his father's arm. "Don't." He shook his head and sighed. "There are gas lines, and that wall doesn't look stable." He looked at what used to be his house. "All my photos are in the cloud. My hard drive is backed up; all my work files are saved. I'm wearing the watch you guys bought me." He shook his head and shrugged. "What's left is just . . . stuff. It's just replaceable stuff." He held up the clock and gave me a sad smile. "Except this."

Tully put his arm around me. He rested his forehead on my shoulder, exhausted. I knew exactly how he felt.

"I don't know where I'll go," Ellis mumbled.

"You can live with us," Tully replied quickly.

Us?

It took me a moment to realise that Tully included me. Sure, I lived there. But up until now it had felt like I was only *staying* there. As if it were a temporary arrangement.

Tully squeezed my hand. "Is that okay?"

Okay?

"Of course it's okay. It's your house. Why are you asking me?"

"Because you live there too."

"Yeah, but it's not my house."

Tully sighed and, ignoring that comment but still holding

my hand, looked at Ellis. "You can stay with us. For as long as you need."

The fire truck came down toward us and one guy got out. "Hey, folks," he said. "Everyone okay here?"

"Uh, yeah," Ellis replied. "This is my house . . . Or was . . . I wasn't here when it struck."

"Do you know if any of your neighbours were home?"

He told them about the Lims and how he'd thought the people across the road were staying, but the Lims had said no, the Wards had left yesterday. The fireman said they'd go check anyway but warned that none of the street was safe and we'd be required to move along.

"Excuse me," I said. "Have you any updates on the power outage? Or the internet?"

He gave me an odd look, so I clarified. "I work at the Bureau of Meteorology and our power was cut. All my systems are down. I lost all comms. I'll need to relay some data to Arnhem Land—"

He stared at me. "You work at the . . . Was it you who did that message?"

Oh.

Tully snorted and clapped my back. "Yes, it was him."

The officer took two giant strides toward me and collected my hand, shaking it somewhat violently. "Well, I'll be damned," he said, grinning. Then he called out toward the truck. "Jimmy, it's the weather station guy!"

Another fireman, who was at the house across the street, came over. He was maybe fifty, fit, and rather good-looking. "What's up?" he said.

"The guy who put the message on the weather radar about the eye of the storm," the first officer said, gesturing to me. "This is him."

Jimmy's chiselled face grinned. "Ah, the blue-eyed weather guy from the news. It was you?"

I heard Tully grumble beside me, but then he inhaled

deeply, which I knew meant he had every intent to unload a mouthful. I tugged on his hand to let him know I had this one.

"Yes, my eyes are blue," I said with a sigh, because that was the detail they took away from all of this.

I shouldn't ever dare to not be surprised. Or disappointed.

"In other *more important* news, do you have any updates on the power and internet outage?" I asked flatly. "I'd like to get my system up and running as fast as possible. The building's intact, but I have no satellites or antennas. I'm sure you can understand the urgency. Flood warnings will remain in place, and I have no access to data or alerts to the east of us, where Hazer is right now."

He straightened up. "The main lines are down. There's optic fibre cable damage on the cable line that comes into Darwin. I believe they're working on it. Could be days for all we know." He glanced back at the truck and his colleague. "We don't even have radio. Even the CB towers are down. They're working on satellite comms but most of the dishes were destroyed, so guessing a timeframe is sketchy at best."

Right. Finally some proper information. Not that it was great news by any stretch, but at least he was taking me seriously. "Thank you." I turned to Tully. "We should go."

"Look," Jimmy said. "Sorry . . . about before. I didn't mean any disrespect. What you did with the message on the radar was real smart, and it saved lives, no doubt about it."

Given he'd said it with sincerity, I met his eyes and gave him a nod. "Do you know if the emergency response office is open?"

Tully pulled on my arm. "Yeah, no. Your work is done today. Let other people do their jobs."

I pulled my arm free, annoyed. "There are still parts of the state—"

Tully held his hand up and raised one finger. "First of all, this is a Territory, not a state. You're new here so I'll let that slide. Second of all, you haven't slept properly in two days. You saved enough people today, and you almost died twice." He held up two fingers. "Twice I thought you were gonna die today, two separate times, which is more than enough, thanks." He fired a filthy look at Jimmy. "And you still get disrespected. So you know what? You've done all you can do today; let other people do their jobs. What you need right now is food and sleep, and what I need right now is you. And my brother lost his house and everything he owns, and half the city is gone. So . . ." His bottom lip wobbled, and I knew then that Tully was well and truly at his limit.

I slid my hand around the back of his head and pulled him against me. "Okay. Let's go."

His mum came over and put her hand to Tully's hair. "Come back to our place. Rowan's cooking some meat on the BBQ. Get some food in your belly and then you can sleep."

Tully looked about ready to argue, but I nodded. "We'll be there, thank you."

He pouted and went to the passenger seat of the Jeep, which meant I was driving. Ellis went with his parents, and they drove off first. "I just want to go home," he said.

I was about to start the engine, but I didn't. I turned to face him instead. "Spend time with your family." I took his hand. "They need to see you, and you need to spend time with them. Especially Ellis. Especially today. It could have been a very different outcome today. If the cyclone had been just a few streets over, your entire family . . ." I dropped my head. "I know you're tired. But just give them one hour."

He didn't say anything for a moment and I wondered if I'd overstepped, but when I looked up at him, he was smiling. It was a teary smile, a tired smile, but it was a grateful smile that made my heart knock against my ribs. "Okay," he murmured.

I nodded and kissed his knuckles, then started the Jeep and drove us to his parents' house.

TULLY PLAYED WITH HIS NIECES AND NEPHEWS, HE CHATTED WITH Zoe and Rowan—siblings he wasn't particularly close to—he had some quiet conversations with Ellis, and his parents hugged all of them a lot.

We checked on the bird in the box and managed to feed it some minced beef and water. Mr Larson said it was a baby magpie, likely unable to fly to escape the storm. I figured if it lived through the night, we could take it to someone to look after.

I sat with his mum while Tully helped his dad take down the boards of plywood from the windows and they tidied up the yard. The old weather station Tully had installed was nowhere to be found, but that wasn't surprising.

"Thank you for making him come back," his mum said quietly. "I know he didn't want to."

"He needed to," I said. "And he'll be glad he did."

She smiled as she watched him lifting off one of the boards. "You have a way with him," she said, still smiling. "You calmed him down so easily today. He listens to you."

"It'd been a stressful two days, that's all," I said, dismissing her claim. "Though he does have a short fuse."

She chuckled. "He really doesn't. He's normally very placid. Cool-headed and easy going; it's what makes him very good at his job. He'd be the one to break up a fight, never start one. He argues with his brother all the time, but that's all in jest. Mostly. I think I've seen him genuinely bristle only three times in his life: once was when he cussed out the news reporters on live TV, and two times were today."

"Oh. Well, he was tired and hungry today," I said, immediately trying to defend him. Then I realised what point she was making. "Those three times are because of me? Are you implying I'm not good for him?" I started to feel a little unwell . . . I was too tired to be having this conversation right now.

She took my hand and squeezed it. "Heavens no, just the opposite actually."

I was so confused. "I'm not following. Sorry, I—"

"He was defending you, Jeremiah." She smiled at Tully, who was now bickering with his dad about how he was holding the board while his father unscrewed it. "He's so in love with you."

Oh, dear god.

"And it's wonderful to see," she mused happily, still watching him. He was still bickering with his father.

"Are you sure he doesn't have a temper, because . . . ?" I gestured to him. He was now arguing a little louder than before.

"Okay, maybe a little bit," she allowed. She patted my leg. "Take him home."

They finally got the board off and Tully dumped it on the pile with the others. Taking him home sounded like a really good idea. "Tully," I said.

He looked straight over at me and came inside. "Are we going? Please tell me we're going?"

I nodded. "I'm tired."

He put his hand to my belly and slid his arm around my waist. Displays of affection in front of people would definitely take some getting used to. Especially in front of his parents.

Then I remembered that I'd kissed him in front of them, and that made leaving sound even better.

We said goodbye to everyone, and Tully got to Ellis. "You coming?"

"I will. Tomorrow, if that's all right. I might stay here tonight," he said.

It was understandable.

"Plus, I'm pretty sure I don't wanna hear what noises'll be coming outta your room—"

Tully snatched the cordless drill off his father and tried to get around the couch to kill his brother. Rowan and their dad tried to intervene, the kids all joined in, laughing and squealing like it was all the best game they'd ever played.

I sighed and gave a nod to his mum. "Thank you for the food."

"Thank you," she said. "Maybe one day you can tell us about the hero story the news crew talked about and that nice-looking fireman mentioned."

I smirked. "He was nice-looking, wasn't he?"

"Hey, I heard that," Tully said. He was no longer holding the drill, but he did have one nephew over his shoulder. "He was nice-looking. Until he opened his stupid mouth." He made a face. "Errrr, the blue-eyed weatherman, said the brown-eyed fireman. What a dick."

"Tully," Zoe chided. "Language."

"How come you noticed his eye colour?" I asked.

"Yeah, Tully," Ellis chimed in. "How come you noticed?"

Tully was about to have another go at Ellis, but Ellis was under a pile of nieces and nephews, and he was smiling for the first time since we'd got back. Tully added another kid to the pile, and with a smile aimed at his mum, we took the box with the bird in it and went home.

It was still daylight outside, but his house was completely boarded up and pitch-black inside. He shone his phone torch around, and everything was just as he'd left it.

No broken windows, no damage.

Not that we could see, anyway. There was certainly no missing roof and demolished house like Ellis' and countless other people's.

We were so very lucky.

Tomorrow we would learn more about the widespread damage, and the death toll numbers would start to come in.

But for now, like the boarded-up windows, we could block

it out and, for a few hours at least, pretend the outside world didn't exist.

We put the box with the bird in it on the floor. "Good luck, little guy," Tully said quietly. Then he led me upstairs. "No power also means no air conditioning," he said. "But it also means no hot water. Hell, I don't even know if we have cold water." He led me straight into his bathroom and put his phone torch up on the sink. "Quickest shower ever, then bed. And I can't believe I'm going to say this, but I'm too tired for sex."

I snorted. "Honestly, same."

He pulled his shirt off. "But not too tired for kisses or cuddles." Then he pulled *my* shirt off. "Right?"

"Right."

He stopped, and putting his head on my chest, he fell against me. I was quick to hold him up. Apparently the cuddles were starting early.

"Thank you," he murmured. "For making me go back to Mum and Dad's. You were right."

"I usually am."

He snorted, barely able to keep his eyes open. I rubbed his back and he got heavier in my arms. "Just wanna stay like this."

"You'll appreciate a shower."

"I'll appreciate you washing me."

I kissed the side of his head. "Okay."

I turned the water on, and yes, there was cold water. No hot. But this was Darwin; the cold water was warm anyway. For me at least. I lured Tully under the showerhead and began to soap us both up.

Scrubbing the dirt, the mud, and the awful day away felt so good—kissing him softly, his lips, his nose, his eyelids—felt heavenly. But exhaustion was setting in, and when Tully swayed on his feet, I shut the water off.

I towel-dried us off the best I could, then helped Tully into bed. I climbed in after him and he wrapped himself around me.

"M' hair's still wet."

"I don't care."

"Been a day," he mumbled. "Thankful we're okay."

I kissed his forehead. "Me too."

"Love you."

His words both thrilled me and calmed me, and even after the day we'd had, I was still too scared to say them back.

I wanted to tell him I loved him. I wanted to say the words so much, but my staccato heart stopped me. Could I run out into a lightning storm without hesitating? Sure. Could I put myself in danger without fear? Sure.

Could I say those three little words out loud?

No.

Instead, I tightened my arms around him and tilted his face up so I could kiss his lips.

"Me too."

CHAPTER ELEVEN

TULLY

I slept like a log. After the week we'd had and the stress of it all—after hunkering down and bein' all tensed up for hours—I was so exhausted. Then in my darkened bedroom—without one sliver of light and having a Jeremiah-sized pillow—I don't think I even moved once.

Not until someone bangin' on the front door woke me up. I pulled on some shorts and went downstairs. "Yeah, hold up. I'm coming." Then I remembered the day before and the cyclone, and I wondered if someone was hurt. "I'm coming."

"I bet that's what he said," Ellis called out. "You better not be naked, for the love of god."

I sighed and opened the door to find my parents and Ellis standing there in bright daylight. It hurt my eyes. "Christ. What time is it?"

"It's after eight," Mum said as they walked in.

"Eight o'clock?"

They got as far as the foyer. "God, it's like a cave in here," Dad said. "No wonder you don't know what time it is."

I scrubbed my hand through my hair and stretched my back before shuffling into the kitchen and flicking the coffee machine on . . .

Goddammit.

"No power means no coffee," I said, putting my head on the kitchen counter. "I hate this already."

"Let's get these boards off the windows," Dad said, getting straight to work.

I sighed. "I'll go wake Jeremiah."

I took the stairs and climbed onto the bed, crawlin' over to his body and kissing his shoulder. "Hey, sleepyhead," I murmured. He mumbled and groaned. "My parents are here, and it's after eight. Doreen'll be wondering where you are."

He shot up. "Eight o'clock?"

I laughed and got off the bed. "I'd offer to make you coffee, but I can't."

He scrambled out of bed. "Doreen's going to kill me." He stopped, confused. "Why is it so dark?" Then his shoulders sagged, as if he just remembered the whole cyclone thing like I had just a few minutes ago. "Oh."

"Dad's here to help me take the boards off."

He pulled on some shorts. I loved that he hated under-wear. "I wish I could help," he said, plucking a T-shirt off a hanger and pulling it over his head. "Doreen's going to be so mad."

I laughed. "No she won't."

He dashed into the bathroom to scrub his face and brush his teeth. "Try not to drink the water," I said. "We'll need to boil it from now on."

He paused with his toothbrush in his hand. "Oh, yes. Of course."

It made me smile that he was so stinkin' smart, so switched on about all the genius stuff, but sometimes the basic stuff was lost on him. It was cute. "I'll see if I can find us something to eat," I said, leaving him to it.

I went back downstairs to some sunlight coming through the back glass door. Dad and Ellis already had one board off the panel. Mum was in the kitchen with some Weet-Bix on the counter. "The milk in your fridge will still be good for now. You may as well use it."

Jeremiah came down the stairs with his boots in his hand. "Morning," he said. "I'm really sorry I can't stay. Doreen's going to murder me."

"Call her Dori," I said with a grin. "Just to see what she does."

Jeremiah stared at me, aghast. "I'll do no such thing. I like my teeth where they are."

I snorted. "You talk like she's gone Lord-of-the-Flies mode and will have your head on a pike at the gate to warn off those less worthy." I turned to my mum. "Doreen is like seventy years old."

He pulled on one boot and stared at me. "Seventy, yes. But she has a shaved head, rides a motorbike and wields a baseball bat, and wears vagina shirts."

I laughed but he went a shade of horrified pale and could barely look at my mother. "I'm so sorry."

Mum shrugged. "I like the sound of her."

I made him some Weet-Bix and pushed the bowl toward him. "You have time to eat. I promise you, Doreen won't be mad. After yesterday, you could do or say anything and she won't care. She was in awe of you yesterday."

He pouted a little, which was hella cute. But he shook off his embarrassment about the vagina comment, pulled on his other boot, and spotted the box on the floor. "Oh, have we checked on the bird this morning?"

He picked the box up and slid it onto the counter and folded back the lid. "Is it still alive?" I asked.

Jeremiah reached in and picked up a very alive, very alert bird. "He sure is."

It squawked and opened its beak, and Jeremiah cradled it to his chest. "It's okay, little one. Don't be stressed." Then he looked at me. "What do we do with it? Is there someone we can take it to?"

I couldn't help but smile at him. "Maybe we should keep him for another day or two, just to be sure. I've got minced meat and stuff in the fridge that needs to be used."

Jeremiah made an uncertain face. "Are you sure?"

The way he was cradlin' it, being so damn cute. God, it gave me butterflies. "Yeah. I'm sure."

Mum was smiling fondly at me, and I knew what she saw. Me gettin' all bent out of shape over him. I shrugged because there was no point in denying it. I pushed the plate again. "Jeremiah, please eat something," I said.

He handed the bird to me and shovelled in a few mouthfuls of breakfast before putting his plate in the sink. "I really have to go. I'm sorry I can't help today. Hopefully the roads are clear and they restore some power soon." Then he made a face. "And if the news crew are there again, maybe Doreen will be mad at them instead."

I hadn't thought of that . . .

"If those arseholes are there again, you call me."

He fished his phone out of his pocket and tapped the screen. "I would if I could, but we still have no service."

Goddammit.

"Maybe I should come with you."

He shook his head. "I'll be fine. They'll have enough stories to cover without bothering me. I'm old news. And I'm sure you have enough to do at your work."

Mum waved her hand. "Your father's already been down this morning. There's some minor damage. Mostly water damage, but the loading docks look okay. The engineers will need to assess them, of course."

Shit.

I put my hand to my forehead. I hadn't even thought about my work.

Guilt hit me hard because I *should* have thought about it. I should have considered my parents' lifework. "Mum, I'm sorry. I didn't even think. Are we able to go down today? Is the admin building okay?"

She patted my arm. "It's fine. You've had enough to worry about. We'll go back after we've finished here."

That didn't make me feel any better.

Jeremiah took the keys to the Jeep. "I have to go. I'll come back as fast as I can and help with whatever's needed. I doubt there's much I can do at the office anyway, apart from cleaning up and assessing the damage. But without power or radio signals or internet, there's not much I can do at all. But I told Doreen I'd be back first thing."

"It's okay," I said. "Be careful."

"Always am."

"That's a lie."

He opened his mouth, then shut it again. "Well, I'll try to be."

I smiled at him again. "At least promise me you won't try to die today."

He sighed. "I don't try . . . It's not deliberate. I simply—"

"Jeremiah," I said, walking up to him. Still holding the bird to my chest, I leaned up on my toes and kissed him. "Have a good day. Be careful out there. I love you."

His eyes went wide, and his whole face went red. He glanced over at my mother. "Tully," he hissed.

I laughed. "Tell Doreen I said hello. And I hope Suri's okay today."

He mumbled something as he backed out, and he turned for the door. He looked back and waved, completely flustered, then made a quick exit.

I laughed, and Mum clucked her tongue at me. "Leave the poor boy alone."

I sighed happily—who would've known that being in love was such a fucking rush—and I went out onto the balcony to see if Dad and Ellis needed some help.

"My god, the sea is so calm," I said. Sure, the palm trees were a mess, but the bay was like glass.

Ellis put one piece of plyboard against the wall. "Crazy, huh?"

"How are you this morning?" I asked.

He shrugged. "Yeah, I'm okay. Luckily I took a bag with a change of clothes to Mum and Dad's, and my toothbrush. Everything I own fits in a backpack, but I'm okay."

I clapped his shoulder. "You're good to stay here for however long you need. My wardrobe's yours until we can get you some new stuff."

He gave me a smile and nodded. "Yeah, thanks. I know you and Jeremiah just moved in together, so if you'd rather I stayed at Mum and Dad's, I'd totally get it."

"What?" I looked at him funny. "Dude. Jeremiah and I are fine. Sure, it's kinda new, but don't worry about it. No one expected your house to be demolished, Ellis. It's fine."

He seemed mollified, then nodded to the bird I was still holding. "Still got your bird, I see."

"Mm. He looks kinda bright-eyed this morning. Needs some food though."

"Are you gonna help us do your windows?" Ellis asked.

"But you're doing a stellar job without me," I said. "I need to feed this little guy."

Mum came out and took the bird. "I'll feed him. You do what you're told. And no fighting."

Ellis laughed. "Go and put a shirt on and some underwear. Jesus, if you freeball it around the house, maybe I will live at Mum and Dad's."

I tried to kick him. "Stop lookin' at my junk."

Dad stood up straight, the drill in his hand. "The battery in this drill has about five minutes left in it, and so help me god, I will use it on the both of you. Now shut up and help me."

We both shut up and helped him.

Ellis made a face from the other end of the plyboard and stuck out his tongue.

I snorted. "You living here is going to be so much fun."

He smiled at me, and we both started to laugh.

I WAS SURPRISED WHEN JEREMIAH TURNED UP AT MY WORK JUST after three o'clock. We'd been cleaning up at the docks and the admin building for hours, but I thought for sure he'd be gone until dark.

I was on the end of a broom when Rowan had called my name and nodded toward the car park. I looked up to see Jeremiah walking my way, and damn, it made my heart skip a beat.

"Uh, hello, stranger," I said, grinning. "While you *are* incredibly gorgeous, I won't be buying anything you're selling, as I already have a boyfriend."

Jeremiah rolled his eyes, but his cheeks bloomed with colour.

"Please tell me he never used that on you," Rowan said. "God, Tully, that was terrible."

I laughed, still grinning at Jeremiah. Rowan didn't need to know that Jeremiah had used that line on me, and it wasn't terrible because it totally worked. "I didn't think I'd see you till later."

"I went past your place and you weren't there. Ellis' street is all blocked off and your car wasn't at your parents' house." He shrugged. "This is the only other place I know in Darwin."

Aww. I stepped in close. "Well, I'm glad you found me." Then I handed him the broom. "They've been makin' me work all day."

He pushed the broom back to me. "Good."

Rowan laughed and pointed his chin to Jeremiah. "I like him."

I sighed. "Nobody loves me anymore." Clearly, pouting wasn't getting me anywhere. "How did you go today? Was Doreen mad?"

"No. She was happy to see me, actually. It was disconcerting, to be honest. A little frightening."

I snorted.

"Suri was there. She was much better today. Jeff and his girls are going to stay with his sister, I think. And Doreen had to stop old Arty from climbing a ladder onto his roof, because that's what anyone who's almost ninety should be doing." Jeremiah rolled his eyes. "We mostly did clean-up and damage reports. We have no antennas, no satellite, nothing." He frowned and half shrugged. "I don't know what we can do. We have nothing to work with. Nothing even to start from."

He looked out toward the docks and shrugged again, like he had something to say but couldn't find the words to say it.

"Hey," I whispered, taking his hand. "You'll be fine. You and Doreen are two of the most resourceful people I know. You'll be back up and running in no time."

His eyes cut to mine, and there was sadness in the striking blue. "What if they send me back?"

Back?

"Back where?"

"To Melbourne. Or to somewhere else? To another office somewhere."

A bomb of rage and fear detonated in my chest. Instantaneous, panicky, and seeping hot. The thought of him leaving, even the mere mention of it, had my blood boiling.

"They won't. They better fuckin' not."

"They didn't exactly give me a choice for this post, did they? They couldn't ship me off fast enough—"

"Then you tell them no," I snapped. "You be the Doctor

Jeremiah fucking Overton I know, who tells people how shit's gonna go down. If they thought you were difficult before—if they thought *I* was difficult before—they haven't seen nothin' yet." I dropped the broom and poked him in the chest. "You kicked arse yesterday. You were fuckin' brilliant, and you saved lives, and that's why there isn't anyone better for the job here than you."

He put his hand to my neck. "Tully," he murmured.

I shook my head. "You can't leave. You have to be here. I just found you."

He smiled at that. "I don't want to leave. But I'm almost glad we have no communication with Melbourne or Canberra. That way they can't tell me that I'm needed elsewhere."

"If they do, I will walk to Melbourne, if I have to, just to crack some fucking skulls."

He sighed and dropped his hand from my neck. "I think we need to talk about your violent tendencies when it comes to me. I'm beginning to think I bring out the bad side in you. Your mother mentioned it yesterday."

Rowan coughed out a laugh. I didn't even know he was still there.

"I'm sorry," I said. "Just thinking about someone hurting you makes me see red. I get so fucking mad I want to rip people apart."

"Well, that's nice," Jeremiah said, making a face. "And disturbing, and completely unnecessary. But thanks?"

I took a deep breath in, then exhaled slowly. "Okay, I'll try to stop threatening people. But they need to stop *actually* threatening you or using you. Or whatever. Then I won't actually need to threaten them, so technically it's their fault."

Jeremiah made a pained face. "I'm not sure that's how it works."

I sighed again. "Fine. I promise I won't threaten physical violence. But you have to promise me you won't leave."

His smile was shy and genuine, and he gave Rowan a quick glance before his eyes met mine again. "I promise. Though I should add the caveat that I promise to do everything within my power and that some things may be out of my control, and that's technically not my fault."

"Fine. And I'll add the caveat that some things may be out of my control too. Like if that news reader comes back and shoves her microphone in your face one more time—"

Jeremiah picked up the broom and shoved the handle against my chest. "Shut up and sweep."

I snatched the broom with a huff, though my petulance was lost on him. He simply turned to Rowan and said, "Tell me what needs doing?"

Rowan grinned. "I really like you, Jeremiah. Come with me."

I stood there with the stupid broom and watched as they walked inside the admin building.

So I swept the damn yard and picked up debris and sweated my arse off in the brutal humidity until I was done sulking.

It took a while.

Eventually, I ditched the broom and went inside. I found them moving filing cabinets off wet carpet, and yes, I liked very much that Jeremiah slotted right into my family—he was working alongside Rowan and my father, after all—but I'd had enough for today.

I needed some alone time with him.

If I was being honest with myself, what I needed from him was a long hug and some reassurance. But I didn't want to have to admit that. I just wanted to crawl onto the couch and cuddle for hours.

Had falling in love suddenly turned me into a giant insecure baby?

Apparently, yes.

Jeremiah and Dad shuffled the last filing cabinet into the

corner when Jeremiah noticed me. He stopped and came straight over. "What's wrong?"

"Nothing," I mumbled. "I just wanna go home."

He frowned and went to put his hand to my face but stopped himself.

I didn't want him to stop himself.

But with my dad and brother in the room, I shouldn't have been surprised. I tried to not let it bother me, but it did.

"Okay, we'll go," he said. "You sure you're okay?"

I didn't answer. I turned to Dad. "We have to go. See yas tomorrow when we're back to do it all over again."

Dad stretched his back. "Yeah, we're all done for today too. Pretty sure I have some beers in the fridge that need drinking before they get hot."

I pulled on Jeremiah's shirt, tugging him toward the door. "Another time, Dad, but thanks. I'll see yas all again bright and early tomorrow."

If they noticed my mood—and I'm sure they did—they never said anything. I wouldn't have known what to tell them anyway. I just needed to leave.

"I'll follow you," Jeremiah said, going straight to the Jeep.

I tried to get myself together on the short drive home, but this feeling, this uneasy, frustrated feeling wasn't going away.

I pulled into my garage and went inside, seeing the storm clouds rolling in again across the horizon. It was almost five o'clock, and I was ready for this whole day to be over. The box squawked, so I opened it up and took out the bird. He squawked some more and I fed him the small balls of minced meat my mother had made.

At least he made me smile.

Jeremiah came in, put his keys and stuff on the kitchen bench, and gave the bird a gentle stroke. "He's a little fighter."

"We'll need to get him a proper cage," I said quietly.

Jeremiah looked at the top of my head and straightened out an errant strand of hair. He smiled as he thumbed my jaw. "Want to tell me what's wrong?"

I frowned. "I don't know what's wrong. I just feel . . ." I shrugged my shoulders and tried to shake off the funk I was in. "I don't know how I feel. Like I need you to hug me. And it's weird, because I've never needed that before. I feel . . . deconstructed. I dunno. And then you mentioned that you might be leaving. Why did you say that? Jesus, Jeremiah, I just found you!"

He took the bird and put it back in the box, then pulled me against him. He wrapped his arms around me, pushed me against the cabinet, and held me so damn tight.

God, he felt so good it made me want to cry.

"I don't know what's wrong with me," I mumbled.

"Nothing's wrong with you," he whispered. "Nothing at all."

I fisted his shirt at the back, and with my face in his neck, I breathed him in, like I could somehow absorb his strength that way. God, this was ridiculous.

"Wanna lie down on the couch?"

I nodded. "Yes."

I felt like a child. God, I was acting like one.

But then he pulled me onto the couch with him and I lay there, half on top of him, with his arms around me and my head tucked under his chin. He rubbed my back and kissed the top of my head every so often.

"Feel better?"

I nodded again. "I just . . . I just needed this. Exactly this. With you. I need to know you're okay, that we're okay. That everything will be okay."

He lifted my face and brought me in for a kiss. "Everything will be okay. You and me, we'll be okay."

"You're not leaving?"

He smiled and shook his head, his eyes soft. "They'll have to drag me out."

I chuckled and he kissed my cheek, my nose, my forehead, and tucked me back in under his chin.

Then we heard keys in the front door. I'd forgotten about Ellis. "You better not be naked," he called out.

"Eat a bag of dicks," I replied.

Jeremiah tried to sit up, but I held him right where he was. "Mm-mm. Don't move."

Ellis came in and all but fell into the single seater next to us. He looked exhausted, and he didn't give one fuck that Jeremiah and I were tangled on the couch together. "What is it with the 'eat a bag of dicks' line as an insult?" Ellis said with a frown. "I mean, sure, tell me to eat a bag of dicks and I'd be like, 'yeah, no thanks, not my style.' But if I told you to eat a bag of dicks, you'd be like, 'hell yes, go turkey-mode, and gobble-gobble.'"

I threw a cushion at his fucking head.

He caught it and laughed. Then before I could say anything, or get up and beat the shit outta him, the TV power button came on, the fridge kicked in, and a few other electrical appliances beeped.

I sat up. "Holy shit. We have power!"

Ellis threw his hands up, victory style, then looked at the TV and quickly deflated. "Oh . . . my PS5." He sighed. "Christ, Tully, why don't you have a gaming console?"

"Because I'd never use it," I said, helping Jeremiah sit up, now that I'd peeled myself off him. I got up to get us all a bottle of water.

Ellis rolled his eyes. "Because you spend all your money and time on storm-chasing shit."

Jeremiah smiled. "Same."

Ellis groaned. "I'm living with the storm boys."

I came back with two bottles of water and a baby bird. I gave one bottle to Ellis and kept the other for me and Jeremiah to share. I handed the bird to Jeremiah and reached for the air-con remote.

Jeremiah stroked the bird's neck, and it squawked a bit. It was young and it couldn't fly yet, but like Jeremiah had said, he was a fighter. "We should name him," I said. "Given he made it through the worst of it, I think he deserves a name."

Jeremiah's eyes met mine. "Really? I've never had to name something before."

"Never?"

He shook his head. "I've never had a pet before."

Jeez.

I leaned against his arm and gave the bird a gentle pat. "Even if we find him a home in a day or so, we can still name him. I'd reckon all the vets and wildlife carers would be pretty busy right now, so a few days won't hurt. He likes that minced meat. Which is gross, but he likes it. Lucky Mum and Dad knew what to feed him, because my entire education relies on Google, and without power and the internet, I had no clue." I checked my phone. "Still no service. It's funny how long the battery lasts when you can't use your phone."

"Oh," Ellis said, grabbing the remote for the TV. "Maybe there are updates on the news or something."

Some channels weren't working at all, but we found the local one. Channel 4, because of course that would be the only channel still working.

Footage of Darwin filled the screen, from the street and from the air. There was just so much devastation. So much loss. They showed people crying, people being rescued, people carrying kids and pets through water. They showed collapsed buildings, and they showed Ellis' street.

Christ, it was hard for me to watch. I couldn't imagine what it was like for him.

Then my favouritest news reporter in the whole country appeared on screen.

Lindsey.

I grumbled under my breath.

And then I realised where she was. She was standing out the front of Jeremiah's work.

"I'm here with Doctor Jeremiah Overton," she said.

And there he was. The love of my life, the man sitting on the couch next to me right that very second, wearing the same clothes on TV as he was wearing right freaking next to me.

"You never told me she hassled you today!" I said. I might have yelled. "I said if those leeches harassed you one more time—"

"She didn't harass me. I asked her to come over."

I stared at him.

Stared.

Until my eyeballs dried out.

"When you lost all communications yesterday," Lindsey said on the TV, "you used some thirty-year-old radar that still used old radio frequency, and you typed in the warning about the shortened duration of the eye, is that correct?"

The screen showed the typed message in the top of the radar screen.

"Yes, that's correct."

"And if that didn't already make you a hero, we have footage of you saving two small children from a lightning strike yesterday," she said. "And not just them; you saved myself and my cameraman."

The footage cut to a shaky view from Shane running up the steps, then panning back in time to see Jeremiah skid in the mud, collect the two kids, and race back before the lightning lit up and blew out the fence.

Ellis pointed at the TV. "Holy shit, dude, was that you?"

"Yes, that was him." I went back to staring at Jeremiah. "You asked her to come speak to you? I'm sorry. But why?"

He shrugged. "Because I had something to say."

I looked back at the TV, to the Jeremiah on screen. Lindsey

was smiling at him in a way that made me want to poke her in the eye.

"This footage has gone viral," she said. "What do you have to say to the people who are calling you a hero?"

On-screen Jeremiah looked right at the camera. "Nothing. I'm not a hero. I just had no other way to let my dad know I was okay. He's in Melbourne. Dad, if you're watching this, I'm fine and I'll call you when the phone towers are back up."

Then on-screen Jeremiah smiled at Lindsey and simply turned and walked back up to the office. Lindsey stood there with her microphone, not knowing what else to say.

I snorted out a laugh because that was funny as hell, but then I looked at Jeremiah next to me, and with a heavy sigh, I dropped my forehead to his shoulder. "God, I'm so sorry. I'm sorry I didn't even think. Your dad must have been worried, and you . . . You must have been so . . ." I looked up at him. "And I didn't even stop to think. I'm a terrible boyfriend. I'm so sorry."

Jeremiah took my hand. "My father would have been mildly concerned at best. I just thought he might like to know, and when someone from Channel 4 came to collect the van, I told them to pass on a message to come interview me. They used me, so I used them. I think she was hoping for some exclusive scoop or whatever. But anyway, it doesn't matter. Hopefully my father sees that."

I still felt bad.

"I'm sure he was more than mildly concerned," I offered. "But still, I'm sorry. We got home last night and crashed, then we were up and gone this morning. I barely had time to speak to you, and then I spent all afternoon sulking like a fucking child. I should have been more considerate."

"You were," he said.

"What? Considerate? Or sulking like a child?" I asked, then regretted it because I didn't want to know. I already knew. "You don't need to answer. I'm sorry."

Jeremiah laughed and he nudged his knee to mine. When I met his gaze, his eyes were happy and soft. He was still holding the bird, which we still hadn't named.

God.

"We should call him Hazer," I suggested.

Jeremiah screwed his nose up, clearly not liking that suggestion.

"I can't believe you skidded across that mud and collected those two kids like they do in the movies," Ellis said, disbelief still clear on his face. "You wanna watch out. The Buffaloes will be looking to sign you up."

Jeremiah squinted at him. "The buffaloes?"

"Football," I offered.

"Oh." He grimaced. "No thanks."

I snorted. "What if we call him First," I suggested as a bird name. "As in he was the *first* time you almost died yesterday."

He rolled his eyes, then looked at the little bird. "Naming something is a lot of responsibility."

Ellis groaned. "For the love of god, you two. Mr Percival is right there." He waved his hand at us. "I already called you the storm boys, so really, what other name *could* you call it?"

My initial reaction was to tell him to sod off. And I wanted to hate the name suggestion, but I couldn't. I looked at Jeremiah and he smiled.

"Mr Percival is kind of nice," he said. "Well, it's appropriate. Though he's not a pelican."

"I don't think that matters," I said. I gave the bird a gentle stroke, though he was very content to be secure in Jeremiah's arms. "Mr Percival."

"You're welcome." Ellis stood up. "I'm gonna cook some pasta for dinner. Sound good? The power will likely cut in and out for a week while they fix shit, so we should make use of it."

"Sounds perfect. I can help," I said.

"Nah, I got it. It'll just be veggies and shit."

"Hold the shit in mine," Jeremiah said. "I'm not a fan."

My god, he'd made a joke to my brother.

I grinned at Ellis. "Yeah, me either. Feel free to make yours extra shitty though."

Ellis gave me the finger. He walked to the glass door. "There's an electrical storm on the horizon. Oh, and now we've got power, did you wanna check the camera you had on the balcony? See what kinda front-row footage you got of the cyclone."

I snuggled into Jeremiah a little and he leaned into me, sliding one arm around me, and we both smiled at Mr Percival. "Nah," I said, feeling very content where I was. "It can wait till tomorrow. This is about all I wanna do tonight. Stay right here."

Jeremiah kissed my temple and, over the top of my head, watched the lightning over the ocean. "Yeah. This is all I want to do tonight too."

I sidled in a bit closer, nudging my nose to his throat. "Well, I hope it's *not all* you wanna do tonight."

He gave me a squeeze and chuckled, then whispered in my ear, "Not *all*."

"Oh," I said, like that struck a memory. "Did you check the app on your phone for the heart-rate strap?"

"No. I forgot all about it."

"Hmm," I hummed, kissing his Adam's apple. "We should see what it says. Though we'll need to establish some control groups, purely for scientific purposes. If you know what I mean."

He gave me a squeeze. "I believe I do know what you mean, yes."

I whispered in his ear. "Resting heart rate, heart rate when you fuck me. Heart rate when I fuck you."

He swallowed hard. "Hm. Yes, those control groups would suffice, I do concur."

God, he made me laugh.

Then we sat there for a little bit longer. Jeremiah chewed his bottom lip, and when he started to tap his foot, it got the better of me. "Maybe we could check the app, just real quick, and see what records we need to beat."

"I'm certain each reading isn't a personal best to beat every time. That's not why I bought it."

"Hm, personal bests. I like the sound of that."

He smirked. "Well, I think the sprint across the yard to collect those two girls, sprinting back, and almost getting hit by lightning will be hard to beat. My heart was beating out of my chest."

I met his gaze. "Is that a challenge, Doctor? Because I do like a challenge."

He glanced back toward the kitchen to see if Ellis was listening. He wasn't, so Jeremiah looked back to me. "Well, a little competition could be fun."

"I'm going to make a chart," I proclaimed loudly. I didn't care if Ellis heard. "With gold stars and everything."

Jeremiah's eyes went wide. "Oh god, please don't."

"Yeah," Ellis chimed in as he stirred a pan. "Please don't. I don't know what you're talking about, but it involves a chart and gold star stickers and he's trying to whisper, so I can only assume he's getting his freak on. Believe me when I say I don't wanna fucking know."

I burst out laughing. "Jeremiah, quick, get your phone. We need to check the app so I know how much stamina I'll need tonight."

"Oh my god," Jeremiah hissed. "Tully, stop it."

Ellis let his head drop with a loud groan. "Staying here was such a bad idea." He turned the stove off. "Pasta's cooked. Come up and get your own, nut sac." Then he rolled his eyes. "Not you, Jeremiah, obviously. I was talking to the six-foot talking haemorrhoid sitting next to you."

I burst out laughing and even Jeremiah tried not to smile

as he put Mr Percival back in his box. We dished up our own pasta, and sitting on the couch eating Ellis' terrible cooking just made me so freakin' happy.

Having Jeremiah in my life and having my shithead brother live with us made me so unbelievably happy.

Granted, these weren't ideal circumstances, with the cyclone and all. But even after everything Hazer threw at us, with all the devastation and the loss, to still be able to sit around and joke and laugh with each other, we were pretty damn lucky too.

"Cheers," I said, tapping my bottle of water to Ellis'. "To surviving cyclones." Then I tapped Jeremiah's. "And to more storms in the future."

Ellis shoved a forkful of pasta in his mouth, then spoke with his mouth full. "You're both crazy."

I laughed. "Maybe. But he's my kind of crazy."

Ellis ignored my sappiness and shook his head at Jeremiah. "I still can't believe you saved those kids from that lightning strike."

"I'm not surprised one bit," I said. "We have footage of him running a hundred metres in the rain and sliding under the wall at the bunker like an action-movie hero."

Jeremiah's cheeks were now a vivid pink.

Such a contrast, from the hero to the shy guy . . .

"About the footage," Jeremiah said.

"The footage from the bunker?"

"No, the footage from your balcony, looking at the cyclone." He shrugged. "Maybe we could take a little look."

I grinned at him. *Hell yes, we could.* "We could hook it up to the TV and watch it on the big screen!" I ditched my pasta and stood up. "I'll go get it."

Ellis groaned. "Oh my god, I'm living with storm nerds."

"Shut up, nut sac," I yelled out.

"Grab me a beer on your way back," he replied.

I grabbed three bottles, and a few minutes later, the three

of us settled on the couch with our beers, my head on Jeremiah's shoulder. "Are we ready?" I asked, pointing the remote control at the TV.

Jeremiah kissed the top of my head. "Always."

THE END

TOUCH THE LIGHTNING

TOUCH THE LIGHTNING

CHAPTER ONE
JEREMIAH

Twenty-three.

Twenty-three people had died in Cyclone Hazer, and a month later, I thought of them often.

Twenty-three.

A number I couldn't get out of my head.

Tully had told me I wasn't responsible for them, and the logical part of my brain knew he was right. "You saved countless more," he'd said. And he'd been patient with me, and he was kind and supportive. He was utterly perfect.

While I felt hopeless. And helpless.

I needed to work. I needed to get back into it and be productive. I needed to be functioning normally.

And my office was not functioning at all.

I had only a department-supplied laptop—since my own was fried from the electrical surge when we were at the bunker, and then of course with the cyclone—but I was grateful they'd sent me anything.

I'd added all the data I'd collected for my personal reports. I'd collated stats and figures on heart rates during storms and the cyclone, from both my chest strap and watch. It was interesting, to say the least. And I'd collected more statistical analysis in my time here than I had in the few years prior.

But it wasn't work.

It was the longest time in my life when I hadn't been actively working, or studying for work, or doing something productive. I needed it.

So yes, the laptop was great, and it allowed me to stay in touch with the bureau and for me to watch radar loops for hours on end. But it wasn't enough to run the office.

All official bureau warnings for the Northern Territory were being run out of Queensland and Western Australia, and I had to wonder if they had any intention of ever re-opening the Darwin office at all.

Perhaps they were waiting for the media hype to have fully dissipated before they announced I was fired.

And there had been media hype.

Which was ridiculous. But yes, the blue-eyed weather guy—whose mother was the famous lightning-strike lady—had managed to send a warning message out via an old radar system by typing it over the office location sequence.

Well, there had been media hype across Australia, and even made news around the world, but not so much here in Darwin.

Given everyone was without power initially, then most news reports and updates pertained to health and safety information, it wasn't surprising my story got buried.

And I was glad it had been.

Tully's family knew, of course. He'd replayed the news footage a hundred times. And Doreen knew because she'd witnessed it.

But no one else gave a damn.

Thank God.

We had enough to worry about. Supermarkets were rationed, but we had power. Our phone lines were restored after a few days, and internet a few days after that. Many people were displaced, many people injured.

A death toll of twenty-three.

Twenty-three.

Twenty-three lives gone forever. Twenty-three holes where someone's loved one used to be.

It was an awful number.

A number I wasn't responsible for. I knew that. But still . . . it was a number I couldn't easily forget.

I also couldn't forget about how, during the middle of the cyclone, I'd had moments of disassociation. Full mental reasoning that the cyclone wasn't happening, that the deafening noise was no longer there.

That I could simply go out into it and risk the lives of everyone sheltering in the office to save a soaked and sodden bird.

A bird who, against all odds, was now thriving.

Mr Percival sat on the back of the couch, his favourite spot, and squawked for more food. We'd sought the advice from a local vet who provided us with more suitable dietary requirements that helped him learn how to feed on his own, and the little guy was growing so well.

He was losing the grey feathers, replaced with the more adult glossy black. He was curious and inquisitive and smart. He liked to perch on my shoulder and sleep against my neck when we watched TV.

Which was where we were when Tully and Ellis got home.

They'd been to work and then they'd had to sort out more insurance legalities for Ellis' house. As most people in Darwin after Cyclone Hazer were finding out, red tape and bureaucracy slowed everything down.

But at least Ellis was insured. Many folks weren't.

"How did it go?" I asked, not getting up.

Ellis threw a wad of papers onto the coffee table and then fell onto the couch. "Same shit, different day."

Tully came around and stopped when he saw me. "That bird is in my spot," he said. Then he came closer and gave Mr Percival a gentle stroke. "Lucky he's cute."

"He's getting better at flying," I said. "I think we should leave his cage on the patio with the cage door pinned open so he can come and go as he wants."

Tully's eyes met mine. "You want to get rid of him?"

"No." Mr Percival ruffled his feathers and decided to jump down to my leg, then across to Tully's leg, where he did his little hoppy dance on his thigh. "I want him to be happy and to be where he should be. Which is flying free with other magpies."

Tully gave me his puppy-dog eyes. "Aw, but you'll be sad."

I chuckled. "I'll survive. But he's not ready yet. He still needs help with eating those grubs."

Tully tried to stroke Mr Percival again, but Mr Percival pecked his finger instead. "Ow. That's not a worm, little guy."

Mr Percival decided to squawk and sing, just as Ellis' phone rang. He stood up and answered it as he took the stairs two at a time. Tully gave me a nudge. "He's been talking to Grace."

"His ex?"

Tully nodded. "He called around to see her after the cyclone, helped her with a bit of damage, tapin' up some windows or something. Anyway, there's been some texts and phone calls."

I had noticed him smiling at his phone lately. "Good," I said. "He deserves some happiness."

"He needs a good railing," Tully said flatly. "Might not be such a cranky fucker."

I snorted. He was so charming. "He just lost his house and everything in it. He's allowed to be somewhat cranky. Plus, he's living with you. His greatest agitator."

"I don't agitate him."

"You do. You're both as bad as each other."

Tully pouted and pretended to sulk. "Now I'm cranky."

I didn't bother with a reply. I knew what was coming.

He gave me the puppy eyes again. "You know what would make me feel a whole lot better?"

"I have a fair idea, yes."

He grinned. "A gold star."

I sighed. *And* there it was.

"Well, at least you didn't say a good railing."

"Oh, believe me," he said seriously. "There is a distinct correlation between the good railing and the gold star."

I laughed. "Is that right?"

He nodded without shame. "And I plan on getting both."

CHAPTER TWO

TULLY

I wasn't kidding about the chart with gold stars.

Jeremiah might have thought it was a joke at first, and he did laugh when I first showed him. But the time I only gave him a silver star instead of gold, he took it very personally and made his mission to earn gold stars every time.

Every.

Single.

Time.

And honestly, his performance was well above the silver star I'd given him, but his efforts since then?

Absolutely worth it.

I know people go on about sliced bread and penicillin, but I can declare, without a skerrick of doubt, the chest strap heart-rate monitor was the best invention ever.

Life had been pretty great, all things considered.

It'd been one month since Cyclone Hazer tore Darwin apart.

One month of living with Jeremiah. One month of learning more about each other. One month of adjusting. One month of watchin' him bond with Mr Percival, feedin' him, watchin' TV with him, talkin' to him.

One month of me fallin' more in love with Jeremiah than I ever thought possible.

The best one month of my life.

Not forgetting the one month of living with Ellis. Even that was fun. He gave me and Jeremiah as much space as he could, but even watching he and Jeremiah become friends made me happy.

It was also one month of disrupted essential services, disrupted food supplies, disrupted rebuilding. There'd been a lot of hard work by everyone, but things were slowly returning to normal.

Except for Jeremiah's office. It was still completely offline, but considering it required a full upgrade and fit out, it was hardly surprising.

But things like non-emergency medical tests were available—tests, like all the STI tests, for example. Tests, which meant Jeremiah and I were given the all-clear to ditch condoms.

Which was why, at midnight, I was face down on my bed with my arse in the air and the heart-rate monitor around my chest, gripping the bed covers and cussin' at Jeremiah to hurry the fuck up.

"I swear to god, Jeremiah, if you're not inside me in the next thirty seconds—"

"I am inside you," he mumbled, sliding his lubed fingers in and out.

I tried to get up onto my knees so I could turn around and fucking argue, because his fingers were not what I meant and he knew it, but he shoved my head back down to the bed, his fist tight in my hair. "Stay down."

Oh, hell yes.

The ECG readings were going to be off the charts.

In contrast to the hair pulling, he ever so lightly ran his hands down my back and pressed his cock against my hole. "Are you sure you want this?"

"I swear to fucking Christ, Jeremiah," I bit out. "If you don't—"

And then he did.

He pushed his bare cock into me, slick and hot and oh so good. All the way in, in one long, slow push. His fingers dug into my skin and he made the hottest fucking sound. *A moan where pleasure is so good it dances with pain . . .*

"Oh fuck," he rasped out.

God, I love it when he swears . . .

The feel of him, skin on skin, knowing it was him inside me and nothin' else, no barrier between us, made me feel hot all over. It burned in my chest, the love I felt solidified into something more, something deeper.

He pushed all the way in, his hips flush against my arse, and he rolled his hips in that way he knew I loved. He stayed still, breathin' hard, before he pulled back a little and did it all over again.

He yanked my shoulder up, so I was on my knees, my back to his chest. And he held me like that, buried inside me, and he kissed my neck, my shoulder, his hands holding me, digging into me. But he groaned in frustration.

And then he pulled out.

"What's wrong?" I asked, confused.

He tapped my hip. "Roll over. I need to see your face."

I quickly obeyed, and he leaned over me, between my legs, and folded my knees up to my chest. And he kissed me, deep and slow, as he sank back inside me.

Oh god, yes.

This. This right here.

I wrapped my arms and legs around him, givin' him my whole body. He was so far inside me, his cock and his tongue, and it still wasn't close enough.

I wanted more.

I ached for it.

"Jeremiah," I whispered.

He groaned and shuddered, and with his forehead pressed to mine, his eyes imploring, he held still, strung tight. "Tully," he hissed. "I'm so close, I can't hold it. Tell me if you don't want this."

I slid my hand to his cheek. "Give it to me."

I could feel his cock twitch, impossibly hard and swollen and so deep inside me. His eyes rolled closed, and he thrust into me, driving upwards, and sweet mother of god . . .

I could feel it.

I could feel him come.

His whole body went rigid, his head pushed back, and the veins in his neck stood out. An animal sound ripped out from somewhere deep in his throat.

I could feel his whole body jerk and pulse as he spilled inside me.

I'd never felt anything like it. I'd never experienced anything like it.

I held his face and when he collapsed on top of me, his breath against my neck, I wrapped my arms around him and held him tight.

He was wracked with tremors, and he moaned as he began to pull out. I kept my legs around him, holdin' him right where he was. "Stay," I whispered.

I never wanted him to leave.

He pulled his head back, his eyes were glazed over and dreamy, and he kissed me. Open mouth, deep tongue, his face tilted so he could kiss me deeper still.

And he began to rock his hips, sliding his half-hard cock in and out, like he was trying to crawl into my body. Like he was tryin' to tell me something . . .

"Jeremiah," I murmured.

His gaze met mine, and his blue fire took me by surprise.

"You have my seed inside you," he breathed.

Jesus fucking Christ.

Wow.

His words heated my blood from my toes to my scalp.

I rarely knew what words would come out of his mouth, but I never expected him to say that.

He slowly pulled out and looked down between us. "And you haven't come yet."

"I don't need to," I replied. "What we just did . . ."

"I want you to do me," he said in a rush. "I want that."

Umm.

The fuck?

"Now?"

"Right now."

I was so stunned I couldn't speak. He'd once said that he'd bottom if it felt right, though we'd never explored that because I was a shameless, needy little slut who loved getting dicked.

Apparently.

He frowned. "Unless you don't want to . . ."

I flipped him over so fast he yelped in surprise, and I laughed. "I want to." I nudged his nose to mine. "Are you sure?"

He nodded. "Very."

Then, like he didn't need words to tell me what he wanted, he rolled over onto his front, spread his legs wide, and raised his arse a little.

I slid my hands up the back of his thighs to his arse cheeks. "You're so bossy."

"I expect gold stars," he mumbled into the sheet.

I laughed and leaned over him so I could whisper in his ear. "I can feel your come in me. You want mine in you?"

His breath caught and he stretched his back, raising his hips. But no, I wasn't lettin' him dictate this whole show. I held him down, pinning him, and grunted in his ear. "I will always give you what you want. Whatever it is, baby. I'll give it to you."

He writhed under my hold, unable to contain his need for it.

I knew how he felt. That give-it-to-me-before-I-die feeling. By the time I got him ready for me, his hands were fists in the bedding and his patience was worn thin.

His impatient whimpers and moans of pleadin' set my body on fire. Knowing I pulled his strings like a puppet . . . God, it was hot.

And then he growled.

I chuckled, because he sounded just like me.

Planting a hand by his head, I leaned over him and dragged my nose across the nape of his neck. "Patience is a virtue, Jeremiah."

He grunted, angry now. "Tully, if you intend to make me beg—"

I pressed the head of my cock against his hole and pushed in, his words catching in his throat.

Now, it had been a long time since I'd topped anyone, but it was never like this.

Never.

And it wasn't because I wasn't wearing a condom. It was because of him.

I ran my hands along his outstretched arms, kissing his shoulder and the back of his neck, and settled my weight on his back. I moved my hips slow, rolling and driving up into him.

I took my time, savourin' every second. Every heartbeat, every breath.

I wanted him to feel how much I loved him. I wanted him to feel adored and cherished and how grateful I was that he was giving me this gift.

A gift he'd never given anyone else.

The fact I was inside him, unsheathed . . . he was so hot and tight, so perfect, it took every fibre of self-control I had to pace myself. I wanted it to last forever.

"I love you," I murmured, taking his ear between my lips.

He whined and threaded our fingers above his head, lifting his hips. "Tully, please."

"Are you sure you want this?"

He gasped and moaned on the exhale. "Yes, please, please."

So I let go of his hands and leaned up, my hands now pushing his shoulders into the mattress, and I began to thrust harder, deeper, longer. There was no going back, no stopping as I chased that peak of bliss, so close, so close . . .

My orgasm ripped through me, powerful and devastating, and so utterly perfect. Buried in him to the hilt, my cock surged and spilled, and he gasped as his body took every drop.

I collapsed on top of him, so wiped out and entirely boneless, I couldn't have moved, even if I'd wanted to.

I barely had the cognitive power to breathe.

I meant to close my eyes for just a second. I meant to rest for a minute and then get up and tend to him, make sure he was okay.

But the next thing I knew, it was morning.

His side of the bed was empty, and when I checked the time, I saw why. I'd slept straight through till seven o'clock, and he'd have been gone for an hour already. And I was sad, because I hadn't checked on him, I didn't know if he was okay. So I rolled out of bed, my body aching in the best of ways.

I grabbed my phone to send him a message when I saw he'd put the chart on my bedside table. I laughed, because there beside my name and last night's date was a very bright and shiny, big gold star.

CHAPTER THREE

Getting the bureau's office set up had been an ongoing nightmare. From supply issues to actually getting the gear delivered to Darwin had been delay after delay.

And don't even get me started on the actual install.

I understood all technicians, builders, and electricians were busy. Darwin needed a lot of repairs and rebuilds, and there had even been planeloads of qualified tradies coming in from various parts of Australia to help.

The response had been amazing.

But it was still frustrating.

One month later and I still had no working office.

I had spent one week at the Darwin airport, helping their control crew re-establish their weather station. It had been important work, fun and rewarding. Being productive and helping in desperate times—ensuring the city's only airport was functioning and safe—did more for my mental health in one week than all the years I'd worked in Melbourne had.

Helping the community, even in the small and non-concerting way I could, made me feel good.

It made the guilt a little easier to bear.

Guilt that wasn't rational, but guilt all the same.

But my god, I needed to work. I needed my office back. I needed to be doing something.

I'd cleaned out most of the old gear that was now in boxes. This whole office was going to be ripped apart, so anything that was worth keeping now sat in Tully's garage.

Admittedly, it wasn't much.

He kept the helmet with the light on it. For what purpose was anyone's guess. It was old and didn't work, but it made him happy, so . . .

A knock at the door startled me, and I looked up at the security screen—the only screen that still worked—and saw who it was. "Jememiah," a little voice said.

A little voice that made me smile.

I opened the door for Presley and Casey, the two little girls from down the road. The little girls I'd collected in a tackle-run to save from a lightning strike.

Presley, the younger of the two, called me Jememiah, and it was cute.

"Hello," I said. "Are you allowed to be up here?"

"Yes," Casey said. "Daddy's here with the roof man."

"Ah, good." I walked down the steps into the yard and, sure enough, saw Jeff talking with a few men who had a trailer of roofing iron. I gave him a wave, and the girls decided climbing into the Jeep was fun, and I didn't even mind.

That vehicle was indestructible, and if the wild pig tracks and potholes at the bunker or, indeed, a whole cyclone didn't break the car, two small girls wouldn't either.

It wasn't as if I had any work to do.

Then Arty from across the road came out with a plate of biscuits, the coloured wafer kind, and offered them to the girls and I. I asked him about his house and his cat, and we chatted a while. Jean and Michael were also doing well, and the couple across from Jeff were too.

And that was the thing about Darwin—the people who called it home.

Tough didn't begin to describe them.

Resilient and resourceful came to mind. Choosing to live in a city thousands of kilometres from any other city, plagued by insufferable heat and monsoons . . . it took a special breed of person to live here.

Like Tully and his family.

They took everything in stride. No problem was too big or too small. They supported each other and they worked hard. They supported their employees—some had lost their homes or cars—and the Larsons did everything they could to help them.

They were good people, and yes, despite having been on my own for so long, living with Tully *and* Ellis had been great. He and Tully bickered as often as they laughed, and despite the name-calling and frequent threats of homicide, they loved each other dearly.

I envied them all.

To have a family that loved as loud as they did was a beautiful thing.

I, on the other hand, had spoken to my father all of three times in the last month. And that included the day of the cyclone when Tully had held the phone to my ear, and the time when our lines were reconnected when he called to say he had seen my interview where I'd told him I was okay.

And once after that when I'd called him.

We'd never been particularly close, but it still stung.

Now that we lived at opposite ends of the country, the effort to stay in touch seemed too difficult. Maybe I hadn't realised just how much effort I'd put in when I'd lived in Melbourne. Or more to the point, just how little effort my father had put in.

I could see now that my relationship with my father was a thread stretched a little too thin.

Yet I didn't regret my move here.

In fact, perhaps it reinforced my resolve. I'd made the right decision to stay.

I'd never felt more loved in my whole life than I'd felt since I met Tully.

"You okay?" Jeff asked.

I hadn't even realised he'd walked up. "Oh yes. Sorry."

"M'girls not annoying ya, I hope."

"No, of course not. They're a joy."

He nodded to the office building. "How are the repairs coming along?"

"Slow."

He sighed. "Yeah. Same here. I got my place waterproof, so that's a start. But the roofing guys reckon they can start next week."

"Oh, that's great news."

Just then, a white Range Rover pulled into the yard and parked near the Jeep. Tully got out, and when Presley raced over to him, he collected her over his shoulder like he did with his nieces and nephews and put her in the backseat of the Jeep.

"Afternoon," Tully said to Jeff, giving me a smile instead of hello.

"A slow day at work?" I asked.

He groaned. "Busy as hell, actually."

"Which explains what you're doing here."

I noticed then just exactly what he had stuck on his collar. And he noticed me notice it, and he gave me that grin that sent the butterflies in my belly into a frenzy.

He was wearing the gold star I'd put on the stupid chart.

"I was comin' to take you out for lunch," Tully said. "Because I knew you wouldn't have eaten."

"Yeah, I gotta get these girls some lunch," Jeff said. "Good to see you both again. Hopefully we'll be neighbours again soon."

"I hope so too," I replied.

He rounded up his two kids, and as I watched them go, I could feel Tully's eyes on me and the smile he was aiming at me, waiting for me to look at him. "And I actually called around to see if you were okay after last night. I meant to treat you better last night, but I fell asleep. I didn't even hear you leave this mornin'."

I met his eyes. "I'm fine. What do you mean you meant to treat me better?"

He shrugged. "To care for you afterwards . . . you know."

Oh.

I pretended I wasn't blushing. "You treated me just fine, if you'll recall. You earned a gold sticker, did you not?"

He laughed and lifted his collar. "Sure did."

"Did you have to put it on your shirt?"

"Hell fuckin' yes, I did." He had exactly no shame. "I earned this."

I couldn't help but laugh. "You did."

He patted his collar. "And this isn't the sticker from the chart. I left it on there. This is a new one."

"Oh, so you think you deserved two gold stars?"

He looked me up and down and stepped in close. His eyes filled with a very familiar heat. "We can go inside your office and I can earn it again right now if you want."

"I thought you were offering lunch?"

"I am." He looked directly at my crotch. "I'm talking about an *actual* happy meal."

I snorted and gave him a shove. "You're so crude."

Then he winced and whispered. "I've had a semi all day. Ever since I woke up. I keep thinking about last night, you doin' me, me doin' you, and my dick hasn't quit since. Especially with the horse riding without saddles, if you know what I mean."

Horse riding without . . .

Oh.

Bareback.

I rolled my eyes.

He groaned. "Oh come on! You gotta admit, it was the hottest thing ever."

I couldn't believe he was talking about this—out the front of my work, of all places. Not that anyone could hear, but still . . .

I mean, what he said was true.

Tully laughed and wiggled in close. "Is that blush on your cheeks your answer? Is your face red because you're embarrassed? Or because it was the hottest thing ever?" He grinned. "Are you remembering how it felt?"

"Oh my god, stop it," I said, grabbing his arm and hauling him up the stairs and inside.

Of course he thought me manhandling him was a treat. He laughed and leaned his back against the useless radar console, offering himself. "You wanna do me again right now? Because you won't get a no outta me." He began to undo his fly. "Or do you just wanna little suck?"

The fact that my dick was half interested in that idea didn't help.

Jeez, what had I become?

I stepped in close, my fingers on the button of his pants. Because having a little suck sounded like a very good idea.

God, I was going to do this . . . in my office, during the day. Me, of all people.

I licked my lips and Tully groaned out a laugh. "Oh fuck yes. I was only joking, but if you're gonna get on your knees . . ."

Yes. Yes, I was going to.

Until my phone rang.

I saw the number on the screen and my heart almost stopped.

National head office.

All thoughts of fellatio were gone. God, I could hardly speak. "Tully."

"What's wrong?"

"What if they . . . ? Tully, they're going to tell me— I can't leave. I have too much work to do, and I have you."

The phone kept ringing.

And ringing.

Until it stopped.

"Jeremiah," Tully said. "What are you doing?"

"I'm not answering it."

"You have to."

"If I don't answer, they can't tell me to leave."

He was clearly confused. "Leave where?"

"Leave here."

"They're not gonna tell you to leave."

I gestured to the very dark dashboard. "It's not as if I can actually do any work."

"They didn't tell you to leave last time they called. You spent a week helping the airport weather-station crew."

"What else is there for me to do here? The repair team still haven't confirmed the ETA."

"Maybe that's what they were calling for."

Maybe.

Except I didn't think so.

My phone rang again. "Why did they have to fix the cellular network already?"

Tully snorted and picked up my phone, hit Answer, and held the phone to my ear.

I glowered at him and sighed. "Doctor Overton, Darwin office."

"Doctor Overton," a familiar voice said. Peter, manager of the national head office. "I trust you're well."

"Yes, thank you." I took the phone from Tully and put it on speakerphone, considering he could hear it anyway. "Any word on the refit? I'm hoping you have good news for me."

"Yes, and no."

"I'm not sure how news can be both, Peter. It really is more of an either/or situation." And I was betting on the bad news being what I'd been dreading.

Yet Tully's eyes were wide and hopeful.

And a little worried.

"Good news or bad news first?"

"I'd prefer neither, if I'm being frank."

"Good news first then."

I waited for him to continue, even though it became apparent he was expecting me to say something when I was not the one leading this conversation.

"Right then," he added. "So the refit of the Darwin office is scheduled and confirmed to begin the week after next."

"Oh, well, that *is* good news."

Tully's smile widened, and he nodded excitedly.

"We expect it will be a three-week job to complete."

"Okay." I wasn't sure what he expected me to say. "One week to start, three weeks to complete. That's reasonable."

"It's pretty good, actually. It's a complete refit; all new wiring and cabling has to happen first. You won't recognise your new office when you get back."

The relief I felt was visceral. They were fixing my office! And they weren't sending me away! But then I thought about what he'd said.

Uh . . .

"I'm sorry." My eyes narrowed at my phone. "When I get back from where?"

Tully was no longer smiling.

"When I get back from *where*?" I asked again, louder this time, when Peter still hadn't replied.

"Well, that's the bad news."

"Peter," I said flatly. "After the month we've had here, I have neither the patience nor the sense of humour for such games."

"The remote weather station at Oxley Island," he said. "As you know, we have a signal, but the radar system is offline. The local police said they could see by boat that the building is still standing but they don't have access to assess the damage. Might just need a simple reboot for all we know. And well, you're the closest manager on the ground . . . and you're not exactly busy right now."

The Oxley Island remote weather station.

Oxley Island was about three hundred kilometres from Darwin, situated off the northernmost tip of Arnhem Land. It was a small island with absolutely nothing on it but the automated weather station on the top eastern side. Which was, apparently, no more than a small, one-room brick building miles from anywhere and anyone.

The island itself had somehow escaped the direct path of Cyclone Hazer, but like most of the coastal parts of the Northern Territory, it had been hit by torrential rain and severe wind gusts. It just wasn't razed to the ground like some parts.

So, not too far away—certainly not across the country— but damn, it sure was remote.

"How long am I expected to be there?"

Tully was still staring at me, his eyes wide but now filled with more uncertainty.

"Well," Peter said. "We're trying to arrange transport. It'd be a full day's drive by four-wheel drive, and there *is* road access, but some of those roads have been damaged. Some are close to impassable if the last report was anything to go by."

Impassable roads in crocodile-infested Kakadu and Arnhem Land. "I know a thing or two about impassable roads out that way," I said flatly.

Tully grinned, nodding earnestly.

I glowered at him and shook my head.

Then Peter said, "And we'd still have to get you boated across from there. Honestly, it'd be quicker by boat from

Darwin. But we'd have to find a local to get you over to the island."

"Boat?" I repeated. I was *not* a fan of boats, but the idea of driving more impassable roads along those swampy mangroves . . . I'd rather the boat.

"Whose boat?" Tully asked.

"I didn't realise this wasn't a private conversation," Peter said.

"Apologies," I said. "My . . . my boyfriend is here." I cringed at having to say that out loud. I still wasn't used to saying it at all.

Tully's grin was spectacular, and his eyebrows almost met his hairline. "Boyfriend," he mouthed.

I sighed.

I didn't call him that often enough, apparently.

"Oh, of course," Peter mumbled.

I didn't like his tone.

"To repeat my earlier question," I continued bluntly, "how long am I expected to be there? It's not exactly convenient to run to the supermarket from that location, so I will need to prepare many things, I suspect. And what about equipment? Do we know what equipment I'll even need to make repairs? If any of it is repairable at all, I should add. If the damage is structural, I won't be able to do anything. If it's a matter of replacing aerials or satellites, then I'm not sure how much use I'll be at all. I'm hardly qualified to install the equipment, Peter. Otherwise I'd have done my office by now."

"It's no longer connected to the mesonet. It could just be a connectivity issue," he said. "Or it might be a write-off. You could get there and do nothing more than fill in a damage report. Maybe nothing's salvageable. It's all old gear anyway."

I snorted. "You've seen the equipment list from the office I'm currently standing in, right? That all needs to be replaced. I can assure you, if the gear at Oxley Island is older than what's here, I'll bring it back to the Museum of Technology, Dark Ages exhibit."

Tully laughed.

"Yes, well," Peter mumbled. "Your office was long overdue for an upgrade."

He could say that again.

"Anyway," he continued. "We'd imagine the work itself at Oxley Island shouldn't take too long: a day, maybe two. But it's getting you there and bringing you back again that's proving difficult."

"If I'm going by boat, wouldn't the boat and the driver wait for me?" Surely they wouldn't drop me off and come back for me.

He made an uncertain sound. "Under normal circumstances, yes. But a lot of charter companies are out of commission with cyclone damage, as I'm sure you're aware."

"I'm aware, yes."

"I might even suggest maybe one of the news stations take you, and in lieu of payment, they could film you and the repairs, documentary style—"

"Absolutely not! I'd rather swim there in crocodile and jellyfish infested oceans than endure that special kind of hell."

Peter snorted. "Yeah, I figured you'd say that. It was just an option."

Tully gave me that gorgeous, insufferable smile. "Well, isn't it just as well that your boyfriend is the favouritest son of the owner of one of Australia's largest shipping companies? We happen to have boats."

"I can't take a cargo ship to Oxley Island," I replied. "Thanks anyway."

He laughed. "No, that's a ship, not a boat. But I do have a boat licence and access to a few different vessels. I can take you."

I stared at him. "You could take me?"

His eyes lit up when he grinned at me. "Abso-freaking-lutely."

Peter was quiet for a second. "Uh, was that offer legitimate? Because I'll need to lodge another permit."

Tully was so excited he was almost bouncing. "Hell yes, it was a legit offer." He patted his shirt collar and beamed. "I knew this gold star would be lucky today. How long can we stay for?"

CHAPTER FOUR

TULLY

It took two days for Jeremiah's and my permits to enter the Arnhem Land islands to come through. It took me that long to organise things at work, even though we were only expecting to be gone for maybe two days at the most, and it *was* a weekend. But my work had been busier than ever, and the days of the week hadn't really mattered since the cyclone.

Everyone worked every day.

But Mum and Dad knew everyone had been puttin' in long hours since Hazer, and they also knew I'd be goin' with Jeremiah whether I had approved time off or not.

He was goin' to a remote island, after all. A remote island that was only accessible by boat and was a true effort to get to —even more remote than the bunker.

There was no way I was letting him go alone.

My dad had two boats, and one in particular was ideal. A twenty-two-metre Sportfisher. It was designed for fishin', but it would be more than perfect for what we needed. Jeremiah thought the boat was fancy—and it was nice, don't get me wrong—but it wasn't the biggest or most expensive in its class. Not that I expected Jeremiah to know these things.

Dad loved his boat; he went deep-sea fishin' any chance

he got. He *loved* it enough that he'd had it taken out of harm's way when the cyclone was due to hit. Like all the ships in our fleet. His fishing boat was no exception.

Growin' up, Dad had taken all his kids fishing, just like he took us hunting, and riding motorbikes, and camping in Kakadu.

Rowan preferred fishing. I preferred camping out at the bunker, and Zoe and Ellis preferred sports like football and CrossFit.

But we all learned how to drive a boat, like we all knew how to ride a motorbike or drive a forklift. Like we all knew how to cook, clean, and sew on a button.

So takin' Jeremiah to some remote weather station on an island for a day or two sounded like a holiday to me. In fact, I was secretly hoping for a two- or three-day stay. Albeit, he had a list of work he needed to do, and a crate of gear to do it with.

All I'd packed was a fishing rod, a change of shorts, and my toothbrush.

I wasn't expecting it to be all fun and games, but I got to tag along, help out, explore the area, maybe do a spot of fishin', and hang out with my most favouritest person. Not to mention the scorching hot ways we'd need to entertain ourselves at night, all by ourselves, alone with no television.

It was all a win for me.

The Bureau of Meteorology offered to pay me, and they did fulfil a bogus invoice I'd sent them. But I'd used the money they'd paid me for my 'charter service' to order a top of the range ergonomic desk chair for Jeremiah, because what they expected him to use wasn't good enough.

The cheaper one I'd bought him before, and Bruce the dog's chair, wouldn't cut it anymore for my Jeremiah.

Which I decided to tell him all about on the way to the marina when Ellis was driving us, because Jeremiah wouldn't be mad at me in front of my brother.

Or so I'd thought.

"Why would you do that?" Jeremiah said firmly. "You were supposed to use the money to cover costs and expenses for this trip."

"Because the chair I fixed for you before isn't good enough for the hours you put in. And the one you inherited when you took over is at least twenty years old, covered in dog hair, and has the impression of Doreen's backside in it," I argued. "And no doubt your head office would only approve basic cheap shit in the new refurb, and I want you to have only the best."

He narrowed those sharp blue eyes at me. "But now I feel bad. You're covering the costs of this trip—the fuel, the food . . . when you said you'd organise all that, I didn't expect you to pay for it. It was covered in the invoice."

"Sure. Honestly, the chair wasn't *that* expensive," I countered. "But the way I look at it is that chair is technically for me as well."

He blinked. "You want to use my office chair?"

I winked at him. "Hell yes. I needed to ensure the chair was the best ergonomic design for spinal support, but also that it held both our body weights because we have to christen your new office."

Ellis laughed.

"Christen . . ." Jeremiah's eyes went wide when he realised what I meant. He glanced at Ellis, then cut me a rather sharp stare as he burned a spectacular shade of red. "Oh my god."

I just laughed. "Boats and ships are christened with smashing a champagne bottle before its maiden voyage. Office chairs should totally receive a similar bang and smash."

Ellis cracked up laughing. "Did you buy the chair from a sex shop? Because those are totally a thing."

I snorted. "No. But if you could send me a link, that'd be great. Gay edition, thanks."

Jeremiah sighed and turned to stare out the window, though the tips of his ears went red.

He was so damned cute.

And he was used to me and Ellis now.

Kind of.

"You still didn't have to waste the money on me," Jeremiah furthered. "The standard-issue office chair would have sufficed."

He was just mad that I'd used the money on him because he was only ever used to paying his own way. He'd had to save for every single thing in his life or go without, and me buying him things made him feel uncomfortable.

"Let him buy you stuff, Jem," Ellis said gently. He knew that Jeremiah struggled with anyone spending money on him for anything. "It makes up for his terrible sense of humour."

Jeremiah levelled him with a stare that said, in no uncertain terms, that Ellis and I shared identical senses of humour. Or maybe it was for the use of the nickname Jem. Rowan's youngest had called him that because they couldn't say his name, much like Presley and Casey who called him Jememiah.

It was cute when the kids said it, apparently. The adults, not so much.

I snorted. "Babe, if I kept the money for taking you to the island, it'd make me a real-life Julia Roberts in *Pretty Woman*."

He turned to squint at me. "What?"

So I explained. "You'd be paying me to stay with you and for the amazing sex we're gonna have," I said. "Which is technically prostitution. And we *will* be having a lot of amazing sex, because two or three days of just you and me and nothing else is a really long time. Now, I have no problem with prostitution or with role playing Julia Roberts if you wanna be Richard Gere. Or we can take it in turns with which one of us wants to be the pretty woman. I have zero problems with that."

Ellis laughed.

Jeremiah slow-blinked before sighing. "Your mind is a frightful place sometimes."

"I've been saying that for years," Ellis said as he pulled the car into a parking spot at the marina.

"You're both welcome." I got out and held Jeremiah's door for him. As he climbed out and when Ellis couldn't hear, I whispered, "I wanna be Julia first though, if that's okay?"

He smiled as I closed the door behind him, and Ellis already had the boot open.

"Hey, dickbag, come get your shit," Ellis said.

"Oh," Jeremiah said, rushing to help, but Ellis was clearly talking to me.

"You're not the dickbag, Jeremiah," Ellis corrected, shoving my duffle bag at me. He slid the black crate of gear closer. "This good to go?"

"I can take that," Jeremiah started. "It's rather heavy."

Ellis picked it up and began walking to the dock. Jeremiah shot me a he-doesn't-have-to-help-me look and I closed the boot and smiled at him. "You'll get used to it."

I would have thought he'd be used to it by now—having my family around so much, doing family stuff for him—but apparently not.

We followed Ellis down toward the dock where a familiar figure stood next to a gangplank.

"Morning," Dad said cheerfully as we got closer.

"Morning," I replied.

"Good morning," Jeremiah said. Ellis walked the crate onto the boat and disappeared inside. Then he looked at the boat. "Oh, good heavens, is this it?"

I knew he'd think it was too expensive or whatever. What could I say? My dad liked to go fishing. "Sure is."

He looked at it again, something on the roof making him look twice. "Is that a radome?"

I laughed. He was such a weather nerd. "Yes."

I even caught my dad trying not to smile. "It's a pulse compression radar," Dad said.

Jeremiah brightened. "Oh? What's the pulse repetition frequency?"

Dad beamed. "Up to five thousand nine hundred hertz."

Jeremiah was impressed, and honestly, I shouldn't have been surprised.

Then Mum appeared on the back deck of the boat. "Morning, boys."

"Hey, Mum."

"Hello, Mrs Larson," Jeremiah said with a smile.

"We've stocked your food for you," she said. "And Jeremiah, darling, I've told you to call me Brielle."

Jeremiah looked pained. It made me smile at him.

"And the tank's full," Dad added.

"You really didn't have to do that," Jeremiah tried.

Dad held his hand for Mum as she stepped off the gangplank, like he did every time. "Yes, we did," she said, giving Jeremiah's arm a squeeze. She understood that Jeremiah struggled with having a family that did things for each other and how it made him feel inadequate. He struggled with dealing with my large family most of the time, but he was trying to get past it. It just wasn't easy for him. Being alone, even with his father, it was so ingrained in him to be self-sufficient.

Many things were ingrained in him. Like his fierce independence and how showing any affection in front of others made him freeze. Whereas I came from a loving family that regularly hugged and told each other we loved them. He did not.

God forbid I ever bestowed the L-word on Jeremiah in front of my family.

He was okay when I told him I loved him now, when it was just us, of course. But no one else. Not even in front of Ellis.

I was still working on that.

Ellis came back over the gangplank and pretended to almost drop my car keys into the water below. He thought he was hilarious. "Very funny, nut sac," I said. "You break any part of my car, you pay for it."

"I won't break it," he said with a grin. "But I will drive through every red-light camera in town."

I put him in a headlock and tried to give him a noogie while Jeremiah talked to my parents. Ellis almost managed to junk-punch me so I let him go just in time to hear Jeremiah say, "I do appreciate it. When Tully told me you'd organised food for us, I worried we'd inconvenienced you."

Mum put her hand to his face. "Oh, you're such a sweetheart."

Oh no. She touched his arm *and* his face . . .

Jeremiah almost took an embarrassed step backwards off the dock. I shoved Ellis off me and went to Jeremiah, sliding my arm around his waist, making sure he didn't fall. "And that's enough scaring him for today, thanks, Mum."

Jesus. He adored my mother, and she had a real soft spot for him, but a compliment *and* a physical touch and a trip in a boat. He was going to need sedating.

He picked up his bag, pretending his face wasn't nuclear red and that he wasn't mortified, and he gave a worried glance at the boat and then to me. "And you assure me you can actually drive this boat. I'm not a fan of boats, as I'm sure I've mentioned. Several times."

"You'll be fine. And yes, I can drive a boat. Just like I drive the Jeep through Kakadu."

Jeremiah paled a little. "Oh joy."

Dad laughed. "Relax. I taught him everything he knows. He's very sensible. There's a satellite phone if you need, and there's also a flare gun. So if he drives irresponsibly or does anything stupid, shoot him with it."

Jeremiah looked at him, aghast.

"He's joking," Mum said, giving Dad a poke.

"Shoot him in the dick," Ellis said.

Mum whacked Ellis' arm but smiled at Jeremiah. "Ignore them."

"Why did you tell Jeremiah to ignore them," I asked her. "I'm the one they're telling him to shoot with a flare gun."

"They wouldn't actually shoot you, Tully," she said.

Ellis imitated holding a pistol. "It's really simple, Jeremiah. Just hold it away from your body, unlock the safety, and aim. At his junk."

I tried to push him off the dock. Fucker was stronger than he looked.

When I gave up and turned around, Jeremiah was already on the boat. "Hey," I said. "I was going to help you across." I grabbed my bag and Jeremiah held out his hand to help me as I crossed the gangplank instead.

"Aww," Ellis cried. "Princess."

Dad shoved him for me.

I stepped into the boat, turned around, and flipped Ellis off. "It's *pretty woman* to you, nut sac."

Dad squinted, confused. Mum sighed. "I don't want to know."

"Thank you for everything," I said to them. "But we should head off if I'm going to get this handsome doctor to his destination before the tide changes."

Dad nodded. "Be careful. Call us if you need. Radio the coast guard if you get into trouble."

"Will do."

"Life jackets," Mum reminded us.

"Yes, Mum."

I took two life jackets and helped Jeremiah with his. I slipped it over his head and fastened the clips, cinching them in at his waist, making him jolt toward me. "Mmm," I hummed, low enough for only him to hear. "New kink unlocked."

He glanced over at my parents to see if they'd heard. They mighta done, given Ellis was grinning at us. Jeremiah shoved me away. "Thank you again," he said to my family. "Ellis, please look after Mr Percival for us."

He gave a salute. "Shall do. Just me and the bird all weekend."

"If you treated your girlfriends better, that wouldn't be the case. Maybe you'll treat Grace right this time," I said, then had to pull the gangplank onboard before he could cross it.

A few minutes later, we were unmoored and ready to go. Jeremiah was sitting down, gripping onto the seat under him as if his life depended on it. He was excited underneath the nerves, and I knew the best way to help with that was to put him to work. "Okay, Navigator, you're up."

He looked around as if I was speaking to someone else. "Um, what? I thought you said you could drive this thing?"

"I can."

"Then what do you need me for?"

"Just come up here."

He grimaced, and after considering his options for a few seconds, he came over to me. He was a bit wobbly, and this wasn't even the open sea yet. I had him stand in front of me, putting my arms around his waist to hold the throttle.

"This is all very high tech," he said. "This navigation system is better than anything in my office. Well, when I had a working office."

I pointed to the screen. He knew how to read this informa-tion. He knew maps and graphs and weather charts better than anyone. I took his hand and put it on the throttle, then his other on the wheel. "Okay, keep her under five until we clear the break wall. And see those buoy markers?"

He nodded.

"You gotta keep port side of those."

"What the hell is port side, Tully?" He cried. "Use termi-nology I understand."

"Left. Portside is left."

"Why didn't you just say that? Why does language change when you're on the water? That makes no sense."

"There's actually an etymological reason why nautical terms are used," I began.

"I don't care," he said. "Not right now. I'll care when I'm on solid ground and not driving a boat. Sorry."

I snorted. "Babe, you're doing great."

"You have more confidence in me than is warranted," he said, but after a while I could see just how much his cheeks were raised, how he was smiling.

"You can do anything you put your mind to."

He shook his head. Of course he'd disagree with me.

"You're driving a boat, Jeremiah."

He turned and grinned at me.

I grabbed the wheel. "Don't look at me. You gotta watch where you're going."

He pulled both hands away. "Oh. Sorry."

I kept him caged in my arms, my eyes on the bow. "We're gonna leave the shelter of the break wall here and go through Van Diemen's Gulf, up between the Tiwi and Vernon Islands, but from there we'll enter open water and skirt the coastline around Croker Island to Oxley Island," I said. "Read the navigation and tell me—"

"No thank you," he said, pushing my arm away and wobbling his way back to his seat. His hair was tousled by the wind and he looked so handsome in the sunlight. Even if he was holding on to his seat for dear life. "You said open water," he yelled over the sound of the engine. "That's where I opt out. Thank you for the offer though."

He was so adorable.

But I knew when not to push. He'd had a few minutes of fun, but he was clearly out of his comfort zone. And it was probably just as well, because crossing into open waters needed all my attention.

The gulf was spectacular today. The water calm and a magnificent array of blues and tropical greens.

It made Jeremiah's eyes stand out even more, dark sapphires against topaz.

I had to go over to him. I held his face up and smacked a kiss on his lips.

He pulled back in surprise. "What are you doing?"

"I just had to tell you you're beautiful."

He pointed to the helm. "Hold the wheel and watch where we're going. You can tell me I'm beautiful when we're on dry land."

I laughed and went back to the wheel, and he sat there and got all flustered and embarrassed, still holding onto the bottom of his seat with both hands. But he smiled as he took in the view. First of the Tiwi Islands and then the coastline as we made our way out to Oxley Island.

I knew he wasn't a fan of boats, but on a calm and sunny day like today—perfect boating conditions—he was enjoying it. Well, enjoyin' it as much as he could with both hands gripping onto his seat.

I'd imagine in rough seas it'd be a very different story, but the water was as smooth as I'd seen it. The sun was bright, the warm breeze played with his hair, and I even caught him closing his eyes a few times as he smiled into the wind.

I wish I'd thought to take him out on the water before now.

But I knew I had a slim chance of ever gettin' him out here again, so I enjoyed it while I could.

I was disappointed it didn't take us longer to get there.

But as we came around the top of Oxley Island, I slowed right down and brought us in closer. I was assured there was an old jetty near the weather station that was still intact.

Another one of those things built to last, like the bunker, before red tape and a lack of common sense came in to play.

But given this jetty was wood and rusted bolts, I kinda

wished common sense played a little bit harder. It was short and it did look robust. The pylons were as round as telegraph poles, which was probably exactly what they once were.

But it was still standing.

Kinda.

I lassoed a pylon and gave the rope to Jeremiah. "Pull us in," I said, going back to the wheel. He clearly hadn't expected me to get him to do that, bein' all wide-eyed and nervous, but like everything he did, he did it well.

I really loved how he just got in and had a go. Never said *oh, I can't do that* or panicked or whined about it. He just used that big ol' brain of his to figure shit out and he did what needed doing.

I manoeuvred us in and cut the engine as he pulled the rope, and I tied it off.

"Be careful of the boards on the jetty," I said. "Actually, let me go first."

But it was too late. He threw the gangplank over and was already standing on the jetty by the time I'd finished speaking.

So impatient.

"Good heavens," he said, inspecting the wood. "Apparently they built this jetty when they brought the radar in by barge about twenty years ago." He looked at it, horrified. "How is this still even standing?"

"I'm surprised it wasn't washed away long ago." I walked across to meet him, and he held his hand out for me.

So sweet.

"Perhaps we should walk along the edge where the bolts are," he said. Then he grimaced. "Where *some* bolts still are."

"Yeah, how about we don't jinx it," I suggested. "Let's go and check out the weather station and see if there's anywhere to camp tonight. Or if we're sleeping on the boat."

With a nod, he led the way off the jetty and onto the wharf. It was a rocky platform, clearly man-made like Jeremiah had said, when they built the weather station and needed to offload gear. Further down was a small beach, dotted with large protruding boulders and rocks. There were a few palm trees, though it was mostly shrubs, and it was hard to tell if the cyclone had mown over them or if it always looked such a mess.

I was thinkin' it could be the latter.

But there, a few metres back into a clearing, with its own two-metre-tall fence built right around it, was the most prominent and probably only feature. There was a small, square, cinder-block building with a flat roof that appeared to be welded on. It reminded me of something from one of those worst-prisons-in-the-world episodes.

"Sweet mother of god," Jeremiah mumbled. He stood there, his arms by his side, his mouth open, and stared at the building. He shook his head, dismayed. "What even is this place?"

"I was just thinking it looked like a cell block, or maybe an outhouse at one of the world's worst prisons. Except for the mess of antennas and radars on top of it."

"Yes, well," he said as he opened the padlock on the gate. "This one is even older than my office."

Jesus.

Did he have any equipment that wasn't older than him?

I knew it made Jeremiah frustrated and disappointed, but it made me really fucking angry.

"If they don't upgrade you with all the newest and bestest of everything, Imma pay a little visit to the dipshits at the national head office."

He held the gate for me. "And who said chivalry was dead."

"Not me." I gave him my biggest grin. "I'm the most chivalrous man in all the lands."

"I'm certain cracking skulls and name-calling falls somewhat short of the chivalrous qualifiers." Then he smiled at me. "Though the sentiment is heartwarming."

I preened and he rolled his eyes before walking toward the building.

"Jeez," he said, now looking at something else in the corner of the yard. "Look at that."

There was a weather box on the ground.

Well, it used to be a weather box. One of those Stevenson-screen types, the white box with louvred slat sides. It was now on the ground against the security fencing in the far corner, half covered with branches and a palm frond. It was hard to tell if it was intact.

I went to clear off the debris, but Jeremiah stopped me.

"Leave it," he said. "For now. I'll need to take some photos first."

"Oh, sure. Good idea."

"Let's have a look inside the building."

"You mean the prison outhouse?"

He managed a smile. "Indeed."

We went to the door of the building, and he was getting the keys ready to unlock the old door.

"Wait," I said, this time stopping him. "There could be critters."

He looked to his feet. "What kind? Are there snakes here? On this tiny island? How did they get here?" Then his eyes almost bugged out of his head and he took a large step backwards. "Are there frogs here?"

"Truth be told, I'm not up to date on the exact eco-life of this island. I'd reckon, given the whole island is covered in these kinds of shrubs that seafaring birds are the main inhabitants. They're gonna take care of the snake and frog problem."

Okay, so some itty-bitty white lies to make him feel better weren't gonna hurt either of us.

"But I should probably just check, just in case."

He handed me the keys and took another step back.

The real truth was, I had no idea what could be in this shack. It didn't look like a human had been here in a few years, at least. But odds were there were other kinds of visitors. And probably the bitin' kind because, let's be real, most critters in the Territory were.

I picked up a fallen branch from a shrub and after opening the door, I nudged it open with my foot, holdin' the branch like a weapon. I'd rather a startled snake get a fang full of dried leaf than my leg, thanks.

But inside . . . there was nothing.

And I mean nothing.

Well, there were some old meters on the wall, like the real old electricity metres from the fifties or somethin'. There was a ladder propped against one wall, and there were swirls of undisturbed dirt on the concrete floor. Jeez, even the spiderwebs here and there looked abandoned.

Jeremiah peered in from the doorway. "I will never complain about my office again." He went in and looked at the meters, clearly tryin' to determine what they were for.

"How is this powered?" I asked. There sure as hell wasn't electricity here. "Solar?"

He nodded. "I guess there's a small panel on the roof." He pointed to one meter that resembled a modem—if they had modems back in the 1970s. "That's a VSAT."

"A what?"

"A very small aperture terminal."

I snorted. "For real? That's what VSAT stands for? Clearly people who got to name shit lacked imagination."

He smiled. "It's a ground station for the satellite dish." Then he tapped the meter itself. "There should be lights, so the connection is broken between here and the satellite on the roof."

"Just a quick question," I said.

He turned to me, waiting.

I gestured to the meters and the room. "What the honest fuck?"

His eyes darted around the room, then back to me. "Uh . . . Was that your actual question?"

"I believe it was, yeah. Look at this shit." I gestured to the meters as if it explained everything.

He looked around and grimaced. "Well, I'm inclined to agree with you because . . ."

I snorted. "Because? Come on, say it, baby."

He smirked, but then dragged his finger across one of the meter screens and held it up to show me the reddish-brown evidence. "What the *honest* fuck?"

I laughed. "God, I love it when you swear. It's like you're being naughty." I waggled my eyebrows at him. "And I love it when you're naughty."

He rolled his eyes and sighed. "I know." Then he narrowed his eyes at me. "Baby."

Holy shit.

"Did you just . . . did you just call me baby? Like for real?"

"I was being sarcastic." He dusted his hands off on his shorts. "Because you call me that, and it's . . ."

I stared at him. "It's what? Don't you like it?"

"I know you're fond of it, but for me, it's unusual." He made a face. "I've never been called that by anyone, and it's not a term of endearment I would choose. If I had the choice."

"What would you choose?"

"Well, to be honest, I'm not sure I'd choose any term of endearment."

I gasped. "Why, baby?"

He gave me the stink eye, then sighed. "I don't know. Your name is already short, and your brother calls you Tull, which is sweet."

"You can call me Tull."

"But now it would feel forced."

God help me. How could he be so cute and so damn frustrating at the same time?

"You like it when the kids call you Jememiah," I said.

He pulled his bottom lip in between his teeth and shrugged one shoulder. "It's cute because they're children."

"Can I call you Jememiah?"

He squinted at me. "I seem to recall when we very first met that I introduced myself to you as Jeremy."

"But you're not a Jeremy," I said flatly, like *duh*. "You're a Jeremiah. Or a Jememiah. Or Doctor Overton. Or baby. Or my personal favourite, which is 'fuck yes, right there.'" I panted. "Harder, harder, oh god."

He rolled his eyes. "You're insufferable."

I laughed. "Speaking of sex—thank you for bringing that up, by the way—I don't think we'll be sleeping in here tonight." I nodded to the concrete floor. "Boat sex it is then."

"I didn't bring it up."

"Shh. Do you want another silver star?"

He stared at me, then cracked up laughing. "You wouldn't dare!"

I took his arm and pulled him out the door. "Come on, let's take your photos. Then we can go explore the island a little bit before you suggest doin' something tragically boring like work."

CHAPTER FIVE

JEREMIAH

I AGREED TO GO EXPLORING THE ISLAND FOR TWO REASONS.

The first, so that afterwards Tully would allow me to get some work done in peace.

And the second was—given the size of the island, the lack of infrastructure, and the repetitive and somewhat destroyed vegetation—I figured it would take all of twenty minutes.

We began down the beach. It was rugged and mostly untouched. I'd hazard a guess that Tully and I were the only people to have set foot on the island in some time. It was small, barely two square kilometres, and sitting out in the Arafura Sea at the mercy of the elements. The island itself was mostly flat, and I could safely assume there was no elevation three metres above sea level. The vegetation, the shrubs and grasses were gnarled and ragged.

"Do you think the shrubs are this damaged from the cyclone?" I asked. "Or is this just how they look?"

Tully chuckled. "I wondered the same thing. This eastern side was protected, somewhat, but I'd say this whole island cops it from all directions on the regular. My dad and his team use weather reports from here for their shipping routes." He made a face. "Well, they did. Before the cyclone.

When I mentioned coming out here, he knew what I was talking about."

All the more reason to finish exploring and make some attempt at sourcing the problem.

I didn't say that. I just kept walking. I mean, how often would we ever get an entire island to ourselves?

"It appeared that old weather radar was still attached to the roof," I offered. "So I'd say there's just an internal miscommunication somewhere. Hopefully an easy fix. Not that I'm a technician by any stretch—"

Tully grabbed my arm. "Stop."

He was looking a few metres ahead, where the sand met the grass and shrubs. But his urgency had me on alert. "What is it?"

"See that?" He nodded ahead. "That track?"

It was a wide track of flattened sand with an odd divot, as if someone had dragged a zigzag with a stick right through the centre.

"I thought we were the only ones here," I said.

"We are." He took a few steps to get a closer look. "The only humans, anyway."

I looked at the track again, then shot him a panicked stare. "What made that? Tully, what animal made that track?"

He grinned. He actually grinned. "That's a croc. Big one too, by the looks of it."

A croc.

A freaking crocodile.

I took his arm in a death grip and dragged him backwards. "Get away from it, my god, Tully."

He was like an excited child. "No, look at how awesome it is! You can see where the tail—"

"No. No, immediately no. No, thank you." I looked at the scrub, then at the water, suddenly feeling very exposed. "We're going back to the building area that is fully fenced. Actually, now that I think about it, that fence wasn't built to keep people out, was it? It's to keep the crocodiles out. Good lord. Why wasn't that ever mentioned?"

He resisted my tugging him along until he relented with a laugh. "There's no crocs there now. They probably just come here to rest or lay eggs. So realistically, you're more likely to be surprised by one walking this close to the water's edge."

I may have screamed and jumped a good metre away from the water.

He snorted. "You just need a long stick. Kinda poke at 'em if you have to." Then he shrugged. "But honestly, if they're determined to get ya . . ."

I turned on my heel and walked back to the safety of the fenced yard. "I have work to do."

"Ah, babe, I was just kidding!"

"We need to have a serious conversation about your sense of humour."

He laughed again but fell into step beside me. "I'm sorry. No more croc jokes."

Once we got back behind the fenced area, I felt immediately better. Until I remembered that I needed my gear. "Well, shit."

"Well, shit what?"

"How do we get our stuff off the boat?"

He cocked his head. "Like you normally would. We walk on and carry it off."

"But there are crocodiles."

"Not on the jetty."

"But the jetty is unstable, and the waters are—"

He took my face in his hands. "Jeremiah, my love. I'd never let anything happen to you."

I rolled my eyes. "You won't let the already decrepit jetty fall away underneath me so the crocodiles can't eat me for lunch?"

"No, I will forbid it." Then he shrugged. "Plus, I'm the

only one who gets to snack on you. Though now that you mention it, lunch is a really good idea."

I was so confused. "Are you talking about sex or actually eating lunch? It's hard to tell."

"I will always opt for sex. Always. But for the record, I wasn't talking about sex. But I am now. Because you brought it up." He grinned. "You have the best ideas. And I've never had boat sex before."

I sighed. "Work first."

"No, lunch first. For real." He patted his stomach. "I'm legit hungry. But then when we're on the boat—" He waggled his eyebrows and did some unruly hip thrusting movement. "—we should put that boat-rocking to good use."

I hated that he made me smile, and I hated that my dick liked the idea. I tried to be stern. "Lunch first."

His grin was spectacular. "This is the best day ever."

I snorted out a laugh. "Let's see if there are any crocs on the jetty before we rush into that statement."

There weren't, of course. But I kept an eye on the bay, giving a double look at every shadow in every ripple on the water. Yes, this small inlet was sheltered from the open sea, and I'd been thankful for that before.

Now I realised it just made it a prime location for crocodiles to come onto land.

We were both careful with every rickety and rotten plank on the jetty, and Tully held his hand out for me to step onto the boat. He pulled the Esky out and opened it.

"Let's see what goodies my mother packed for us," he said. He pulled out some wrapped bread rolls and handed them to me. "Ah, sweet chili chicken and Asian greens on a roll. Mum knows my favourite." Then he handed me a takeout container. "Dunno what's in that."

I opened it. "It's your mum's cold pasta and chorizo salad."

I'd mentioned once that I'd thoroughly enjoyed the cold

pasta salad she'd made . . . and now she'd made it again.

He shook his head and kept rummaging, pulling out a second container of something different. I opened it to find cold roast chicken, all neatly sliced.

Tully sighed. "And this. Good lord, how long did she think we were going for?" He pulled out a bunch of bananas and then some bottled water. Then he grinned. "And look. A bag of the little Snickers."

It was absurd to me, and very foreign, that a parent would do such a thing as go to all this trouble and effort for their grown child. I could understand essential items—even my dad would probably do that—but never favourite foods and treats.

I doubted my father knew what my favourite food even was.

"I won't have to cook ya rice and spiced beef like I did at the bunker," he said.

"I really liked your rice and beef," I said, my voice quieter than I'd intended. "If I had to eat it forever, I'd still be grateful."

He looked at me then, a container of cut oranges in his hand forgotten. "Hey," he said with a frown. "You okay?"

I nodded. "Your mum spoils you. You're very lucky."

He slid the container of oranges onto the small table and took my hand. "I know how lucky I am. But honestly, this is more for you than me. Pretty sure if it was just me, I'd have gotten a Vegemite sandwich and an apple. Or maybe even told to get my own."

But still . . . "I mentioned to her once that I liked her salad. And the Moroccan roast chicken she did. And she made them again for us today. One time I mentioned them, Tully. Just once. And she did that for me."

He squeezed my hand and smiled. "She adores you, Jeremiah."

I had to swallow back unexpected tears.

"Oh, baby." He leaned over and rested his chin on my shoulder, softly kissing my cheek. "I'd say don't get too cocky about it," he joked. "Because she dotes on all her kids and their partners." He threaded our fingers. "But she knows you grew up without a mum, so I think she dotes on you a bit more than the others."

I nodded again, having to wipe away one foolish tear that had escaped. "My dad wouldn't even know what my favourite food is." I shook my head this time. "But that's not his fault. Growing up, I didn't really have a favourite. I was grateful for anything we had. Some things he cooked better than others, but I was still grateful. When I was old enough, I'd cook dinner for when he got home. Just simple things like mashed potato and sausages. He must have choked down some terrible cooking," I said with a teary laugh. "But he never complained."

Tully lifted our joined hands and kissed my knuckles. "What's your favourite food now? Of all the things you could have, what would you wish for?"

I smiled at him. "Rice and beef, a la house specialty of the bunker."

He laughed. "I'm being serious."

"I am being serious." I sighed and met his warm honey eyes. "Maybe it's the memories that go with it. Meeting you, chasing storms, and falling in love. And you cooking that every night. They're the best memories of my life."

Tully stared at me, really stared. A slow and shy smile tugged at his lips. "You just said the L-word."

I resisted groaning and I tried to pull my hand from his, but he gripped mine tighter. "No, no," he said. "No take backs, no returns. You said it. Let me savour this moment forever." He closed his eyes and inhaled deeply, then exhaled loudly. "There. Officially savoured."

I did roll my eyes that time. "Are you done?"

"Yep." He let go of my hand, but he leaned in for a kiss

and waited for me to meet him halfway. Which I did, of course, and he smiled. "Thank you. I love you, and if you want spiced beef and rice any time, you just have to ask."

"I think I'd like it to be a bunker thing. Every time we go there, it can be our thing."

"You wanna go back?"

"Of course I do! I loved it. I wish we could have stayed longer. Perhaps next time we can. Weather permitting, of course."

He was practically buzzing with excitement, his eyes lit up, his grin wide. "Hell yes. Oh my god. I fucking love you. I love going to the bunker, and I love that you wanna go there with me." Then he got a far-off look in his eye. "You know, I wonder if I could convince my dad to buy a helicopter. I could get my licence and I could fly us in for weekends and stuff, and we could go all the time and—"

"Absolutely not."

"But then you wouldn't have to go down the mountain in the Jeep."

"Tully."

"Yeah?"

"Let's just eat lunch."

He repacked everything back into the Esky, sans the bread rolls and a bottle of water each. We ate in silence for a while, but I could tell by the furrow of his brow and thinking-while-chewing face that he was still mulling over the helicopter thing. "A helicopter would make—"

"No."

"But—"

"No buts. The Jeep is perfectly fine. More than fine. All discussions of helicopters are off the table."

I'd never heard of anything so ridiculous.

And expensive.

But mostly ridiculous.

He pouted as he chewed. "A fun boyfriend would say

yes."

I snorted out a laugh. "A boyfriend who didn't care about frivolous spending or your safety would say yes. A real fun boyfriend would have packed the heart monitor strap to see if boat sex is a factor in varying results."

His eyes shot to mine. "Did you pack it?"

I smiled as I took a bite of my lunch. "I did. But which of us gets to wear it is the real question."

He laughed. "You're the funnest boyfriend ever. And just so you know, when we get home, I'm ordering a second one online so we can wear them at the same time. You know, purely for scientific purposes."

"Mm-hmm. Purely."

It took some convincing Tully that I should at least look at the weather box and radar on the roof before we retired to the boat for the evening.

"I get it," he'd griped. "Work comes before I come."

"No, before the crocodiles do," I'd countered. "I'm assuming they might like to come to land at dusk. I'd like to be on this boat before that happens."

And he couldn't really argue with that.

So back to the weather station we went. He held my hand this time as I stepped off the boat, smiling and pleased with himself for helping me the same way his dad had helped his mum.

But we carried my crate and gear to the cinder-block, cell-block outhouse, as Tully called it.

He wasn't exactly wrong.

The first task was to check the Stevenson-screen weather box. Tully made sure there were no uninvited critters using the box as a nest, and thankfully there weren't.

The box itself wasn't damaged, but the stand was well and

truly broken. Inside the box, everything seemed to be intact. There were two glass minimum and max thermometers fixed to the back wall, plus three small remote sensors connected to the small hydrometer, a barometer, and a hygrometer, and I could only guess the reading units were in the cell block.

"Jesus H. Christ," Tully said. "How old is this?"

I shrugged. "I don't know. But the remote sensors can't be too old. And when I say *too old*, I mean not new, but not as old as my prehistoric Doppler in my office."

"I could order you a better system off eBay."

That was likely very true. "How's the stand?"

He righted the metal frame and it barely held its own weight. "I don't think we can fix it," he said, inspecting it. "Maybe I can rig something up, but it wouldn't last another big storm. Certainly not a cyclone. It needs a stronger base, anchored into a concrete bed."

"Mm," I said with a shrug. "I'm not sure if there's a point in even attempting to rig something up. Like you said, it needs to be done with the proper gear and equipment."

"And funding."

"Correct."

He inspected the box and the stand and sighed. "If we can get the sensors online again, then I'll try to fix the stand. If the box is dead, there's no point."

This was true. "Also correct. I should get up on the roof and inspect the damage to the antennas and satellite dish."

Tully carried out the ladder and held it for me while I climbed up. As soon as I could see on top, I could see what was wrong. There were several antennas, two were now laying on the far edge, only attached by wires, and the tracking satellite dish was damaged. "The LNB is disconnected," I said, climbing up the last rung and lifting myself onto the roof.

"The low-noise block?" Tully asked. "Please be careful up there."

"This roof is a lot sturdier than the jetty," I said. "And yes, the LNB has completely come off the feed arm. I should be able to reattach it. But some antennas are down."

I took a bunch of photos with my phone before trying to fix the LNB, but it wasn't as simple as just reattaching it. The port jack was broken off inside it. "I don't think the noise block is repairable," I said, loud enough for Tully to hear. "But the antennas might be. They're still here, at least." I walked to the edge so I could see Tully. "Remember how you MacGyvered the booster at the bunker? These antennas might just need MacGyvering."

"Okay, I'll come up, hang on."

"Let me get down first." I climbed down and showed him the photos, and with a nod, he grabbed a few tools before he went up.

Did I find it extremely attractive that he was so handy?

Yes.

Was the fact he could fix things a turn on for me?

I was beginning to think it might be.

"You know," I said, "there's a lot to be said about the sexy handyman persona. A man who can use tools and isn't afraid to get his hands dirty. I never realised I had a thing for such appeal."

Tully's smiling face appeared. "You okay down there?"

It didn't help that he was holding a pair of pliers.

"I'm great. How are you up there?"

He laughed and snapped the pliers. "Do you have a fetish I didn't know about?"

"I wouldn't call it a fetish," I argued, thankful we were all alone on this island. "But if you were to also perhaps look at purchasing a tool belt, I wouldn't be mad about it."

He laughed. "Would I get extra gold stars?"

I pretended to have to consider this. "Hmm, maybe. Would you be naked under that tool belt?"

"I can be naked right now," he said, pulling his T-shirt

over his head. He threw it down to me, and by some miracle, I caught it.

"Keep your shorts on. I don't think dangling your bits on that hot tin roof will do either of us any favours."

He burst out laughing. "But then you'd get to kiss them better."

I snorted. "What difference does that make when you know I'll kiss them anyway? You don't need to put yourself through what I would imagine is a rather excruciating lesson."

He grinned. "I'll hold you to that."

"I don't doubt you will."

He was still grinning. "Want me to come down now and you fulfil your promise, or should I fix your antenna first?"

"Antenna, please."

He sighed. "So cruel."

But he disappeared from view, and after a few moments, I decided to climb up and watch him from the ladder.

Until he tried to kneel on the roof and hissed at how hot it was. "Here," I said, throwing his shirt back to him. "Kneel on that."

He was very obviously surprised to see me peering at him through the top two rungs of the ladder. "Are you perving on me?"

"It's not perving," I replied. "Think of me as the OH&S officer in this working agreement. I'm supervising."

He laughed, but he shoved the shirt under his knee and went about fixing the antenna. He had a cordless drill and some screws and had it fixed again in no time. "The backing plate's a bit bent, but she'll be right," he said. "Now, if you wouldn't mind supervising from inside and see if anything's back online."

Oh, yes. That's probably a good idea . . .

Except there was no change, no miraculous fix. Everything was still dead.

"Nothing," I yelled.

"Let me see if I can fix the satellite thing," he replied.

I went back out and up the ladder to watch him again. He was standing now, shirtless in the sunshine, his muscular torso glistening with sweat, his hair being tousled in the wind. How, in this lifetime, this man was in love with me, I would never know.

But for some ridiculous reason, he was. I knew this fact all too well because he told me, with his whole chest, at least once a day.

I wished I could say it back to him. I wished I could be so carefree with my declarations of affection, but every time I tried, the words wouldn't come out.

I wanted to tell him as often and with my whole heart the way he told me.

But still, I couldn't.

It was fear that stopped me. Fear of putting myself out there—which was stupid because I was already well and truly out there for him. It was fear of being exposed and admitting my vulnerability.

And that was probably the biggest difference between Tully and me.

I grew up believing that to show any emotion was a sign of weakness.

Tully grew up believing that love was the ultimate strength.

"Whatcha lookin' at?"

I blinked in surprise and grabbed the ladder I forgot I was standing on. I'd totally spaced out.

"I was looking at you," I said. "I just got distracted."

"Picturin' the totally hot boat sex we're gonna have, huh?"

"Something like that."

"How about you do your boat-sex daydreamin' on the ground?" He had the broken jack port in his hand. "I'd rather you didn't fall."

"I'm fine," I said. "I have hold of the ladder. But the wind is picking up. Perhaps you could get down off the roof too."

"Let me just see if I can salvage this," he said. He was holding the end of the LNB, trying to extract the broken jack, trying to reattach the broken pieces together. "Would electrical tape fix this?"

"I highly doubt that. I think it's a replacement job."

"Did they send you a new one of these noise things?"

"A low-noise block? No, they did not. They didn't send me much of anything."

He grumbled about that, but reassembled the jack into the port, trying to get a reconnection. "It really just needs a new connection. It's the little prongs that are bent, see?" He held it out to show me. "Unless it snapped the internal wiring. Then it's a replacement job."

He was so clever. So inquisitive, and—

"Are you picturing me with a tool belt again?" He was grinning at me.

"Possibly."

"Wanna check the meter things?"

"Yes, of course."

I climbed down the ladder and went back inside, but nothing was spinning, nothing was flashing. "No change," I yelled.

"Hang on," he called out. "How about now?"

A green light, faint as could be, flickered, then died. "Wait! What did you do? Do it again!"

A second later, the same green light flickered on, stayed green for half a second, then died again. "Yes, that!" I said. I went outside so I could speak up to him. "There was a brief green light on the tracking sensor. It comes on for a second, then goes off. So there's some kind of signal."

"Okay, let me try again," he said.

It took a few attempts, some disassembling and reassembling and some electrical tape, but he managed to get one green light to stay on. "Hold it there," I yelled, excitedly. "We have one solid green light."

"Awesome!" he said, tossing his shirt down to me, then climbed down the ladder. As soon as his feet were on the ground, I gave him a kiss, then pulled him into the room.

"Look!" I showed him the single green light. "You did that."

His smile faded as he stared at the old white box. "But there should be four," he said.

"Well, yes. But even one light tells us that there's a connection."

"But why aren't all the lights on?"

"I'd say there's a connectivity issue with the wiring. And that's a job for a technician."

"Lemme see if I can do somethin' with those antennas."

Back up he went, and after some MacGyvering with the antenna and aerials and securing the bases, he had them all upright at least.

I watched the different sensor units, not holding out much hope but excited all the same.

"How's that?" he yelled.

"Nothing."

There was more grumbling from the roof. "Okay, what about now?"

"No." But then another sensor light blinked on. "Wait! Yes, right there!"

"Right there, baby. Yes, yes," he yelled in a provocative tone.

And another sensor came on.

"There! You got another one."

But after some more cussing and sighing, the last one wouldn't come on. All up, three out of five was better odds than I could have hoped for.

When Tully climbed down off the ladder, I pulled him inside again. "Look at what you did!"

He smiled. "I'm pissed about the last two."

"I'm not. This place needs a full upgrade and install. We fixed more than we rightly should have. If all we'd done was come here and taken some photos and filled in a damage report, I'd still call it a success. But we have readings." I couldn't help feeling a little proud. "There better be some happy people in head office."

Tully laughed. "There better be, yes. You can tell them that your boyfriend did a super impressive job, and we'll just keep the fact that between you and me that all I really did was jiggle some wires and screwed a few antennas back into place."

"Believe me, I'll be telling them exactly everything you did."

"I took some photos for your report," he said, showing me on his phone. "But now I guess we better try and fix that box stand, or the readings sent back to head office won't be correct."

This was true. Stevenson-screen weather boxes had specific location and height requirements to achieve the most accurate results.

"It's gotta face south, right?"

"That's correct. How do you know that?"

He made a face as we went back outside. "I'm a storm guy, remember? And we made one in high school for science class."

He carried the box over to where the stand had broken off at the ground, then took his shirt from where he'd tucked it into the back of his shorts and wiped his face with it.

"Ugh, it's gettin' hot," he said, and immediately we both looked up at the sky.

There were dark clouds coming in from the west. Cumulus, low and dark.

Storm clouds.

Our eyes met, and he grinned.

CHAPTER SIX

TULLY

As soon as Jeremiah's gaze went from the incoming storm to me, we both smiled.

An incoming storm while we were on some remote island, without another single person for miles, could only mean one thing.

And bein' so far from anywhere, with no internet or nothin', we had no idea how long this storm would last, how deep the trough was, or how good or bad it was going to get.

"I say to hell with the stupid weather box," I said. "Time for awesome boat sex."

He checked his watch with a smirk. "Well, it is getting on in the afternoon." Then he looked out to the water and his smile died. "And I'd rather be on the boat before any crocodiles decide to take shelter on land."

"Solid plan."

He closed the door to the cell block, left the box right where it was, and pulled the gate closed. And it wasn't until he crossed the jetty to the boat that something occurred to him.

"Oh my," he said, his arms out for balance. "The boat . . . the turbulence . . ."

I laughed. "Uh, it's not called turbulence on a boat," I said, jumpin' in beside him and holding onto him. "The seas get choppy in storms. You know this. You issue weather warnings for sea swells all the time, do you not?"

"Well, yes," he said, gripping onto the doorframe into the cabin. "Theoretically, I'm well aware, thank you. But in practice, I'm never on a boat. My god, Tully, is this even safe? Should we leave?"

I bit back my smile because he was clearly stressing. "Babe, we'll be fine. We're securely moored, and this boat is designed for these conditions."

And the truth was, this wasn't even choppy yet. But I didn't tell him that. He was already a little pale.

"How about we get you into the cabin?"

"Good idea."

I got him situated and closed the door, and he relaxed immediately. But as the skies grew darker and the boat began to rock a little more, his grip on the seat cushion tightened.

"Want something to eat?" I suggested.

He grimaced. "Probably not."

"Some water?"

He shook his head, and his knuckles were now white.

I was beginning to think that our awesome boat sex was probably out of the question.

"Okay," I murmured, peeling his fingers free of the seat. He transferred the death grip to me instead. "Um, ouch."

He looked at our hands. "Sorry."

"Would you like me to show you the radar," I said, pointing at the screen. "And you can see the storm, see the numbers and stats, and you'll know that you'll be okay."

He shook his head again, his mouth a thin line. "It's not the storm."

Ah, damn.

"Jeremiah, you'll be fine. You're with me."

He nodded.

"I know you don't like boats."

"Well, technically, it's probably not so much the boat as it is the crocodile-infested water the boat is currently bobbing up and down in."

"Would you feel safer if we headed out?"

His eyes shot to mine. "But you said this inlet is protected against the wind, and I therefore assume the storm."

"That's true."

"So, which is worse? Open sea in a storm, or a partially protected inlet which may or may not be home to crocodiles?"

"Well . . ."

Don't tell him crocodiles also exist in the open sea. Don't tell him that. Don't say it.

"Oh my god, there are crocodiles everywhere, aren't there?"

"Not technically everywhere."

"For the love of all that is holy."

My knuckles were starting to grind. "Can we lessen the death grip? Because, ow."

He released my hand from his vice-like grip. "Sorry."

"Would you feel better if you wore a life jacket?"

He made a face. "Not particularly." Then he seemed to reconsider. "Maybe."

"Let me get it for you."

"And you. I'd feel a lot better if you wore one too."

"Okay."

Yep. Awesome boat sex was well and truly out of the question.

I helped him into his vest and clipped mine on, and he did seem to breathe a little easier. But then thunder rumbled overhead.

"I think this will be the first storm I've not actually enjoyed," he said. Both his hands were balled into fists on his lap.

I sighed and took his hand, trying to unfurl his fingers.

There was only one way to help him, and that was distraction.

"When you went to South America to see the Catatumbo storms for your thesis studies, did you go on any boats then?"

"Yes."

"And did you not experience any storms when you were on a boat?"

He blinked a few times. "I think so, yes."

"And were you this worried then?"

"Not that I remember." Then he looked at me, annoyed. "And I know what you're thinking. That it's foolish that I'm worried now."

"I would never think it's foolish."

"Then why did you bring it up?"

"I just thought I'd point out that you were fine back then, and you'll be fine now."

"But I didn't have you then."

"What difference does that make?"

"Because."

"Because why?"

"Because I'm worried for you."

"Are you saying you love me? I'm pretty sure you're saying you love me."

He rolled his eyes, but his grip on my hand had lessened somewhat. "Are you trying to distract me?"

I laughed. "Yes. And it's working. Because I'm getting some feeling back in my pinky finger."

He let go of my hand completely. "Sorry."

"Don't apologise." I shrugged. "If that didn't work, I was going to suggest throwing these seat cushions on the floor and distracting you in carnal ways."

He almost smiled, until thunder rumbled overhead, louder this time.

Closer.

He grabbed my hand, and his grip was vice-like again. "Does this boat have lightning rods?"

"Yep. It has—"

"Good."

I noticed then that he was doing that mouth thing, where it tasted bad, and sure enough, lightning cracked and lit up the sky.

"We'll be fine," I whispered, but the boat rocked more, the water slapping the hull.

"What's that noise?"

"It's just water."

"It's not a crocodile testing the structural integrity of the hull?"

I snorted. "No. This isn't *Jaws*."

Which was the very wrongest thing I could have ever said because his eyeballs almost exploded out of his head. "Sharks? Oh my god, Tully, why would you say that?"

I had to prise my hand from his death grip before he actually broke some bones. "I realise now that I shouldn't have said that."

He really wasn't having a good time.

The thing was, this was a purpose-built fishing boat. It wasn't built for comfort, per se. I mean, it was very comfortable, but it was no luxury yacht with full-length beds. It was built for fishing. And given we were both wearing life vests, we wouldn't fit together if we lay on the bench seat. Our cuddle room was limited.

"Okay, stand up," I said, getting to my feet.

He did so, reluctantly. "Why?"

I pulled the thin seat cushions off the seats and laid them on the floor, then unrolled a sleeping bag, unzipping it so it was more like a blanket. "Lie down," I said, sitting on the floor. I waited for him to join me and then I spread the blanket out over us.

I pulled him into my arms, his head on my biceps, and despite the life-vest situation, I held him the best I could.

Rain pelted the windows and we rocked as thunder rumbled overhead. But he breathed deeper and the tension in his body began to melt away.

"Feel better?"

"Yes. Much."

I patted his head, rubbed his arm, and hooked my leg over his as the boat rocked and the storm raged.

"Enjoying the storm now?"

"Not particularly. I mean, this is nice. And I appreciate you accommodating me."

I wanted to laugh but thought better of it. "I'm not accommodating you." I kissed the side of his head. "You say it like it's a chore or an obligation. I want you to feel safe. I don't like it when you're scared, baby. I'll do anything to make you feel better."

Thunder boomed and the sky lit up with a crack of lightning, but he buried his face in my armpit. "We're missing a really good storm, babe."

He pulled his head back and risked a look upward until he made a dry heaving sound. "Ugh, why is the sky moving like that?"

I chuckled and tucked him back into my side. "It's the boat that's moving. Not the sky."

"Please don't talk about it," he mumbled.

"Sorry."

We were quiet again while the rain lashed at the windows and the waves rocked us. It was probably louder inside the cabin, truth be told, but we were warm, dry, and we had each other.

"We should have brought a tent," Jeremiah said. "We could have set it up inside the fenced area."

"We'll do that next time."

He laughed, and maybe, just maybe, he sounded a little

crazy. "There will be no next time. I'm never getting on another boat, sorry."

"Not ever?"

"I like terra firma, thanks all the same. And if head office ever suggests I come back here, I'll be explaining my *hell no* in great detail."

I laughed. "Will there be expletives?"

"Most likely."

I patted his hair down on the back of his head and kissed his forehead. This distraction ploy was working a treat. I had to keep it going. "Okay, super-serious question time."

"Is it about sex?"

"No."

"Then, yes?"

"If it was about sex, would you not answer?"

"I'd answer, yes. But if the question was a proposition or suggestion to partake in sex right now, then my answer would be no."

I snorted out a laugh. "That wasn't my question."

"Then ask away."

"If I were a breed of dog, what would I be?"

He froze. "What?"

"If I were a breed of dog, what breed would I be?"

"What kind of question is that?"

"A very serious and important kind of question."

He was quiet for a second. "A golden retriever. Shaggy blond hair, cutest smile, big brown eyes, kindest heart. The very goodest of boys."

I laughed. "Sounds like you're a bit fond of me."

He smacked my arm. "Oh shush. What kind of dog would I be?"

I sighed, long and loud. "What's the smartest breed?"

"I'm not entirely sure. Alsatians rank high, I believe."

"Like a police dog? *No*, you're more of a border collie."

"Are you saying I herd sheep?"

I laughed. "No. Ooh, I know. You're a kelpie. Smart as hell, analytical thinker, can be savage if you need to be."

"But I'm still herding sheep."

"And if I were a cat, what kind of cat would I be?"

"One that can run fast because, if I'm still a kelpie—"

I burst out laughing. "No interspecies breeding allowed."

"Oh my god, Tully. Why would your brain even go there?"

"Okay, next question, if we were to wake up tomorrow as a different species, would you still love me?"

"Well, yes, though there would be many varying factors. And so you're aware, love doesn't equal sex, and sex doesn't equal love. They're not mutually exclusive, you know."

"I know. But you still didn't answer. What are the varying factors?"

"It would depend on the difference in species. Are they compatible in any way, or are they natural born enemies?"

"Okay, you're *way* overthinking this. It was really just a simple yes answer."

"Then yes."

"But what if I were a frog?"

He shuddered. "Then no. Sorry. You're on your own."

I laughed and pulled his face back to kiss him. "You absolutely would still love me."

"Not if you had suction cups for feet. I absolutely would not." He shuddered.

I laughed again, and his gaze went up to the roof. To the gentle splatter of rain, the grey skies that were no longer moving so much.

"Uh, I think the storm is over," he whispered. "The boat's no longer bobbing like a cork."

I smiled at him, unwrapped my leg from his, and stroked his hair. "You okay now?"

"Your art of distraction game is strong. Thank you. I freaked out, sorry."

I kissed him. "Don't apologise. The first time on a boat in a storm is scary for anyone." I sat up, my back against the seat, and he did the same opposite me, his leg resting against mine. "Are you hungry now? It's getting late."

"A little."

I leaned over and pulled the Esky closer. "Mum's pasta salad sound good?"

"Perfect."

With the container between us and armed with a fork each, we managed to demolish half of it.

"So, can we discuss the if-I-was-a-frog thing?" I asked. "Because you're supposed to be my prince charming, which means you're supposed to kiss the frog to turn me into a real boy."

"I think the real-boy storyline is Pinocchio."

I shrugged. "Sentiment is the same."

"Any other animal but a frog."

"A slug?"

"Fine."

I grinned at him. "I'd kiss you no matter what animal you were. Even if you were a face-eating lion. I'd risk it."

"Valiant, but foolish."

"Thanks."

He shoved a forkful of pasta into his mouth and spoke around it. "What about a praying mantis?"

"I dunno. Do they speak with their mouth full?"

He laughed and swallowed it down. "I can't be certain. But they do rip off their mate's head after copulation."

I stabbed some pasta and sausage. "Are you having psychotic tendencies I should know about?"

He smiled. "No. But I'm having copulation tendencies. After you were so very kind and sweet to distract me when I thought we were about to be croc food. I was thinking I could show you my gratitude."

I grinned at him. "Copulation tendencies and gratitude are my three favourite words."

He took the container and our forks and slid them onto the seat behind him, then straddled my thighs. "I am very grateful for the way you look after me," he said, tilting my chin up and kissing my lips. "And I spent all day admiring your body and your muscles and how capable you are."

"I'm definitely buying a tool belt when we get home."

He chuckled and undid my life vest, one slow clip at a time. I was more rushed with his, unclipping it and sliding it over his shoulders, momentarily restraining his arms at his sides and pulling him down for a hard kiss.

His eyes flashed with blue fire, and I laughed . . .

Until he slid his hand around the back of my head, pulled my hair so my face angled upwards, and he kissed me. Teeth, tongue, slowly grinding his hips, seeking friction.

I gripped his arse, pulling him down as I drove my hips up to meet him. He grunted, the most obscene sound, and he deepened the kiss.

I dug my fingers into his arse cheeks and realised . . . he wasn't wearing underwear. Again.

My god, this man.

Commando really was my favourite thing.

I flipped him over onto his back on the cushions on the floor and kissed him again, settling my weight between his legs. He brought his knees up, his hands on my arse, and he took my tongue in his mouth.

So fucking hot.

I rubbed my cock along his, hard and hot, but I wanted more tonight. I wanted to be inside him. I wanted to come in him. I wanted to make him mine, over and over.

"Where's the lube?" I murmured, kissing down his jaw. "I wanna sink myself inside you so fucking bad."

He stilled, saying nothing until I stopped licking his neck and looked at him. "I didn't bring any. I thought you did."

"No, I thought you . . ."

He began to smile.

"Oh, thank God you're joking," I said.

He laughed. "I'm not. I didn't pack it."

I blinked. "Then why are you laughing?"

He put his hand to his forehead. "It is kind of funny."

I rolled my hips, letting him feel just how funny my dick thought it was. Then I had a thought. "I wonder if there's anything in the Esky we could use."

He wrapped his legs around me. "You're not using your mum's food as lube."

"Ugh, babe," I whined, falling onto my hand by his head. He was still hard and so was I, and this position wasn't doing us any favours. "You shouldn't wrap your legs around me like that."

He bit his bottom lip and brought my nose to his. "How good are you at maths?"

Huh?

"What?"

"Maths. How's your subtraction?"

"Normally pretty good, but right now I'm just confused. Please don't make me do maths. I'm not thinkin' with my big brain right now."

He smiled. "What's seventy minus one?"

Even my lust-addled and confused big brain could work that out.

I kissed him with smiling lips. "I'm gonna seventy minus one you so hard."

He laughed and unhooked his ankles behind me, so I manoeuvred myself on my side, my face in line with his erection in his threadbare shorts and his warm breath on my aching dick.

I slid my arm under his hip and pulled the front of his shorts down to free his gorgeous cock. I was so enraptured by this sight, by what we were about to do, that his warm, wet mouth took me by surprise.

"Oh fuck," I cried as he sucked me in.

And it would've been so easy to get lost in the pleasure, the heat and the glide, how he sucked . . .

I had to remember to focus on him.

So I took him all the way in, sucking and swirling my tongue, opening my throat. He moaned around my cock, his body trembling, and I didn't ease up. I worked him hard and fast, holding the backs of his thighs, his arse, as I swallowed around him.

He grunted, his body jerking in my arms, and his tongue worked its magic on me. So hot and wet, and he could suck so hard. I was close. I wanted to come so bad but I needed him to come first.

I snuck a finger in to draw a line along the seam of his balls to his hole. He bucked his hips, groaning around my cock, his entire body went rigid, and he shot his load down my throat.

His groan, his tightened throat, the way he held me was enough to end me. My orgasm ripped through me and I tried to pull out, I tried to warn him, but he only held me tighter as I came.

He grunted with every spurt, with every wave of pleasure.

Until he finally released me and we both collapsed, breathing hard. My head was still spinning.

"You okay?" I asked.

"Mm. I think you broke my throat."

I barked out a laugh but sat up and helped him sit up too. I gently touched his throat. "Does that feel okay?"

He winced when he swallowed.

"Let me see. Open wide."

"No. Opening wide is what broke it."

I didn't mean to laugh, but given he was talking and

joking, I was sure he was fine. "Okay, it's not broken. And just for the record, I tried to pull out and you pulled me in deeper."

He made a face and shrugged. "I'm not sorry in the slightest." But then he winced again when he swallowed.

"Let me get you a drink." I opened a bottle of water for him and he sipped it. "Better?"

He gave a nod. "I'm still not sorry."

I snorted. "Okay, but maybe rest it for a bit."

"Are you telling me to shut up?"

I chuckled. "No. Just take it easy. No singing."

"Have you ever heard me sing? Ever?"

"No."

"And for that, you can be thankful."

I leaned over and gave him a soft kiss. "I love you."

He gave me a smile and nodded, his cheeks red, immediately uncomfortable. "Same."

I knew he loved me. I did know that. But man, I had to admit, it started to hurt a little not hearing him say it. And it wasn't his fault . . . I knew that too.

So I tried to make a joke out of it and pretended he'd shot me in the heart. "Oh, so close, but yet, so far."

CHAPTER SEVEN

JEREMIAH

I'D NEVER EXPERIENCED INEPTITUDE. I'D NEVER FAILED AT anything. Well, social situations aside. I'd excelled at all academics. I'd excelled in my career. I'd excelled in any task I'd set my sights on.

But I felt as if I was failing Tully.

I was not a good boyfriend. I wasn't capable of reciprocating his affection declarations, and it was hurting him. He needed it, very clearly thrived on it, and I fell woefully short.

He tried to laugh it off, but I could see the hurt in his eyes.

He'd told me he loved me, as he had declared many times. And I'd replied with, "Same."

Same.

I hated that I was like this.

Before I could make things any worse, he stood up and held out his hand. "Come on, let's go outside and see."

He helped me to my feet. "See what?"

"See what we can see, see, see."

The way he sang it led me to believe it was a nursery rhyme. A child's song I'd never heard.

"Never mind," he mumbled.

Clearly, I'd failed at that too.

Outside, much like the direction my mood had taken, was getting dark. "Does this boat have lights?"

He nodded. "Yes. But we have an LED lantern. Better to use that than the battery on the boat."

He found the lantern and, opening the door, went out to the stern. There was still enough daylight to see, barely though. The skies were overcast and grey, clouds low, but no rain, and the water was dark. It wasn't as rough as before, but it wasn't calm by any means.

He turned the lantern on, holding it out and scanning the beach.

I was almost afraid to ask. "Any visitors?"

"Not that I can see. No eyes staring back at us anyway."

"It's not necessarily the ones you can see that bother me."

He turned and rubbed my back. "We're safe here. If you need to pee, go stand on the bow and aim with the wind, not into it."

"I'm not peeing off the front of the boat."

"Would you like to fill an empty water bottle again? You could give this one to the crocs too. We should absolutely patent Croc-ade. Pee-coloured electrolytes with crocodile teeth punctures on the label. Could be the new Red Bull."

I ignored that and didn't even bother rolling my eyes. "I'll be fine."

"If you gotta pee, you gotta pee. And if you should require a bathroom for any other reason, I suggest you do it now before we lose all light. There's a camping shovel, the kind that folds up, for you to go into the bushes and dig a hole."

I stared at him, and he tried to keep a straight face but failed. I gave him a playful shove. "You're not funny."

He laughed. "There's an enclosed head."

I squinted at him. "Is that a boating term I should be familiar with?"

Tully snorted. "Come on, I'll show you."

He revealed a hidden door and how there was, in fact, a full toilet on board. It was approximately the same size as the bathroom in my old apartment in Melbourne. "I don't want to know how much this boat cost, do I?"

He chuckled. "Probably not."

"Well, considering it's absurdly expensive—and you know I saw the radome on the roof—and now that we're not going to capsize, can we have a look at the weather radar system?"

He grinned at me, the soured mood from before seemingly forgotten. "Of course we can."

He showed me how to turn it on, and I was impressed with it too. Though, honestly, given my time in Darwin, I'd be impressed with any radar system that wasn't as old as I was. "This has a better system than my office."

"Well, that wouldn't be difficult, considering your office isn't operational right now. But they'll be starting soon, and it'll be state of the art. Everything."

"I hope so."

We watched the radar for a short time. There was a cloud band right across the screen. The rain had moved east and there didn't appear to be much left in the tail. He kissed my shoulder. "Feel better now that you can see it?"

I nodded. "Yes, thank you." I turned to him and pulled him closer. I might not be able to say some things out loud, but I could say this. "Thank you for before. You never ridicule me or make fun of me. And you know exactly how to make me feel better. I want you to know how much that means to me."

He smiled, not a full-wattage grin, not even really a happy smile. And I realised then the difference between his honest smiles—like the ones that made my heart skip a beat—and the one he wore now. They were so very different. "I know," he murmured. Then he put his finger to my lips. "You're supposed to be resting your throat."

So yes, I was failing at being a boyfriend.

I needed to do better. I needed to be better, try harder.

For him.

So I took his hand, turned it palm side up, and nervously drew a heart with my index finger.

Tully chewed on the inside of his lip before a smile broke out. A genuine smile this time. "Did you just draw a butt?"

I rolled my eyes and he laughed, pulling me in for a hug. He kissed my temple, and any hurt from before seemed to have dissipated. And that was Tully Larson—hurt for a brief moment before letting the sunshine-side of him win again.

My god, I didn't deserve him.

"It was a heart," I mumbled into his neck.

"It was a butt." Then he ran his hand to my arse and squeezed. "I happen to like butts."

I sighed, long and loud. "I'm tired. It's been a long day."

"Wanna call it a day?"

"I think so."

"Can I still hold your arse if we lay down?" He gave me another squeeze for good measure.

I snorted. "Fine."

When we lay down, I used Tully's arm as a pillow and sighed as tiredness crept over me. The gentle rocking of the boat was even kind of nice. "We're heading home tomorrow, yes?"

"Don't wanna stay for a few days?"

"I really don't."

Smiling, he kissed my temple. "We can try fixing that weather box stand in the morning, then head back with the change of tide in the afternoon. Sound okay?"

"Perfect. Thank you for bringing me out here. I don't mean to sound ungrateful, because I'm so thankful you're here with me. And I cannot believe head office thought I could come out here with anyone that wasn't you."

"Well," he said with a sigh, "even if someone else brought

you out here, I'd still be coming with ya." He rolled onto his side and pulled me into his arms properly. His eyes were closed. "No one gets you to themselves but me."

I smiled as I drifted off to sleep. "No one but you."

***

I WOKE UP TO AN AWFUL ROCKING, AND FOR A NOT-FULLY-awake-moment, I'd thought I'd woken up drunk.

Drunk, I was not. I was still on this damn boat.

I was alone too.

"Tully?" I called out, getting up.

It was barely daylight, though still overcast, and the door was open. I walked out on somewhat unsteady feet, having to hold on to the wall. I couldn't see Tully anywhere. I tried not to panic. I couldn't see any crocodiles, but ugh, the water was rough; fast and uneven waves were rocking the boat. I went to the very back, about to step onto the rickety jetty. Panic started to rise in my chest. "Oh my god, Tully? Where are you?"

"Hey. I'm up here," he called out from the other end of the boat. Up on the bow, sitting with his feet over the edge like a madman. He was holding a fishing rod?

"Please don't dangle your feet near the water," I pleaded. "Crocodiles can jump, you know. Are you crazy? I thought you'd gone overboard and were missing, presumably taken by a crocodile, and you know I wouldn't know what to do."

He laughed.

Because of course he did.

"I was going to catch us a fish."

I looked around, trying to let my face show how displeased I was with that idea. "Oh good. Any bites?"

He laughed louder and began to reel his line in. "No bites. I thought with the overcast skies and choppy water I might have some luck."

He fixed his line and stood up, walking down the edge of the boat toward me, and I tried not to have heart failure watching him. He walked—barefoot, mind you—as if he were on solid ground and not a thin, narrow railing on a boat that was rocking in rough waters.

I held my hand out to him. "Please get down. You're scaring me."

He jumped down, grinning, and he took my hand to look at my watch. "Huh, elevated heart rate. Not my preferred method of raising your heart rate." Then his eyes met mine and he let out a disappointed sigh. "We forgot to wear the chest strap yesterday during our seventy-minus-one math lesson. We might need a repeat today . . ." Then he made a face. "Oh, how's your throat this morning?"

"My throat's fine."

"So we can have another math lesson? We both get gold stars at the same time."

I snorted. "I'm not opposed. As long as you fulfil the promise you made yesterday."

He squinted at me, confused. "What promise?"

"That you bury yourself in me when we get home and have lube."

His eyes widened, as did his smile. He palmed his dick. "Damn, babe. We could go home right now."

"We need to fix the weather box."

"Fuck the weather box."

I laughed. "It won't be the weather box that gets it, I can assure you. Should we have some breakfast? I'm starving."

He ditched his fishing rod and followed me inside. "No, I'd like to revisit the deep-dicking conversation. And the math lesson."

I found the container of orange segments, opened it, and held one slice up to Tully's lips. The boat was rocking so much that I almost missed his mouth. "Oh god, I'd really like to not be here anymore. On this boat, on this island." I had to hang onto the seat. "The sooner we try and fix the box, the sooner we can go, yes? You mentioned waiting for the tide. Do we have to do that?"

"No, it just means we'll have to navigate around sandbars. But that's okay." He held onto me by the arm. "You okay?"

I shook my head. "I'd very much like to go stand on some solid ground."

"Okay. Lemme just check the weather radar. It's still overcast out there, but the wind might determine if we have to leave now."

Splendid idea.

"Yes, yes. Sorry, I didn't think of that."

I didn't think of anything when I was stressed, apparently. Not in cyclones. Not on rocking boats. Tully thought clearly and rationally all the time, and all my mind could do was gather enough synapses for me to hold on to the seat while the boat rocked.

"Come and have a look," Tully said. "It'll make you feel better. Temp is twenty-four degrees. Humidity is at sixty-three."

He held his hand out for me and put his arm around me when I stood in front of the radar. A rain band covered the Top End, shades of blues and patches of greens meaning light to moderate rainfalls expected in the next hour or so. "Westerly wind speeds of ten to fifteen knots," I said. "Is that okay?" I knew what those numbers meant, but not what it meant to being on an actual boat in the middle of it.

"We need to leave by the time this comes in," Tully said, pointing to the deepening trough on the radar. "According to this, swells outside are at a metre already, and if we leave it too late, they'll be two metres, and you won't wanna be in that."

My stomach rolled. I didn't want to be in this now.

He squeezed my shoulder. "We need to be gone by ten, okay?"

I checked my watch. It was almost six thirty in the morning. Three and a half hours? "Easy."

He put on his boots, then took my wrist and looked at my watch. "Okay, before your watch overheats, we need to get you onto dry land."

"Are there crocodiles?"

He gave me a sad smile and shook his head. "Nope."

I was almost certain he was just saying that.

He put his hand to my chest, to see if he could actually feel my heart thumping; I was sure of it. "You okay?"

I nodded with more conviction than I felt. "Yes. Let's get this stupid weather box on its stupid stand so we can leave."

He helped me off the boat, then helped me along the jetty, all because my legs weren't connected to my brain, apparently. Even on dry land, it felt as if my knees would give way.

Tully held my elbow, trying not to laugh. "You good?"

"My legs have lost all structural integrity." My left knee wobbled right on cue and almost brought me undone.

He laughed as he helped me stay upright. "Walking helps. Come on, jelly legs."

We walked to the gate in the fence. Well, Tully walked; I wobbled like a newborn foal. And Tully put me straight to work.

He really was very good at distracting me. He knew exactly what I needed to get me out of my head. The frame the weather box stood on needed extra bracing, so he sent me in search of some branches or driftwood with strict instructions to not go too far.

He needn't have worried about that.

I wasn't keen on going too far at all. The very last thing I wanted to stumble upon was a crocodile nest in some shrub. There wasn't much in the way of vegetation to pick from, but Cyclone Hazer had made a mess, which made picking out some branches and twigs much easier.

I came back to the yard just as Tully was stomping a metal

peg into the ground. All that was left of where the base had been fixed into the ground were two pegs, and he was adding a third.

"Found it by the fence," he said as he used the heel of his boot to stomp it down.

"Be careful," I urged. "Skewering your heel with a rusted metal spike would be extremely low on my idea of fun."

He laughed. "I got trusty boots. And no sledgehammer." He grunted with the last stomp and panted, his hands on his hips. "But if I can get the frame attached to the base, make it sturdier, and we are good to go."

I dumped my armful of sticks. "You're going above and beyond what is expected."

He picked up the first longer stick. "Well, they're gonna hafta come out and replace it anyway, but at least if we can get some kinda accurate reading, then comin' out here weren't for naught." He shrugged. "And if this stand falls over as soon as we leave, I don't give a fuck."

He set about bracing the frame with sticks and zip tying them together. It wasn't pretty, but it was a damn sight better than what I could ever put together.

And it worked.

We got the weather box placed on the frame, he fixed that with screws and zip ties, and after a good hour or so, it was done.

I went into the outhouse and checked the meters. "It's good!" I yelled.

Tully came in, all sweaty and concerned. "What's up?"

"You did it!" I said, giving him a kiss on the cheek. I was so proud of him. He did this. He fixed it all. It wasn't perfect and technicians would need to come out and get it all up to code. But he'd fixed it. This station would now be pinging accurate readings to the bureau.

The sky rumbled overhead. "Okay, that's our cue," Tully

said. "I'll get the crate. You lock everything up. And let's go home. Where there is beer and lube."

I laughed. I wasn't looking forward to the trip home at all, but the beer and lube sounded like a great way to spend the afternoon.

After hot showers, of course.

We packed up the crate and I took some more photos before locking the outhouse door. Tully carried the crate and headed toward the boat while I pulled the gate closed. And just as I got the padlock through the bolt hole, I had a very strong, very sudden taste in my mouth.

Oh no.

I looked upward to the cloudy sky. Cumulonimbus clouds, low and darkening. It was drizzling rain, and thunder grated along the sky.

Something didn't feel right.

It didn't sound right, as if everything was in a vacuum. It made the hairs on the back of my neck tingle.

Oh god.

"Tully!" I yelled. "Get to the boat! Now!"

He turned as he was halfway to the jetty. "What was that?"

The copper suddenly filling my mouth was putrid. Far too strong, as if my mouth was filled with blood.

"Run!" I yelled, trying to get my body to move. To run, to sprint. To save him.

Then the sky went white, and everything went still before the silence exploded.

And then there was nothing.

CHAPTER EIGHT

TULLY

Jeremiah spun, the same way his mother had spun in that awful footage on Collins Street.

He danced the same way his mother had, his arm extended outward as he fell to the ground.

The deafening sound of the lightning, the blinding whiteness of it, was nothing when all I could see was Jeremiah being spun like that.

The void of sound as he crumpled to the dirt.

I hadn't even realised I was on the ground. The crate was knocked over. Had I been knocked off my feet?

I didn't remember falling.

I only saw him.

I clambered to my feet, scrambling to run back to him, sliding to where his body lay, his leg twisted underneath him. But his eyes . . .

So stark, so blue.

Open and staring.

"Jeremiah," I said, shaking him. "Jeremiah!"

Nothing.

No, no, no.

"No," I yelled. I shook him. I begged and touched his face.

Nothing.

So I banged my fists on his chest with all the strength that I had.

He sucked back a breath, as if he'd been rebooted, and he blinked.

Then he groaned.

I sobbed, fisting his shirt, my forehead on his chest. "Jeremiah, just breathe, baby. Just breathe for me."

He groaned again. The breath from his lungs sounded like an expiring tyre.

I stared at his face, making sure he could see me. "Baby, please. Stay with me, okay? You gotta stay with me."

He groaned again. His breaths were shallow, raspy. He tried to speak. Then he tried to sit up but couldn't. I shook my head. "Stay there," I said. "Don't move."

He needed help, and I had three choices: get him onto the boat and drive him back to Darwin myself, put out a radio call for help, or call for a medevac.

Medevac, Tully. Now.

I needed a phone.

Mine was on the boat where I'd left it yesterday. We had no service here because we were on a remote island in the middle of the fucking ocean, and I hated the bloody thing anyway. Jeremiah's phone was in his pocket because he'd been taking photos . . . I patted him until I found it and pulled it out . . . it was hot. And completely dead. No, not dead. It was fried.

Fuck!

Wait. The satellite phone.

On the boat.

Dammit.

"Jeremiah, listen to me," I said. "Stay right here. Don't try and move. I'll be right back."

He groaned.

I didn't want to leave him, but I had no choice.

I sprinted for the jetty, not caring about which boards I trod on. I made it to the boat, ripped the door open, and found the phone in the console—seeing the emergency beacon and flipping it on—before racing back to Jeremiah.

He was now half sitting up, which probably was a good sign, but as soon as I slid in the dirt beside him, he fell back to the ground.

Christ.

I dialled 000, trying to stay calm.

"Police, ambulance, or fire," a woman's voice said.

"Police. Ambulance, coast guard. I don't know. Someone. I need a medevac—"

"Sir, what's your emergency?"

"My boyfriend just got struck by lightning," I said, tears burning in my eyes. "We're on Oxley Island at the weather station. He's breathing now, but he's in a lot of pain. He doesn't look too good." I sobbed. "Please send someone. Please hurry."

I DON'T EVEN KNOW WHAT HAPPENED IN THE MINUTES AFTER. IN the eternity after. I'd never been so happy to hear a helicopter in my life. I cried with relief at the sound. In fear too.

I'd never been so fucking scared.

Jeremiah was a little more aware. He was breathing okay but he still couldn't seem to speak, and he kept trying to sleep.

He was so damn weak.

By some miracle, the chopper landed up on the beach, and two medics ran over to us. They wore the green overalls and white helmets, just like you saw in the movies.

And they took him, just like you saw in the movies too.

I somehow had the cognizance to ask them where they were taking him.

Royal Darwin Hospital.

I was supposed to wait for the coast guard boat to arrive, but there was no way.

No fuckin' way.

The coast guard could arrest me or fine me or do what the fuck ever they had to do. But I wasn't waiting.

I collected the crate and threw it onboard, unmoored the boat, switched off the location beacon, and hit the engines.

I radioed the coast guard as I drove out toward Croker Island. I gave them the boat registration and told them my intended destination. I told them to call off the emergency, the vessel was fine, and I didn't need their help because I was fine.

I was not fine.

I was so very far from fine.

I steered the boat through the rain and rough swells with more speed and less caution than I probably should have for what felt like hours, and I had to keep remindin' myself to slow down because I'd be no use to Jeremiah if I capsized.

And I needed to see him.

As I came in south of Melville Island and as my phone beeped with a signal, I dialled my dad.

"Hey, Tull," he said.

As soon as I heard his voice, I burst into tears. "Dad, Jeremiah's been taken to the Royal hospital. I'm coming back now. I'm just at Melville Island. I'll bring the boat into the marina, but I'll need a car or a lift to the hospital."

I don't even know how I managed to speak or how he managed to understand me. But he was on it like I knew he would be.

I came into the main marina dock where he'd told me to go. There was no time for parking and mooring in our allocated bay. I didn't even shut the engine off. As soon as I got close, Dad stepped on board, I stepped off, and he took over.

Mum put her arm around my shoulder and ran me to my waiting car.

"We'll be right behind you," she said, opening the passenger door for me.

Ellis was in the driver seat.

Like a military operation, my family had never let me down.

And I knew Ellis would have had a hundred questions, but he took one look at me and just nodded. "Christ. It's okay, Tull." He drove my car like he'd stolen it, and it still wasn't fast enough.

I wanted to tell him thank you. I wanted to tell him what had happened, but I didn't trust myself to speak.

"They choppered him in, yeah?" he asked.

I nodded.

"Then he's in the best hands."

I nodded again, wiping away a tear. "He better be okay. He just has to be."

Ellis slid his hand up my shoulder and squeezed the back of my neck. "He will be."

"Fuck, Ellis. He wasn't lookin' so good."

He gave me a gentle shake as we drove into the hospital grounds. "Hey. He'll be okay. But I tell ya what, I'll drop you off at the A&E and go and park the car. You need to tell them he's your husband, okay? Tell them you're married so they have to let you in to see him. They don't give a fuck otherwise."

I nodded, trying to pull myself together.

He pulled up at the emergency doors. "I won't be long. I'll find you."

I got out and went inside, heading straight for the triage window. The nurse took one look at my wet, dirty, tear-streaked face. "Can I help you?"

"Yes," I said. Then I remembered what Ellis had just said.

"I'm here to see my husband. The medevac helicopter brought him in. He was struck by lightning."

Now, I don't know if it was what I said or how I could barely speak at all or if it was the look on my face, but she stood up and nodded toward the access door. "I'll buzz you through."

Ellis came running in at the right time, just as the security doors opened, and we went through, but the look on the nurse's face stopped me in my tracks . . .

Jesus, no.

"Is he . . . ? Where is he? Is he okay?" I couldn't quite catch my breath. "Is he . . . ?"

"This way," she said.

She still hadn't answered, and now my legs wouldn't work and Ellis had to all but make me walk. Through the corridors, the awful smell of hospitals, the fluorescent lights, the coldness of it all.

"I just need to know if he's okay," I said, trying to swallow back tears and the need to be sick.

The nurse stopped at what I now realised was the critical care ward. "Stay here, I'll get the doctor."

"Where is Jeremiah?" I asked, but she was gone. I went to follow. I needed to find him.

"Hey," Ellis tried, pulling on my arm. "We have to wait."

Why wouldn't anyone tell me where he was? "Jeremiah!" I yelled, heading toward the door. "Jeremiah!"

A doctor appeared with the nurse. A tall woman with a concerned scowl. "Excuse me," she said.

"I need to find Jeremiah Overton."

"Were you with him when he was struck by lightning?"

"Yes, I—"

"What can you tell me about it?" she pressed on. "Was it a direct strike? How close was—"

"Is he okay?" I asked, but my voice wouldn't work. "Is he

alive?" I asked, louder this time. Ellis still had hold of my arm.

"Yes," she answered, and I almost went to my knees.

My god.

Thank God.

"Okay, let's sit you down," Ellis said, ushering me into a chair in the hall.

There was quiet talking around me. I heard my name over the blood pounding in my head, then the doctor leaned down to speak to me. "Mr Larson, my name is Doctor Jillick. Were you hit as well? How close to your husband were you at the time of the strike?"

I shook my head. "I don't know . . . maybe twenty metres. I think I fell down, but he . . . he spun. He was near the metal fence, and he spun and crumpled." I had to scrub at another tear. "Like a puppet when you cut the strings. He just . . . crumpled. And he was starin', and I don't think he was breathing. I don't know. I think I thumped his chest a few times and I just really need to see him. Please."

The doctor spoke to the nurse and the nurse disappeared, but then the doctor was shining her penlight in my eyes and holding my wrist—no, taking my pulse.

"I'm fine," I said. "I just really need to see Jeremiah."

"You said you fell down," the doctor said, still holding my wrist. Then the nurse was back with a machine, and she put a pulse thingy on my finger and an arm band on for blood pressure.

"Mr Larson?" Doctor Jillick repeated. "You fell down?"

"Uh, yeah, I was carryin' the crate of gear back to the boat, and then I wasn't. I was layin' in the dirt. I dropped the crate, I think. I dunno, I was too busy focusin' on Jeremiah to notice what happened to me."

"Okay, your pulse is a little above normal but regular. Your blood pressure is high—"

"Yeah, because I've had a bit of a rough day, not gonna lie."

"I'd like to get you checked out properly—"

"And I'd like to see Jeremiah," I said, standing up.

Ellis stood with me, holding my arm. "Tull, we need to make sure you're okay."

"I'm not okay," I cried. "I'm *far* from okay. I need to see him. Why won't they let me see him?"

And then I thought, *fuck it, I'll just find him myself.*

I sidestepped the doctor and went for the doorway opposite the nurse's station, but Ellis stopped me with his hold on my arm. I tried to break free, but then the doctor was in front of me.

"Mr Larson," she said sternly. "Don't make me call security."

"I just need to see him," I said. "For one minute. That's all. I just need to see him." I had to wipe tears off my face again. I tried to breathe but it came out as a sob. "If he's not okay . . ."

Ellis pulled me in for a hug and I fell into him, his strong arms holding me tight, holding me up, and he held me while I cried. "I just need to see him," I mumbled.

"I know."

He held me for a bit before he led me back to the chair, and I was suddenly so freaking tired I could barely keep my eyes open.

Then Doctor Jillick came back. "Okay, you have one minute. You can see him for one minute. There were traces of heme pigments in his urine, so we've administered alkalisers to minimise renal complications. We're monitoring his heart, so don't be alarmed by the machinery. Lightning injuries tend to get worse in the few hours after before they get better."

I stood up, my heart in my throat, suddenly afraid to see him. To see how badly he was hurt. I couldn't get my legs to work.

"Mr Overton?" the doc said.

Ellis was beside me. "Come on," he said, urging me forward. "I'll go with you."

I swallowed hard and managed a nod. My feet felt heavy, my steps wooden. But I followed the doctor into the large room. There were a lot of cubicles, most with the curtains drawn, and the doctor walked to one in particular and stopped.

"One minute," she said, then pulled back the curtain. "He was very lucky. His ECG has shown some irregular function, his brain function is normal. We're running more tests and keeping him closely monitored."

She talked about entry points and exit points and the affected organs, but I couldn't quite grasp what she was sayin' because what I saw almost killed me. He was lying there, half a dozen machines beeping beside him, connecting wires to his torso. But he had a bandage wrapped around his head, covering his eyes.

His beautiful eyes.

"It's precautionary," the doctor said, and I realised that my hand was touching my own face, my eyes. "Eyes and ears are susceptible to damage in lightning strikes."

Yeah, of course.

"His pupils were dilating, and he was following movement. We don't believe he sustained retina damage."

I took his hand, but he didn't react. "Hey," I whispered. "It's me. I'm here. I'm right here."

Machines beeped and his lips cracked open. But his hand . . . his hand squeezed mine.

My knees almost gave out and I had to lean on the bed. I lifted his hand to my face and I sobbed. "You're gonna be okay," I said through my tears. "I'll be right here. You get some sleep. I'm not going anywhere."

Very slowly, he squeezed my fingers.

I'd never felt a more precious touch.

I leaned in and kissed his temple. "I love you," I whispered. The heart monitor beeped and I barked out a laugh. Then I kissed his bandaged eye. "Get some sleep, baby. I'll be right here."

The doctor walked me out and Ellis put me back in the chair. He fell into the seat beside me and rubbed my back. "Mum and Dad are on their way in," he mumbled, holding his phone. "I told them where we were."

I nodded, feeling better now that I'd seen him, but my god, I couldn't stop the tears.

"Mr Overton," Doctor Jillick said. "I'd still like you to get checked over."

I shook my head. "I'm fine, honestly, doc. I've just had a rough day." I scrubbed my hands over my face. "Thank you for letting me see him."

"No headaches?"

I shook my head.

"Difficulty breathing? Did you lose consciousness?"

"No."

"Blurred vision?"

"Only when I cry," I said, tryin' to be funny, but it didn't help that I was on the verge of more tears.

Ellis snorted, his hand on my knee.

The doc pursed her lips but gave a nod. "I would suggest perhaps going home for a few hours, but I—"

"I'm not leavin' him."

"I assumed you'd say that."

Just then, Mum and Dad pushed through the doors, Mum leading the charge. She stopped when she saw us, and god, it just started me crying all over again. I stood up and she collected me in a fierce hug.

"He's okay," Ellis said behind me. "Well, he will be."

"He's not out of the woods yet," Doctor Jillick corrected him. "He can expect to be here for forty-eight hours, minimum. He was very lucky."

"Oh, love," Mum said. She pulled back and cupped my

face, only to drag me back in for another hug. "Of course he'll be okay."

The doctor cleared her throat, and Mum let go of me. "Can I suggest a visit to the cafeteria," the doc said. "You can see him again in an hour or so. If there are any changes, I'll let you know."

"I told him I'd be right here," I said, but Ellis put his hand on my shoulder.

"She's asking us nicely to come back in a bit," he said. "So you don't have to leave the hospital, that's all. He's sleeping anyway, right?"

The doctor gave him a thankful nod and Mum thanked her, then led me out, her arm around my shoulder.

They sat me at a table in the cafeteria, Dad soon putting a coffee in front of each of us. I knew they'd need an explanation, so I tried to start at the beginning.

"He didn't even do anything crazy," I said. "He didn't run out in the storm. Hell, it wasn't even raining. It was just overcast, and we'd checked the radar beforehand. There was no lightning activity." I shrugged. "We were locking up the yard because he wanted to come home. Just about to get on the boat. And then he . . . he . . ."

Mum gave my hand a squeeze.

"He was putting the padlock on the gate, and I walked ahead with the crate with all his gear." I shook my head. "And he yelled something. I didn't understand what he said. But he was doing that thing with his mouth." I imitated the way he did it. "When he can taste it. Before lightning, he gets an awful taste in his mouth. Then he screamed at me to run, and there was a huge bang, like a bomb went off, and a flash . . ." My chin wobbled and I blinked back more tears. "Then I was on the ground. I think it knocked me over. I dunno. But he was lying there." I couldn't stop the tears. I didn't even try. "The sight of him just lying there, all twisted, with his eyes open, staring, unseeing. I'll never forget it."

When I looked at my mum, she had tears rolling down her cheek.

"You did the right thing," Dad said gently. "You got him help."

I wiped my snotty nose with the back of my hand and Ellis handed me a serviette. I looked at my dad and nodded. "Sorry about just leaving the boat to you. I can go and clean it up later, I just—"

He shook his head. "It's fine, Tull. Don't you worry about anything."

"I activated the emergency beacon locator," I said. "I'll need to replace it."

He reached over and patted my hand that Mum still held. "You did the right thing."

I let out a shaky breath. "Thank you all, for coming to help. I don't know what I would've done."

"We're just glad you're okay," Mum said. "And we're glad Jeremiah is too."

"The doc wanted to check Tully out, but he refused," Ellis told them. "'Cause he got knocked over. Blowback or something like that, she called it."

"I'm fine," I added quickly.

"Tully," Mum started.

"I'm fine, honestly, I feel fine. Just worried about Jeremiah, that's all." I gave Ellis a look because he could have freakin' waited to tell them that. "I think he stopped breathing. When it happened. I dunno if it stopped his heart or if it was just shock, or what." I shrugged. "He was just staring, his mouth open. Maybe it was shock. I don't know. I pushed on his chest, I think. I dunno. It's all a blur."

Mum's tears started again. "But you got him here."

"And I was supposed to wait for the coast guard. The guys in the helicopter told me to wait for them. But I cancelled the request or I'd probably still be out there." I shrugged and looked at Dad. "You'll probably get a bill for that, so just give it to me."

"Don't worry about that," Dad said. "Drink some of your coffee. When did you eat last?"

I shrugged again and sipped my coffee. "I'm fine. I'm not hungry, to be honest."

Ellis disappeared and came back with a sandwich.

And then I got teary again, because I had such a wonderful family and Jeremiah was lying in that bed all alone. And I remembered something else.

"Oh god."

"What is it?" Mum asked.

I leaned my head right back and dug my thumb and finger into my eyes. How was I supposed to tell Jeremiah's father that what happened to his wife—the godawful horrible thing that ruined their lives—just happened to his son?

"Jeremiah's dad," I said. "I need to call him."

CHAPTER NINE

JEREMIAH

Everything hurt.

Everything.

My bones. My brain. My skin.

Everything.

I remembered Tully's face. Grey clouds behind him. A drizzle of rain. His wet hair. His tears.

His fear.

Then nothing.

Then there were lights and people staring down at me. A hospital. I remembered the doctors telling me to close my eyes, it would help, they said. They would cover my eyes because it would help, they said.

It sounded as if they were underwater.

Then everything was dark and the only thing that existed was pain.

Until that didn't exist anymore either.

But then there was a familiar touch. A hand in mine. A familiar voice. He sounded so sad. He was crying. But he was adamant and strong, and I clung to that.

He wasn't going anywhere.

He'd be right here.

Right here.

He wasn't leaving.

"Get some sleep," he said. "I'll be right here."

I clung to that with all I had left in me.

I woke up to more sounds. Beeping. Far-off voices. It sounded obscured but better than before. There was still only darkness, but someone had hold of my hand.

I didn't need to see to know who.

I squeezed his hand. I tried to speak, despite how dry my mouth was, how dry my throat was. "Hey."

"Jeremiah," he whispered. Tully's voice was like hearing heaven. "You're awake," he said. "Thank God."

I lifted my hands to my face, trying to find why I couldn't see.

His gentle fingers stopped me. "It's a bandage. The doctors said it was just precautionary." He squeezed both my hands and I felt the bed dip. His voice was much closer now, his breath warmer, and a soft kiss pressed to my forehead. "You're okay, baby. You're gonna be fine."

I sighed, resting, basking in the fact he was here. That he held my hands. That he loved me.

I tried to stay awake, to stay coherent, but the heaviness dragged me under again. Everything felt off-kilter. My heart, my breathing.

But I'd be okay. Tully said so.

And he still had a hold of my hand.

I woke up again to more voices. Quiet murmurs, familiar and warm. I knew he was close, but my hands were empty.

"Tully?"

"Oh, hey," he said, quickly taking my hand. "You're awake. You sound better."

A hand touched my other shoulder. So gentle. "Oh, Jeremiah, we've been so worried."

Mrs Larson.

She was here?

Tully snorted. "Mum's here. Dad and Ellis too, but they just went to get some drinks."

I still couldn't see, but my back hurt. Not like before. But as if I'd been lying down too long.

"Need to sit up," I said, trying to do exactly that.

I felt stiff and sore all over, and my head was woozy. My chest felt jittery.

"No, stay there," Tully said. "I'll go get the doctor."

He dropped my hand and Mrs Larson patted my other arm. "Oh, we're so glad you're okay. Tully's been out of his mind with worry," she said softly. "We made him go home and shower, at least, because he stank. But he came straight back."

"How long . . . ?"

"You were brought in this morning. It's now after six in the evening."

I tried to get my head around that.

"Do you remember anything?"

I tried . . .

"Just Tully."

Mrs Larson cry-laughed. "Of course." She patted my arm again. "You were brought in by medevac helicopter."

Helicopter?

I had flashes of being carried. Men with white helmets . . .

I shook my head.

I was dizzy and my heart felt fluttery.

Mrs Larson spoke quietly. "Tully called it in, then drove the boat back. I think he broke the speed barrier, but you're both okay and that's all that matters."

I wasn't sure what to say. Everything seemed so hazy.

"Oh," Mrs Larson said. "Before the doctor gets here, Tully told them you were married so they'd allow him to stay. Just so you know if the doctors or nurses refer to your husband."

My what?

"Husband?"

She patted my arm. "Shh."

"Oh, Mister Overton," a strange woman's voice said. "You're awake."

"It's doctor," Tully said. "Doctor Overton." A brief pause. "Oh, he's not a medical doctor. He's a genius doctor."

"Oh," the woman's voice said. "Doctor Overton. My name's Doctor Jillick. The medical kind."

I should hope so . . .

"Glad to have you with us," she said. "You gave us all a bit of a scare today."

"Need to sit up. My back hurts," I said. I tried for the bandage again. "Take this off."

An unfamiliar hand stopped me this time. Doctor Jillick, I assumed. "Okay, we'll sit you up first and I'll ask you some questions before we remove the bandages. How does that sound?"

"As if I have very little choice."

Tully snorted, though it sounded like he sobbed. "He's fine."

The bed began to incline, and I was soon half sitting up. I wasn't sure if it was better or worse. *Better, I think.*

"Can you tell me if you have pain?"

"Uh. Yes, though it's hard to localise. It's just . . . all over."

Tully took my hand again. The left, this time. Doctor Jillick was on my right.

Trying to garner some sense of space helped, and I tried to think about my body.

"My back. Lower back."

"It could be kidney related. We're running more blood and urine tests. You had some pigmentation present in your urine, which we've counteracted."

"Alkalisation."

There was a pause as if she was surprised I'd know this. "Yes."

"My head hurts," I said. "A dull headache. No sharp pain. I feel dizzy. My chest hurts—left side. My heart feels skittish. My right knee hurts. My teeth hurt. But I ache all over. My bones ache. Should a skeleton ache? I'm not sure it should."

Tully lifted my hand to his face. It seemed to hurt him to hear.

"Your brain activity is normal," Doctor Jillick said. "Your ECG is on the weaker side of normal and there is some atrial fibrillation, but that's not uncommon with lightning injury. We have you on medication for that, and we'll continue to monitor you for forty-eight hours. You have an electrical burn entry point on your left side near your ribs, which would explain the pain. You also have exit wounds on the soles of both feet," she said. "They're small, approximately five millimetres each, full-thickness burn."

Wow.

"A dull headache is expected," she continued, "and may not subside for a while, for weeks even. It's very common for headaches to persist after a lightning-strike injury. All things considered, you were very lucky."

A lightning strike.

I don't know why I was surprised to hear her say it.

There was a moment of silence. "Doctor Overton," she said, her tone different this time. "Do you remember being struck by lightning? You seemed surprised when I said that just now."

"I remember," I began, trying to recall. "I remember Tully's face . . . and seeing the sky. Nothing else."

He pressed my hand to his cheek. "You told me to run," he said.

I tried to remember more, but I had nothing.

"We were on the island," I murmured. "Then I was here. I'd like to take this bandage off now." I pulled at the gauze again, and no one stopped me. I wanted to see what *here* looked like.

I needed to see Tully.

"Let me," Doctor Jillick said, and then she unwound the bandage from around my head. "Keep your eyes closed for me. And don't be alarmed if your vision's not normal. You may need to adjust."

I kept my eyes closed.

"The lights are low; things may appear dark. Open them, nice and slow," Doctor Jillick said.

I did as she said. My eyelids felt heavy and I realised now that, yes, my eyes hurt too.

I was in a bed, there were white curtains for walls. A woman with dark hair and a stethoscope stood by the bed, observing me, and Mrs Larson stood at my feet with tears in her eyes. But there, holding my hand, was Tully. He looked tired and hopeful.

Beautiful.

"Hey," I whispered.

He burst into tears and stood, pulling me in for an awkward hug, my face against his neck. His familiar scent and warmth made my head spin and my heart felt too full and jittery.

"Okay, he's had enough excitement for one day," Doctor Jillick said, urging Tully to pull back before she pressed buttons on one of the machines next to me. At least the beeping stopped.

Tully put his hand to my face and kissed me softly. He scanned my eyes, searching for something.

"Are they still blue?" I asked.

He grinned. "The bluest."

Then Ellis and Mr Larson came through the curtain, surprised but happy to see me. "Lightning McQueen," Ellis said. "You're awake."

Mr Larson elbowed him.

"Okay, this is far too many people," Doctor Jillick said, checking her watch. "You have two minutes, then everyone has to leave. Even husbands, sorry." She gave Tully a pointed nod. "This is the critical cardiac ward. Non-standard visiting hours apply."

"Even husbands, Tully," Ellis repeated with his usual grin.

Mrs Larson levelled him a look that shut him up. Even Mr Larson grimaced.

But something else . . .

"Cardiac ward?" I asked.

It was only then that I realised I had a chest full of sticky pads and wires.

Why was my brain so slow?

Doctor Jillick met my gaze, her stoic face giving nothing away. "Your heart stopped. You were wearing a heart monitor watch and a chest strap. We don't have the numbers from the chest strap, but those watches give us all kinds of information. Your heart rate went from eighty, to one hundred and forty, to zero. Hard to tell if it was the lightning strike that caused your watch to stop or your heart, but given the accounts by your husband and the point of entry at your ribs, it's likely." She looked at Tully then. "His soreness is a direct result of the electrical entry and the shock to his heart, not from any attempt at compression."

My heart stopped.

My heart.

Compressions?

I looked at Tully. "You . . . ?"

He nodded and half shrugged. "I wouldn't call it compressions. It was more that I punched your chest a few times because you weren't . . ." He shook his head, tears in his eyes. "I'm sorry if I hurt you."

Doctor Jillick shook her head. "I can assure you, Mr Larson, it wasn't you."

Tully nodded, and his chin wobbled. He didn't look convinced.

I put my hand to his face.

"You were very lucky your husband was with you," Doctor Jillick added.

I smiled at Tully, his face in my palm. "My husband."

"Okay, we'll get going," Mrs Larson said brightly. Changing the topic, probably. "Tully, Ellis will wait for you at the car. And Jeremiah, we'll be back in the morning. Get some rest, sweetheart."

I managed a smile and a nod as they left—Mr Larson led Ellis out before he could speak—and Doctor Jillick gave Tully a stern glare. "One minute."

Tully kissed my palm, and when we were alone, he met my eyes. "She says one minute a lot." He looked so tired, as if he'd had the worst day. "Jem, about the husband thing," he whispered.

"Your mum told me."

"Don't be mad or freak out," he added. "It's just quicker and easier."

I dropped my hand and patted the bed. "Can you sit up here?"

He sat on the edge of the bed. "You okay?"

I was so tired and short of breath. "Lie down with me."

He didn't need telling twice. He crammed himself on the edge of my bed, half lying on me, his head in the crook of my neck.

If I had one minute left with him, this was exactly how I wanted to spend it.

We didn't speak; anything that needed to be said could wait. We just lay there, his body, his warmth, all that I needed right then.

He made everything better.

Until Doctor Jillick pulled back the curtain, took one look at us, and sighed. She gave Tully a nod of her head that said it was time to leave.

He whined, but he got up. He kissed my forehead, then my lips. Right in front of her, and I didn't even care.

"Get some sleep. I'll be back at breakfast time."

Doctor Jillick said, "Visiting hours are—"

"I'll be back at breakfast time." He kissed the side of my head. "I love you." Then he paused for a second, staring into my eyes before pulling away. He gave me a nod with such sadness on his face, then disappeared behind the curtain.

Doctor Jillick talked about me trying a light dinner and how tomorrow, if my ECG continued to improve, I'd maybe get moved to another ward.

But I couldn't get the look on Tully's face out of my mind. Was he sad because he had to leave?

Probably.

But it looked like more than that.

"Doctor Overton?"

"I don't know if I'm terribly hungry," I said. The scent of the food being served to other patients was awful, and I was having trouble keeping my eyes open.

"Well, if you move to another ward, your husband can stay."

My husband.

My heart fluttered at the word, and I was suddenly utterly exhausted. "Then maybe I could try and eat something." My words sounded garbled, and I got butterflies in my chest, and I was very dizzy. I was having trouble keeping my head up.

"Jeremiah, look at me," Doctor Jillick said. She sounded mad. And far away.

I tried to focus, but the jitteriness in my chest stole my breath.

Then everything went dark.

CHAPTER TEN

TULLY

I ALMOST DIDN'T ANSWER THE PHONE.

Nobody answers unknown numbers, and for a moment I considered not answering it at all, but it was a local landline.

I'd been home for all of thirty minutes. I was in the kitchen and Ellis was insisting I eat somethin' before going to bed. It'd been one helluva day and I didn't really feel up to talkin' to anyone.

I half expected it to be a news reporter and I wasn't gonna answer it. Then I thought maybe tellin' someone to fuck off seemed like a good idea.

"Mr Larson," a voice said. "This is Doctor Jillick."

My knees buckled and the room tilted.

"I want to reassure you that your husband is stable, but we believe he's suffered a delayed ventricular arrhythmia episode. He's having a cardiac MRI—"

The room began to spin and I couldn't hear what else she said.

"Mr Larson?"

"I'm coming back," I said, looking for my keys.

"I would ask you not to, Mr Larson," she replied. "The

ICU doesn't take visitors at this time. He's receiving the best possible care."

"That's great," I said flatly. "But I'm coming back. I'll sit in the hall if I have to."

I'd sit in the fucking car park for all I fucking cared.

I still couldn't find my keys.

I disconnected the call and was tryin' real hard not to lose my shit. "Where are my fucking keys?"

Ellis held them up, and for a split second I thought he was going to say no . . .

But he didn't. "I'll drive you."

I WASN'T JOKING WHEN I SAID I'D SIT IN THE HALLWAY.

I wasn't allowed in to see him, which wasn't a great surprise. I wasn't even mad. It took every ounce of control I had not to cry.

But in the hallway, I sat.

And that's where I was when my mum came in just after six in the morning. I must have dozed off because I startled when she sat down next to me.

"Oh, Tully," she whispered. "Ellis called us."

I nodded, trying to think clearly. I scrubbed my hand over my face. "I don't know how he is. I'm not allowed in to see him."

She rubbed my back. "He seemed okay when we left him yesterday," she whispered.

I nodded. "I know. Delayed symptoms, delayed reactions. I dunno. It's common with lightning injuries." I shrugged. "The doc said he had a ventricular episode or something. Must have been right after I left. He was tired. I should have paid attention. I shouldn't have left."

"You didn't have a choice, love."

I blinked back tears, and my nose burned. "He needs to be okay."

She nodded, fighting her own tears. "He will be."

I sighed, my head falling into my hands. "He's studied lightning his whole life. And you know, it doesn't scare him at all. He'll run into a storm and lightning could rip the sky apart right over his head and he wouldn't even flinch. And he knows when lightning's gonna strike, Mum. He gets a funny taste in his mouth. It's a thing that happens to some people who've been struck . . ." I let out a teary laugh. "You know, on the island, he told me to run. Not himself. He has no self-preservation skills at all. I mean, at all. And after Cyclone Hazer when he saved those two kids, I made him promise me that he had to start thinkin' about me, and he couldn't just run out into a freakin' storm like that."

I shook my head, not even sure what or who I was getting mad at.

"He told me to run. So at least he was thinking of me, I guess."

Mum didn't say anything, just listened and let me vent. I wasn't making much sense, but god fucking dammit.

"I tell him I love him all the time," I said. "But he's never once said it back to me. I make jokes about it and try not to let it bother me, but . . ." I shrugged. "I told him last night, before I left. I said, 'I love you,' and he . . . he said nothing."

"He wasn't very well last night," Mum said. "He was clearly not feeling well. I don't think that's anything to go by."

Maybe not.

But still . . . I couldn't stop thinking about it.

"He grew up so different to me. His whole life was . . . changed the day his mother died. And that's understandable. Anyone's life would be. I get that. But his mum died so publicly. He's reminded of it every other day, and it follows him everywhere, especially at his job. And you know if the media finds out that he was struck by lightning, my god, they'll have a field day."

"Then we don't let them find out. We protect him."

I nodded slowly.

She took my hand. "Do you think he doesn't love you?"

I couldn't stop the tears then, and I tried to wipe my cheek but it seemed pointless.

"I think he does. I joke about it because what else can I do? And I know he's not good with saying it. Talkin' about his feelings was never really allowed when he was growing up. He can't say stuff out loud, and I try to not let it bother me, but . . ." Fucking hell. "I guess it does."

"Oh, Tully," Mum whispered. "That man tells you he loves you every time he looks at you. You're just not listening to his language."

I wasn't sure I followed. "What?"

"The way he looks at you," she said with a gentle smile. "He might not be able to say the words, but the way he looks at you . . . just screams how much he loves you. You need to listen in other ways. Listen to his love language, Tully. It's all right there. The way he looks at you when you're not looking at him. The way he smiles when you laugh. If you could see that . . . Tully, it's written all over his face."

I knew this.

I wasn't stupid, and I wasn't blind.

I saw the way he smiled at me, the way he looked at me. I could count all the little things he did for me, the way he looked after me. The way he touched me . . .

I sighed and scrubbed my hands over my face again. I was tired and stressed and scared.

"Ignore me," I mumbled. "I'm bein' stupid."

She patted my hand. "You're not stupid, love."

"It's not his fault. I don't blame him." I looked at her then. "It'd just be nice to hear it one time, ya know?"

She smiled sadly at me. "I know."

It took me a second to realise that someone was missing. "Where's Dad?"

"He had to go into the yard to check everything was done. The engineers are coming back tomorrow, and you know he's been waiting. He'll be here when he can."

Oh, work. I hadn't given work a thought. "Yeah. Fair enough."

"When does Jeremiah's father get here?"

"Tomorrow afternoon at three o'clock. He doesn't know yet. Jeremiah doesn't know. I didn't tell him yet."

"I'm sure he'll be grateful. They both will be."

I wasn't sure about that.

"I really want to see him, Mum. When can I get in to see him?"

She checked her watch. "It's almost seven."

The double doors opened and I was surprised to see who walked in. Rowan and Zoe. They stopped when they saw me, their eyes going to Mum.

"Is he . . . ?" Rowan asked.

"We haven't been allowed in yet," Mum answered. "All we know is that he's stable." She gave my knee a shake. "And that he's in good hands."

I must have looked like a wreck because Rowan walked over to me, pulled me to my feet, and hugged me. Strong and warm, he patted my back. Then Zoe gave me a quick hug too.

It just made me all teary again.

"Ellis called us," she said, her eyes full of concern.

I nodded just as a doctor came out. I hadn't seen him before. "Mr Larson?"

I turned, my stomach in knots, my heart banging to the point of pain. "Yes."

He smiled, taking in all the expectant faces staring at him. "Am I talking to everyone, or . . . ?"

"Yes, please." I doubted I'd hear or understand any of it.

He gave a nod as though he assumed as much. "Last

night, his ECG revealed an irregular wide complex tachy-cardia with a variable—"

"In English, doc," I said. "Please."

He smiled again. "Last night, his heartbeat became so fast and irregular it caused him to lose consciousness. A delayed electrical shock reaction, more than likely. He was treated with defibrillation."

Oh my fucking god.

"You had to shock him back to life?"

I suddenly felt faint. Or like vomiting.

My mum tightened her hold on me.

The doctor gave a nod. "He was lucky the doctor was with him when it happened. His heart rate is now back in the normal range, though he's weak and we can expect him to be tired and lethargic for some time."

"But he'll be okay," I tried again.

"His heart has sustained some muscle damage," he said. "His recovery will be slow, and I'm hesitant to say he'll make a full recovery, because the truth is the full extent of lightning injuries aren't often known for weeks or, in some cases, years."

"What do you mean muscle damage?" I asked. "The whole heart is muscle, so what does that even mean?"

"The MRI also showed signs of takotsubo cardiomyopa-thy. More than likely brought on by the tachycardia and the defibrillation. That's not unheard of."

Tako . . . cardiomyopathy.

I'd heard of the cardio part, but I didn't know what it meant.

"Is that . . . takesumo-something. What is that?"

"It's a heart condition, brought on by an extremely sudden stress, where the heart's lower left ventricle changes shape and enlarges." He shook his head. "Honestly, we can't say exactly what brought this on. Could have even been from the tachycardia episode on top of the thirty million volts he took in the lightning strike. From the markings on his chest, it looks like it hit him on the left side of the ribs, directly near the heart. He's very lucky to be alive at all."

"Sorry, doc," I said, still trying to get my head around any of what he'd just said. "Is it bad? The tako . . . thing? That's different to the tachycardia?" I was so confused.

He gave a nod. "Yes. Two different conditions. The tachycardia—the irregular heartbeat—has been corrected, for now. Takotsubo cardiomyopathy, the enlarged ventricle, is a temporary condition and should heal in a few months. It's not likely he'll require surgery. He's been administered medication, but with a healthy lifestyle and proper rest, it is completely manageable."

"That's good, yes?" I asked.

The doctor gave a nod. "All things considered, yes." He looked at us all in turn, his gaze returning to me. "His heart rate is regular, but—"

But it was good last night too, I thought.

"He's very weak and tired. He'll need complete rest."

"And his recovery?" Mum asked. "Do we need a recovery plan? What do we do now?"

The doctor paused, his gaze meeting Mum's with a smile. Like he appreciated that one of us was keeping up. "There will be a recovery plan, yes. As for the full recovery . . . We can't answer that definitively. People who survive lightning injuries may suffer side effects for weeks or even years afterwards. Some never fully recover."

"I know. He knows," I added. "It's not the first time he's been hit."

The doctor stared at me.

Shit.

"He was two years old. It wasn't recent. He . . . he studies lightning. He's a fulminologist. A meteorologist. He's a doctor . . ." I felt every second of the sleep I'd missed. "Can I see him? Please? I just really need to see him."

He had a nurse lead me through the very quiet, very horrible ICU. The doctor stayed back to talk to my family, no doubt asking all about what I'd just said. And they could tell him everything—about Jeremiah's mother, about him being the meteorologist who saved lives during Cyclone Hazer, about him going viral for almost getting struck by lightning when he saved Casey and Presley, about any of it—I didn't care.

I just needed to see him.

He was lying back at a slight incline, his eyes closed. There were more machines now. But the blankets were only up to his waist, shirtless with white monitor pads stuck all over his chest.

But holy shit . . .

His chest and up his neck were covered in a red vein-like pattern that I'd read about but never seen. It looked like lightning but on his skin.

Lichtenburg figures.

Spreading out from his left side, they crawled outward, like macabre capillaries. Like lightning had painted itself on his skin.

It was a phenomenon common in lightning injuries, and I knew they weren't painful, but they were very confronting proof that the lightning had touched him. What it had done to his circulatory system. What it had done to his heart.

Proof of how close he'd come to dying.

I took his hand, and he slowly opened his eyes. He saw me, slow-blinked, and his lips pulled upward in a smile. "Hey."

My nose burned and my eyes welled with tears. "Hey. You gotta stop tryin' to die on me, okay?"

He smiled a little more. "Okay."

"How are you feeling?"

"Better now. Heart not so jittery," he said. "Good drugs."

I laughed despite my tears. He did seem a little drowsy. "We need to look after your heart, you hear?"

He slow-blinked again, his gaze fixed on mine. "Yeah."

"You've got some pretty cool Lichtenburg figures all over your chest."

"I do?"

I took my phone out and snapped some quick photos, then held the screen up so he could see them.

"Well, shit," he said.

I laughed because it wasn't like him to swear. I kissed the side of his head. "You're gonna have a whole lot of data to study after this. They ran bloods and brain scans and all kinds of tests."

He didn't reply to that, and when I studied his face a little, his eyes were trained on mine. Almost like he was seeing me for the first time.

"You okay, babe?" I asked.

He smiled again, slow and dazed. "I love you," he murmured.

My heart thumped and my pulse rapid-fired in my veins. *He just said . . . He just said the words. He just told me he loved me.*

He was high, mind you. On whatever drugs they'd given him. But he'd said those three words I'd been dyin' to hear.

I barked out a laugh and wiped a tear from my cheek. "I love you too."

He slowly lifted his hand to my face, his eyes scanning me like he was tryin' to commit it to memory. "It's true. Always been true."

I nodded, holding his palm to my cheek. "I know. But thank you for saying it."

"Should have said it before now." He was getting tired again, his blinks getting longer. "Not afraid anymore. Need you to know it."

I cried into his hand, nodding, and I kissed his palm. "I know, Jem. I know. But I gotta say, it's real nice to hear it."

He smiled and closed his eyes. "So tired."

"Go to sleep, baby." I kissed his forehead. "I'll be right here."

"Right here," he mumbled.

I brushed his hair from his forehead as he slept, taking in his beautiful face.

I didn't even notice the doctor was standing at the foot of the bed. He kinda startled me. "He's asleep," I said, like he couldn't see that himself.

"He'll be very tired for a while," he said.

"But he'll be okay, right?"

The doctor's expression gave nothing away. "He's young and very healthy. He shouldn't have survived at all. The fact he's made it this far . . . his odds are good. Other concerns may present themselves, but for now, he's stable. Maybe you should get yourself some breakfast. The nurses tell me you've been in the hallway all night."

"I can come straight back though, right?"

He gave a nod. Even smiled. "Sure."

I followed the doctor back out to the hall where my entire family stood. Dad and Ellis were there now too. All their eyes zeroed in on me, waiting for some kind of news.

"I spoke to him. He said he feels better and that the drugs were good, and he swore," I said with a teary smile. I tried to get a hold of myself, but seeing the concern on their faces, all I had was more tears. "God, I'd really like to stop fucking crying."

Mum gave me a hug, and then Ellis joined us, and he fake-whispered, "What kind of drugs?" I nudged him, but I knew he was joking. "Come on," Ellis said, his arm around my shoulder. "You need food. Did you sleep at all?"

"Don't think so."

"Then we'll all have breakfast," he said. "Like the freaking Brady Bunch."

And we did. All six of us.

I couldn't remember the last time the six of us had sat around a table and eaten breakfast together. Not since I was a kid.

But it was real nice.

My siblings and I didn't always agree, but all our differences aside, I knew they loved me. And Jeremiah. They loved him too.

It bolstered me, gave me strength to get through the next few days. I knew they'd be tough. Tougher for Jeremiah still.

I managed to eat something and I choked down a terrible cafeteria coffee, but I needed to get back to him. Everyone hugged me and they waited until I was the one to walk away.

And holy hell, walking back into that awful ICU was frightening.

All those machines and the terrible smell of sickness and mortality . . . I was glad when Jeremiah's nurse pulled the curtain around, blocking it all out.

Just me and him.

I sat beside his bed and took his hand.

His eyes were closed, he looked peaceful. The wires and sticky pads stuck all over his chest were a reminder that his peacefulness was chemically induced. The morbid patterns on his pale skin were fascinating and beautiful and terrible.

His thumb stroked my finger, and I looked up to find him watching me.

"Are you perving on me?" I asked.

He smiled. "Yes."

"Just as well." I stood up and kissed his forehead. "I missed you."

He huffed out a quiet laugh. "Missed you too."

I sat back down, his hand in both of mine. "My family all said to say hi and that they love you, and they want you to rest and get better."

He stared at me.

"All of them," I added. "They were all here. Even Rowan and Zoe. They came for you."

He gave a slight shake of his head. "They came for you."

"They came for you, Jem. Mum's been here almost as much as me. Dad had some stuff to take care of at work but he came straight back. Ellis has been doing the rounds, keeping everyone up to date, and he's been an absolute rock. Well, as much as a nut sac can be an absolute rock."

Jeremiah snorted quietly.

"They love you," I said. "Like I love you."

His fingers squeezed mine. "Like I love you," he whispered.

I met his gaze, and he met mine right back. No looking away, no blushing, no eye-rolling.

"I don't know why I was so scared to say it," he murmured. "I thought it was foolish and unnecessary. I was wrong."

I kissed his knuckles, then I stood up and kissed his cheek, his eyebrow, his nose, his lips.

"I should have told you every day," he whispered.

"You can. Starting today. I'll make up another chart and we can add gold stars for every time you say it."

He smiled for a moment; then it faded. His eyes filled with sadness and regret. "I thought I was going to die," he whispered. "And you being here kept me here, I'm sure of it. Kept me tethered here. Knowing you were here. Knowing you loved me." He shook his head, his eyes full of tears. "I had to tell you. You needed to hear it, and I'm sorry I was a fool before."

I swallowed back my tears. "I'm trying to not cry anymore today, and you're not helping." I sat on his bed and tried to give him a hug, but it was awkward, so I lay my head on his chest instead. "I want to hear your heart," I mumbled. "I want to hear it strong and forever."

His hand found my hair, and his blinks were already getting slower.

"You almost did die," I said. "Twice. They had to use the paddles on you, like they do in the movies."

His fingers stopped in my hair. "I don't remember . . ."

"Probably just as well." I listened to the *thump th-thump* of his heart, the most precious sound. "I'm glad I didn't see it. I don't think I'd have survived."

"I'm sorry," he whispered, a tear rolling down to his temple.

I wiped it away. "But you're okay now. The doc said your heartbeat's back to normal and we just need to watch it and be careful, and you'll probably need medication for a while, and if that's what we have to do forever, then so be it."

He nodded.

"And I was thinking that we can get you a new watch and somehow sync it to my phone as well, so I get your heart-rate alerts too. I dunno if someone's invented that yet. Or maybe you can wear a chest strap every day and I'll get the readings on my phone. That might be better."

He chuckled softly. "Sounds good."

I sighed, putting my head on his chest again, listening. "I can see straight up your nose."

He laughed then, and I sat up, taking his hand again. "I missed your smile," I murmured. "And your eyes. And everything about you. I was really scared, and I'm thankful more than words can say that you're still here."

"Me too." His eyelids half closed. "I'm tired, Tully. I'm so tired."

I put my hand to his cheek and gave him the best smile I could manage. "The doc said you would be, and that it's normal, and that you should rest and sleep a lot. So don't fight it. I'll be right here. All day. Until they kick me out."

He smiled as his eyes closed. "Right here," he mumbled as he fell asleep.

So I sat there, watching him sleep, watching the machines like I had any clue what any of them did. But I watched those little heart lines as if they meant the world to me.

Because they did.

They were steady and consistent, pulsing the sweetest beeping sound in the world.

I watched them, and I watched him.

Until an hour or so later when his eyes opened again, and he smiled. "Still right here," he said.

"Just like I promised." He was thirsty, so I got him a drink of water and helped him sip it through the straw. He seemed a little brighter, so I took his hand and kissed his knuckles. "I forgot to tell you something."

"Oh, what's that? That you love me, or that you can see up my nose?"

I chuckled. "Well, both of those still apply, obviously. But I called your dad."

He seemed surprised by this. "You did?"

"Of course. And he's coming to see you. He'll be here tomorrow."

CHAPTER ELEVEN
JEREMIAH

My father was coming.

My father was coming here to see me.

Tully had called him, which I understood. But he'd also insisted my father fly into Darwin as soon as possible. Tully had arranged and paid for the ticket without hesitation. I didn't like the fact he'd paid for it, but it was very much a Tully thing to do.

We both knew there was no way my dad could afford it on his own, and he'd have to take days off work, which he never liked to do.

Yet, he'd agreed to come.

Perhaps because Tully had asked him and not me.

Not that I had ever asked him. I didn't want to inconvenience him . . .

I tried not to think about it.

He wouldn't arrive until later tomorrow afternoon, so I had a good twenty-four hours to get used to the idea. Twenty-four hours to rest and regain some strength.

I felt so weak and tired. It was disconcerting how just lying in bed and breathing could be tiring.

The doctors came and went, telling me everything that

had happened and that would need to happen in the next forty-eight hours. I'd be hooked up to these machines for two days, then maybe I could move to another ward.

Tully sat by my side, listening and nodding. He held my hand and smiled at me, a beacon of reassurance in an otherwise dark and frightful time.

And I *was* scared.

Scared what this meant—for me, for him, for us. For my work, for everything.

Yet Tully never baulked, never faltered, never flinched.

He'd said he'd been scared enough the first day, he'd cried a river of tears. Now he was all positivity and sunshine.

He sat on my bed and fed me small triangles of sandwiches. He said they were 'coronary friendly,' and his nose scrunched up as though tomato and cucumber on wholemeal sounded atrocious, but they were the sweetest, most delicious thing I'd ever eaten.

They did kick him out for a few hours, but I slept the whole time he was gone, only waking up when he came back in. He was with Ellis this time, and Ellis took one look at me and stopped.

"Holy shit, that's so cool," Ellis whispered. He was staring at my chest, and I moved to pull the sheet up. "Sorry, dude, but have you seen yourself?"

"Leave him alone," Tully said, fixing my sheet for me. "Yes, I've shown him."

Ellis ignored him, took his phone out and reversed the camera so I could see myself. My chest. The Lichtenburg figures. The red lightning mapping out the veins and arteries under the skin.

"Does it hurt?" he asked.

I shook my head. "No."

I tried to sit up and Tully helped with the bed. It made it easier for me to look down at myself. The marks were concentrated on my left side, sprawling out like red lightning across my torso and neck.

"Always thought these were cool too," Tully said. "Until I saw them on you." He shuddered. "I don't like the reminder. Maybe I'll look back at some photos in a few years and think it was cool, but not now."

I looked up at him. I'd have thought he would have loved seeing them—they were a rare phenomenon, after all—but he really didn't. I reached for his hand. "They'll fade. Apparently."

"Well, I think they're cool," Ellis said. I think he'd taken some photos. "You look like one of those hotted-up cars with the flames up the side."

I snorted, but Tully grumbled and ignored him. He kissed the side of my head. "Did you sleep okay?"

"Mm."

"The nurse said you're doing well."

"If sleeping can be considered an accomplishment."

Ellis snorted out a laugh, then remembered to keep the noise down. "I better get going. Mum said she'll be around this arvo to see ya." He gently patted my leg. "Good to see ya doing well, Jem. You got a bit of colour now." And then he leaned in and whispered, "And don't listen to him. The mean-machine flames are fucking cool."

Tully looked for something to throw at his brother. I could see that he considered the drinking cup from the tray, and I think Ellis saw too, because he grinned and waved as he disappeared out the curtain.

I smiled at Tully. "At least he didn't call me Lightning McQueen."

He rolled his eyes and sighed. "Yeah look, about that. I think he ordered balloons to be delivered. He tried for flowers but they're not allowed in this ward. Something to do with pollen and allergies and incredibly ill people. So anyway, he ordered balloons, and from the stupid grin on his stupid face when he told me, I think we can assume it's either Lightning McQueen related. Or pornographic. It really could go either way."

I chuckled, and he cupped my face and kissed my lips.

"Ugh, my breath must be terrible," I mumbled.

He clearly didn't care. "So I was doing some research on diets for a healthy heart, and it looks like we'll be eating a lot of grilled fish and salads. Which is fine by me. But I also thought about exercises we could do, and I know you used to swim when you were in Melbourne."

"Well, yes, but—"

"Because people can't talk to you while you're doing laps. I know. I remember. But I was thinking we could install a lap pool at home, on the strip that fronts the ocean."

"No."

"As long as we make it crocodile proof—"

"No."

"But then you could do laps for exercise and I could watch you, because I like it when you're wet, not gonna lie."

"Tully, you're not putting a pool in for me."

"It would be for me as well."

My nurse peeked around the curtain. "Oh, good," I said. "Can you please tell him that putting in a pool for me to exercise in, while being a lovely gesture and all, is a ridiculous waste of money?"

She looked at him. "I don't care about the pool, but you come in here and argue with my patient and I'll give you a lovely gesture of my own."

Tully pouted like a four-year-old, and I smiled. "I win."

The nurse came in, checked the machines, checked my IV bag, and put her hand on my arm. "Everything okay? Does your husband need to go?"

I smiled at Tully. "No, he can stay."

Tully was still pouting. "I'll be good."

She gave a nod and left us alone, and Tully sat in his chair. "The pool conversation can wait until we get home."

I sighed and held out my hand for him to take. He slid his fingers through mine and I tightened my hold on his hand. "I love you," I whispered.

He perked up, his pout now that smile that won me over from day one. "I'll never get used to you saying it. I think you're gonna need to say it every day just to be sure."

"Okay."

He kissed the back of my hand. "You're tired again. You should close your eyes. I'll be right here."

I was tired, that was true. "Yeah. But I'm hungry," I said.

Tully stood up. "Then I'll get you something. You name it."

I pointed to my lips.

He grinned and leaned in, kissing me.

"And another sandwich would be great."

He kissed my forehead. "Your wish, my command."

He disappeared out the curtain and I must have dozed off again, because when I opened my eyes, he was sitting beside my bed, his arms crossed, his chin on his chest, sound asleep.

There was a cucumber and tomato sandwich on my tray table and a small apple juice.

And a huge bunch of balloons on my side table.

Lightning McQueen, of course.

AFTER EATING AND TAKING ANOTHER NAP, I FELT SO MUCH better. I was getting stronger and able to stay awake longer as the day progressed.

Mr and Mrs Larson called in to say hello, and after Tully fed me dinner, they took him home. And when I say he fed me dinner, I mean that he sat on the side of the bed and spoon fed me dinner.

I wasn't even embarrassed or annoyed.

It just made me happy.

And playing the charade of husbands didn't bother me at all.

In fact, I was getting used to it.

Liked it, even.

Perhaps it was cliché, but almost dying made me realise what was important. I didn't want to waste any more time.

More to the point, I didn't want to cut my time short. Not that I ever did so deliberately, but there had been times when I'd been reckless or blasé.

Those days were over.

I wasn't sure what it meant for my career. I would always be a meteorologist. I loved what I did. I loved my work at the bureau, and I loved the magnificence of Mother Nature.

But as for my personal quest to study the effects of lightning on the human body . . .

Well, I think I'd learned all I needed to know.

I'd been incredibly lucky to survive at all. Tully had been there to save me, and yet my brush with lightning, my very nearly dying because of it, had almost killed him too.

Not physically. It hadn't stopped his heart as it did mine, but I'd broken his. I'd put him through hell.

And if he wanted to sit on the side of my bed and feed me gentle spoonfuls of food, then I would never object.

The installation of a pool was still a hard no, though.

I had to draw a line somewhere.

"Someone looks a little brighter tonight?" the doctor said. He came in, smiling, checking my charts on his iPad.

"Feel much better."

"Heart rate's good," he said. "No light-headedness or pain?"

I shook my head. "No."

"Good."

"How long will I be in this ward for?"

"We'll take another ultrasound of your heart tomorrow, then we'll see about maybe moving you back to the cardio ward, depending on what we find. How does that sound?"

"Good."

"One step closer to going home, huh?"

I nodded.

Home. Wherever Tully was, was home to me.

"I'd really like that."

"I spoke to your partner about home care."

"Husband," I corrected automatically. It was a lie, but it gave me a thrill to say it.

I'm surprised the ECG didn't beep.

"Sorry, husband," the doctor said sheepishly. "He said twenty-four-hour home care is an option."

Of course he did.

"If it gets you home quicker," he added.

That made me smile.

"I explained it would require an ECG machine similar to this one and he had no objections."

I tried not to smile so big. "Of course he didn't."

He nodded slowly, checking the chart again. "I asked him why you were wearing an athlete's chest strap monitor."

Oh no.

"Uh."

He chewed on the inside of his lip. "First, he blushed and his brother laughed. So I could only assume . . ." He smirked at me. "Then he explained that you monitor your heart rate during electrical storms and that you've had a few close calls with lightning before."

I inhaled deeply and let it out with a sigh. "I did, yes. But I think those days are over."

"He said you chase storms together."

"He's a storm chaser. I'm a meteorologist."

He nodded. "Yes, who issued the warning alert for the cyclone. Created quite the hype if I recall."

At least he didn't mention my mother, though if he knew who I was from Cyclone Hazer, it was like he knew anyway . . .

"And saved two children from a lightning strike," he added.

"Yes, well, I think I'll be staying indoors from now on," I said. "My fulminology days are over. If I were a cat, I'd be on my ninth life." I inhaled deeply, realisation that my studies were over really sinking in. "After my last close call, Tully told me I needed to consider him instead of almost dying to save other people. I think I'll do just that."

He nodded slowly. "Well, as a doctor, I'm inclined to agree with him. No more lightning strikes. I can almost guarantee the next one won't be so kind."

I considered telling him I hadn't deliberately endangered myself in the name of science. Not this time, anyway. But what was the point? It didn't make any difference now.

In the end, all I could do was sigh.

He checked my burns, my small exit wounds on the soles of my feet. According to the doctor, they looked like cigarette burns. As if someone had extinguished cigarettes on my skin. The one on my ribs was much the same.

Fascinating that the entry and exit of so many volts could be so concentrated, so small.

The Lichtenburg figures were beginning to fade from my neck, though were still darker at my ribs.

My ribs hurt the most now, which was probably a good sign that the rest of me had stopped hurting, that the pain was mostly gone. My heart and chest were still tender, and it helped to keep my breaths measured.

But the doctor was happy with my progress.

"Get some sleep," he said. Then before he turned to leave, he nodded at the balloons. "Someone has a sense of humour."

I smiled. "Yes, he does."

Sleep didn't come easy, as tired as I was. I could doze off

well enough, though my mind kept returning to my earlier realisation.

My fulminology days were over.

I still had my job, of course. And I would always love meteorology. But I couldn't risk another strike injury.

Not that I'd risked myself this time. And maybe that was what annoyed me the most. I hadn't run out into a clearing in the midst of electrical activity. I hadn't wrapped myself in foil, as Tully had once suggested, to go and stand out in a storm with a death wish.

I'd simply been in the wrong place at the wrong time.

Like my mother had been.

I wasn't sure what it meant for me and Tully.

He loved storm chasing. He'd lost previous relationships because of his commitment to it. He'd spent weekends and every holiday out in the wilderness to simply be in any storm he could find.

And he'd said that he couldn't believe how lucky he was to have someone he could share that with.

But what if he could no longer share that with me?

Sometime in the middle of the night, my nurse came in with a frown. She checked my machines. "Everything okay?" she asked. "Your heart's a little fast; blood pressure's on the rise."

"I'm okay," I said. "Just thinking."

"Thinking or worrying?"

I snorted.

"All you're doing is adding stress on your heart. So how about we try and sleep instead?"

"Hm."

She gave me a smile. "No worrying allowed. Or I'll tell that gorgeous husband of yours."

That made me smile. *Husband.* "No tattletales, please."

Happy with the machines and whatever output I was now

showing, she patted my arm. "Get some sleep. You've got a big day tomorrow."

An ultrasound, with hopefully good findings. Maybe moving to another ward.

And my father's arrival.

A big day indeed.

Tully's bright and smiling face greeted me after breakfast. He planted a kiss on my forehead, then my cheek. "What did they make you eat?"

"Cold toast and black tea."

He made a face. "Christ."

"There was a porridge-like substance but—" I shook my head. "I stopped eating craft glue when I was in preschool."

Tully laughed, his brown eyes shining.

"Wow," he said. "You were ahead of the class. I didn't stop eating craft glue until year three, at least."

I'd do anything to keep him smiling like that.

"I was a gifted child."

"Can I get you anything from the cafeteria? From an actual café? A proper coffee?"

"Maybe later." I took his hand, just wanting to hold it.

He perched his backside on my bed and played with my fingers. "You okay? The nurse said you didn't sleep too well."

"She's a dibber dobber."

"Jem?"

I sighed. "I just spent a lot of time thinking. I can't do much else."

The hold on my hand got a little tighter. "Thinking about what?"

"About what I do now."

"What do you mean?" He was worried, a little pale even. "Are you talking about us?"

Oh god. He thought . . .

"No, not like that. Not about us."

He sagged, visibly relieved. "Christ, Jem. I was about ready to call for the crash cart. You almost gave me a heart attack."

"Well, you're on the right ward."

"True." He put my hand against his chest. "Feel that?"

I could feel the thrum of his heart under my palm. I smiled, then nodded to the ECG machine. "Mine comes with pictures."

He smiled but his eyes scanned mine. "What were you thinking about? You're still kinda scarin' me, not gonna lie."

"Well, I . . ." I wasn't sure how to say this, and I could only guess honesty was the best policy. "I'm not sure I can continue with my fulminology studies."

He seemed confused by this.

"Okay." He squinted at me. "I'm not sure what you're saying. Are you talking about your work at the bureau?"

"I'm not sure," I said. "I'd like to stay. I love my job, and if they ever get around to upgrading my office . . ." I looked at our joined hands. "What I'm saying is, I don't think I can continue to monitor storms. Outside of office hours, that is."

He opened his mouth and gave a small shake of his head.

I licked my lips, my mouth dry. The disappointment on his face was a bitter thing to swallow. "I'll always support your love for storm chasing," I said. "And I'd once dreamed of spending every weekend, every vacation with you. At the bunker, where it's just the two of us in the middle of the storm season in that small bed. It's all I ever wanted."

He was frowning now, shaking his head. "If you want that, why can't we?"

"Because I almost died. And you made me promise last time that I'd consider you before I tried to get myself killed again. So that's what I'm doing." I squeezed his hand. "Seeing you so upset, knowing what I put you through. It made me realise that you were right. I need to consider people other than myself. Which is not something I'm too familiar with, to be honest. I've never had anyone . . ." I lifted his hand to my lips. "So if that means my research days are over—or field trips, at least—then so be it."

"Jeremiah," he murmured.

"It's not a bad thing. I can still study and research, but running out into electrical storms . . ." I shook my head. "Not if it ever hurts you again. I can't do it. And I'm not sad about it. My priorities are quite clear to me now. And my priorities are you, and my work, of course. But standing out in a clearing holding a metal rod to the sky during a storm is now not so appealing."

"Jem," he whispered. "I never meant that you had to stop. I'd never ask you to stop."

"I know. And I would never ask you to stop either. I know you love it, and I know you've had relationships where they've not understood. I'm not like them. I do understand and I want you to keep doing whatever you love. I'll always support you."

"But you won't come with me," he said, frowning.

"Tully, I can't go through this again. I can't put you through this again."

He nodded slowly, his eyes getting that hardened, focused, possibly angry gleam. "See, here's the thing, Jeremiah," he said. "I've been chasing storms my whole life. Since I was a kid, doin' all kinds of crazy shit with my dad and then when I was old enough to do it on my own. And I ain't ever been struck by lightning."

"Neither had I," I countered. "And for the record, I wasn't doing crazy shit. It was a freak electrical discharge. Just because it isn't raining or storming overhead doesn't mean lightning can't strike."

"Exactly," he said. "You just said it. It was a freak accident.

There was no way you could have predicted it. You didn't mean for it to happen."

I may have now only just seen the corner I'd painted myself into.

He smiled as if he knew, though it was still a little sad. "It wasn't like you were out there holding a metal pole up to the sky, actively seeking out a strike point. Not like when you wanted to trek into mangroves holdin' a bunch of metal equipment. Or that time you ran out into a storm to fix your weather station and almost got hit. Those were deliberate acts of stupidity."

I snorted. "Thanks."

"Or the time you saved Casey and Presley. That was deliberate and stupid, but you saved those kids so I'm giving you a pass."

I smiled but he was also helping my point. "All these times are just proof that I need to stop."

"No. It's proof you need to start thinking. So we keep goin' to the bunker, and we can take all the monitoring gear." He leaned in close, his eyes trained on mine. "And we make love on that small bed while the storms rage outside."

My ECG machine beeped.

He looked at it. "Oops."

My nurse appeared like a genie from an ECG bottle. "What did you do?"

Tully got off the bed, his hands behind his back. "Just making sure it still works, that's all. A civic duty, if you will."

She glared at him, then she smiled at me. "Is he bothering you?"

"Yes."

He gasped. "Husband! How could you?"

She looked at me. "There's another visitor waiting out in the hall. I told her there's only one at a time and that you were here."

"Her?" Tully asked. "Mum wasn't coming in till this arvo."

"I can't remember her name," the nurse said. "Tall, older lady, shaved head. Shirt has a dinosaur on it. Was her name Doreen?"

Tully grinned at me. "Our favourite lesbian."

I laughed and it hurt my ribs. "Ow."

He kissed the side of my head. "I'll go get her and she can say hi, and I'll go and get you a proper coffee."

They were both gone, and I barely had time to think about everything Tully had said before he came back with Doreen. "Here he is," Tully said. "Now please talk some sense into him."

"Sense about what?" she asked.

"He doesn't think he should come storm chasing with me anymore," he replied. "Tell him that's a load of shit."

Someone in the ward said something about his language and Tully disappeared behind the curtain, leaving Doreen standing there. She was holding a bag in her hand, wringing the handle.

I'd never seen her look so awkward.

"How ya holdin' up?" she asked.

"Had better days," I replied. "But I'm getting better."

She was still fidgeting with the bag. "Tully said it was a close call."

"Yeah. Lucky he was there."

She nodded. "So you gonna quit or something?"

"What? Quit the office? No." I shook my head. "You can't get rid of me that easily."

She finally smiled. "Well, good. Glad to hear that. They tell me the install's about to start. Some optic cable guys came by to measure something."

Finally.

"Oh, that is good news."

"But don't you worry about none of that. I'll keep 'em on their toes for ya, make sure none of them are slackin' off."

I smiled. "Good. Thank you."

She nodded, looking around awkwardly again. "Couldn't believe it when I heard. I was gonna come in yesterday, but Tully said today might be better."

"Thank you for coming in," I said. "It's a lovely surprise."

She nodded to the balloons. "Lemme guess. Tully gotcha those?"

"Ah, no. His brother."

She nodded as if that made total sense. "Kinda funny."

I smiled at her. "It is."

She winced. "You know I'm not a fan of hospitals."

"I got that impression, yes." It was only then I noticed her shirt. It did indeed have a dinosaur on it. It was pink, white, and orange—the lesbian pride colours—with long eyelashes, and underneath it was the writing *lickalotapus*.

I expected nothing less.

"Love your shirt."

She smiled, for real this time. "Thanks. It's new." Then she only just seemed to remember that she was holding something. "Oh, I got this for you. I got it when I ordered mine. Was gonna save it for Christmas or a birthday or somethin', but it didn't feel right comin' to see ya and not bring something."

She handed it over. Inside the bag was a shirt, which I could see had the words *I love Dick* written on it and a picture of Dick Van Dyke's face.

I laughed and my ribs twinged. "I love it, thank you."

"No worries." Then she rocked back and forth on her heels, uncomfortable again. "So, uh, did it hurt?"

I didn't mind her questions. She was, after all, a meteorologist. Her curiosity was natural. "I don't remember it. The pain afterwards, yes. When I came to, I guess, for the want of a better word. There was pain. Everywhere."

"Was it a direct hit?"

I shook my head. "Side splash. Got me in the ribs." I lifted my left arm, and she looked and winced.

"Jesus."

"Right near the heart."

"And the Lichtenburg marks?"

"You mean my Lightning McQueen racing flames?"

She smiled at that, but then looked at my torso. "Jesus, Mary, and Joseph. It's unreal. Any exit wounds?"

"A matching pair on the sole of each foot."

She shook her head, seemingly lost for words. "You were lucky, huh?"

"Yes."

"So, no more storm chasin', huh?"

I shrugged. "I don't know. I saw what I put Tully through, and I can't do that again. I need to think of him now too. I don't think he's happy with my decision, but . . ."

"Give it some time," she said. "It's not so much the storm chasin' you gotta quit. It's the doin' stupid shit like runnin' out in a lightnin' storm that you gotta quit."

I snorted. "Thanks. I'll keep that in mind."

"I'm just sayin', if you love it, if it's part of what makes you *you*, then if you quit, then you're quittin' part of yourself. And that can lead to resentment and if you blame yourself or Tully, or maybe he'll blame you. It ain't good either way."

"What's not good either way?" Tully asked as he walked back in, holding a takeaway coffee cup. "Nurse said they're comin' to put some dye in ya for the echo-thingy ultrasound. I asked if the dye would make you glow in the dark. She said no. But I did ask if the coffee was okay, and yes, you can still drink this." He put the coffee on my table. And then he saw the shirt. He held it up. "Oh my god, this is the best thing I've ever seen. I'm gonna need one in every colour."

"It's not yours," Doreen said. "It's Jeremiah's."

"We share a wardrobe," Tully said. "What's mine is mine and what's his is mine."

Then, because Tully was Tully, he pulled his own shirt off over his head and pulled on the *I love Dick* shirt. He patted it down and grinned right at me. "You like?"

I couldn't stop smiling at him. "I love."

He beamed, giving Doreen one of his grins, and she rolled her eyes.

Tully rolled his other shirt into a ball and shoved it in the bag. "Anyway, the nurse said we gotta go. I'll come back as soon as they let me in." He leaned down and kissed my forehead. "Love you. See you soon."

"Love you too," I said.

He was still beaming, and he laughed when my ECG line stuttered upwards. "Oops."

My nurse appeared like magic again, her glare fixed directly at Tully. "Is your husband being a menace again?"

I saw Doreen do a double take at the word husband, and Tully must have seen it too. He quickly took her arm. "Come on, Dory. Time to go." She managed a wave before they disappeared.

My nurse tsked after him. "Does that grin of his get him whatever he wants?"

I chuckled. "Yes, it does."

She patted my arm. "Okay, let's get you ready for this test. What did we call it?"

"One step closer to going home."

CHAPTER TWELVE
TULLY

Leavin' the hospital without Jeremiah got harder every time. He was gettin' better, and I didn't need a doctor to tell me that. He was brighter, smiled more, talked more, slept less, and didn't wince every single time he moved.

I walked Doreen to the car park and thanked her again for coming to see him. She wasn't the big bad meanie she made herself out to be, though I doubt I'd be calling her Dory again anytime soon.

She threatened a specific kind of bodily harm and then laughed. Not like it was a joke, but in a 'do it again, I dare ya' kinda way.

I wouldn't be tempting that fate any time soon.

Knowing Jeremiah would be busy for an hour or so, I headed to the office. I'd basically abandoned my job in the last few days, so pickin' up some slack while I could was a good idea.

Keepin' busy was too.

I opened my emails, fully expecting a barrage, and I wasn't disappointed. I'd only got through a handful when Rowan walked past my office, saw me, and stopped.

"Oh hey," he said, coming in. "I didn't think you'd be in this week."

"I'm not here now," I replied. "Just tryin' to make a dent in my inbox."

"Everything okay at the hospital?"

"Yeah, he's just havin' some tests done. I'll go back soon."

He only just seemed to notice my shirt. "Uh, nice shirt."

I laughed. "Thanks. It was Jeremiah's. Now it's mine."

He made a face that said 'Jeremiah would never wear that' but didn't say it out loud. "Ellis said his dad gets in this afternoon."

I inhaled and sighed. "Yep."

"Is that not a good thing?"

"It is." I puffed out my cheeks with another sigh. "Well, I hope it will be. They have a kinda strained relationship. Never been very close."

He nodded slowly and came in to sit in the chair across from me. "It must've been difficult for both of them after Jeremiah's mum died. And I'm not excusing his dad's behaviour at all . . ."

I wasn't sure where he was trying to take this.

"What?"

"I know if it was me, if I were in his shoes, well, I'd like to think . . . If Diah died, I'd like to think it'd make me hold my kids tighter, love them harder. But you just never know. I'd be a forever-changed man too. It'd break me. And I'm pretty sure after seeing what you went through with Jeremiah these last few days, it'd break you too."

I . . . I was speechless.

Rowan shrugged. "And we have a big family that steps up when we need it, and I can't imagine how hard it was for Jeremiah, having no one and growing up like that. I'm sure his father did all he could do to provide for him the best he knew how." He ran his hand through his hair. "I don't know what I'm trying to say."

I wasn't sure either. "Are you okay, Rowan?"

He let out a breathy laugh. I couldn't ever recall seeing him embarrassed, yet here he was. "Yeah, I am. I'm just saying maybe Jeremiah's dad isn't a bad person. And I know you're inclined to be protective of Jeremiah and god help anyone who dares to look at him wrong, but maybe now you can sympathise with his dad a little."

"I wasn't gonna be rude to him."

"I know. I know you wouldn't. But he lost the love of his life, just like you almost lost yours." He shrugged again. "Maybe when we meet him this afternoon, we can show him that Jeremiah—"

"Wait. When *we* meet him?"

"Yeah well, Mum thought it might be nice if we all came around for dinner."

"Oh, did she now?"

"Did you want it to be just you and him at home tonight? With Ellis?"

Oh god. "That's a good point."

He chuckled as he stood up. "I'll bring some duct tape. Just in case."

I snorted. "Thanks."

He walked to the door. "Say hi to Jeremiah for us."

"I will."

He left me to wonder if that wasn't the weirdest conversation I'd ever had with my eldest brother. I'd never been close to him. We'd always been at different stages of our lives and never had much in common.

Until now.

I got through another three emails when Mum found me. She knocked and walked straight in. "Oh, Rowan said you were in."

"In the flesh." I checked my watch. "For another thirty minutes, maybe."

"So I was thinking . . ."

"About dinner? Rowan told me."

She smiled as she sat down. "I thought it might be nice. I know he'll be tired after travelling and he'll want to see Jeremiah, of course. But we can have dinner all ready at your place when you get home, and we'll be gone by eight thirty. How does that sound?"

I wasn't sure . . .

"It'll be nice for him to see how accepted Jeremiah is in our family, don't you think?"

"Well . . ." When she put it like that . . . "I guess."

And Jeremiah will be glad he's not there to witness it.

"Any dietary requirements?"

"Not that I know of. Mum," I said. "He's not the fancy type. Please don't go all out to impress him."

"I won't."

"I just don't want him to think that we're pretentious or that we think we're too good for them. I don't want Jeremiah's dad to think—"

"Tully, stop stressing about it. I'm sure he'll see you for who you are, and his only concern will be that you treat his son well. Which you do. That's all any parent wants. He'll be fine."

Ellis chose that exact moment to walk into my office. "Oh look, it's my second favourite nut sac."

Mum sighed. "How could anyone ever think we're pretentious?"

I snorted. "Ellis will be on his best behaviour, won't you?"

"For dinner tonight?" He grinned. "Of course."

Oh great.

"You know, maybe tonight's not such a great idea—"

"I know when to behave myself, jeez," he grumbled. "So how was Lightning McQueen this morning?"

I was gonna rebuke him, but honestly, what was the point?

"He was good. He's getting better, though he didn't sleep

too well last night." I sighed. "He said he doesn't wanna go storm chasing anymore. He said he doesn't wanna risk gettin' hurt again because of me."

Mum gave me a sad smile. "He's had quite a scare, love. And he saw how it affected you. I'm not surprised he's having second thoughts."

Ellis completely dismissed it. "Oh please. Give him two weeks and he'll be back out there on the patio watching storms with you. He gets that same stupid, excited look on his face you get when thunder starts to roll."

I snorted. "Gee, thanks."

Mum gave a pointed nod to my computer. "You know you can just leave that."

"I know. But it helps to feel productive." I checked my watch again. "I gotta head back soon anyway. I told him I'd be there as soon as they'd let me see him."

"Did you want me to get his dad from the airport?" Ellis asked.

I considered it for half a second. "As much as I don't wanna leave him, I think I should pick him up. Good first impressions and all."

Ellis grinned at me. "Meeting the father-in-law, huh? Are you nervous?"

God yes.

"No."

He snorted. "If you're gonna lie, you need to get better at it."

I let out a puff of air. "Thanks."

Mum stood up, signalling for Ellis to do the same. "You'll be fine, Tully. He'll love you. Come on, Ellis. We're keeping him from getting anything done."

"Do you need me to grab anything for dinner tonight?"

"Not a thing." Mum ushered Ellis out the door. "Give Jeremiah our love. Oh, and Tully?"

"Yeah."

"Before you pick up Jeremiah's father, you might want to reconsider the shirt."

Ellis clearly hadn't paid my shirt any attention. He looked at it now and cracked up laughing, and Mum led him out the door.

I sighed at my now empty office. I hadn't got a lot of work done but they did give me a lot to think about.

I KNEW JEREMIAH WAS IN PAIN AS SOON AS I WALKED IN. He tried to sit up a little when he saw me, and he gasped and winced.

I took his hand. "What's wrong?"

He shook his head. "Nothing. They just made me move a lot. On my side, and they had to push against my ribs. I'm fine."

I brushed the hair off his forehead. "Can I get you anything?"

He pointed to his lips and pouted.

I laughed and kissed him. "Better?"

"Yes."

I kissed his forehead for good measure. "So what did the docs say?"

"Full report to come, but prelim was good. Nothing worse, slight improvement, rhythm normal and blood flow good."

"That's great news."

He smiled, tired but happy. "It is. He mentioned moving to another ward, but I really just want to go home."

"I want you to come home too. I said I'd hire a full-time nurse, and I mean it. Just for a few days or a week, or however long it takes. At least you'd be home. Mr Percival misses you."

"He does?"

I nodded. "Well, he squawks a lot. I don't speak magpie."

He smiled and squeezed my hand. "I'd like to go home."

"Want me to bust you out? Because I will. I can wear some scrubs and put your sheet over your head, wheel you right out the door. No one would know."

"I think they might."

"Well, I could ask about getting you discharged legitimately, but it's not as much fun."

"I'm supposed to stay off my feet," he said. "I have to be careful of the exit wounds. I'm supposed to be doing leg exercises, which would be fine if my ribs didn't hurt so much."

"Want me to bend your legs for you?"

He raised one tired eyebrow. "I'm almost certain that's not what they had in mind."

I snorted. "That's not what I meant at all. You've got a dirty mind."

He chuckled but his cheeks flushed pink.

I sighed and ran my thumb across his cheekbone. "Blush is my favourite colour on you."

He looked up at me, slow-blinkin'. "That kind of talk isn't helping with my dirty mind."

That made me laugh. "Wanna give that ECG machine a workout?"

He snorted, but then he winced and held his ribs. "Maybe another time."

"I wish I could do something to help."

"You being here helps. It really does."

I kissed his temple. "Can I take you out of this room at least? In a wheelchair?"

He brightened for half a second, like that was the best idea ever, then he sighed. "I'm not sure. I'd have to ask. Maybe when the doctor comes in. If they're taking me to a different ward, I'd imagine they'd want me up and about more than I have been."

"Do your feet still hurt?"

"Not so much."

"I can help you walk. Take you to the bathroom." Then I whispered, "And hold your dick when you pee."

That made him smile. "You might have to shower me too."

"Hell yes I will." The banter was fun but he was getting tired, so I sat in the chair beside him and took his hand. "Well, when we get you home, I'll park you up on the comfy couch with all the snacks and movies you wanna watch."

"And books."

"All the books you want."

"I miss my phone. I miss reading."

"Oh, babe, you should have said." I put my phone on his table. "Use mine, download any books you want."

"I can't take your phone."

"I'll survive. Just until I get you another one."

"Do you even know where my phone is? You said it got fried, right?"

I nodded. "Yeah. It's dead. It didn't like fifty-thousand volts, apparently. We can check the sim card though."

"Same as my watch."

"I'll get you a new one of them too. And a new chest strap. Though it won't be for scientific purposes now. It'll be medical, so I make sure we don't overdo it. I fully expect gold stars though. There's a lot to be said about taking it slow."

He didn't sigh, he didn't argue, he didn't get mad. He just watched me with soft eyes and a warm smile. "I love you," he murmured. "I don't know what I'd do without you."

Just then, the familiar rattle and smell of the lunch trolley came into the ward. "I'm going to feed you some lunch first. And then when they make me leave, what you can do without me is get some sleep. I'll be back after three," I said. "With your dad."

His eyes widened, then he deflated a little. "I forgot."

Standing up, I kissed the side of his head. "Babe, it'll be

fine. And you should consider yourself lucky that you're in here, because my parents insisted that he meet my entire family for dinner. At our place. Including Ellis."

"Oh dear."

I nodded. "Exactly."

I waited at the airport, like I had many times before. Not so long ago waiting for Jeremiah. Now waiting for his father.

I was ignoring the nerves, pretending it wasn't making me feel sick. But I was thinking maybe eating lunch had been a bad idea.

Calm down, Tully. It'll be fine. Everything's gonna be fine.

I'd only ever seen one photo of the man before, but I didn't need it. There was only one man who came through the Arrivals door that could be Jeremiah's dad. No mistaking it.

He was tall and thin, wearing trousers and a white button-down shirt. He had dark grey hair and striking blue eyes.

Not as blue as Jeremiah's, but still . . .

He was simply an older version of Jeremiah himself.

He was scannin' the crowd, nervous and out of place.

"Mr Overton?" I said with a smile. I offered him my hand. "Tully Larson. We spoke on the phone."

He shook my hand. "Oh yes, yes, of course. Uh, thank you for coming to pick me up, and for the ticket, of course."

Seeing that he was as nervous as me made me feel a little better.

"You're more than welcome." I looked at his carry-on bag. "Are we waiting for any more luggage?"

"No, no. Just this."

"Perfect. Then we should get going. Jeremiah's excited to see you." I gestured to the exit.

He gave a nod and we walked out. "Is he . . . is he any better?"

"Much better than he was," I said. "But he's still . . . well, he's still laid up." I got to my car and pressed the button for the boot to open.

He put his carry-on in and wiped his palms on his thighs. "Nice car."

I almost laughed. "You know, Jeremiah looked at it much the same way. I've also got a Jeep that's about twenty years old and he prefers to drive that, but this one has air conditioning."

"Ah, yes. This humidity is no joke."

I opened the passenger door for him and smiled. "Jeremiah said the exact same thing."

I climbed in behind the wheel and getting us out of the car park was a good distraction. I didn't have to worry about what to say for a minute or two, at least.

"Darwin's had a rough time of it," he said as we made our way into traffic. "I tried to catch it on the news, but the Melbourne channels stopped showing it when it wasn't news anymore."

"You saw Jeremiah's interview where he told you he was okay, yeah?"

He furrowed his brow. "Well, yes. Though he probably shouldn't have wasted important resources for that."

It was hard not to smile at him because, my god, he and Jeremiah were so alike. "That news crew owed him. A ten second interview to let you know he was okay was the least they could do."

He scowled before schooling his features. "Yes, with the lightning strike. I saw that too."

"When he saved those two kids?" I nodded. "He's a bit of a hero in this town."

He watched the passing scenery for a few long seconds:

the still-damaged buildings, the construction work. "It didn't help him much this last time though."

I withheld my sigh. I wanted to say *so* much, but knew I had to bite my tongue.

"There was no storm when he was hit," I offered gently. "No thunder, no rain. He wasn't reckless or foolish. It was just a freak accident."

He nodded solemnly, his mouth a grim line. "I've heard that before."

And there it was.

A painful truth that he'd lived through this before.

As simple as that.

We drove in silence the rest of the way. There was nothing I could say, nothing I could add.

As we pulled into the hospital car park, I saw him in a different light. Yep, he was a lot like Jeremiah—that was true —but there were differences too.

His father was gaunt, the lines on his face were ingrained with almost thirty years of grief. There was a dark cloud over him, and though he'd smiled when I first met him, I could see now that it was just a conscious effort at an expected facial expression.

Whereas Jeremiah still laughed, he still had light in his eyes. His father didn't.

I had to wonder if he'd smiled at all since Jeremiah's mother died.

And Rowan's words came back to me.

"If Diah died, I'd like to think it'd make me hold my kids tighter, love them harder. But you just never know. I'd be a forever-changed man, too. It'd break me. And I'm pretty sure after seeing what you went through with Jeremiah these last few days, it'd break you too."

And I knew exactly what Rowan had said was true.

Jeremiah's father broke the day his wife died. I didn't know what kind of man he was before, but I'd hazard a guess that the light inside him died alongside her. And I understood, I could sympathise. Because Jeremiah almost died and it damn near almost broke me too.

So yeah, like Rowan had also said, I could maybe sympathise with Jeremiah's dad a little.

I pulled into a parking spot and shut off the engine. "Let's go see him. He was sleeping when I left him, so hopefully he's had a good rest."

Mr Overton gave another nod and we headed inside. His nervousness ratcheted up a notch with every step, and he stopped dead when he realised I was taking him to the ICU.

"ICU?"

"Yep. They're hoping to move him out today. He had some tests done this mornin' and he was waiting to hear back from the doc."

"Is he . . . can he . . . ?" He looked considerably more gaunt now. "I should have asked before now. When you said on the phone that he wasn't well . . ."

I put my hand on his arm. "He's okay. He's going to make a full recovery. He's talking, eating, and drinking. He's still got his sense of humour. They're talkin' about getting him up and walking. He's just here because of his heart."

"His heart . . . ?"

Oh god.

"Yeah, the high voltage gave his ticker a jumpstart. So he's hooked up to machines that measure every beat. It's mostly precautionary," I added, trying to placate him a little.

Jeez.

I sucked at this.

Oh . . .

And then I remembered something else.

Ah, hell. Here goes nothing.

"Oh, and uh, yeah, before you go in," I hedged, lookin' around to see who might be within earshot. "The hospital might be under the impression that Jeremiah and I are married?"

He stared.

"We're not," I added quickly. "It's just so that I can be here with him, ya know? Makes it easier, that's all."

His brows did that unimpressed thing again, his mouth a disappointed thin line. "Right."

So that went well.

"Okay, let's not keep him waiting."

I got him signed in and led him into the ward. I held the curtain for him and followed him in.

Jeremiah was still in bed, and it looked as if there'd been some attempt to brush his hair. As soon as he saw his dad, he tried to sit up straighter and winced immediately. "Dad," he said. There was hope in his eyes, and for a brief second, I got a glimpse of a small boy who'd have given anything in the world to make his father happy.

His dad took one look at him, nodded, and began to cry.

CHAPTER THIRTEEN

JEREMIAH

Seeing my father upset, seeing him show any kind of emotion at all, took me by such surprise I wasn't sure how to react.

Seeing him cry made me cry too.

Instant tears, my heart heavy, a lump in my throat.

I tried to reach for him but it hurt my ribs, and he quickly took my hand. "Sorry, son," he said, wiping his cheeks, trying to compose himself. "Just got a little shock to see you, that's all."

I'd never seen my father cry. Not ever.

"It's okay, Dad," I said.

Tully wheeled my table over closer to me, and there were now tissues on it. He kissed the side of my head. "I'll just be out in the hall."

I watched him leave, the curtain swishing after him. Dad stood there, uncertain and clearly not sure what to say. "He seems a nice fellow."

I laughed, still teary. "He is." I still had hold of his hand and reluctantly let it go. "Take a seat. How was your flight?"

He sat down as if the seat would bite him. "I'm sorry

about before," he said quietly. "I just . . . I don't know what came over me."

"It's okay, Dad," I said again. "I've missed you. I'm really glad you made the trip."

He shifted in his seat. "Yes, well . . . Tully insisted I come. He paid for it, which I didn't expect him to do that, and I can pay him back the money."

"He'd probably be offended if you tried. And he is insistent. If you'd have said no, he'd probably have gone to Melbourne to bring you up here himself." I smiled. "He's a good man, Dad. He saved my life."

His eyes cut to mine. "He, uh, he said you weren't doing too well. When he first called me. He said he thought it best if I make the trip."

I nodded. "Yeah. It was pretty scary."

His gaze bored into mine. That hesitancy, that awkward habit of his to not hold eye contact was gone. "Lightning, huh?"

I sighed, dreading this conversation that we had to have. "Yes. I know."

"I almost lost you both to it. Do you know what that would've done to me?"

I tried to keep my breathing low, my heart rate down, but damn. Being hooked up to every machine made it hard to disguise. My blood pressure began to rise, and I knew my nurse was just a few seconds away.

"I'm sorry, Dad. I didn't mean for this to happen. I didn't want this—"

And there she was. Breezed in around the curtain and ignored my father completely. She had one hand on my arm, the other pressing the machine. "Jeremiah, my darling, what are we doing to your BP? Are you trying to stay here in the ICU?"

"Sorry, I—"

Dad stood up. "I should go," he said. "I didn't realise my being here—"

"No, Dad. Stay. Please. My research is over," I blurted out. "I'm done. I can't do this again. I can't put Tully through this again. Or you."

Dad stood there, stunned. Disbelieving. "But your work. All those years you put into it."

"It doesn't matter. None of it matters."

He shook his head. "Jeremiah."

My nurse patted my arm. "Keep your heart rate down," she said, then gave my father a parting glare as she left.

Neither of us said anything for a few moments.

"I'm staying in meteorology," I said. "I love my job and I've done good work here, Dad. The people here are great. They like me, they respect me. But my field research is over. I don't need data or statistics on keraunopathy or even keraunomedicine, because I know all I need to know."

He looked at the machines, the curtain, then finally at me. "I don't want you to give up on your dreams. As much as I don't like it or understand it." He shook his head. "You've dedicated your whole life to . . ." He waved his hand at me. "To this."

"And it almost killed me."

He sat back down, and a blanket of acceptance settled over us.

"What will you do?" he asked.

"My job. That won't change." I sighed. "And I will look at my medical records, at the data. There were brain scans and ECGs, et cetera, and maybe one day I'll compare statistics. But my days of chasing lightning in some self-serving attempt to beat it are done."

"What about Tully?" he asked quietly. "I thought you said he enjoyed it as well, that it was something you did together."

"It is. And if he wants to go, then maybe I'll go with him." I swallowed hard. I knew I would, as much as it scared me.

Because it mattered to Tully and he shouldn't give up part of who he was to be with me, like Doreen had said. I didn't want him to resent me. So I would go, but I would be careful, like Tully was. "But no more reckless behaviour. I can admit to being reckless and foolish before. It was inconsiderate of me, and I can see that now. I need to think about people other than myself. Like him, and you." I reached for his hand, and hesitantly, he gave it to me. "I'm sorry, Dad. If I ever let you down. Or if I ever disappointed you. Or made you worry."

"Jeremiah," he said, shaking his head.

"Please, Dad. Listen. I had a real wake-up call. And maybe Tully taught me how to say what I feel. I should have said this long before now. I'm sorry if my studies ever caused you concern. And moving forward, I will try to be a better son. I want you to know that I appreciate everything you ever did for me. All the hours you worked, everything you provided. I know you did that for me."

He shook his head again, his chin wobbling. "I tried to make it enough. I couldn't give you what other kids had. I know that."

"It was more than enough, Dad. We got by just fine."

Another tear escaped his eye and he quickly wiped it away. "We did, huh. We got by okay. You grew up to be someone your mum would have been proud of." He sniffled and his eyes welled with tears. "And I'm proud of you too."

I squeezed his hand and swallowed back my tears. "Mum would be proud of you too. It wasn't easy, but here we are."

He took a tissue and wiped at his fresh tears. "Here we are."

With another squeeze of my hand, he let go and sat down. He took a moment to compose himself and to take some deep breaths. This wasn't an easy conversation for us, but I'd said what I needed to say.

And he'd returned the sentiment, which was new ground for us both. I felt as if a weight had been lifted off my shoulders. Did my father and I have a perfect relationship? No. Would we ever? Probably not.

But we were us, and we were going to be fine. I intended to include him more, involve him more. Even if it was a weekly phone call, or maybe I could teach him how to do video calls.

"So," he said. "Tully's a nice young man."

"He is, Dad. I love him."

He blinked in surprise. "Right, yes. Well, I'm glad. I'm happy for you. He, uh, he has a nice car."

He's trying. He's actually trying to talk about my boyfriend.

Another first.

I chuckled, my heart warm. I half expected one of those damn machines to beep, but it didn't.

"He's great, Dad. He's kind and thoughtful and generous. He loves with his whole heart. He has a great family; they've been very welcoming to me. Taken me in like one of their own."

He nodded slowly. "That's . . . that's nice." He shifted in his seat and fidgeted with his hands. "I'm happy for you."

"You'll see what I mean when you meet them tonight."

"When I . . . tonight?"

I snorted. "Ah, yes. Um, about that." I let out a slow breath. "They're holding a welcoming dinner for you at Tully's house tonight. It's only casual and what you're wearing is perfectly fine." I said that because I knew he would ask. "But I should include a fair warning. There's a lot of them and they're loud. But they're amazing people, and they will make a fuss over you, and it's honestly less painful if you just let them."

I smiled at the look of horror on his face. It was where I inherited the same look from. "Oh."

"Mrs Larson promised everyone would be gone by eight thirty. Or so Tully said."

The curtain pulled back and my doctor stood there with

Tully behind him. The doctor was smiling and Tully was grinning, so I assumed it was good news. Though Dad stood up, wringing his hands again.

"It's okay, Dad. It's good news." I looked at Tully and he nodded. I met the doctor's eyes. "You're moving me to a different ward?"

"The results of the TTE are good, and the bloodwork's good. Cardiac enzymes are back to normal levels."

Thank God.

"That is good news."

The doctor nodded, then gave Tully a smile. "As much as someone wants you to go home today, I think one or two more nights in a different ward would be best. We need to get you up and moving, make sure the pressure on your feet doesn't affect those burn wounds and that other bodily functions are okay. The tests for your renal enzymes also came back clear, so once we get you using the bathroom on your own, walking on your own, then you'll be free to go home."

Tully was just about to burst. "Did you hear that? He said *home*. You just gotta stand up and pee."

The doctor closed his eyes for a second. "That's not—"

I put my arm out. "Tully, help me up."

Tully laughed and came straight over. "How about we lower the bed first and get you sitting up with your feet on the floor? See how you feel?"

I nodded. "Perfect."

My ribs twinged, but it helped if I kept my arm tucked against my side. But I managed to sit up with my feet on the floor.

Tully kept his hand on my shoulder. "How does that feel?"

I glanced at the monitors to see if they'd betray me. Thankfully they didn't. "Feels good."

The doctor sighed and gave my dad a smile. "There's no

greater motivator than the word *home*." Then he looked at me. "How about we get your catheter out?"

Having a catheter removed wasn't a great deal of fun, but being free of it was a big relief.

One step closer to going home.

I sat on the edge of the bed again, my feet on the floor, and Tully and my nurse held onto me while I stood up.

My dad stood there, looking all kinds of helpless, but he smiled when I did.

I managed a few small steps but I couldn't stand for long, and while the idea of going home sounded like heaven, I knew realistically another night at least in hospital was probably a good idea.

I was so unbelievably tired.

That small amount of exertion had taken a lot out of me, and my nurse kept a close eye on every machine I was hooked up to. By the time I'd been moved to a normal ward, I could barely keep my eyes open.

I was still attached to one heart monitor, but nothing else.

One step closer to going home.

Tully put his hand to my cheek. "Jem, you need some sleep," he said gently.

Given he'd done and said this in front of my father, I should have been embarrassed. The old me would have been horrified, and my dad looked as if he'd witnessed something incredibly private.

But all I could do was smile. I held Tully's hand to my face and sighed. "I am tired."

"Then we'll go," Tully said. "And we'll be back bright and early tomorrow, and we'll practice more walking. As much as I want you to come home, we're not gonna rush it. However long it takes, okay?"

I nodded, exhausted. "Okay."

He kissed my temple. "Love you."

Again, in front of my father.

"Love you too," I said, fighting to keep my eyes open. "Love you too, Dad."

First time in my life I'd ever said those words.

I wanted so much to see his face, but my eyes betrayed me. After a long beat of silence, his warm hand squeezed my arm. "Sleep well, son."

I was so happy, even in my almost-asleep state.

Then Tully's voice, fading as they walked away, said, "So I need to explain something before we get to my place. I have a brother, Ellis . . ."

I woke up just after five in the morning, hungry and determined.

I was going home today.

I knew it would be tough, and I would need to take precautions and be sensible. But I was determined to get the all-clear from my doctor.

I'd missed the family dinner last night—well, Tully's family and my father—and I didn't want to miss another thing.

I was certain everything went well. I knew my father would be overwhelmed but gracious, and of course the Larsons would take the very best care of him.

I just wished I'd been there to see it.

So, if I was going home today, I needed an early start.

I had a new nurse now, along with the new room, new ward, new everything. When I buzzed for an attendant, a middle-aged, robust woman came in with a smile. "Everything okay, Mr Overton?"

I didn't bother correcting her on my title. "Yes. I'd like to use the bathroom and perhaps have a shower. Before the breakfast rush, if that's okay. It's been an embarrassing number of days since I last showered." I tried sitting up on the edge of the bed, my feet on the floor. "My . . . husband . . . and my father will be here first thing and I'd like to be presentable. And preferably not have swamp breath."

She laughed. "Then let's get you showered and minty fresh."

And if I thought having a hot shower after five days at the bunker was heaven, then this shower was out of this world.

Even if I was sitting in a chair stark naked and had a nurse checking in on me.

That hot water, the razor, the soap, the toothpaste . . .

Heaven. On. Earth.

But by the time Tully and Dad came in, I was sitting up in bed, with freshly washed hair, a new gown, eating some wholemeal toast.

Tully did a double take when he saw me. He put a bag beside the bed and looked me up and down. "Uh, excuse me, while you're incredibly good looking and the, yes, dress is flattering, I'm looking for Jeremiah Overton."

I snorted at his term for my hospital gown.

"Who is this new man?" he said, kissing my head.

I laughed. "I found him in the shower. It was the best shower of my life."

Tully was very much about to comment on that—in all likelihood something rude—but I made a point of ignoring him and looked at my dad instead. "Morning," I said. He was standing at the end of my bed and smiling, which made me incredibly happy to see. "How was dinner last night?"

He glanced briefly at Tully but then back at me. "It was very nice."

I looked between them. "What was the look for? What happened?"

Tully laughed. "Nothing. It was all great. Mum made sure everyone was gone by half eight and Ellis was on his best behaviour."

Dad smiled, nodding. "I thought Ellis was polite and well-mannered."

"Well-mannered?" I studied Tully's face for a hint of humour. "No name-calling, no wrestling, no belching? No threats of grievous bodily harm?"

Tully laughed. "The threats of bodily harm were all given before we arrived. Mum made it pretty clear. Ellis was good. And when everyone left, he ducked out to see Grace."

"Oh? Things going well, I hope?"

Tully clucked his tongue. "We all hope. For all our sakes." Then he rubbed my arm, my shoulder. "You feelin' okay today? How are your feet?" He took a look at my soles. "They look good. Was standing and walking okay?"

"It was manageable. I'm just letting them dry properly. Apart from my feet, showering and walking took considerable effort and energy, and I will be taking a nap soon, I think. But . . ." I met Tully's gaze. "I'd really like to go home today."

Tully grinned and picked up the bag. "I packed you some things, in case today was the day." Then he looked at my dad, then at me. "I'll go grab us a coffee. Mr Overton, black with one sugar?"

"That'd be great, thank you."

He gave me a smiley kiss on the temple and left me alone with my father.

"So, tell me honestly, how was last night?"

Dad was still smiling, not something I saw on him very often. "It was very nice. Honestly. They're all lovely people. I mean, there were a lot of kids and noise. But the madness is part of the charm, right?"

I chuckled. "It is."

"And his house . . ."

That made me laugh. "I know. It's very big and expensive."

"I take it they have a lot of money," he said quietly. "Not

that they paraded it or anything. Actually, they're very down-to-earth people. But, well, you know . . ."

And I *did* know. When you grew up and lived with only the bare essentials, and sometimes not even that, someone with money was easy to spot. And it wasn't just the flash cars or expensive jewellery. A lot of it was behaviour that came from a privilege they weren't even aware of.

"I do know," I replied. "When I first met Tully, he wore old clothes and drove an old banged-up Jeep. Then he took me to his house. It was quite the separation from who I assumed he was. But he's just a normal guy, Dad. They all are."

He shrugged one shoulder. "They said the family business was shipping. Not sure what that means."

"You know the shipping containers and freighters with the knight's helmet?"

He nodded, then his eyes went wide. "*Those* Larsons?"

I chuckled. "Yes. Don't worry, I almost died when he took me to his office and I realised. He'd never told me who his family was. He just said he works in imports and exports. Which isn't a lie. They just don't flaunt it. Actually, I don't think it even occurs to Tully to flaunt it."

Dad was still taken aback. "Well, I never . . . I had no idea."

I smiled and patted his hand. "Proof that they're just normal people."

He nodded, then remembered something. "Oh, I met your bird, Mr Percival. Cheeky thing he is."

"He is." I was glad to be able to rest my head on the bed. I'd done a lot this morning and was already tired again, even though it was barely 7:30 am. "He's a real character."

"Want me to put your bed down a bit?" he asked, concerned. "You can close your eyes for a bit."

"Maybe later," I said. "I'm glad you're here."

His eyes met mine briefly before he looked away again, embarrassed. "I'm glad I'm here too."

"How long are you staying for?"

"Three days. It's all I could get off work."

He'd always worked so hard, and it helped make up my mind. "I really need to go home today."

Tully came in with a tray of coffees and a smile that made my heart thump. I glanced at the machine; it didn't beep but there was a spike.

It made Tully laugh. "I'm definitely gonna get us one of these machines. Do you think they'll let us keep this one?"

"Highly unlikely."

He handed us our coffees. "Yours is on skim milk," he said. "We're heart-healthy people now."

Oh good lord. "Are you going to police every single thing I eat and drink for the rest of my life?"

He grinned. "That's the plan."

I hadn't meant for the *rest of my life* to imply anything, but the gleam in his eye and the softness of his tone implied exactly that.

Then he startled, as if he'd just remembered something. He picked up the bag and took out a shirt. "Your leaving-hospital shirt."

It was the *I love Dick* shirt.

Because of course it was.

He turned it around to show my father, whose eyeballs almost fell out of his head. "Oh my."

Tully just laughed, no shame, not much decorum either. "Today's the best day ever."

CHAPTER FOURTEEN
TULLY

Jeremiah's dad was so much like Jeremiah it wasn't funny.

Composed, quiet, always-thinking, assessing, and seriously introverted. Smart, too. But he was also courteous and kind.

And under that hard exterior was a big squishy marshmallow.

I hadn't expected him to burst into tears when he first saw Jeremiah in hospital. To be honest, I think his outward show of emotion surprised everyone, himself included.

But it warmed my heart to see.

I was only too happy to leave them alone for some time to talk. Finally, twenty-something years too late, but better late than never.

The Jeremiah that woke up in hospital was a new man. After almost dying twice—first when he was struck by lightning and the second time when his arrythmia damn near flatlined him—he was determined to say what he felt.

He'd told me he loved me. Several times, now. And he'd said it in front of other people. Even his father.

Like he'd been given a second chance at life and wasn't gonna waste a minute.

He told his dad that he loved him too.

Shame it took nearly dying to do it, but wow, what a transformation.

I guess getting struck by lightning would do that.

But his father . . .

If I had to guess what Jeremiah's father was gonna be like, I'd have imagined him exactly as he was.

Stoic, unsure of people, unassuming, and happy to blend into the background.

After all, how far could the apple fall from the tree?

But there he was with my family, where he was the guest of honour, thrown out of his comfort zone by kids running around the house, adults chatting and laughing, a mountain of food, and my parents who put him at ease.

Dad spoke to him about AFL, and Mum talked to him about inconsequential everyday things. They were pros at this type of thing; making people feel at home, showing kindness and charm that made Mr Overton feel right at home.

He was a factory worker and had been for thirty-plus years. He'd lived in the same house in Melbourne all that time. He never mentioned Jeremiah's mother, and perhaps he didn't have to. The sadness in him was in his eyes, and I remembered what Rowan had said.

He clearly remembered too, because when we were at the BBQ on the patio, he handed me a beer. He didn't say anything, just gave me a smile and a nod—perhaps telling me I'd done the right thing by having Mr Overton stay, by having a family dinner, and by truly understanding why he was the way he was. Then he'd clapped my shoulder and went back to refereeing his kids' game of Twister.

I couldn't have imagined that I'd have found common ground with Rowan either, but through this whole ordeal, he'd been everything I'd needed him to be. Maybe he always had been, and I'd just been too immature and self-absorbed to see it.

Yeah, maybe I'd learned a valuable lesson too.

"Whatcha thinking?" Jeremiah asked.

I must have zoned out, because he and his father were watching me.

"Not much. Just between cyclones and lightning strikes, I think I'm done with life lessons for a good while. Ready to just coast through for a bit, where everything is cosy and boring."

"Cosy and boring sounds great," Jeremiah said, squeezing my hand.

"How much longer till the doctor comes?"

"Five minutes since you asked last time."

I groaned like the child I was, apparently. "I'm gonna go look for him."

I stood up just as the door opened and the doctor walked in . . . pushing a wheelchair.

"Yay!"

Yeah. I actually said yay.

I wasn't even remotely embarrassed.

"Sorry to keep you waiting," the doctor said. "I believe it's discharge o'clock."

I helped Jeremiah to his feet and eased him into the wheelchair. "Do you feel okay?"

He smiled up at me, tired but *so* happy to be leaving. "Yeah."

The doctor looked at Jeremiah's shirt. "Nice shirt."

Jeremiah rolled his eyes and gestured to me, like it explained everything.

I put my hand to my heart. "I happen to be a very big fan of dick."

"Van Dyke," Jeremiah added. "You forgot the Van Dyke."

I snorted, because I absolutely did not forget it, and poor Mr Overton clutched the bag and the balloons, offering the doctor an apologetic smile.

The doc laughed, then handed Jeremiah a clear bag with

several bottles of pills and what looked like scripts. "We'll see you back in two weeks. Keep a diary of your bpm and blood pressure. Don't forget."

"He won't," I said. "I drew up a chart for that kind of thing. It has colour-coded stars and everything."

Jeremiah pressed his lips together and sighed. "I'll keep a diary. Thank you, doctor."

He tried to wheel himself out. "Hey," I said, grabbing the handles. "Let me do that."

We left the hospital and I wheeled him into the sunshine outside. He closed his eyes and tilted his face toward the warmth. "Oh, that feels so good."

I gave him a moment to enjoy it. "Ready to go home? The car's just there."

He nodded and let me help him into the passenger seat, then he let me help him get out and into the house. Then I helped him onto the couch. I brought him a blanket, a tray with drinks and low-sodium snacks and some fruit, and the remote control. "Use the downstairs bathroom and don't try climbing those stairs without me, okay?" I checked the blinds. "Are these open enough? Would you like them closed?"

Jeremiah chuckled. "Tully, I'm fine, thank you. Everything is perfect."

I took Mr Percival out of his cage and he quickly perched himself on my finger, squawking that it was about damn time. I walked him over to Jeremiah. "Here's this little guy. He missed you." Mr Percival agreed by swooping to the couch, then hopping along to Jeremiah as he chorused his happy magpie song.

Jeremiah laughed when Mr Percival hopped onto his shoulder and pecked at his neck and then tried to steal some sliced apple.

"Ah, it's good to be home," Jeremiah said. He was tired, that was pretty obvious, but he hadn't stopped smilin' yet.

I didn't miss the way his dad caught the word home and his understanding of what it meant.

This was Jeremiah's home now.

This house. Darwin.

Me.

His dad joined him on the couch, and he smiled at the silly bird who was trying to steal more apple.

I decided now was a good time as any. And I knew Jeremiah would probably be mad but . . . "So I got you something," I said.

Jeremiah watched me as I came around the couch, holding a white Apple bag and a brown paper bag.

I sat on the coffee table in front of him. "And you're not allowed to be mad because of your blood pressure and heart rate, so . . ."

His gaze went from the Apple bag to my face. "What did you do?"

I handed it to him. "Technically, Ellis bought it. I mean, I asked him to and it was my card, but he did the buying, so you have to be mad at him and not me."

He pulled out the first box. It was a new phone. And a new watch.

"Yours were fried," I said, now giving him the brown paper bag. "The hospital gave these to me. And the clothes you were wearing. But I thought you might like to see these."

Inside were his old phone and watch and the chest strap.

"None of them work anymore. And the guy at the Apple store said the phone was actually fried. As in, some of it was melted on the inside. He wanted to know if it'd been microwaved." I shrugged. "Ellis said it was. Pretty much. Yeah."

Jeremiah was quiet as he turned his old phone over in his hand, inspecting it.

"Even the sim card was fried," I added. "I couldn't get

your number reissued on a new sim because you weren't with me, so you'll have a new number now."

He nodded, then met my gaze. "Thank you."

"At least those news reporters won't be calling you now."

He smiled ruefully. "True."

Then he looked at the watch, at the dirty wristband, at the black screen. He tried to turn it on and sighed when nothing happened.

He took out the chest strap, and without even looking at it, he put it on the couch beside him. "Didn't buy another one of these?" he asked. There was a spark of humour in his eyes.

I grinned at him. "It's on back order."

He gave me a tired smile until his dad picked up the old phone. "Must have been a hell of a zap to fry a phone. And a watch," Mr Overton said quietly. "You were very lucky, huh?"

"Yeah," Jeremiah whispered. His eyes cut to mine and he smiled. "Very lucky indeed."

He could barely keep his eyes open, so I moved the tray of food and put the blanket over him. "Get some sleep."

He nodded, his eyes already closed, and two seconds later, he was out.

I carried the tray into the kitchen and Mr Overton followed me. He was nervous and clearly had something to say. I gave him time to put his thoughts in order.

"I never thanked you," he said, fidgeting his hands, then folding his arms, then uncrossing them again. "It would have been a very different story if not for you. You were there with him when it happened, and he told me you saved his life."

"I was with him. I dunno if I saved his life, but I put in the call for medevac." I shuddered at the memory. "It scared the hell outta me, not gonna lie."

"You love him very much," he said. It wasn't a question. "I can see that."

Jesus. This was not the conversation I expected to be having with his father.

"I do."

He smiled sadly. "I'm glad." Then he swallowed hard and kept his gaze fixed on the ocean views out the window. "He spent his whole life studying, reading, researching. He was never a very sociable child. I worried that was my fault. I worked shiftwork and he was home alone a lot. And when he first told me he liked men, I worried even more for him."

Ah, shit.

"I thought he'd be destined to be alone like me, and I didn't want that for him. I wanted him to have a family, and to know what love was." He turned to face me, making eye contact for a second before glancing away, grimacing a smile. This wasn't easy for him to say, but with a deep breath, he continued. "I needn't have worried, because he has that with you. All of it. Everything I wanted for him. He has that here."

Hmm. *Here.*

"He's a long way from home," I offered. "But what if we come to Melbourne once a year? And you can come here any time you'd like and stay here for as long as you want. Just give me the dates and I'll make it happen. Jeremiah would like that. I've only been to Melbourne once. It was a while ago now. Maybe we could catch a footy match."

He smiled genuinely then. "That'd be nice. I'd like that too."

We were quiet then, and I wasn't sure what to say. He'd come all this way to learn that he'd very nearly lost his son the same way he'd lost his wife, and now he was losing him to me.

"He's happier here," he said eventually. "In Darwin. He was never really happy where he was. As if he was constantly going against the grain. His colleagues were a contentious bunch. He never got along with them."

"They were a bunch of arseholes who never appreciated him." He looked at me, startled, and all I could do was shrug. "It's true."

He smirked and was quiet again, his gaze out to sea. "Do you . . . do you ever get sick of the view?"

I laughed. "Never."

"Can't say I would either."

———

I'D NOT REALISED JUST HOW MUCH I'D MISSED SLEEPING NEXT TO Jeremiah until I helped him into bed, sliding in beside him, holding him tight. His head was on my chest, my arms around him, and something settled in my bones.

Something that felt like coming home.

"I missed you so much," I murmured. It was late and he'd tried to stay awake after dinner, but he'd dozed on the couch again until I'd helped him upstairs and into bed. "I missed this so much."

He hummed. "Doctor said no sex for a while. Nothing arduous, anyway."

I snorted. "So having competitions as to who can get the highest heart rate is out?"

"I think I won that game."

I gave him a squeeze and kissed the top of his head. "I don't care about the sex," I admitted. "It'll happen when you're ready. I'm just glad you're here. Lyin' in bed with you like this is enough for me."

He kissed my pec. "I'm glad because laying here is about all I'm capable of doing."

I chuckled. "I love you."

He sighed and nuzzled in a little closer. "I love you too. I'm so thankful for you." His voice got slower, quieter, as he drifted off to sleep. "Every little thing. Love every little thing."

I kissed his forehead this time and smiled at the ceiling. "Love every little thing about you too."

Watching Jeremiah talk with his dad and watchin' them smile made me happy in ways I couldn't describe.

Was their entire relationship magically fixed overnight? No. But it was a really good fucking start.

Even when he had to say goodbye to his father at the airport, Jeremiah was still smiling. I mean, he was kinda sad to see him go—and they had hugged goodbye—but when I got him into the car after we'd watched the plane leave, he let his head fall back on the headrest and he gave me a smile.

"You okay?"

"Yeah." He held out his hand, which I was quick to take. "I am. You know, I think we'll be okay."

I kissed his knuckles. "I think you will be too."

"And you and me," he added. "I think we'll be okay too."

"You bet your arse we will be."

He snorted. "Can we drive past my office?"

"You sure?"

He nodded with a tired smile. "Yeah. I just wanna see it."

"Okay."

So I drove him to his office. The gate was open, Doreen's bike was under the carport, and a utility van was parked alongside it. It looked like an electrician's van, with ladders and gear on top.

Doreen came out and grinned when she saw it was us. Her shirt had a picture of a cat-shaped bottle with the words *pussy liquor* on it. I got out of my car laughing. "Possibly my favourite shirt yet."

She looked down at it. "It's a ripper, ain't it?" Then she looked at Jeremiah. "What are you doin' here?"

"Just thought I'd call past. I'm not staying." He nodded toward the van. "Work's started, I see."

"Early days. But yeah, he's fixin' something to do with the mains and a new transformer." She shook her head and shrugged. "Needed a full upgrade for your new computers and shit."

Jeremiah was obviously pleased to hear this. "Thank you for being here. I should be back at work soon."

"Uh," I objected. "The doc said two weeks."

"Yes, two weeks until full-time work. He said nothing about calling in and checking on progress. It's not like I can help them or do anything."

"You just take it easy," Doreen said. "I can come and open a gate for 'em. It's not like I'm busy these days."

"And I do appreciate that—"

"Are you arguin' with me, son?"

He sighed. "No."

She gave a victorious nod. "Good."

I coughed to cover my laugh, and Jeremiah took his phone from his pocket. "I have a new number, if you should need to call me."

"Lemme grab mine," she said, disappearing back inside.

Phone numbers all sorted and a quick update on the street —Arty was still a stubborn old goat, and work had started on Casey and Presley's house—it was time for Jeremiah to go home.

"I wish I wasn't so tired," he grumbled.

"I know, babe. But you're doin' better every day. We'll get you situated on the couch and you can take it easy. I'll make us an early dinner." I helped him inside. "How does home-made pizzas sound? I got those pita bases and low-fat cheese."

He snorted. "They sounded good until the low-fat cheese part."

Ellis met us in the living room. He was just heading some-where. "Is that dinner about tonight?"

"Yeah, homemade pizzas. Why?"

He grimaced, blushing a little. "Well, I asked Grace if she wanted to come over for dinner tonight."

I grinned at him. "Oh, that sounds very . . . domestic. Will she be staying the whole night?"

His eyes narrowed at me. "Listen, nut sac—"

I laughed. "I'm just stirrin' ya. That's good news, Ellis. I'm glad you're sorting things out with her."

He studied me for a long beat. "Can you not bring any of that shit up in front of her? About how I was a dick to her before? Or try to embarrass me. Or her." He clenched his teeth. "I swear to god, Tully, if you embarrass her—"

"I'll be on my best behaviour." I gave him a salute. "Promise."

"I'll make sure he's well-behaved," Jeremiah said.

Ellis sighed. "I'm going to grab a few things. Need anything for pizzas?"

"Garlic bread and real cheese would be great," Jeremiah said as he walked toward the couch.

"Babe," I started. "You need to watch your heart."

"Garlic bread and real cheese would make my heart happy," he mumbled. "And maybe it will give me energy for later."

I stared at the back of his head.

Did he just . . . ?

"Did you just imply . . . ? Jeremiah!" In front of my brother.

Dear god.

Ellis snorted. "Pretty sure he did, yeah."

Okay then. "Well," I allowed. I nodded to Ellis. "Get him garlic bread and real cheese."

He laughed as he walked to the door. "Oh, it's supposed to storm tonight," he called out before he left.

Hmm.

I jumped on the couch with Jeremiah, snuggling right in so we'd both fit, and I pulled the blanket over us. "Did you hear that? It's supposed to storm tonight."

His eyes stayed closed, he rubbed my back, and the corner

of his mouth lifted ever so slightly. "Perfect night to stay indoors."

"You, me, and pizza," I said with a sigh. "And a storm outside. Sounds perfect to me too."

He was quiet for a long beat. "I want to watch storms with you," he murmured. "But I'm not ready to go out in them yet."

I gave him a squeeze. "It's okay, Jem."

"I can have both, right?" he whispered.

Oh my god, yes. "You sure can have both."

"What you said was true. And Doreen. She said the same thing. I can still go storm watching with you. But I'm done being reckless. Not with my heart, and not with yours."

I sighed happily. "That's all I ever wanted."

EPILOGUE

TWO YEARS LATER - TULLY

Paul and Derek's camp had been lucky to escape any real damage during Cyclone Hazer. They were far enough out not to be in its direct path, and had sustained minimal damage.

Thank god.

Pulling up at their camping ground gave me just as much of a thrill as it always did. Even more, probably, now that Jeremiah was with me. We'd come at the beginning of the wet season last year too.

That trip had been Jeremiah's first true outing back in the furore.

Almost ten months after his brush with lightning, he'd wanted to come to the bunker with me. He was scared and he never set foot outside the bunker as soon as there was a cloud in the sky, but he was there with me.

And that was all I ever wanted.

I didn't need him to be a scientist out here. I just needed him to be happy—and being out here made him happy.

So now we were back, two years after the lightning strike. We had enough gear to last us a week, but if we had to leave earlier, then so be it. The weather was supposed to be warm and humid with afternoon storms.

Perfect.

And my secret, my surprise, the small box in my duffel bag felt like a large elephant in the Jeep with us. I wanted to tell him . . . I wanted to show him . . .

"You good?" Jeremiah asked.

I shut off the engine and gave him a smile. "I'm great."

Paul came out, holding two large containers stacked on top of each other. He saw it was us, and he grinned. "Hey, strangers."

We got out of the Jeep, Jeremiah rushing to take the top container from him. "Here, let me get that."

"Thanks."

I followed them through to the outdoor kitchen.

"How've you both been?" Paul asked. "You, Jeremiah—" He looked him up and down. "—look good. No more brushes with death, I take it."

He laughed. "No, thankfully."

I slid my hand along the small of his back. The truth was, Jeremiah did look good. Really fucking good. He was happy. His new office was a dream come true and he now had two other staff. Howard and Georgia were both young and smart, really driven, and they brought a great energy to the office. And they both admired Jeremiah a lot. They respected him.

It was an office full of weather nerds, but Jeremiah would come home buzzed instead of beaten. He also talked to his dad more than ever. We'd been to Melbourne three times, and his dad had been back to Darwin twice since that first time.

He also had a stellar fucking sex life, I might just add.

So when Paul said that Jeremiah looked good, he wasn't wrong.

Derek came out of their tent, the closest to the kitchen. "Thought I heard voices," he said. "Welcome back."

We all shook hands and said hello, and ten seconds later, Jeremiah and Derek were off, looking through Derek's telescope.

"How's he been?" Paul asked quietly. "No problems?"

They knew all about the possible long-term health and medical complications that came with being struck by lightning. Some took months or years to develop, like cataracts and organ complications.

"None, thank God. He's been great. Passes all his physicals with flying colours."

"And how is he with storms now?"

I nodded. "Better. He still won't go out in them. Can't say I blame him."

"But he's here," Paul offered. "To go camping at the bunker for a week in storm season."

I chuckled. "Yeah. He still loves storms. And he still studies the data. He's just safer about it now which, to be honest, is a good thing. No more crazy shit." I sighed. "I ain't gonna lie, a week of no interruptions, no work, no prying family, just us, one bed, and a storm every afternoon? He's not passing that up."

I thought about telling Paul of my plans, my surprise for Jeremiah, but for some reason I didn't. Now would have been the perfect time—and I did want to tell someone—but the only person I really wanted to tell was Jeremiah.

Paul smirked with a cheeky twinkle in his eye. "Yeah, about that. When I said he looks good, honestly, if it were possible, I'd say he was pregnant. He's glowing."

I laughed loud enough that Jeremiah and Derek both turned to look at us. "Well, we keep trying," I said, rubbing my belly. "Both of us."

Paul threw his head back and laughed. "But not for the lack of trying."

"Absolutely not." I gave him a nod. "And you two?"

Paul looked out to where Derek stood, and he sighed, a serene smile on his face. "We're great. He's great."

We both stood there smilin', like two fools in love.

"Oh, look at this," I said, taking my phone out. "We had some visitors last week."

I showed him the photos of two adult magpies on the patio railing with two adolescent chicks. "Someone got himself a family."

Paul looked at the pictures, then at me. "No way! Is that the bird you were looking after?"

I nodded. "Mr Percival."

We'd left his cage on the balcony, like Jem had suggested, with the door open so Mr Percival could come and go as he wanted. His days away got longer until it was a few days at a time that we didn't see him, then even longer.

But last year he'd come back with a friend, like he was bringing his girlfriend home to meet his two dads.

And then this year, there were babies.

"That is the coolest thing," Paul said.

"Yeah, it's pretty amazing. Jem was stoked."

"Might be time to take the plunge and become dog dads, or cat dads."

I snorted. Maybe . . .

"Speaking of taking the plunge, got everything organised?"

His grin was back. "Yep. Not much to organise to be honest. And you guys booking in, it was perfect timing. We really do appreciate it."

"It's our privilege." I clapped him on the shoulder. "Tell me what needs to be done."

THE MINISTER ARRIVED BEFORE SUNSET, AND AT THE EDGE OF THE ridge, overlooking the vast wetlands below, the sky a glorious palette of pinks, oranges, and yellows, Jeremiah and I stood witness to Paul and Derek's wedding.

I couldn't help but stare at Jeremiah as they talked of love and forever, as they vowed to love and cherish each other for all their days.

Jeremiah in the fading pastel sunlight was one of my favourite sights in the world. Wet Jeremiah, and hot and sweaty Jeremiah, and turned-on Jeremiah were also my favourite kinds of Jeremiah.

Even the mad Jeremiah and annoyed Jeremiah.

I loved them all.

But there, against the most beautiful backdrop, stood the most beautiful man. Sure, Paul and Derek's wedding was lovely, but damn . . .

Jeremiah.

"I do," Paul said, making me pay attention.

"I do," Derek echoed, softly kissing Paul. "For now and forever."

And then, just like that, they were married.

Jeremiah and I both clapped and hugged them, and after the minister had gone, we ate seafood from the grill and drank champagne and toasted to the night sky.

But lightning flashed far out on the horizon as storm clouds moved in, and I could feel Jeremiah's nervousness rolling off him. I took his hand and pulled him toward our tent. "We're gonna head in," I said to Paul and Derek, but they didn't care.

They were too wrapped up in each other, slow dancing under the stars to music only they could hear.

Once we were inside our tent, I put my hand to Jeremiah's cheek. His face softened under the fairy lights. "You okay?"

He nodded. "Thank you for understanding."

I kissed him softly. "Any time."

He put his forehead to mine. "It was a beautiful ceremony."

"It was."

And god, I wanted to tell him.

It was right on the tip of my tongue, and my mind burned knowing that little box was right there in my duffle bag.

Should I tell him now?

I could . . .

But no. I wanted to be at the bunker.

Jeremiah ran his finger down the side of my face. "You sure you're okay?"

I nodded. "I am."

"You sure? Because I'm tired and I wanted to fall asleep with you inside me," he murmured. "But if you're not up for that . . ."

I barked out a laugh and took his chin between my thumb and forefinger. "Oh, I'm up for that."

THE NEXT MORNING, NOT LONG AFTER SUNRISE, I LEFT JEREMIAH in bed and went in search of breakfast and found Paul and Derek in the kitchen. Derek had Paul pushed up against the counter and was sucking on his neck. He didn't even stop when he saw me. He simply smiled.

Paul laughed. "Morning."

"Yes, it is," I said. "Don't stop on my behalf. I'm just here for some . . ." I opened the fridge. "Food."

"Are you leaving this morning?" Derek mumbled, his mouth still on his husband's neck.

I snorted. "Yep. Soon as Jem wakes up." I took some fruit and yoghurt and clapped Derek's shoulder. "If you're not around, we won't come knocking to say goodbye."

"Good," Paul mumbled, and when I got to our tent, I turned back to see Paul was now facing Derek, his hands on his face, in a deep kiss.

I was smiling when I went inside, and Jeremiah grumbled at me from the bed. "You weren't here."

"Morning, sleepyhead," I said. "I was getting you some

breakfast. Paul and Derek are putting on a bit of a show in the kitchen. We should probably leave."

He sat up. "Oh. A show? Any good?"

I laughed. "Didn't you have enough last night?"

He shook his head and fell back onto the bed. "Never, apparently."

I peeled the lid off the yoghurt, added a spoon, and handed it out for him. "Eat up. We have to get down the ridgeline."

He took the yoghurt and sat up again, frowning this time. "Oh yippee. My favourite wild pig track. Nothing like a vertical descent down the mountainside to wake me up."

I peeled the banana and pretended to deep throat it before I licked the length of it. "I have plans for you this afternoon, so hurry up and eat."

He stared at the banana, then shook his head. "Using promises of sex as a bribery tool is incredibly manipulative."

I bit the banana. "But it's effective. Now eat."

Half an hour later, fed and showered and packed up, we were back in the Jeep. Paul and Derek were nowhere to be found, so we didn't get to say goodbye, but I did beep the horn on our way out.

And down the side of the mountain we went.

Jeremiah only swore and gave me the stink eye a few times, and soon enough we were pulling up at the bunker.

He was smiling now.

He really did love it here. The seclusion, the ruggedness of it. That it was basic and rudimentary essentials and nothing else.

We got the side walls up and I checked for any uninviteds. I made sure the shower and toilet were frog-free, and Jeremiah gave everything a bit of a clean.

By mid-afternoon, it was stinking hot and we were both shirtless and sweaty, and he looked as happy as I'd ever seen him.

Maybe this was my favourite kind of Jeremiah . . .

We had one laptop monitoring the weather, and we did bring his new automatic weather station. He also wore his watch and we'd brought the chest strap, strictly for medical reasons, but he wasn't wearing it.

He was looking at the weather radar, and I was lying on the bed, tryin' not to think about what I needed to show him, wondering when would be the perfect time. Was there ever a perfect time?

Every time I thought of it, my nerves buzzed around in my chest like a box full of bees waiting to explode.

"There's increased storm activity about to hit," he said. "Lightning activity likely."

I sat up. "We'll be okay here, Jem."

He nodded, though that line between his brows told me he didn't really agree with me.

And then he started pacing.

I stood up and went to him, stopping his pacing with a tight hug. "You know you're safe here, and you've been in electrical storms since. Wanna tell me what's really bothering you?"

"Nothing."

I took his wrist and looked at his watch. "Uh, your stress beacon here says otherwise."

He grumbled. "I hate this watch."

I pulled his hips flush with mine and held his gaze. "We had storms here last year and you were fine."

He frowned again but wouldn't look at me. "I know. I just . . ."

"Jem," I said, chasing his gaze until he looked at me. "What are you worried about? Tell me."

"I'm not worried. I just . . ."

"You just what?"

"Paul and Derek," he whispered.

"What about them?"

"They got married."

"They did, yes," I said.

I would have smiled if he didn't look so serious. Thunder boomed in the distance and it startled him.

I tightened my hold and gave him a bit of a shake. "Babe, what's the matter?"

"Did you ever think it was possible?" His eyes searched mine. "When you were younger, growing up. Did you ever think getting married was something that would ever happen to you?"

"Sure."

He deflated. "Well, yes. You're bisexual. It was always possible for you." He shook his head and tried to pull away. "Forget it."

I held him even tighter. "I won't forget it. This is clearly bothering you. And honestly, what the hell? Whether I married a guy or a girl. Whether I was gay, bi or straight, why does that matter?"

His eyes searched mine and he sighed. "I'm sorry. That was . . . I shouldn't have said that."

More thunder rumbled across the sky, closer this time.

"Jem, I always pictured myself with someone forever. Like my mum and dad. I always wanted what they have."

"I never had that. I never saw what that kind of love was like." He shook his head. "Even when I fell in love with you, it never occurred to me that it was possible for me. Not even knowing we were going to be witnesses for Paul and Derek." His lip pulled down, sadness filling his eyes. "Until I saw you standing there, smiling at me. And I thought . . . maybe. Maybe that was something we could do now."

Oh hell.

Oh fucking fuckity fucking hell.

He put his hand to his forehead. "And maybe that was something you might want to do? With me? One day. It doesn't have to be now."

Thunder cracked overhead and Jeremiah turned to the storm. "Do you mind? I'm trying to have a moment here!"

I burst out laughing and sat him on the bed. "I want to show you something," I said. "And tell you something."

I went to my duffle bag and took out the box that had been burning a hole in my brain since I got it in the mail, and I went to my knees in front of him.

"A month ago, after we'd booked in with Paul to come here and he called me back to ask if we would be the witnesses to their wedding, I spoke to your dad. I called him . . ."

"My dad?"

I nodded, nervous as hell. Those bees in my chest were really trying to break free. "I told him I'd been thinking about asking you to marry me. I wanted him to know. I wasn't asking permission, as such, but I did want him to feel included and to remind him that he wasn't losing you." I let out a breathy laugh. "And he went all quiet and I thought for sure he was gonna say no. But he said he was surprised it'd taken me this long. And he offered me this."

I held up the box, but Jeremiah was stuck staring at my face.

"Jem?"

He startled. "Oh, I'm sorry, what? Did you . . . did you ask my father?"

"I did. I've been thinking about this for a while, and well, Paul and Derek kinda beat me to it, and I didn't want you to think I was just asking you because of them. It just kinda gave me the push to do it. Anyway, your dad sent me this."

I offered him the box again, and this time he took it. "What is it?"

It was an old jewellery box. "Open it."

He lifted the lid and stared at the ring. He blinked quickly a few times before his eyes found mine. "Tully."

"It was your mother's wedding band," I said. "Your dad

thought you might like it. He said you had your mother's hands, but if it doesn't fit, we can get it resized. If you want." He was stunned, clearly. He stared at me, then back at the ring, but he still hadn't said anything. "Or not. It's okay if you—"

A tear rolled down his cheek. "This is my mother's?"

I nodded.

"Oh my god, Tully," he said, a shaky hand over his mouth as more tears fell.

"I'm sorry. I didn't mean to upset you."

He laughed through his tears and took the ring out of the box. Then he handed it to me and offered me his left hand.

"Is that a yes?" I asked.

"You technically haven't asked me anything."

I snorted. "Jeremiah, will you marry me? Say you'll be with me forever. That we'll come here forever, to this place. That we'll chase storms forever. That we'll love each other and protect each other forever."

He nodded with more tears and a laugh, and I slipped the ring on his finger. It was a tight fit. "Oh, you might have trouble getting that off," I said.

He shook his head. "I'm never taking it off."

I stood up and pushed him back on the bed, following him so I could kiss him. His legs went around me, and I kissed him, our tongues in a familiar tangle, his hands in my hair.

As the storm raged on outside, as rain lashed the walls and thunder rumbled low and deep, he made love to me. Slow and deep, he slid in and out of me, taking me to that place only he could.

And when I was close, when my body was at the precipice, he froze. So far inside me, to the hilt, his eyes wide, and he licked his lips. "Lightning. Taste it with me."

He crashed his mouth back to mine, giving me his tongue

as the sky outside lit up with a symphony of thunder and lightning.

Just for us, the storm played on. Cymbals and drums, lights and song. Music only we could hear.

As it would for us, forever.

THE END

THE STORM BOYS SERIES

Thank you for reading Tully and Jeremiah's story!

Outrun the Rain

Into the Tempest

Touch the Lightning

Go back to where it all began with Paul and Derek?

Second Chance at First Love

THE STORM BOYS SERIES

ABOUT THE AUTHOR

N.R. Walker is an Australian author, who loves her genre of gay romance. She loves writing and spends far too much time doing it, but wouldn't have it any other way.

She is many things: a mother, a wife, a sister, a writer. She has pretty, pretty boys who live in her head, who don't let her sleep at night unless she gives them life with words.

She likes it when they do dirty, dirty things… but likes it even more when they fall in love.

She used to think having people in her head talking to her was weird, until one day she happened across other writers who told her it was normal.

She's been writing ever since…

ALSO BY N.R. WALKER

Blind Faith

Through These Eyes (Blind Faith #2)

Blindside: Mark's Story (Blind Faith #3)

Ten in the Bin

Gay Sex Club Stories 1

Gay Sex Club Stories 2

Point of No Return – Turning Point #1

Breaking Point – Turning Point #2

Starting Point – Turning Point #3

Element of Retrofit – Thomas Elkin Series #1

Clarity of Lines – Thomas Elkin Series #2

Sense of Place – Thomas Elkin Series #3

Taxes and TARDIS

Three's Company

Red Dirt Heart

Red Dirt Heart 2

Red Dirt Heart 3

Red Dirt Heart 4

Red Dirt Christmas

Cronin's Key

Cronin's Key II

Cronin's Key III

Cronin's Key IV - Kennard's Story

Exchange of Hearts

The Spencer Cohen Series, Book One

The Spencer Cohen Series, Book Two

The Spencer Cohen Series, Book Three

The Spencer Cohen Series, Yanni's Story

Blood & Milk

The Weight Of It All

A Very Henry Christmas (The Weight of It All 1.5)

Perfect Catch

Switched

Imago

Imagines

Imagoes

Red Dirt Heart Imago

On Davis Row

Finders Keepers

Evolved

Galaxies and Oceans

Private Charter

Nova Praetorian

A Soldier's Wish

Upside Down

The Hate You Drink

Sir

Tallowwood

Reindeer Games

The Dichotomy of Angels

Throwing Hearts

Pieces of You - Missing Pieces #1

Pieces of Me - Missing Pieces #2

Pieces of Us - Missing Pieces #3

Lacuna

Tic-Tac-Mistletoe

Bossy

Code Red

Dearest Milton James

Dearest Malachi Keogh

Christmas Wish List

Code Blue

Davo

The Kite

Learning Curve

Merry Christmas Cupid

To the Moon and Back

Second Chance at First Love

Outrun the Rain

Into the Tempest

Touch the Lightning

TITLES IN AUDIO:

Cronin's Key

Cronin's Key II

Cronin's Key III

Red Dirt Heart

Red Dirt Heart 2

Red Dirt Heart 3

Red Dirt Heart 4

The Weight Of It All

Switched

Point of No Return

Breaking Point

Starting Point

Spencer Cohen Book One

Spencer Cohen Book Two

Spencer Cohen Book Three

Yanni's Story

On Davis Row

Evolved

Elements of Retrofit

Clarity of Lines

Sense of Place

Blind Faith

Through These Eyes

Blindside

Finders Keepers

Galaxies and Oceans

Nova Praetorian

Upside Down

Sir

Tallowwood

Imago

Throwing Hearts

Sixty Five Hours

Taxes and TARDIS

The Dichotomy of Angels

The Hate You Drink

Pieces of You

Pieces of Me

Pieces of Us

Tic-Tac-Mistletoe

Lacuna

Bossy

Code Red

Learning to Feel

Dearest Milton James

Dearest Malachi Keogh

Three's Company

Christmas Wish List

Code Blue

Davo

The Kite

Learning Curve

Merry Christmas Cupid

To the Moon and Back

Second Chance at First Love

Outrun the Rain

SERIES COLLECTIONS:

Red Dirt Heart Series

Turning Point Series

Thomas Elkin Series

Spencer Cohen Series

Imago Series

Blind Faith Series

Missing Pieces Series

FREE READS:

Sixty Five Hours

Learning to Feel

His Grandfather's Watch (And The Story of Billy and Hale)

The Twelfth of Never (Blind Faith 3.5)

Twelve Days of Christmas (Sixty Five Hours Christmas)

Best of Both Worlds

TRANSLATED TITLES:

ITALIAN

Fiducia Cieca (Blind Faith)

Attraverso Questi Occhi (Through These Eyes)

Preso alla Sprovvista (Blindside)

Il giorno del Mai (Blind Faith 3.5)

Cuore di Terra Rossa Serie (Red Dirt Heart Series)

Natale di terra rossa (Red dirt Christmas)

Intervento di Retrofit (Elements of Retrofit)

A Chiare Linee (Clarity of Lines)

Senso D'appartenenza (Sense of Place)

Spencer Cohen Serie (including Yanni's Story)

Punto di non Ritorno (Point of No Return)

Punto di Rottura (Breaking Point)

Punto di Partenza (Starting Point)

Imago (Imago)

Imagines

Il desiderio di un soldato (A Soldier's Wish)

Scambiato (Switched)

Tallowwood

The Hate You Drink

Ho trovato te (Finders Keepers)

Cuori d'argilla (Throwing Hearts)

Galassie e Oceani (Galaxies and Oceans)

Il peso di tut (The Weight of it All)

FRENCH

Confiance Aveugle (Blind Faith)

A travers ces yeux: Confiance Aveugle 2 (Through These Eyes)

Aveugle: Confiance Aveugle 3 (Blindside)

À Jamais (Blind Faith 3.5)

Cronin's Key Series

Au Coeur de Sutton Station (Red Dirt Heart)

Partir ou rester (Red Dirt Heart 2)

Faire Face (Red Dirt Heart 3)

Trouver sa Place (Red Dirt Heart 4)

Le Poids de Sentiments (The Weight of It All)

Un Noël à la sauce Henry (A Very Henry Christmas)

Une vie à Refaire (Switched)

Evolution (Evolved)

Galaxies & Océans

Qui Trouve, Garde (Finders Keepers)

Sens Dessus Dessous (Upside Down)

La Haine au Fond du Verre (The hate You Drink)

Tallowwood

Spencer Cohen Series

GERMAN

Flammende Erde (Red Dirt Heart)

Lodernde Erde (Red Dirt Heart 2)

Sengende Erde (Red Dirt Heart 3)

Ungezähmte Erde (Red Dirt Heart 4)

Vier Pfoten und ein bisschen Zufall (Finders Keepers)

Ein Kleines bisschen Versuchung (The Weight of It All)

Ein Kleines Bisschen Fur Immer (A Very Henry Christmas)

Weil Leibe uns immer Bliebt (Switched)

Drei Herzen eine Leibe (Three's Company)

Über uns die Sterne, zwischen uns die Liebe (Galaxies and Oceans)

Unnahbares Herz (Blind Faith 1)

Sehendes Herz (Blind Faith 2)

Hoffnungsvolles Herz (Blind Faith 3)

Verträumtes Herz (Blind Faith 3.5)

Thomas Elkin: Verlangen in neuem Design

Thomas Elkin: Leidenschaft in klaren

Thomas Elkin: Vertrauen in bester Lage

Traummann töpfern leicht gemacht (Throwing Hearts)

Sir

THAI

Sixty Five Hours (Thai translation)

Finders Keepers (Thai translation)

SPANISH

Sesenta y Cinco Horas (Sixty Five Hours)

Los Doce Días de Navidad

Código Rojo (Code Red)

Código Azul (Code Blue)

Queridísimo Milton James

Queridísimo Malachi Keogh

El Peso de Todo (The Weight of it All)

Tres Muérdagos en Raya: Serie Navidad en Hartbridge

Lista De Deseos Navideños: Serie Navidad en Hartbridge

Feliz Navidad Cupido: Serie Navidad en Hartbridge

Spencer Cohen Libro Uno

Spencer Cohen Libro Dos

Spencer Cohen Libro Tres

Davo

Hasta la Luna y de Vuelta

Venciendo A La Lluvia

En la Tempestad

CHINESE

Blind Faith

JAPANESE

Bossy

PORTUGUESE

Sessenta e Cinco Horas